A Nameless Curse

Book One of The Realms Curse Duology

GW Prouse

ProuseBooks

To those who have hidden
bits of their memories and
found them again. Whether it was to
forgive, forget, survive, or heal...
you're stronger for it.

Author's Note: Some of the subject matter contained in this book
may be difficult for some readers
as it includes depictions of gore, mentions of torture, enslavement,
and on page death.

Just in case: This book is a <u>SLOW</u> burn! Be patient with the
characters. They are dealing with stuff.

TALAMH
TINE
DOMHAIN
SAOL
N

ÉARDROM
AER
SCATH
VISCE
THE OILEÁN ISLANDS
DORCHA

Chapter 1

Felicity grazed her fingers over the vial sewn into a hidden pocket within the seam of her three-quarter-length sleeve. As the carriage rolled along the packed dirt road of Domhain, she attempted to smooth down the flowing silk skirts of her hunter-green ballgown. The Tower stylists had chosen the color to accentuate the tint of red in her mahogany hair and her tan complexion. It was as much a costume as the smile she displayed.

Although the ride hadn't been long, Felicity tapped her foot in anticipation as she observed the passing landscape when a marble manor expanded into view. Figures dressed in resplendent attire exited fine carriages and began their ascent up a long staircase dotted by lanterns to a grand entrance of pillars and two large wide open front doors. The terra cotta shingles adorning the roof were probably imported from Domhain's northern neighbor Tine—the Fire Realm and one of the eight realms of Talamh.

She sniffed, lip curling. The outlying towns they had passed were nothing more than ruins in comparison. Homes and business establishments had been made from stones scaffolded down like steps to jagged rocks creating an outline of what was meant to be a building. Faeries and humans walked along dusty streets or huddled together over cooking fires. It was early summer, the remnants of spring drifted through a cool breeze that bent patches of grass. It wouldn't remain that way for long, and soon people would be exposed to the elements.

In her line of work, guilt was an emotion Felicity learned to ignore. She could only control so much and bringing change to the realm of Domhain was not within her abilities. In the end, she might grant them some hope. Her target was part of the problem and held blame for the people's suffering. When this mission was complete there would be no remorse on her part.

Her fingers played with the crystal pendant she always wore around her neck. Pressure built within her chest, but she forced her shoulders back and took slow breaths to calm her erratic heartbeat. There were few times that she could remember being nervous on assignment. Although she was more experienced now, she wasn't complacent. The tiniest detail could give her away. And something was off about this mission.

With a sigh, she closed the curtains, not only to block the view but to hide. Her skin prickled in anticipation. She pinched her hazel eyes shut and willed the glamour to fall—cheekbones rose, the edges of her heart-shaped face sharpened, and ears elongated to a point. The chain that connected the stud on her lobe to the cuff on the helix of her right ear stretched too. The glamour was nothing more than an image shown to others. Like a second skin, and her body itched as it fell, causing her to shiver as she revealed herself.

It had been years since she'd taken her true form beyond the privacy of her room. Even longer since she'd shown it to anyone outside of the Tower's council. The three council members were the exclusive few who knew the truth of who and what she was—fae.

Her glamour was the only magic the Tower's council knew about, and it allowed her to blend in among the guild of human spies and assassins. It was also one of the reasons she was skeptical about this mission—not that she had said so aloud. In her history as a recruit and now an initiate, they'd never asked her to use her fae heritage and certainly not in the open. It had felt like a protected secret and one she had appreciated, at least for the lack of turmoil it would otherwise cause.

This was why she couldn't wait to rise in the ranks and be named a Dearmadta—one of the Master Spies. The title would allow her to pick and choose her assignments. Since she never wanted to leave the guild, her home, she needed to protect her identity from others. The Tower would house her only if it was not more trouble than she was worth.

With a crunch of gravel, the carriage arrived at the steps of Advisor Boister's lavish estate, drawing her attention back to the task at hand. She lowered her chin, and the corner of her mouth rose to form a mischievous grin—costume complete.

Felicity didn't question her own abilities. Even with the doubts and unanswered questions, the Tower had never steered her wrong before. After a deep breath, she pushed all distractions to the back of her mind. She needed to be on her game and ready for anything.

When the door swung open, she gave the footman a radiant smile and exited—until her silver heel caught on the smooth white stones. She grasped onto the footman's shoulder to catch her balance, a squeal breaking from her lips.

"Oomph." The attendant's grip on her hand tightened while his other arm shot out to catch her.

He assisted her upright, and she looked up at him through dark lashes. "I'm sorry."

"Quite all right, milady." The footman's cheeks flushed, and when he was certain she was settled, he released his hold. "Happens all the time."

A few arriving guests glanced in their direction to catch the footman whispering to a blushing female. With a thankful nod and sheepish smile, Felicity turned and ascended the staircase alone, fighting back a grin of triumph.

She slowed at the fifteenth step and glanced up at the top still so far away. Her shoes pinched her toes, and Felicity cursed them. It was the price she paid when the Tower stylists had a vision but not the proper size to fulfill it.

Felicity was close to tearing the shoes off her feet when a flash of silver caught her attention. She paused and carved through the other guests to the side of the staircase. Her eyes widened as a smoky gray fox slipped between the round stones that cascaded along the side of the opulent ascent. A thrill rushed through her as their gazes met. It tilted its head for a moment, and she resisted the desire to step forward and attempt to brush a hand through its soft fur—if it would even allow such a thing.

Before she could act on the wish, it darted from view. Felicity blinked, wondering if she imagined it. She gathered herself and turned ahead to the grand entrance. The mission—yes, the mission needed her attention. Not a little fox that should be far from her mind at this moment.

The entrance doors of the villa were opened wide for the arriving guests. Using her peripheral, she noted the stares that followed her ascent but didn't allow her steps to falter. Whispered voices commented on the green shade of Felicity's dress and more than one guest mentioned the style of her hair.

"Very modern," one female said to another behind her gloved hand.

The crowd was led through the grand foyer of granite walls and windows inset with mosaics of greens and brown earth. The colors then fluctuated to a blue sky and a dragon in tinges of green flew from behind a glass cloud—an ode to Domhain's lost heritage. It had been called the Earth Realm, but now the once abundant land had turned mostly to stone—nature reinventing itself. Peaks had lifted from the ground, jutting out shards of thick rock in haphazard directions. Lakes and rivers had dried until pebbles and fossilized algae were the only sign of what used to be.

Felicity stopped in line, taking a silent step forward as individuals were introduced and welcomed by their host. Music wafted up to the waiting guests, a soothing aura that rose and fell in a beat and curled around Felicity. It drew her in, calming her previous anxiousness and settling her mission to the forefront of her mind. She breathed in the scent of fresh bread intermixed with citrus—the fruit likely imported from the orchards from her home realm Saol. She flicked her wavy hair behind her shoulder and added a small, nuanced sway to her hips as she made her way towards the herald.

Before she reached him, she recalled the instructions given to her by Harrison, her handler, prior to her departure. *Remove your glamour to fit in with the crowd. He prefers fae over humans.* He'd said this with a straight face, but Felicity could hear the discontent in his tone. Then he sighed and told her step two. *Connect with the target. Don't lose him or you'll have to work hard to gain his attention again.*

Tricky—but not impossible.

As she came to a stop, the herald peeked at her over gold-rimmed glasses and held out his hand, awaiting the invitation with her name on it. One brow lifted as he looked back up at her. "Oileán? I didn't think any of our island neighbors were able to attend?"

A guard stationed a few steps behind him—one of four Felicity had noted thus far—tilted an ear in their direction.

Felicity blushed. "Last minute trip. My father couldn't take my continuous pleading any longer. In the end, I believe he was thrilled he could send me away just to get me out of his hair."

She took a deep breath, prepared to continue a long tirade of a tale but the herald's pursed lips stopped her and he waved her ahead as he cleared his throat. "Lady Felicity Dwauer, of the Oileán

Island Territories." His voice carried over the hum of chatter in the cavernous ballroom.

As soon as Felicity's name was announced—her supposed location stated—the room quieted and everyone's attention diverted towards her. A few whispered behind cupped palms to their neighbors. It was rare that a member of the Oileán territories visited the mainland. If her previous grasps for attention hadn't worked, this information would seal the deal.

The silk of her dress brushed against her skin as she cascaded down the stairs and smiled at those willing to meet her gaze. This was what she was good at—setting herself apart from the other guests while also drawing them in. It was the only reason she could fathom why she was sent on this mission in the first place. Any of her fellow initiates could kill an advisor in cold blood—human or otherwise—but not many could do it discreetly while being the center of attention.

She took in the room as she descended. Tables were arranged in a large U-shape along the far wall and set for dinner. Many guests swayed to an ensemble of flutists and violinists. Others mingled in circles near a large fountain that cascaded water in a rainbow pattern. Three exits. Only a handful of guards, most stationed at the main entrance.

Their host stood at the bottom step to greet each guest. When his gaze met hers, her stomach churned as his grin turned to a leering smile. He was built like a rotund boulder. His short, light brown hair was styled in spikes atop his head. His pale-yellow jacket looked like urine against his gray skin. Someone needed to tell him that it wasn't his color—not that it would matter soon.

Felicity curtsied when she reached him. "Advisor Boister." With a demure smile, she straightened, her eyes trailing over his body before settling on his face. She blushed and held out her hand. "It's a pleasure to meet you. Such a lovely home."

"The pleasure is all mine." His lips brushed her knuckles, the touch lingering as he looked over her figure.

A corner of Felicity's mouth lifted a little higher, and his gaze settled on her lips.

"Save a dance for me?"

Felicity giggled and covered her face with one hand to hide flushed cheeks. "I wish I could, My Lord. But if you want to dance with me, we best do it now." With a snap of her wrist, she opened her fan and fluttered it. "It seems I've drawn attention, so I can't make promises of my availability." Felicity leaned in and whispered, "Intrigue and curiosity, you know?"

He chuckled as he held out his arm. "Confident in yourself. I like it."

Felicity slipped her arm into the crook of his. "But what about your other guests?" She glanced back at those left waiting, giving her best look of absolute apology between flutters of her fan as they walked away.

Boister chuckled. "And miss out on the chance to dance with you? My night would be ruined before it began." He clapped his hands and the orchestra halted the upbeat song they'd been playing before starting again with a bright, cheerful waltz. The upper-class fae liked to give off the air of pomp and circumstance.

The advisor rested his palm upon her upper waist, the other gripped her hand. Felicity gazed over his chest, playing the appreciative female as Harrison's words repeated in her mind. *At one point he'll attempt to pass off an envelope to another guest. It should be on his person, but you need that missive first.*

If she had to guess, the advisor was the type to think no one would be the wiser and what she needed would be hidden in the inside pocket of his coat. She met Boister's gaze with a shy smile that he ate up as his eyes perused her body. He growled as he pulled her closer to him and the dance began.

As they twirled, Felicity noted a wide range of the faerie castes interspersed throughout the room. The fae were more prominently present with their regal posture and humanistic qualities, then the pixies with glimmering wings, and a clurichaun with their short stature and pointed teeth who carried a tray of bubbly drinks from one group to the next. A few humans were present, some as guests while others wore the white tunics and black pants of a server.

Then she saw her. A woman dressed as any of the other hired servers entered from a side door with a tray ladened with glasses brimming with bubbling wine. Except Felicity knew her. Sometimes her guild felt the need to send backup. If the spy learned her truth, there was no way she would keep her mouth shut when she returned to the Tower.

The council had warned her that there was a chance her heritage would be exposed after this mission. Another reason Felicity had internally questioned those she usually trusted wholeheartedly.

Felicity's fellow initiates wouldn't like the truth. They already believed she received special privileges with the number of missions she received, but keeping such a secret as being fae would only bring chaos to the guild. Felicity had tried to nix the idea of assistance—she worked alone—but the council obviously denied her request.

Humans and faeries didn't exactly despise each other. At least not in the way that had led to wars being fought. There was a time that the human and faerie realms had lived in a cursory peace. But peace doesn't last forever and before trouble could come to pass, an agreement had been made to close the veil between worlds resulting in many humans returning to their own lands. There was the occasional uproar by the humans who wished to cross now, but also an understanding that it was for the best, so they muttered curses at their ancestors instead.

Felicity may have been one of the fae, but she felt a separation having grown up amongst humans. The music jarred her back to the present. This wasn't the time for these types of thoughts and the growing pinch of her shoes reminded her that she would prefer this evening be over sooner rather than later. Now she needed to dodge the view of this server. With a quick shift of her body, she hid her face into the advisor's neck and turned him to block the view of the other spy.

He snorted, his hand lowering a fraction against her side. "What brought you to the mainland?"

Felicity lifted her head to meet his gaze. "Adventure I suppose. I've never left the islands before." Training sessions shifted in her head. *Give details but keep them simple.* "I saw the invitation for the ball and couldn't turn down the opportunity." She hoped her outward expression showed a youthful excitement while she began to calculate how best to retrieve the missive.

"I've never seen so much marble in my life. Is it all from Domhain?"

The advisor dipped her, sweeping her in a slow arc. She took the chance to search her surroundings, not catching sight of the server. When he pulled her upright, Boister's arm wrapped around her lower back. "Most of it is. There was a lot of excavation along the mountains to find enough to create this masterpiece. When you live as long as we do, extravagance is necessary. I'll have to give you a tour of the estate if you stay for a while." There was hope in his expression. Hope that would die tonight with the light in his eyes.

"That would be lovely."

Blisters had begun to form on her heels by the third song. The advisor hadn't tired but did grab drinks between dances, his breath now laced with wine. After emptying each glass in big gulps, he would place the goblet down on the tray before the server disappeared. At each intermission, he'd procure a glass for her, but Felicity only took a small sip before placing it beside his empty one. If he noticed, he didn't comment. Felicity had to pivot, twist, and turn Boister away from the other guild member, adding to her sore feet and the beginning of a headache.

She had already ascertained that the envelope was exactly where she expected—a slow brush of her palm along his chest revealed the indentation of the parchment. The final stages of her mission repeated in her mind in Harrison's voice. *"Before the meeting takes place, discreetly kill him with this."* He held up the vial now hidden in her sleeve. *"...but remain within the ballroom. Ensure he's taken his final breath, then get out of there."*

"When is the meeting?"

"We don't know."

Thus far, the advisor hadn't even looked among the guests for his contact or drifted from her side. While it was not exactly the easiest place to pickpocket without alluding to something else, she needed an exit plan before making her move. Whoever was meant to receive that envelope would more than likely be handed it, not remove it from his pocket themselves. Unless they planned to get close—which meant she needed to stay closer.

"Let's eat," he announced after the fifth dance. She wasn't given a chance to comment before he took her hand and led her towards the head table. Others watched, probably trying to ascertain why their host had found her so interesting. Felicity wondered the same as he hadn't given her another moment to speak. To burrow her claws in further since their initial conversation. Felicity glanced about the crowd, looking for the server again and not finding her within view. With each ticking minute, the coolness of the vial permeated through the fabric to her skin—a reminder.

Soon.

"And who are you?" A gray mustached male leaned forward on the other side of Advisor Boister. He took a bite of the roasted pig, juice splashing onto his cheek. He really should consider using the folded napkin that sat beside his plate.

Her shoulders drew back, bristling at his tone. "Lady Felicity Dwauer, milord. I'm visiting from Oileán."

She gave him a warm smile, but he narrowed his gaze, the curled tips of his gray mustache lowering into a frown. He opened his mouth, but as if knowing her plight, a trumpet interrupted him. The music halted, and all attention turned towards the staircase. The advisor jumped to his feet, eyes wide. Felicity followed his gaze to the top of the stairs.

The herald stepped forward, and his voice echoed through the room. "The Crown Prince, Alarian."

Judging by Boister's excited glance, there, standing at the entrance of the ballroom, was the one individual who could turn this entire mission to shit.

Chapter 2

Everyone, including Felicity, stood from their seats or stopped dancing to bend into curtsies and low bows as two males began their descent. The first, a step ahead of the other, was dressed in expensive fabrics: dark brown vest and trousers trimmed with copper threading. He left the vest unbuttoned as it hung over broad shoulders, a cream tunic peeking through gave off an air of informality. His dark and fiery auburn hair was shorter on the sides with light waves on top, a strand curled over his brow. Sun-kissed skin made the freckles across his nose stand out—visible even from the distance.

He searched the crowd as he walked until his attention settled on her. His head tilted and her own gaze slid over him from head to toe before meeting his eyes again. Her lips pursed, chin lifting. With a sly smile, he turned back to the crowd.

Thankfully. She didn't want or need the attention of a prince. She had to admit, though, he sure could make an entrance. What his arrival would mean for her was still to be determined. Her gaze flicked to Advisor Boister who stood in awe. *Did the mission just prove to be more difficult?* Felicity knew little about the prince beyond that his family ruled over the eight realms and presided within Éardrom—the Light Realm.

"And Ward," the herald continued as the second male followed down the steps.

No title. No accolades. *No name?* She frowned. The spy within Felicity became curious, overclouding her previous concerns. His near-black hair lazily brushed his forehead, a few wisps dipping over one eye. He wore a black suit lined with silver threading in simple swirls along the hem and lapel. With hands folded behind, he kept a bored glare pinned on Prince Alarian's back.

The prince waved his hand, a signal for everyone to take their seats. When the orchestra started a new song, some continued to dance, casting glances in the direction of the new arrivals.

The advisor gripped Felicity's bicep. She was still chewing fresh berries as he forced her to her feet and dragged her around the tables towards his newly arrived guests. "The prince actually came. I thought the chance was slim since he didn't respond to the invitation. Would you care for me to introduce you?"

If it had been plausible, her answer would have been no, but leaving Boister's side wasn't a gamble she was willing to make. Not if she wanted to complete this mission. He bumped into a table and stumbled, signs that the copious amount of alcohol he'd consumed was beginning to take effect. Even if the prince's arrival might damn her plans—she needed to remain close.

Prince Alarian had settled on a chaise at the far corner of the room behind the orchestra with females already flocked to his side. One had snatched a vine of grapes from a server and sat on the edge near his knee, attempting to catch the prince's attention by feeding him. Felicity resisted the desire to scoff at their fawning. Yes, he was a prince, but was this excessive behavior necessary?

"He's the most eligible bachelor in all of Talamh," a fae whispered loud enough for any nearby to hear.

The prince ignored the gossip as he held his hand out to a passing server who bent forward to offer him a drink.

Ward stood behind the chaise with a serious, flat expression that caused most revelers to steer clear of him.

"Your Highness," Advisor Boister bowed once they reached him. "I'm honored you were able to attend. I can find you a more comfortable location if you prefer?"

The prince waved his hand as one might shoo away a fly. "Not necessary." He sipped his drink and then cocked his head, his gaze narrowing on her.

Felicity dipped into a curtsy as Boister pulled her forward. About to fall into the prince, she side-stepped, pivoted her heel, and caught her balance.

"This is Lady Felicity Dwauer of the Oileán Territories." The bastard hadn't even noted her fumble.

The prince pushed aside the fawning female's hand and stood. He took Felicity's hand from the advisor and pressed his lips to her knuckles, gaze meeting hers as he straightened. "It's a pleasure to meet you, Lady Dwauer. I didn't know we had visitors from the island territory."

"The pleasure is all mine, Your Highness." By the smell of alcohol on his breath, it was obvious he had celebrated prior to his arrival. By the way his gaze roamed over her body, she knew it was dangerous to tarry long in his presence. *He* wasn't part of the mission.

"The pleasure is mine, I'm sure." The orchestra began another song, and he took a step forward but almost stumbled into her. A gust of wind rushed between them, forcing the prince upright and Felicity to take a step back. Ward dropped his hand to his side, scrutinizing her as what she could only ascertain had been his air magic, stilled.

She ignored both of them and stepped nearer to the advisor. With a tilt of her head, she batted her eyes at him. "I hoped for another dance, milord." Even though she was starving, she didn't want to return to the table and give the male with the gray mustache a chance to question her further. And she needed to get the advisor away from the prince, retrieve that damned envelope, and finish this mission.

She was so close.

Boister gave a satisfied smile in Felicity's direction. "Excuse us. ..it seems the lady cannot wait for another dance."

"Save one for me?" the prince asked, stopping her in her tracks.

Felicity's grip tightened on Advisor Boister, and he patted her hand in response. With a flash of her best smile, she curtsied again. "We shall see how the evening continues. It appears you have many awaiting your attention." She steered the fumbling advisor away before the prince could comment further.

Prince Alarian chuckled behind her, undoubtedly distracted by said females vying for his consideration. Thankfully, the advisor didn't seem to mind that she'd drawn him away from a chance to further flatter the prince.

Advisor Boister darted a glance over his shoulder. "You don't want to dance with him?"

"Have you given me a reason to leave your side?" Felicity smiled warmly. It took sheer will not to wave away the stench of his horrid breath.

The advisor puffed up like a peacock. *Could it really be this easy?*

A prickling sensation brushed down her neck. With a peek over her shoulder, she expected to find the prince staring again only to meet his companion's gaze. Ward stood still as he watched her—not in the leering way as the prince had, but with his brows drawn together and mouth pursed.

Shit. She'd seen that look before and knew it meant it was time to disappear. Remaining in his line of vision would only heighten any suspicion he may have, and she didn't need another obstacle. Felicity veered the advisor onto the dance floor, keeping an eye out for the other spy, until they were enveloped by the crowd.

After a round of the bell chiming the half-hour, the lights dimmed, and the music changed to an eerie cadence. The dances became a swaying movement of bodies pressed together, the sharp and jarring change in the sound matching the guests' mood. Some fondled others while a few had pressed their partners against a wall, tongues down the other's throat. Food laid out on the long tables mostly went ignored. The sight of it only made Felicity's stomach grumble in protest.

Not that the advisor had noticed. He had become less inhibited, his lips pressed against her neck, trailing kisses down to her shoulder. She'd leaned into him, sliding a hand between the lapel of his jacket when he attempted to grab her ass. Felicity gave a gentle push back, not to anger him but put a little space between them and redirected his roaming hands with subtle movements.

"Playing hard to get," he purred in her ear before his teeth nipped her neck. "I like it."

She choked back rising bile and stepped away. He didn't notice the slight as another server passed by and Boister took a glass from the tray and gulped down the contents. There was no need for her to wait any longer—at the very least to get his grimy hands off her. She was beginning to wonder if he even remembered his planned rendezvous. His head rested on her shoulder, breathing heavy. They were no longer observed at every turn, the guests involved in their own debauchery and much more enthralled by the prince. In a way, his royal highness had become the distraction she needed.

It was time to make her move and hopefully without drawing the attention of the guild's backup.

Felicity reached for a glass off the tray, and took a sip, licking at the candied sugar on the rim. Under a hooded gaze, the advisor gave a guttural growl. He moved in closer as she swayed to the music, keeping them near the edge of the fray yet still visible and finished the contents of her own glass in one gulp.

"Do you want another?" The advisor breathed, his chest heaving.

"Only if you have one with me." Felicity bit her bottom lip and his gray skin hardened like stone, his magic coursing through his body in a wave as it moved over exposed skin. His control was weakening—she had him right where she wanted him. Oblivious.

Before he could flag down another server, she pressed into him, resting her hand against his chest along the hem of his coat. Heat sizzled off his skin, warming her fingers. "You know, this is the first time I've been to the mainland."

She slid her hand under the coat, resting it on his stone chest. His gaze pierced hers, his pupils dilating. "And how do you like it here?"

Oh, he made it so easy. She lowered her chin, peering up at him through her thick lashes, her fingers clutching the tip of the envelope. As she slid it out, she kissed him and the male wrapped his arms tight around her body, stilling her roving hand to be stuck between them.

Wonderful—like his breath wasn't bad enough.

For a moment, panic rushed through her. She forced herself to relax and released some of the pressure between their bodies as she deepened the kiss. When she created enough space, she removed the envelope and slid it down the cleavage of her dress into her corset.

She stepped back, blushing. "I'm sorry. I was too forward." She crossed her arm under her chest, resting her hand on the edge of her sleeve, drawing his attention towards her breasts. With his gaze lingering on the intended location, she removed the hidden vial, encasing it in her palm.

"No, not at all," he slurred, straightening his coat as he stumbled slightly. "How about one more drink, then I can show you the rest of my estate?"

She nodded her agreement as he reached for two glasses from a passing tray at the same time another fae reached for one. He jerked back as their fingers brushed, the glass toppled, and the contents splashed all over Felicity. She gasped, her grip tightening on the vial, hiding it from view as she looked down at the wine dripping down her front.

The other female covered her mouth in surprise. "I apologize."

Boister grabbed a glass from the server. "Think nothing of it."

Felicity bit her tongue to stifle her frustration. She also kept an extra eye on this new arrival, curious if she was the contact the advisor was waiting for.

As the full-bodied female cocked her head in Felicity's direction, purple hair cascaded over her shoulder and her pearlescent skin shimmered in the candlelight. "Please let me help you." She twisted her hand a few inches above Felicity's dress, and the liquid siphoned off and evaporated. Felicity had never seen magic used this way nor met someone from Visce, the Water Realm. She couldn't pull her attention away as her dress dried and the wine seemed to evaporate in thin air.

Felicity smiled. "Thank you."

She regarded Felicity with a feline grin and nudged the advisor. "I can't help but wonder who this female is who's taken so much of your attention this evening?"

The advisor hiccupped, the contents of his glass sloshing. At least he hadn't finished it yet. With an inward curse, Felicity gave the female a warm smile. "Lady Felicity Dwauer. You are?" Of course this mission couldn't be effortless—she'd been so close.

The advisor reached an arm around Felicity's waist and nuzzled into her neck.

The female sidled closer. "Lady Molyle." Her blue eyes searched hers. "I'm glad to have met you. Did you want another drink? I noticed how much you enjoyed your last one."

An idea began to form and Felicity grinned. Maybe this interruption could be useful after all. "We could share."

A visible shiver passed over Lady Molyle. She took a sip, Felicity noting a tattoo of sea kelp on the side of the female's neck peeking out from the trim of her dress. She held the glass out to Felicity.

Advisor Boister watched the exchange and pulled Felicity in tighter to his side—his possessiveness becoming a living thing. She ignored him as she took a sip, slow and steady. Both pairs of eyes lingered on the bob of Felicity's throat as she swallowed.

Leaving a small amount in the glass, she eyed them both under heavy lids. She handed the cup back to Lady Molyle before gently pushing the advisor's glass to his lips. Felicity bent her wrist just right, the contents of the vial slipped in before she enclosed it in her palm and pulled back her hand. Felicity removed his hold from her waist and with a gentle twist, she kissed his wrist while he drank.

Lady Molyle's attention returned to Felicity, her lips parting as their gazes met.

"She's mine tonight, Lady Molyle," the advisor stammered. "I don't usually share."

Lady Molyle bit her lip, her pleading smile turning to horror as her eyes widened and her hand covered her mouth. A glass fell and shattered against stone.

Felicity turned towards the advisor.

And screamed.

He dropped to the floor, his body convulsing, green blood and froth dripping from his mouth. While everyone's attention was on the advisor, she dropped the vial, stepping on it to ensure the glass broke and mixed the evidence among the shards of glass. Felicity cried, covering her face with her hands as she collapsed beside him. More guests came out of whatever debauchery they were involved in and crowded around the fallen fae. Lady Molyle gripped Felicity's shoulders, but she pulled away from the female, reaching for Boister.

"Someone help him," Felicity pleaded, her damp eyes widening in shock.

The convulsions stopped and it seemed to signal the others into action. A pixie stepped forward and stared down at the male while others held the crowd back. Advisor Boister coughed, gasping for air as bile and the leaf-green blood flew. Felicity ignored what landed on her dress and cheek, letting loose another pleading gasp.

Then the advisor stilled.

Felicity sobbed, trying to catch her breath. "Is he...?"

The observer, his face pale and wings drooped, placed a hesitant hand on Boister's chest and then checked his breathing. His expression fell. "I'm sorry—he's dead."

"How?" Crawling towards him, Felicity bent over the advisor's body with shaking fingers and brushed his forehead. "We were just dancing…"

Another female pushed through the crowd and settled on the floor beside him. Her nose bunched. "Between the convulsions and foaming at the mouth it looks as though he's been poisoned."

With a gasp, Felicity covered her mouth. "What?"

Lady Molyle touched her shoulders again. This time Felicity allowed herself to be pulled away and clutched to the female's arm as she shook her head. She pinched her eyes closed to force out more tears.

The male with the gray mustache broke through the onlookers with his finger pointed at Felicity. "You were the only one with him."

Felicity had expected this. He had been curious about her when they sat down, and she knew he'd be the one to make accusations. With a whimper, Felicity buried her head into Lady Molyle's shoulder.

"How could you," Lady Molyle snapped. "I was with them the entire time. She could have done no such thing."

Felicity hiccupped against the female for added effect while hiding a smile into the female's sleeve.

Collecting herself, she pulled back, wiping away tears until someone handed her a handkerchief. She dabbed her eyes, searching the crowd. "Check with the serving staff. They were the ones passing the drinks."

Gray Mustache grumbled a few words under his breath, then ordered one of the guards to do as she recommended. This was the perfect way to get Felicity's backup out of here, and hopefully before the spy had seen her in her fae form.

Lady Molyle helped Felicity to her feet, leading her away from the body. She shuddered and the crowd ate it up, surrounding her, adding their own words of comfort.

Prince Alarian appeared, toeing at the advisor's boot before Ward pulled him back while he rolled his eyes. The prince sniffed. "Should cover this up at least. A ghastly sight, don't you think?" He leaned into Ward, his smile extending into a vicious grin, needing the male to keep him upright. He hadn't danced once, but it seemed he had continued to enjoy the drinks. "This is one way to end a party, I guess. If he wanted us to leave, all he'd had to do was ask."

Felicity hid her smile behind her hands, letting out a small blubber of a cry. Molyle pulled her into her shoulder and shushed her.

At the sound of footsteps, Felicity glanced up. A human dressed in the server's garb stepped through the crowd, a guard at his side. The guard pressed the man into the center of the crowd. "Tell them what you told me."

The server swallowed deeply. "There was another server. We thought she had been added on by the staff. She's now unaccounted for."

The male with the gray mustache groaned. "I warned Boister." He ran a hand over his face. He pointed towards the door, his words for the guard. "Send others to search for the missing server. Track her down immediately. Search the roads in each direction." Regarding Felicity for a moment, he sighed. "I apologize for my rudeness, milady. Is there anything we can get for you?"

"I just want to go," Felicity cried.

"Of course." He turned towards the server. "Call for the lady's carriage. I believe this party is over." Gray Mustache grumbled under his breath as he shooed people away from the advisor's body. Felicity was certain she heard him mutter more about Boister ignoring his recommendation to hire more security.

Lady Molyle led her towards the steps, and Felicity felt a pin-prick on her back again. When she peered behind her, making sure to give one last grieved glance at the advisor, she caught Ward watching with a look she couldn't place—his eyes wide and mouth gaped. Felicity didn't delay, no matter how much she wanted to understand that expression. Soon it wouldn't matter because she'd never see the male again.

Chapter 3

The carriage reached the opposite side of the pass through the Balla Mountains that separated Domhain from Saol—Felicity's realm. As the dawn light began to glow over the horizon, the haze lifted above the landscape of citrus orchards, farmland, and green fields where cows and sheep began to stir. Roosters crowed the hour as the farms came alive with the morning sun.

Barely visible through the low-hung clouds was the Tower's outline—the single spire extending into the sky. Felicity had become as much a part of the Tower as it was of her during the last fifteen years.

She'd been abandoned on the Tower's doorstep at what was believed to be the age of five in nothing but ragged clothes and an oversized cloak. Raised within the guild's walls, she'd strived to advance through the ranks as quickly as she could. Four years later, she became the youngest recruit the Tower had ever seen. Her peers attributed it to special privileges after having grown up among the trainers, but Felicity knew not to doubt herself. Five months ago, she became an initiate and received her first mission. Soon she'd reach Graduate status and be well on her way to being a Master—a small group considered the most infamous spies and assassins within the eight realms.

Then she wouldn't be sent on measly jobs like poisoning an advisor but instead have the freedom to pick her missions. She was the Tower's weapon. But she wanted some choice in the matter, even if she never planned on leaving the only place she had called, or would ever call, home.

In preparation to give her report, she went over the logistics of the mission. The guards? *Four and useless.* The guests? *About one hundred fifty and from different castes.* Unnecessary babysitter posing as a server? *One—she could have handled it herself.* Special guests? *A drunken prince and a suspicious male.*

She pinched her eyes shut and rubbed her temples in an attempt to brush off that last look Ward had given her—the one she hadn't yet deciphered. It shouldn't matter. He would return with the prince to Éardrom on the northernmost tip of the continent. It would be years before there was even a chance their paths could cross again.

When they reached the Tower's gate, the doors opened by a system of pulleys operated by hidden recruits she could smell with her fae senses. There were eight: hidden upon rafters, within shadows, and among the bushes. Her glamour was already back in place. The use of this magic helped to abate the growing queasiness and headache from her infrequent use of glamour—a common side effect and weakness she despised. A heaviness settled in her chest, and she leaned her head back, concentrating again on the report.

One problem at a time.

When the carriage rolled to a stop, Felicity didn't wait for the footman before exiting and heading straight towards the team of horses. In one hand, she held the horrid now-bloodied shoes, and in the other, two carrots she'd stashed in the carriage at the beginning of this escapade—one for each horse.

"Damnit, Felicity." The driver bounded down. "You going to clean those bits? Cuz' I'm not doing it again."

She hid her smile as she brushed a hand over each of the horse's noses as they crunched on their treats. "I have to get in and give my report."

The driver grumbled under his breath. It was Idan's usual response but seeing as she was the only one who ever gave the horses any attention, she knew his gruff exterior was a façade. When she arrived later to help, Idan's temper wouldn't change but his annoyance would be long forgotten. The two of them had grown to have an understanding in the past years. Neither spoke much to the other, but she could spoil the horses from time to time if she carried her weight around the barn.

When she reached the side entrance near the back end of the circular stone tower, she knocked twice to warn them she was coming before opening the door. After stepping down a short flight of stairs, she entered a small room that held little beyond a table and a few stools. The tattooist pointed to a divider—the usual routine unnecessary to explain. It had been the same since she had become an initiate. She slid behind, removed the envelope and placed it on a stool before taking off the ballgown and slipping on the undergarments and wool shift waiting for her.

When she came back out, she stilled, and all her training took precedence—her chin rose, her expression emptied as she met the gaze of the man waiting for her. *What was he doing here?*

Harrison gestured to the stool, the tattooist readying his instruments. "I'm taking your report this morning."

This was unprecedented, but so far, only the basics of this mission had made sense. She hesitated, just for a fraction of a moment, and then took a seat and held out the envelope she'd acquired.

Harrison took it, stuffing it into his breast pocket before leaning back against the worktable. Her gut grumbled—not from hunger. Even with the glamour back in place, her stomach wasn't settling. In these rare cases, it meant she would need a private session in the training hall but that wasn't going to be an option anytime soon. She needed to ensure Harrison believed everything was all right. The last thing she wanted was for him to question if she was ill.

It took all her self-control not to vomit all over the tattooist. He prepped to add the twenty-ninth star to the moon on her hip—one for each mission she had completed since her initiation. The twenty-eighth star had been added the previous morning. Yet another reason for her to question the Tower sending her on this mission. It was unheard of for an initiate to be sent out again so soon. Only those at Graduate status were requested to do such things and only on rare occasions.

The tattooist removed the bandage, brow furrowing at the sight of the nearly healed star. Although her magic didn't allow the immediate healing many fae had, it was still quicker than a human's ability. Unbeknownst to the tattooist, infinitesimal granules of salt were added to the ink used for her markings. Felicity bit her lip, waiting for a comment, a question...anything. Instead, the man sniffed and continued about his work as though nothing was amiss.

As a member of the council, Harrison knew the secret of her fae heritage, so he might be here to quell any questions. Or so she hoped. Not that her secret would remain one for long if the server spy had discovered the truth.

Harrison rested his hands along the edge of the worktable and watched as the man disinfected the area for the new addition. "It's done then? The advisor is confirmed dead with none the wiser?"

She told him what was necessary, repeating the information she'd practiced, withholding only Ward's expression. That didn't seem like vital information. "The only one who suspected was a male with a gray mustache. I didn't catch his name, but he changed his mind after a little bluffing and some witness reports." Felicity gritted her teeth when the needle hit a sensitive portion of her outer thigh and another bout of nausea rolled through her.

"Witnesses?" Harrison straightened. His usually immaculate clothing was ruffled and looked similar to what he had worn the previous day. It was obvious he hadn't slept. He ran a hand through tousled hair, the gray speckles near his temple illuminated by the lantern light in the otherwise windowless room. "Does that mean you were seen?"

The tattooist snorted, and Felicity couldn't help but smile. She wasn't known as 'The Weapon' for nothing.

Her brow furrowed. "No." She bit back the sarcastic comment on the tip of her tongue. "Your extra eyes were useless by the way." *Except as a scapegoat*, she didn't add.

Harrison tilted his head. "You were informed that it was a step we might have to make."

Not that she could refute the request to remove her glamour in the first place. She bit the inside of her mouth and clenched it shut. It took sheer will not to move or let her anger rise to the surface. It was the only emotion she allowed to show—all others stifled out of her. To be hidden from view from everyone else. Unless they were part of her act, of course.

The tattooist wiped the last of the ink from her skin with a piece of soft parchment. Content with his work, he covered the new tattoo with leaves lathered in aloe and then wrapped her leg with a bandage, certain to cover the nearly healed star.

The man turned to clean his tools, but Harrison cleared his throat. "If finished with the tattoo, you're excused." The tattooist nodded, leaving them with the musty stench of earth within the underbelly of the Tower.

And there went her first assumption as to why Harrison was here—to dispel any curiosity away from her quick healing.

Despite the mid-summer season, Harrison rubbed his hands together to ward off the morning chill. With Dorcha as their eastern neighbors, it was always cold in Saol. The Dark Realm was in eternal winter, and the weather permeated over their craggy snow-peaked mountains, keeping Saol cool throughout the year. It allowed the farmers to produce the majority of the agriculture for many of the realms since it never was miserably hot.

Harrison pulled the tattooist's stool out and sat upon it. "It's just the two of us now. I want you to speak freely without judgment."

This could be a trick—a test. She watched for the crease between his brows. It was his only tell and one that had to be caught quickly because it was always gone in a split second. It wouldn't be the first time the Tower lulled her into a false sense of security to see if she would crack. But she didn't believe Harrison would do that. He'd been her handler for the past ten years and never gave her a reason to doubt him.

"Why was I sent on this mission? I'm not a Graduate and Bishop claimed favoritism—is it true?" Words spilled like the vomit she was holding back.

The sharp lines of his expression relaxed. "It wasn't favoritism, Felicity. Bishop was angry because he wants there to be equality while the rest of the council knows that isn't an option. As for why you were chosen—partly your heritage but more importantly, you're flawless."

She gritted her teeth, the compliment passing over her. Bishop, liaison to the realms, was a thorn in her side. He didn't like her and the feeling was mutual. But it was the comment on her heritage that nearly caused the stool she sat upon to splinter in her grip. She was about to lose the last secret she protected if she didn't watch out.

This secret she had kept wholly her own. Not even the council was aware of it. Maybe it was because the Tower might use it in their arsenal like they had her heritage.

She would need to be prepared for the repercussions of the truth being uncovered and hoped the council would be as well. If anything, the guild wouldn't appreciate the secret being kept from them, but it had been a choice made by the Countess—the leader of the guild—for as long as Felicity could remember. And one thing you never did was ask the Countess why she chose to do something.

Harrison sighed, knowing he had lost her attention.

How had she allowed herself to relax? That wasn't like her. The familiarity that crossed over Harrison's face had put her at ease. Drawing back her shoulders, Felicity took on her neutral expression again. Was he trying to catch her off guard?

"We had our reasons for asking what we did of you tonight, Felicity. It wasn't a choice any of us took lightly. You trust the Countess, do you not?"

Felicity nodded. Even after tonight, she knew the Countess had her best interests in mind. "I'm the Tower's weapon to be used as you see fit. If you had your reasons, I shouldn't question them."

Harrison stood and held out a hand towards her. She looked at it for a moment, then back up at him before she stood on her own. He dropped his arm to his side, sadness flashing in his expression, gone as quick as the warmth that had entered moments before.

"For the future." Harrison nodded.

"With my honor and my blood," Felicity finished the oath to the Tower as Harrison headed towards the exit.

"Get some rest. You deserve it." He left the door open behind him.

Uncertain of what had just transpired, she waited a few moments before she left the room. Why had he taken her report? His presence only heightened her curiosity about the mission itself and she had more questions than answers. An ache pulsed through her muscles, reminding her she hadn't slept in hours. Maybe a clear mind and good sleep would help her piece things together. She could get away with a few hours of rest if her twisting stomach allowed it. Then maybe the world would feel normal once again.

***

When she woke a little later, Felicity careened over the side of her bed and vomited up the contents of the previous evening into a basin. Wiping her mouth with the back of her hand, she fumbled upright, almost tipping it over. Tonight, she would need a private training session or her weakening body would get worse before it got better. It was the burden she carried to protect the secret she withheld from everyone.

After she rinsed off her face and neck, she ran a comb through her hair before braiding it over her shoulder. There weren't any mirrors in their private rooms, so Felicity had no idea if the blood from the advisor's spittle remained hidden in a crevice. Once dressed, her crystal pendant tucked under the collar of her tunic, she began the exhausting descent to the main floor, muscles opposing to the trek and feet aching and sore from those horrid shoes.

She passed through the food hall but only grabbed a roll from the basket at the end of the line, stomach protesting at the sight of the fresh berries and the now cold bowls of oatmeal. The few present, mostly graduates, didn't pay her any mind which meant her identity might still be hers—or the news of her heritage hadn't yet spread like wildfire.

Making her way to the training hall, she stuffed the last bite in her mouth, trying to abate the nausea rolling through her system. This session wouldn't release the discomfort, but it would allow her to use some of the pent-up energy remaining from the previous night. Dancing may be a form of exercise, her muscles may also ache, but it wasn't enough to replace the training she'd missed the day before. Besides, there was no way she could show weakness within these walls and missing another session would cause others to question her ability.

She waltzed inside and passed the smaller training circles outlying the larger center ring. Sawdust billowed up from scuffles and dragged feet as recruits and initiates sparred. As she passed, heads jerked in her direction and a few eyed her from their periphery. Felicity ignored them.

During the first few weeks after her initiation, every time she returned from a completed mission, she'd been welcomed with a sense of reverence. Awe. After her tenth mission, when others had only completed five or six within the same amount of time, the admiration turned to suspicion and now only hate and jealousy remained. For a group of spies and assassins who'd been taught to forget emotions, their expressions didn't lack any in her presence. Bishop knew there was a problem between her and the others, but he didn't know the half of it. She heard some of what they whispered behind her back—words she chose to ignore.

Sparring partners awaited a signal from the center ring, a trainer watching from the outskirts with his hands clasped behind his back. She stopped beside him. Without a glance in her direction, he nodded. "Do you want a go?"

Sweat and dust clung to the graduates as they faced off. At the sound of the training whistle, one rushed the other. Spectators watched from the outskirts, awaiting their turn. Felicity anticipated the second's dodge, and the resounding crack of a broken nose echoed throughout the space. The scent of blood intermixed with the musty odor of sweat. None of the four windows opened, and the drafty cracks in the old stone walls weren't enough to offer a reprieve from the stench. It wasn't helping her sensitive stomach. "Naw. I wanted to work on the Tree today."

The trainer nodded, gruff expression unchanging. "Harness up."

At the back of the training hall was a suspended obstacle course nicknamed "The Tree." Two large trunk stanchions were connected by platforms that branched out until they reached heights of up to fifteen feet. Some of the branches were rounded while others were connected with ropes that teetered and wobbled. Long braided cables hung vertically to climb and swing from one platform or rope to another.

Felicity wound her braid up into a knot on the top of her head as she considered the direction she wanted to go. After tightening the straps of the harness around her torso and legs, she stood on her tiptoes to tie a safety rope around a metal ring. She gripped a nearby cable and began the climb, muscles burning through her arms and chest. When she reached the second level, she grabbed hold of a makeshift rope bridge and started in the direction of the trunk where she could access hand and foot holds to the top.

"Hey!"

Felicity ignored the bellow from below and continued her ascent.

"We want the course."

She stopped her climb and looked below to find her fellow initiate Garder and two others. They had been friends once—until his jealousy got in the way. Now, like the others, he usually gave her a wide berth. "Then come up. Plenty of room," she shot back.

"There isn't enough space for us and your ego."

Felicity ground her teeth. Why did they have to choose today to fuck with her? One of the others was chuckling alongside Garder while the third rubbed the back of his neck and averted his gaze. Frustration welled, attempting to break through. *Use the anger, don't let the anger use you.* This was one of the first lessons they'd been taught but some obviously still had difficulty with the concept.

She tightened her grip on the rope she'd been using and swung her body to the left until her foot caught hold of one of the branches. "If you can't share, then you'll have to wait."

"We'll fight you for it?" This voice wasn't Garder's but his laughing friend.

Felicity shrugged. "Have to catch me first." She stifled the smile playing at the corner of her lips.

The third shook his head and stepped back. "It's all you guys. I'm not messing with *that*."

"Suit yourself." Garder and his friend buckled on their harnesses and started their climb.

Felicity reassessed her surroundings. Fewer branches jutted out near the stanchions, which wouldn't give her much room to move about. But if she went back towards the center, they could surround her. It would force them to separate and although she'd have to watch her back, it would give her more space to maneuver.

By the time she had reached her new location, the other two had split, one coming up from her left and Garder on her right. She settled herself on a suspended branch, her hands gripping two vertical cables, waiting like a spider in her web as they moved in. Her gaze narrowed.

Garder was the first to reach her. He kicked swiftly, his white-knuckled grip on the rope keeping him in place. She dodged it, twisting her body away from him. When the second leapt at her from behind, she hopped off the edge to a lower level, grabbing the ropes to catch herself. Her arms ached and she bit back a groan. His hand slipped on the rope she'd just abandoned. He swung around to save himself and almost knocked into Garder.

"Watch it," Garder growled between tight teeth.

Felicity grabbed Garder's ankle and yanked his foot out from under him. He floundered, his other hand grasping his friend's shoulder to catch his balance. Unprepared for the weight, the second fell. Garder caught himself on the now vacant handhold as the other screamed until the slackened rope tightened, stopping him from smacking his face into the ground. The third helped the second stand. He wasn't laughing anymore.

An audience had congregated at the foot of the Tree. Even the trainer watched with a thoughtful look on his face.

Garder climbed down beside her. She pivoted right before being punched in the face but caught it in the shoulder instead. With a quick duck under the second punch aimed at her temple, her fist connected with his gut.

"Damn you." He grabbed her arm and yanked her towards him, attempting to unbalance her. Using the momentum, she kneed him in the groin, letting her footing clear the edge of the branch. As she fell, she shot her arm out and gripped the edge of the platform. When a few cheers and groans followed her move, Felicity heard the chatter of bets being placed.

Garder clutched his groin, his face bright red. Underneath his platform, she calculated her next move. Straining her already tense muscles, she swung her legs to give herself momentum. The branch moved as she rocked. Garder stumbled, grabbing a plank above to steady himself. Felicity leapt to another rope. Her arms screamed in protest as she pulled up. Bile rose in her throat, and as fun as it would be to see the crowd scatter, she swallowed deep.

Weakness wasn't allowed.

"Pathetic," he hissed it like a curse. "Tired after all the preening from the council. Two missions too much for you?" He began to straighten and by the glint in his eye, she knew what he planned to do. They hadn't sparred together in weeks, but his tells hadn't changed. He charged, his stride lengthening with surprising balance on the teetering branch.

"Nope." She braced for his attack. With one leg wrapped in the rope and grip tight, she kicked the platform with her other foot.

He tried to account for the disruption as the platform he'd been running on jerked left and right. His eyes widened when his foot slipped—too late. He attempted to catch himself but missed the rope, his side smacking into one of the platforms as he fell.

Garder didn't scream as the other had. He growled and grunted as he was forced to a stop a few feet from the ground. Others rushed over to assist him, but he pushed them away. "Leave it," he grumbled loud enough for Felicity to hear.

"Felicity."

Everyone stilled, including Garder who had just found his footing.

She met Harrison's gaze just a few feet outside of the crowd and froze as she spotted the man who stood at his side. Ward, once again, had that unidentifiable expression on his face. *What were the odds that he'd been at the advisor's party and here?* This couldn't be a coincidence. Her anger withered at the sight of them, replaced by an uncertainty she wasn't familiar with.

"Come down here," Harrison called up. He left the fae male alone to speak with the trainer. By the time she reached the ground, Harrison's lecture could be heard throughout the hall. "If one of them had been hurt—or worse? You just stood by and watched."

Felicity tuned him out, her own head muddled with the reality of Ward's presence. She wiped the sweat off her forehead with the back of her hand. By the time she had removed the harness, everyone else had gone back to their sparring, though many darted furtive glances in the direction of the fae male.

Ward shook his head as Harrison returned and she stopped in front of them. "You can't be serious?"

"Is there a problem?" Harrison asked.

"It couldn't have been her. She..." Ward paused, lips pressed tight. With a deep breath, he met her gaze with a piercing one of his own. "There must be a misunderstanding."

Misunderstanding? If anything, *she* should be asking what was going on—not this stranger. But her training kicked in and she kept her mouth shut. She was here to follow orders.

Harrison ground his teeth and looked Felicity up and down. "Do you need to see a healer?"

She shook her head. Besides a few bruises and scrapes, she was fine.

"Good. Follow me." Harrison turned but before he took a step, Ward gripped his shoulder, forcing him to a stop.

On instinct, she slipped between them, facing off against the fae male.

"Felicity," Harrison warned from behind and her eyes widened at her own response. She stepped aside and lowered her gaze to the ground. Harrison cleared his throat. "Come along. The others are waiting."

A heaviness settled in the nauseated pit of Felicity's stomach. Each step felt like a pulsing drum in her head. The last individual she'd ever thought she'd see again was here. She frowned. He hadn't expected to find her. What did that mean? More importantly, what did he want from her?

Chapter
4

Harrison led them to one of the meeting rooms used for elite clientele. Brightly colored tapestries hung from the wall behind the head chair and a large rectangular table was settled on a woven rug in the middle of the room. Centered above the table was an ornate brass chandelier that extended from the stone ceiling with hanging crystals emitting rainbows from the glow of lit candles.

A sense of uneasiness washed over her—initiates weren't called to this room—but outwardly she remained unfazed.

The Countess sat erect at the head of the table, gray swirls intermixed within dark brown locks settled in a bun on the top of her head, not a hair out of place. Between her petite frame, the crinkle of laugh lines around her mouth and the creases above her brow, many underestimated the leader of the Tower. To assume her weak would be the last mistake anyone made.

Felicity knew that if the Countess was here, whatever the reason for this impromptu meeting was serious.

But more surprising was who sat beside her—Prince Alarian. He was definitely hungover judging from the disheveled hair dangling over one eye, partially untucked shirt, and the lazy grin resting on his perfectly shaped mouth.

It could only mean one thing—Felicity was in deep shit.

Was there a detail she had missed? *Connect with Boister, get the envelope, poison him, ensure he was dead, then get out.* Straight forward enough. So, why was she here now in front of the Countess and the prince?

Harrison cleared his throat and Felicity dropped into a polite curtsy, her shoulders tightening as Ward stalked past.

"Please rise," the prince beckoned. She complied and surveyed the room. Harrison stayed beside her with hands clasped behind his back. Cursing herself for not noticing before, she spotted Bishop on the Countess's other side. Two more rules crossed her mind: *Know where all the players were within a room upon entering it. Plan for the worst and know where your exits were located.*

"Well, isn't this a surprise?" Prince Alarian's smile widened. "I'm impressed. Here I was expecting it to be someone of complete inconsequence and yet it was the female at the advisor's side the entire evening that dealt his killing blow."

Bishop, jaw clenched, hissed with disdain from his perch.

Felicity had long learned to ignore the liaison, if only to keep her anger in check. But the prince—it was as though his words stroked a flame deep within and she gritted her teeth in response. Why did everyone underestimate her? From the way he spoke, he must have been the one to procure her for the mission, but she'd previously never been called to stand before a client. Anonymity was key in her line of work.

Maybe it was because he was the prince?

Harrison rocked from one foot to the next, his nervousness palpable. She'd never seen him this way and it gave a heightened uneasiness to her already nauseated stomach.

The Countess nodded in Felicity's direction. "Your test required the best, so we offered it."

Test? Felicity kept the question from her expression. Instead, she studied a spot in the middle of the table, uncertain where to look in this uncharted territory.

Bishop cleared his throat. "Should we allow her to listen in?"

Harrison rolled his eyes. "You're always quick to shut her out. If Prince Alarian has no qualms with her attendance, you shouldn't either."

"Attendance?" Ward asked, his tone annoyed. "She's standing right here."

The Countess rested a hand on the table. "A cuff is placed on our initiates' ear. Once the locking word is uttered, a spell will block their ability to hear. It protects them from the knowledge of the political workings within the realms. Our initiates are trained in court intrigue and social norms, but politics are excluded to ensure they remain unbiased on missions with certain sensitivities. We've taught them basics such as trade routes and what the resources are for each realm to allow for smooth conversation in social circles."

Felicity's stomach flipped. A rush of warmth slithered under her skin, spreading through her. With counted breaths, she attempted to relax the heightened rigidness of her body. She knew this. Trusted the Tower. It didn't mean she liked it, though.

"How do you unblock their hearing?" Prince Alarian stared at Felicity as if she were a prize horse. Already trained, already broken. Felicity resisted the desire to bite her bottom lip. *Use the anger. Don't let the anger use you.* The lesson repeated through her mind again and again.

"By saying her name out loud. She cannot undo it herself—the magic won't allow it." The Countess folded her hands in her lap. "Now to get to business—are you satisfied with her performance?"

Ward opened his mouth but the prince cut him off. "Satisfied? I'm still in utter shock that such a proper little thing not only swiped the envelope but also killed the advisor right under our noses. Her performance was impressive. Believable to the bitter end. With the way Ward here watched her like a hawk tracking a kill, I'm surprised he didn't realize it was her." He chuckled. "She'll fit right in with the court. We can continue her facade of being a visitor from the Oileán islands, frightened and heartbroken after her experience at the advisor's ball."

Ward snorted. "You can't be serious." His gaze narrowed on her, and Felicity met it, her lips pursed. "They might not have been aware last night, but you would be putting her in danger. She's demi-fae, and none are known to reside within Oileán. The court will sniff her out within a week."

Felicity resisted the urge to vomit, hands clenched at her side.

The Countess shook her head. "She's not demi-fae. The little magic she contains allows her to glamour herself. In a guild of humans, we needed her to blend in while she was here."

Blinking, the mission—test—and the conversation with Harrison from that morning rushed through her mind, but she tried to concentrate. There had never been a reason to question the Countess before. She turned her attention to the grooves and grain of the table. It had been sanded recently. A few spots still needed a fresh coat of stain.

Loyal. Weapon. Home. All words that described what this place was and who she was because of it.

"Any other magic?" the prince asked, fingers steepled as he continued to look her over.

"Beyond the glamour—no."

His grin widened. "Good. My father wouldn't be pleased otherwise. We don't want him to question who's the deadliest in the room. He doesn't like competition."

The only knowledge she had of the royal family was that the prince was the king and queen's only child. Ward, however, was still a mystery. Maybe he was a friend or companion of the prince?

Harrison cleared his throat and eyed Bishop. "There are some requirements and she'll need opportunities to train. Here are a few other important notes regarding her stay with you."

Bishop handed the prince an envelope enclosed with a wax seal of a wolf wearing a collar of a snake tied in a braided knot eating its own tail. An ouroboros—the insignia of the Tower. The liaison pushed a parchment towards the prince. "Do we have a deal?"

Stay? Deal? What was happening? A chance to work for royalty would be a step closer to achieving her goal, but to leave the Tower—that was something else altogether.

Without looking down, the prince pulled the paper towards him. "I'll need that word to initiate the spell." He looked over the parchment, ignoring the quill extended to him. Instead, one materialized in a puff of shadow beside his ear and he plucked it out of the air to sign the agreement.

"Of course." The Countess smiled. "It's sámhach."

Everything became fuzzy and inaudible—the only indication of a conversation was the movement of their mouths. Felicity gritted her teeth and memorized the table.

***

Once back in her room, Felicity bent in front of a trunk at the end of her bed, pulled the floorboard beside it loose, and removed the key from its hiding place. With a click, the lock popped open, and she dragged the cloak clear from the trunk. She held up the gray wool fabric and brushed her fingers over the drops—stained memories she didn't remember.

There was no connection behind it. Nothing to draw her to where it came from or whom it had belonged to. All she knew was that she had been found wrapped within it on the Tower's doorstep. It was hers now. The only memento she had of her past. A few shadows of memories remained from a time of laughter and love—but no faces or recollection of who or where they were from.

She rolled the cloak up and placed it to the side as she began to stack up the supplies she would need to take with her.

Packing took mere minutes, and there was still room in Felicity's trunk. With heightened senses from her need to visit the training hall, she expected the knock at the door.

Harrison didn't wait for permission but entered, took a seat on the trunk at the edge of the bed, and then gestured for her to sit. Felicity hesitated for a moment before doing so. His gaze searched her, trailing over every inch of her face. Felicity didn't move, uncertain why he was looking at her this way.

"I'm sorry," he whispered. At the cock of her head, he continued, "You should be aware of what you're getting into."

It had been odd when the usual report wasn't waiting in her room, but she hadn't doubted her mission would be presented to her soon enough. She needed this conversation to be over quickly. Her body pulsed, an ache spreading through her limbs as she did what she could to control the brimming secret she longed to protect. They would be leaving first thing in the morning, and Felicity needed to sneak to the training hall tonight for a private session. Her last chance to abate the illness before it became worse.

Harrison sighed. "There's an uprising against King Roald. He's certain some within his court have aligned themselves with the rebels and are spying on their behalf. Your job is to make yourself part of the court and relay the names of the guilty to the king."

"I'm going to Éardrom? To the palace in the Light Realm?" She wouldn't usually ask questions, but this was so out of the norm, she couldn't help herself. "And last night was a test?"

He nodded. "The prince felt it necessary."

"How long will I be gone?" She didn't want to leave. Éardrom was on the other end of the continent, and she'd never traveled so far north. However, it wasn't the fear of the unknown that worried her but the secretive nature of the mission itself. She had a place within the Tower, the lines were drawn and clear-cut.

The events of the last two days were blurring them to non-existence. Anger replaced fear and her muscles tensed. What weren't they telling her?

"For as long as necessary. Don't let anyone know you can create a glamour, Felicity. It'll be too dangerous. Not even the king can know. That information was shared with the prince and his ward only." His tone was short and terse.

This only brought more questions, but moisture glistened in the corner of his eye, distracting her. Felicity turned away, uncomfortable with the unexpected show of emotion. "Understood."

Harrison reached across and she shuddered as his hand stopped a mere inch from her face. He hesitated before leaning closer to fill the gap, brushing a strand of hair behind her ear. She shouldn't let him. He was a handler. But there was a comforting familiarity in that gesture. He swallowed. "I know this job will define you."

"For the future," she whispered the oath of the Tower, wanting normalcy in a moment that was anything but.

"With my honor and blood," he finished with a faint smile. His lips parted and his gaze bored into hers, expression fierce. "Felicity—"

Another knock forced the awkward moment to a crashing end as both rushed to their feet. Felicity jerked her attention from Harrison as he opened the door and the Countess stepped in. If Felicity had been confused before, she was now dumbfounded. When the Countess wanted to speak to you, you were called to her.

The Countess' gaze thinned on Harrison. "You're dismissed."

With an abrupt nod, he left. When the door closed behind him, Felicity willed the thrum through her body to calm, another wave of nausea running through her system.

"Was Harrison here to give you the particulars of your mission?" The Countess looked more regal than Felicity believed the prince ever could.

She didn't know if she should offer the Countess a place to sit, so she stood across from the woman, remaining at attention. "Yes, Countess. I need to infiltrate myself into the court and discover who is working alongside the rebels—the traitors to our king."

"*The*, not ours," the Countess whispered. Before Felicity could ask what she meant, uncertain if she should even attempt to question the woman, the Countess continued, "Before you left, I wanted to inform you that with this recently completed mission, you've proven yourself within all aspects of the guild's requisites. In previous missions, you have shown your ability in strength and speed. Last night, you not only used stealth but did so while remaining within social norms. You're now awarded the status of graduate."

Felicity's shoulders drew back, and she lifted her chin despite the uncertainty, fighting back a smile. Finally. A step closer to the directive she'd worked so hard for. A sense of relief, after everything, settled momentarily in her chest.

The Countess folded her hands in front of her. "With these abilities, I know you shall excel beyond any within your field and are well on your way to being inducted as a Dearmadta. This mission will be the ultimate test of your knowledge and skills. Every bit of your training will be necessary as this will not be easy. Many obstacles are about to come your way, so trust yourself above all others and don't doubt your senses."

Felicity met the Countess's gaze. "I am the Tower's weapon."

The Countess rested a hand on Felicity's shoulder and squeezed it. "You're far more than a weapon, Felicity," she replied before departing, the door shutting behind her.

She stood there, staring at the spot the Countess had just vacated. Her words reverberated in Felicity's mind—the thrill of proving herself mixed with the anxiousness of what was to come. Using her fae senses to ensure no one else was coming, Felicity lowered her aching body against the wall next to her bed. The last two days had been more exhausting and mind-boggling than she could ever remember. Removing the half roll from breakfast out of her pocket, she tore it into pieces and left one near a crack in the stone wall. Crossing her legs in front of her, she placed another on her knee.

Little whiskers popped out from the hole, followed by the brown body of a field mouse. It bypassed the first and bounded up to the bread on her knee. It sat back on its haunches, watching her with warm eyes as it munched on its meal.

Felicity leaned her head back against the wall. "I have to leave. Don't know for how long but take care of yourself. In the meantime, this should be enough to last you a few days, so don't eat it all at once."

The mouse munched but kept its attention on her. Felicity smiled as little crumbs fell onto her pant leg. "Hopefully, I won't be gone for too long. Be careful and steer clear of the kitchens. The cats are still there." Felicity laid her hand next to her knee, and the mouse stuffed his mouth before hopping onto her waiting palm. She sat him down on the ground by the first piece and placed the remaining bread beside the hole. "See you around, Squeaks."

Straightening, a warmth ran through her limbs and spread through her muscles. It took a moment for Felicity's body to catch up with her thoughts. With all the questions puzzling around in her mind, there was one thing Felicity knew for certain: she needed to sneak to the training hall while it was meant to be closed. Privacy was key in these sessions.

Chapter 5

For nearly five days, Felicity rode her horse behind Prince Alarian and Ward's carriage as they traveled alongside a river on one side and the forest of Scáth—the Shadow Realm—on the other. The mist and shadows surrounding the trees acted as a barrier for the travelers and none ventured closer than necessary.

Their small party sensed an unseen presence within the forest—a tickling that brushed along Felicity's spine. She spent most of her time searching for any indication of the figures, but none moved, giving no sign of their location within the thick greenery. She didn't know much about the fae of the Scáth realm. They were more secretive than the nymphs and changelings that called Visce, the Water Realm, home.

Besides Felicity, Prince Alarian, and Ward, there were only two guards in their party. Although their rigid posture was at attention, their expressions remained relaxed, and they kept up an easy banter as they traveled. Either the males were powerful, or they didn't know of the dangers lurking out of sight.

Felicity knew not to judge any of them by their outward appearances and spent her time trying to dissect their character. The prince was drunk more often than not, and Ward spent most of his time sulking than keeping watch. It didn't mean she put down her own guard around them, however.

Once they reached the rolling hills of Aer, the guards emitted a nearly synchronous sigh of relief. There were only small patches of trees, an occasional thicket of bramble and fallen branches within the otherwise open plains of the Air Realm. A cool breeze battled the summer heat, appreciated due to the little shade on the road. They camped outside most nights, and Felicity slept under the stars, beside the horses. She whispered to them about the home and farms she'd left behind.

Soon she would meet the king of the eight realms in Éardrom. The only reason she could fathom why the prince had traveled to the farthest guild was the limited chance anyone would recognize her. It was one of the many questions Felicity hadn't asked. The group of travelers rarely spoke to her beyond "We are stopping here for the night" or "Someone has to piss."

On the fifth day, with the arrival to the palace finally within reach, she was sequestered to the carriage. Ward rode her mount while she settled into the seat across from the prince. Her backside was appreciative of the respite, even if the stale stench of ale and sweat exuding from the disheveled male caused her stomach to churn.

Could he have at least considered a bath? It would have been easy enough. The inn they had stayed in the previous night in the realm of Aer had its own plumbing system. Something Felicity had only ever heard about. When water had sprung into the tub from the pipe, there had been a moment of awe followed by utter bliss as she submerged into the warmth.

Prince Alarian released a loud snore, his eyes shut, mouth wide open, and head flung back against the coach. She smiled as his head bobbed from side to side, body slouching to the right or left as the carriage bumped, sped up, or hit the occasional rock and divot in the road.

Felicity hadn't minded the solitude. It had given her time to contemplate what was to come while also dealing with the rising nausea. She was exhausted. With her glamour no long in place, the ache of not using her magic had returned. It had been too long since she had a training session—the last one the night before they left the Tower. The watchful eyes throughout their travels hadn't helped, and she didn't trust the privacy of the inn. The prince was usually off at a tavern, leaving her with Ward for company—if you could call him company.

Before they left the inn that morning, a grimacing Ward delivered a dress, in a beautiful deep red, to her room. He'd nearly tossed it in her face. "For your introduction today." Then, murmuring under his breath, he'd stalked down the hall to his own room.

She'd given his retreating form an obscene gesture before he shut his door. It was obvious he disliked her, but she couldn't pinpoint the reason why and hoped she wouldn't have to deal with him much longer. Although, his disdain was similar to those at the Tower, so at least it brought her some familiarity.

The wheel clunked over a particularly harsh bump, and Prince Alarian almost fell over. Felicity bit her bottom lip to stop her laugh, her hand covering her mouth.

Ward rapped his knuckles on the outside of the coach. "Wake up. We're arriving at the gates."

With a look out the window, Felicity's jaw dropped in awe—not at the palace itself but at the view. A field of thick grass in the process of changing from green to brown surrounded the occasional willow trees that dotted the horizon, their long branches waving with the breeze. Reeds tall enough to hide a small child stretched into the distance until they ended at a sudden drop. The expansive ocean lay beyond, the blue and teal waters rolling into white suds. With a small gust, a salty scent wafted through the carriage. It took her breath away.

"You like it?" the prince drawled. "Everyone is impressed by the splendor of the Light Palace."

Felicity blinked as she turned her attention ahead to the building itself. It was dazzling, to say the least. Tall spires reached into the sky and milky stone gave off its own light from the sun's rays. Stained glass windows reflected prisms against the stone adding a rainbow of colors to the stark white. A darkness seemed to settle along the edges as though the shadows played there.

Good. She needed the shadows. In her line of work, they were friend not foe.

"It's exquisite," she replied, noncommittal.

Prince Alarian chuckled, but he was already looking out the window at the passing landscape when she turned to him.

"Are you ready for your debut?" he asked, straightening his tunic. "Hopefully you're capable of a repeat performance. Otherwise, this crowd will eat you up. It's not every day I return home with a female."

Felicity hadn't contemplated this. "I'm certain you know it's best you behave. Wouldn't want there to be an unfortunate accident," she said in a flat tone.

This time he faced her. "Feisty, aren't we?" He ignored her placid expression and laughed again. "We're going to have so much fun together."

Before she could utter another warning, the carriage came to a steady stop. "Welcome to the hornet's nest." The corner of his mouth lifted into a sly smile.

The carriage door opened, and the prince stepped out. Felicity stood to follow, bending at the waist so as not to hit her head and found his hand waiting to assist her down. Part of her wanted to slap it away, annoyed with the idea that he would think she needed or wanted his help. But this was her mission to fulfill, and there was a part to play. His grip was firm but gentle, his skin smooth. The lack of callouses either meant he could heal himself or was as lazy as she perceived. Likely both.

She held a hand in front of her face as the sunlight blinded her for a moment. It felt familiar—as though it called to her. When her eyes adjusted, she noted how many had come to witness the return of their prince. Guards stood at attention, acting as a barrier for the growing crowd forming along the walkway into the palace grounds. Many fawned over him, some glared at her while others waved as Felicity and the prince walked towards the entrance. Harrison hadn't mentioned that she was meant to play this part alongside Prince Alarian and wondered how she'd found herself in this situation.

As if he could read her thoughts, the prince gently steered Felicity closer, wrapping her arm through the crook of his. He leaned in to whisper in her ear. "Let them believe what they want. It'll be easier to allow them to weave their own tales than to make up our own. Especially since we're keeping your supposed name and homeland in case any recognize you from the advisor's party."

Felicity nodded, a blush creeping up into her cheeks as he moved away. She had learned how to adapt, to be flexible, in certain situations. It would be best to keep an eye on the prince before he attempted to pull her into something more devious. She was determined to remain a step ahead of him.

Ward moved in behind her as they ascended the steps. His presence felt like a heavy cloak on her shoulders, and she assumed he must be glaring at her back again. It seemed to be the only thing he found worthy of his time in Felicity's presence.

At the top of the stairs stood two tall oak doors with gold filament etched into a pattern of the sun. They were pulled open by two guards dressed in the royal garb of red and gold. A dragon wrapped around the sun glistened on their shields. Upon entering a long hallway, Felicity's eyes were drawn to the tall ceilings. Lights in glass bulbs glowed, although dim, of their own volition. Another one of the things Felicity had heard of but never witnessed.

The hallway had multiple floor-to-ceiling windows on each side that led to a set of wooden doors. Another hallway continued off to the right. Felicity's attention was drawn to the view on the left, where the expansive stone wall five times her height snaked around the perimeter of the grounds and guards stood at attention on the battlements. The outer wall followed to the plains that led to the bluff overlooking the ocean. The rocky drop must be a deterrent for climbing invaders.

When it became difficult to see the view, Felicity gave the hall a quick scan. Guards were stationed every few feet between tall pillars of marble. Beyond the pillars was the same white stone making up the curved arches over the windows and ceiling. As far as Felicity was concerned, the hall didn't need decor with a view like that.

As they reached the double doors, the prince removed her arm from the crook of his elbow but held her hand out in front of them.

"And now the fun really begins." His serious tone drew her attention, a contrast from the usual playful inflection.

When the doors opened, her stomach flip-flopped, but she hid her uncertainty with an inhale, straightening and lifting her chin. *Make them believe she belonged.* It was one of the lessons she'd been taught and had been the greatest asset in her arsenal.

Within the throne room, the windows on the left-hand side showcased the glittering masterpiece of the ocean, but she forced her attention away from the view to take in the room itself. The largest, most exquisite chandelier hung in the center. It was crafted with pearls and diamonds, casting rainbows of colors against the white stone walls. At the other end of the room, on thrones of cherry wood, sat the king and queen.

Her peripheral took in the few court members present while keeping her attention on the sitting royalty. Most watched Felicity and the prince with cynical expressions—the females in particular. Others barely spared them a glance. By the way fans had snapped open and hands covered mouths, gossip had already begun to spread.

The prince stopped at the bottom of the stone steps and kissed her hand. A moan behind her drew her attention as a female fainted within the crowd. The courtiers gasped, and it took well-trained resilience for Felicity not to roll her eyes but instead to smile primly. Ward stopped a step behind.

"Father, Mother, I would like to introduce you to Lady Felicity Dwauer of the Oileán Island Territories."

Felicity lowered into a curtsy. Prince Alarian headed up the steps of the dais, keeping a watchful eye on his father. He stopped beside his parents. "Lady Dwauer, let me introduce you to His Royal Majesty King Roald and Her Royal Majesty Queen Marquette. Rulers of the Eight Realms."

"You may rise." The king stood as his son took the empty seat beside him.

While she straightened, she raised her gaze to observe their appearance. King Roald was of a similar build to his son, age being the only obvious difference. While Prince Alarian had a careless posture, the king held an air of prestige. He gave his son his dark auburn hair, the splatter of freckles across his nose, a chiseled jawline, and broad shoulders. The remaining attributes came from his mother. Along with her light tan skin, he had his mother's green eyes. Darkness clung to her and her smile didn't reach her cheeks. By her piercing gaze and the prominent way she sat, Felicity was certain the queen controlled the entire room.

The king cleared his throat. "Welcome to the Light Palace, Lady Felicity Dwauer. When my son sent word of your unfortunate experience, I was glad he extended an invitation for you to be a guest within our court."

Even though the king's words were thoughtful, there was a forcefulness in his tone. This wasn't the male she had come to work for, but an act for the crowd. Felicity wondered who within this court was aware. And more, who was plotting against him?

"I appreciate your kind hospitality."

"We hope your travels were uneventful," Queen Marquette said, gesturing to a valet who stepped forward. "Please take the time to settle in your room to rest. We look forward to getting to know you better at dinner this evening."

Felicity curtsied again before the valet and Ward led her from the room. She felt the gazes of the court following her as she left. Her introduction had been easier than she'd thought. Felicity hoped dinner would be just as smooth.

Once the doors closed behind them, and after a quick conversation with the valet who ran off in a different direction, Ward slowed until he was beside her. "The king will allow you time to unpack before he speaks to you privately."

"I can meet now if he prefers not to wait." Felicity folded her hands behind her to give the practiced sense of composure, hiding the growing anticipation to start her mission. With Ward so close, she felt on edge.

"He won't be able to step away right now." He led her down the hall off the main entrance—the one she'd noted before. "If he didn't want to wait, you would know," he added under his breath.

She forced her attention on her surroundings. They took two sets of stairs, another right turn, then a left, before stopping after three doors. "This is your room. Your trunk should be inside. More clothes have been ordered for you and should arrive by tomorrow." He stalked across the hall and touched a doorknob. "This is my room."

"Is that a warning?" Felicity unclenched her fists as she reached for her doorknob.

"If you feel the need to take it as such, then so be it." Without another word, he stepped inside his quarters. The door shut behind him with a resounding click.

Felicity grumbled under her breath, then entered her room to find her trunk settled on the floor at the end of a lavish four-poster bed. A cushioned settee was nestled into a nook of bay windows beside a set of doors that opened onto a small balcony. The distant sound of ocean waves could be heard as they crashed against rock. A fireplace stood near the windows, and in front of the hearth were two chairs settled on a wool rug. It was the most opulent room Felicity had ever stayed in.

There was another door on the opposite side of the room. Peeking within, she found the bathing chamber, eyes widening at the pipes for plumbing. A warm bath was going to be so nice without the hassle of hauling water. In the corner sat a full-length mirror. With a sigh, she shut the door, not daring a glance at her reflection.

Felicity inspected the room, looking for peepholes, false walls, or other security concerns when a knock forced her to stop her search. A fae female with bright blue skin and cream-colored hair that brushed her shoulders entered. She dropped into a quick curtsy. "Sorry, Milady. Your handmaiden, Meira, apologizes as she's unable to attend to you and asked me to get you settled."

Felicity shot a glance towards the trunk sitting on the floor at the edge of her bed. "There is little to attend to. I'll take care of it."

The handmaiden stepped further into the room. "I assure you, it's no trouble at all."

Felicity slid her body in between the fae and the trunk. "Really, I have it under control. Could I please have some tea, though? I find I'm needing a little something." If anything, it would take the edge off of the twisting in her stomach.

The female shot a glance at the trunk before turning back to Felicity. "Of course. I'll return soon."

Alone, Felicity pulled the key loose from the chain around her neck, alongside the pendant. There were some things she needed to keep private—especially from unreliable eyes. With a twist, the lock popped, and she opened the trunk. A few clothes were laid out on top, and it took mere minutes to hang the four dresses Felicity had been given by the Tower's stylists.

Underneath was the blood-stained cloak. She usually wouldn't have brought it, but she couldn't leave it behind. Moving it aside, she stuck her finger into a small hole at the edge of the base and pulled, removing the fake bottom. Felicity ran a finger over the leather of her training and scouting attire. With a deep breath, she moved the clothing to thumb the hilt of the short sword underneath before checking the bow and strings and then counted the daggers and arrows. Everything was accounted for.

With a slide of her hand, she felt the comforting outline of the sheathed blade in place at her thigh—always close. Her dress didn't have a slit like the others she'd brought. That would be one of the first things she'd need to take care of. But for now, she needed to get these things put away before prying eyes returned.

Chapter 6

It was late into the afternoon before Ward came to fetch her to meet with the king. He brought Felicity to a room that was simple in comparison to the rest of the palace. The stone floor was covered with a threadbare rug. On one side of the room, a bust of some prominent fae male stood on a pillar. On the other side was another of a bestial fae—probably from Domhain, judging by their half-male, half-animal qualities. The space wasn't as pristine, the air stagnant. Unlike the rest of the castle, it was obviously not a room often used.

When the king entered with his son in tow, Felicity's head spun as the ache that had begun in the pit of her stomach spread upward as she lowered into a curtsy. Swallowing deep, she tried to ignore the growing discomfort, righting herself as King Roald took a seat at the head chair, the prince standing to the right of his father.

Ward remained by her side with his hands clasped behind his back. No guards entered the room, leaving the four of them alone.

"What is your real name?" The king rested his hands on the arms of the chair.

"Felicity, Your Majesty."

His eyes narrowed with a tilt of his head. "No surname?"

"I'm an orphan. There was no reason to give me any other name." The Countess had suggested she must have chosen to forget her family beyond the friendly shadows of her past. Since she was left behind, there was no reason to consider otherwise.

King Roald turned to his son. "She proved herself with your little test?"

"More than proved herself. She was beside the advisor the entire evening and barely raised a brow of suspicion." Prince Alarian grinned as though he expected a pat on the back for his find.

The king's gaze narrowed on his son. "Don't think I'm happy with your plan—but we'll discuss that later." His attention snapped back to Felicity. "How did she kill my advisor?"

Prince Alarian shrugged nonchalantly. "You'll have to ask her."

The king's mouth puckered as he waved a hand in her direction. Felicity took the gesture as an invitation to speak. "Rowan berries—a poison made from them, Majesty. I slipped them into his drink."

"He was always careless at celebrations—drank too much, too fast. Did you have a server slip it in?" There was judgment in his tone. "What about the smell and taste?"

"No. I added it to his glass myself." Felicity kept the irritation from her voice. Bishop had questioned her abilities in the past, and she'd taken pleasure in proving herself. This would be no different.

"And the other I cannot answer. It's a secret of my guild." Her loyalties were to the Tower—king or no king. The color and taste were almost absent once mixed with alcohol, but she would never admit that the advisor's inebriation had helped.

The prince cleared his throat. "She did it while having a conversation with Lady Molyle of Visce and Advisor Boister, Father. There was a witness to her every move. Neither Lady Molyle nor Ward caught her slipping it into his cup."

King Roald's mouth twitched. His gaze narrowed, eyeing her up and down. When he spoke, it was to his son even as he continued to eye Felicity. "If she fails, it's on you. She's your responsibility. Therefore, whatever mistakes she makes are your mistakes. If she doesn't prove her worth, then you have failed to prove yours." The king regarded her with cold eyes, but Prince Alarian's smirk never faltered despite the warning. Ward was a silent observer behind her; she almost forgot he was there. The only reminder was the occasional whiff of his scent—citrus on a fresh spring breeze.

King Roald regarded her as he tapped his fingers in succession on the arm of his chair. "There are those who oppose my rule. Some within my court are conspiring against me. You're to weed out who they are and bring me their names. Even better if you bring me the rebel scum they work with. You may do this by any means necessary, but if you're caught you're on your own."

Felicity recognized the challenge in his tone—the warning the words held. "As The King commands."

"There are a few requests by her guild." Prince Alarian procured a letter from his pocket. The wax seal of the Tower's insignia was melted into an indiscernible puddle but unbroken. Felicity shot a glance towards the prince, but he gave no indication that he noticed.

The king didn't note the damaged seal and snapped it cleanly in half. He scanned the letter and with a snort, he looked up at her. "Due to your special circumstances, I cannot allow you to train during the day, but the training hall will be available to you after midnight." He nodded at Ward. "When you want to go, Ward will accompany you."

Felicity's shoulders tightened. She had hoped for the opportunity to train alone. As if to remind her, her stomach rolled and joints ached, screaming beneath her skin. Outwardly, she hid her pain. At the Tower, she'd had the chance for the privacy she needed to release the discomfort that welled up inside her. She'd find a way to do so here as well—she didn't have a choice otherwise. The crystal pressed to her chest seemed to warm at the thought.

"You are allowed to search the grounds and palace. If you are caught by my guards, you'll be treated as any other intruder. To be clear, the sentence is death. We do not know who to trust, so only my family, Ward, and the two guards who accompanied you will be aware of your true identity. If any others discover it—I consider that a failure on your part. Just as many of my new guests are treated with a sense of protection, you will be escorted everywhere during the day."

Her jaw tensed but she remained still, letting his threat fuel her resolve.

He glanced at the letter again before he continued, "The letter states you're unaware of the political aspects of this court. Why is this?"

Felicity opened her mouth, but Alarian cut her off. "Her guild wishes that their recruits remain unbiased. They promise she knows enough to keep up with court conversation."

King Roald's brow furrowed, then nodded. "Understood. With the company of females you'll keep, there is little need for such things anyway. Ward will inform you of any information you *need* to know." He shot a snide glare at Alarian. "Since my son decided to make a spectacle of your arrival, you'll need to be seen together from time to time. I can't have his reputation questioned further than it already is. Not when we have his future to consider." The king's jaw ticked as he pushed himself from the chair. "I also see there is something about a cloaking spell for private conversations?"

She felt Ward's agitation. Why she had thought the council would've left out such information, Felicity didn't know. It was probably Bishop who'd ensured it was in there. True, the prince and Ward knew but a part of her hoped Prince Alarian would've been too hungover to recall the finer details of the meeting.

The prince grimaced but only for a brief second. "Yes, Father."

"Well, what is it?" the king grumbled.

"To break the spell, you need to say her name." The prince's gaze settled on her, but she didn't meet it. "And to engage the spell, you need the word sámhach."

Everything became muddled and quiet. Felicity gave no outward sign of her annoyance as her attention fell to the table as silence enveloped her.

After a few moments, the king's voice echoed in the room. "Felicity."

At the mention of her name, she looked up to meet his gaze.

A dim smile spread along King Roald's face at her obedience. "I should consider such magic for my own meetings." He waved his hand. "Take her away. She needs to prepare for her first dinner. Ward, I'm expecting you to do your part."

"Of course." Ward opened the door and nodded for her to exit first. He followed her out, then took the lead. "I'll accompany you to dinner. We don't want it to appear as if the prince is about to announce an impending marriage. Right now, the court will be curious about you, and we don't want them to hate you before a proper introduction."

She bit back a snide remark regarding pining courtiers—an unnecessary response. While she followed in silence, she folded her hands over her stomach. Concentrating on each step, her gut churned and her skin flushed. If she wasn't careful, she'd vomit right here in the hall.

"Are you all right? You look like you're about to be ill?"

"Is that what you say to all the ladies?"

He shook his head, turning away. "Watch it—we say 'female' here when in reference to faeries. We only say lady as a title or when we speak of humans. You don't want them to have the means to question your identity."

She bit the inside of her lip, upset he had pointed out a mistake—one she knew not to make. "I won't make that mistake again. My purpose is my mission."

Ward snorted. "Loyal to your cause?"

"No. Loyal to my guild." She lifted her chin, her jaw clenched against the rising nausea.

He regarded her for a moment, stopping her in her tracks. When she opened her mouth, she had a snappy retort at the edge of her tongue before he began walking again.

When they reached the halls that held their rooms, she didn't wait for Ward to add anything and closed her door. After making certain no one was present, she drew the curtains closed and almost ran to the bathing room to heave up the contents of her stomach. A moment. All she needed was a moment.

She closed her eyes, removed the crystal from around her neck, and held it in her hands. Her skin began to glow, magic spreading throughout her body. Felicity shuddered as it begged for release from her fingertips. She concentrated the sparkling white light towards the prism in her palm and the room was suddenly aglow with rays that reflected off the glass lanterns and mirror. Felicity withheld the desire to extend the amount of light spent—the one part of her magic that she had learned to control. Then she called it all back in, snuffing the room into darkness.

It was easier when using her glamour at the Tower to curb the urge that beckoned her. The ache and discomfort subsided with her magic. It would have to be enough for now. Enough to hold back the weakening of her body. If she didn't use it soon, her magic would consume her, and the last secret she had worked hard to protect wouldn't be hers anymore.

Chapter 7

The previous night's dinner had been an easy-going affair. Only a few members of the court were included at the table in the intimate dining room. Well as intimate as a dining room in a palace could be. Felicity sat at the twenty-foot table between Ward and Lady Avyanna Solfire, a fae noble from Tine who kept the conversation light and easy. The female was curvy and beautiful. Her white dress contrasted nicely against dark skin and deep orange hair that fell in waves to her waist. Felicity noticed on more than one occasion that Lady Solfire attempted to catch Ward's attention, but he never once spared a glance in her direction.

After a training session overseen by a silent Ward late into the night, Felicity was ceremoniously returned to her room where she slipped under the covers and fell into a dreamless sleep.

She was awoken by her handmaiden Meira, a fae with green skin and moss hair. As the handmaiden bustled about, she chatted away. Most of it was about the meals planned or Felicity's schedule for the day. At one point Meira mentioned she was originally from Domhain before she had arrived with the royal family.

If Felicity played it right, and the two of them created a rapport, Meira may let gossip slip. Felicity listened intently as the hand-maiden styled her hair then assisted her into a mauve dress Felicity had brought from the Tower. All the while Felicity nodded, giggled, and smiled at just the right time.

Her new attire arrived shortly after Meira left. Felicity was surprised to find pairs of trousers, a few tunics and undergarments that would make more demure ladies blush. This was the most clothes she had ever owned at once. A strange giddiness fell over her at the choices in color and styles.

Felicity heaved her trunk onto the edge of the bed to rifle through until she found her favorite dagger. She strapped the scabbard onto her thigh and put the weapon in place. It was as much a comfort to have it close at hand as it was a necessity.

At a knock at the door, she straightened her skirts, snapped the trunk shut and locked it. Felicity stalked across the room, replaced the chain around her neck and slipped the key into her bodice alongside the pendant.

She answered the door to Prince Alarian, who waltzed right past without a second of hesitation. "How are you settling in?"

In private, Felicity didn't feel the need to be proper and didn't keep the annoyance from her voice. "What are you doing here?"

He looked about the room, his attention settling on her trunk in its precarious position at the edge of the bed. "Have they brought you enough clothing? You know, for dinners, parties, and such."

He gazed over her current outfit. "This, at least, will do for tea in the garden."

"Yes, but you couldn't have come to assure my attire is appropriate." The hidden dagger pressed against her skin—a subtle reminder of what she wished to do with it flashed in her mind. An image of it landing into the wood of the mantle beside the prince's head made her smile. She wondered how quickly he would run from the room then.

His grin widened, and he chuckled. "Of course not. I was curious how you felt about your mission. Any questions? Concerns?"

Felicity crossed her arms. "I have a job. I've been trained not to be curious or have concerns. It's straightforward enough: find the rebel informants, report them to your father."

Prince Alarian nodded. "Straightforward." He peered towards the window, then back to her. "I also came to tell you that the remainder of the court will arrive in three days. Oh, and you should also know that you and I'll be leaving in six days to attend a party in Aer."

"Excuse me?" Her gaze darkened. If Prince Alarian noted the change, he didn't care.

"Many of the court members will be there. It's the perfect opportunity for you to meet the delegates and make an appearance on my arm." He settled in one of the chairs near the fireplace, facing her with an impish grin. "Dark corners and quiet rooms—all the fun places for mischievous deeds."

She was beginning to hate that smirk of his. "My purpose here is not to parade around court with you, Highness." Felicity's teeth ground together. "I'm here to fulfill your father's orders, not yours. If he deems it important then I'll attend, but not otherwise."

"He's already agreed. Best to find appropriate attire. Meira would know what's proper since the fashion in Aer is different than here." He folded his arms in front of him.

With a protest on the tip of her tongue, another knock at the door interrupted her. Ward entered, gaze narrowing on the prince before he slipped into the room to close the door behind him. "I knew it. What are you doing here?" His voice a harsh whisper.

She grazed her finger over the indentation of the hilt of the blade and crossed her arms over her chest. Now wasn't the time to threaten them, even if it was tempting. Maybe the opportunity would present itself later. Even better; if one were a rebel, maybe the king would allow her to slit their throats herself. She brightened at the thought before realizing the chances of that were dismal. Felicity gritted her teeth—the image of kicking their asses out of her room was enough for now.

"What are you *both* doing here?"

The corner of the prince's mouth rose. A sly glint settled in his gaze. "Just making sure you're prepared." He rested one ankle over the other before turning to Ward. "We don't want the courtiers to question her current standing within the court."

Ward's face reddened. "She can handle herself without you becoming involved. You should leave before you start a scandal."

Prince Alarian chuckled. "I could escort her to tea. It would have all the females abuzz—they wouldn't leave her alone. Besides, what type of scandal will we start when you and I both leave her quarters? What would they say?" He covered his mouth in mock shock.

Although the questions were directed towards Ward, Felicity intercepted the conversation. "That it takes two males to handle me. Now, if you'll both leave, I need to prepare for tea."

Prince Alarian lazily straightened, snickering as he crossed the room. He stopped when he was even with her and gave her body another pass over with those green eyes. "Do you need to take a dagger to tea?"

Her teeth clenched. Ward growled, and Felicity mentally cursed him. She shot the prince a look as his gaze narrowed as it met hers. She didn't know how he'd sensed the blade, her gaze thinning on him. Another thing to consider with the company she was meant to keep. "I will take a dagger to tea and everywhere else I go."

Prince Alarian laughed as he reached the door. "It suits you." He gestured to Ward. "Come, we've been dismissed from the lady's quarters. I can tell it's best we listen."

Ward was still watching her. "I will return to escort you to tea."

She nodded. "Fine."

He glanced between her and the prince. "Do you have any questions about your mission?"

She groaned with exasperation. "No."

Ward rubbed the back of his neck. "Just wanted to ensure that you understood your assignment."

"Get out," she seethed.

Prince Alarian chuckled. "She has it handled. You really shouldn't worry so much, Ward." He opened the door, waving for Ward to follow along.

The two males left, leaving her alone with her frustration. If they continued to interfere, she might just lose her mind. *Use the anger. Don't let the anger use you.* Those words were becoming more difficult to live by.

***

Felicity arrived for tea in the center of an overgrown garden. Gardeners worked nearby, trimming back hedges or pulling thistles that had overtaken the plants. Flowers attempted to break through the thick overgrowth that dangled shriveled and brown as though the life had been squeezed from them. Tall pristine trellises she assumed were new hid the view of the plains leading to the ocean. Why they would cover up such a sight, Felicity didn't know. Even the ivy seemed to have deigned the trellises as unnecessary, their vines spreading outward instead of upward. The scent of fresh-turned soil filled her senses.

Why were they sitting out here?

Ward stood outside the circle of females who watched Felicity with curious gazes, needlepoint in hand. Felicity assumed the high-backed chair was saved for Queen Marquette as it was still empty, the female not yet in attendance. A wooden slatted table sat in the center of the makeshift circle of chairs. Upon it was a white porcelain tea set with silver rims. Ward gestured to an open seat on a bench beside Lady Solfire. The female brushed her bright orange hair over her shoulder as she gave Felicity a wide smile.

"Ladies, I wanted to ensure Lady Dwauer found her way. Enjoy your tea." Ward stepped back from the group, leaving Felicity to take on whatever challenge sat before her. Based on the variety of looks being given, there would be plenty of them.

Lady Solfire cleared her throat. "We're so glad you could join us, Lady Dwauer. The queen is unable to attend today, but tea will arrive soon." She gave a faint nod to the ladies to her left. "This is Lady Mistward and her daughter Miss Isleen of Dorcha." Both women had milky white skin, piercing blue eyes, and hair as dark as midnight during a new moon.

Felicity smiled politely to each of them, which only Miss Isleen returned before Lady Solfire turned her attention to the woman at Felicity's right. "And this is Lady Chartow of Aer."

A breeze brushed past, caressing Felicity's skin at the introduction before wrapping around the female's body and gliding through her long blond hair. She was the eldest of the group with wrinkles beginning to form at the corners of her eyes. Instead of spectacles worn by many ladies at court, she wore an interesting contraption. One side of the frames was similar to a regular pair—glass with a metal rim—but the other had a metal gadget with gears. It emitted an occasional clicking sound as a small version of a spyglass twisted and turned, extending or retracting.

"It's to see the stitches better," the female commented, noticing Felicity's stare.

Lady Solfire cleared her throat. "Many of the Aer fae are inventors. They come up with such wonderful creations."

Felicity blinked and nodded, remembering the plumbing that she had been lucky enough to enjoy during her travels to the palace. "It's a pleasure to meet you all." She strived for warmth in her voice, relaxing her shoulders.

"Is it true you are from the island territories?" Miss Isleen intercepted. "I've always dreamed of going. You must tell me all about it."

Felicity resisted the urge to bite her lip—*shit*. "What is it you want to know?"

Miss Isleen sat forward. "Everything. The color of the water, the landscape. Is it true they have flowers as bright as the sky and in shades the colors of rainbows?" The words flew from her mouth at a speed almost impossible to decipher. "Do the locals really swim with the mermaids and—" She halted, her mother placing a firm hand on her daughter's arm.

The smile came easier than Felicity expected, considering the situation. She wracked her brain, trying to remember all she had learned about the territory. Most of the island realm was known for its trade of wine and fish. That wouldn't do much to appease the youngling if Miss Isleen's hopeful gaze hinted at anything. Felicity stifled a small cough. "May I tell you a secret?"

Miss Isleen's eyes widened. "Yes," she whispered.

"I could never paint the perfect picture of the islands. Just as it was to come here to the palace for the first time—I hadn't expected the splendor or the ocean view. I never imagined being a guest of the king, but here I am." Felicity batted her eyes. "To take away the opportunity of seeing it with your own senses"—she exhaled— "I could never do that to you. Someday you'll go there and when you do, you'll have your own words to describe its beauty."

Miss Isleen looked at her in admiration, as if Felicity was one of those mermaids she imagined. Her mother cocked her head in Felicity's direction, uncertainty plain on her face. Felicity *might* not be finding common ground with the proper individuals.

"How long will you be visiting?" Lady Mistward's eyebrows rose.

Lady Solfire sighed. "We're glad you're here. Truly." She shot a glare at Lady Mistward. "*Some* are curious about the prince's intentions with you."

"Hmph," Lady Chartow added. "If we considered his attentions with every young female, we would be here all day. He hasn't been serious about any of the past ones, and I have it on good authority that he visits the brothels on the regular."

"Only because your husband has been known to do the same," Lady Mistward countered under her breath. It was clear Lady Chartow hadn't heard as she was already back to her needlepoint.

"Behave," Lady Solfire hissed in their direction. "We shouldn't speak against our prince. When the right female catches his eye, he'll settle down. And who's to say Lady Dwauer isn't the right one?"

Felicity, for one, but she bit her tongue, the pain helping withhold the snide remarks regarding their precious prince.

Lady Mistward snorted. "Well, my daughter would be a perfect choice. If he ever took the time to notice her."

Miss Isleen puckered, her face becoming paler. Something Felicity hadn't thought possible. Her mother continued, "He needs someone willing to settle down here. Are you moving to the mainland, Lady Dwauer? Do you have family waiting for you at home?"

Felicity was going to have to watch herself around this one. Curse the damn prince. She inhaled, her thoughts turning to the Tower. "Somewhat. If that is what you would call them. My parents have both passed. I was raised by my aunt." The Countess would blanch if she heard Felicity calling her such a thing.

"You will return to care for her?" Lady Mistward's lips pursed.

Lady Solfire rolled her eyes. Her attention darted away as a server arrived with finger sandwiches. "Let's eat, shall we? Put discussions of the prince aside."

Felicity couldn't agree more. She grabbed a sandwich with dainty fingers, glad for something else to busy her tongue.

"Are we still talking about that lazy boy?" Lady Chartow chuckled. "Drink, females, and sleep are all he cares about. With the increase of rebel attacks, if anything befalls the king and his youngling is placed on the throne, the kingdom will be flattened overnight."

All the other ladies hissed, looking in shock at Lady Chartow. Lady Solfire shuddered as she poured the tea. "Don't speak ill omens of our king or against his son. If the queen was here, what would she think?" She passed a cup of tea in Felicity's direction, then to the others. "We need to remember our place, especially when we have a guest."

Silence spread over the group. Lady Mistward sipped her tea and continued to eye Felicity like a bug that needed to be crushed under her fashionable shoes.

Lady Solfire held up a small bowl. "I forgot to ask if you wanted sugar."

"Please." Felicity smiled as Lady Solfire spooned some into her cup. "I didn't think the prince was still a youngling."

Any fae over the age of fifty was no longer considered a youngling. There was usually a large celebration when they reached this first milestone. Felicity only knew this because she had been commissioned to steal a necklace containing confidential information from a demi-fae at a coming-of-age ceremony as one of her first missions.

Fae were nearly immortal. It was usually poison or fatal injuries that brought them to their last breath, and only if they didn't have the magic to heal themselves. While all fae healed faster than humans, only a few had the ability to mend themselves—Felicity wasn't one of them. It didn't mean they couldn't fall ill or be weakened to the point of death, but it wasn't an easy feat.

Lady Mistward straightened. "He isn't." She tapped the rim of her cup with her finger. "My daughter will be celebrating her coming of age ceremony this winter solstice. The prince is nearing his seventieth year."

"What of Ward?" Miss Isleen asked, eyes shining bright. "How old is he?"

Of course the young female would notice the male shrouded in mystery. Felicity recognized the young girl for the meaning of her name—a dreamer.

Lady Solfire's face went blank. "A few decades older than the prince, Miss Isleen." There was a hollowness in her tone. She turned to Lady Mistward. "Your daughter has much life left before her. There is no need to be tied to any male just yet."

Felicity thought that Lady Solfire may be the one female who could make this entire experience less miserable. Lady Mistward mumbled under her breath but the others ignored her.

As Lady Chartow removed her spectacles, she set them on the empty seat beside her. "The males within this house need to count their years. They could be numbered."

Lady Mistward and Lady Solfire shared a glance without saying a word. Felicity took a nibble of her sandwich. Maybe it was best the queen had not been there. There was little doubt that Lady Chartow wouldn't have spoken as plainly if Queen Marquette had been present. Felicity knew who her first mark should be. She cut a glance towards Lady Chartow, the female ignoring the steaming cup in front of her, still chewing.

Miss Isleen broke the silence. "Is sugar cane better on the islands? I heard it is delicious. Just a pinch is enough to sweeten the sourest lemon."

"I don't know about that sweet." Felicity smiled, almost wanting to change the subject back to the prince again.

Felicity spent the remainder of the tea dodging questions from Miss Isleen on island facts, discussions regarding the change in the weather, and the expectations for the Lughnasadh celebration to mark the beginning of the harvest. She couldn't understand why it was already on their minds as it was weeks away, but she preferred it over the debate of the prince's many relationships or island trivia. If this was only half the court of females, what else would Felicity endure?

Ward arrived to escort Felicity back to her quarters when the sun was near the midpoint of the sky, the others going their separate ways. They didn't speak, and she was surprised he hadn't asked her how it had gone.

Once Felicity arrived in her room, she ran a bath. The warm water was a small comfort to the constant ache in her body. She soaked for an hour. The click of the gears from the mantle clock on the fireplace echoed in the otherwise silent space.

When the clock chimed the fifth hour, her entire body felt as though it was pulsing, an ache beginning in her chest and spreading to her lower limbs.

She stepped out of the tub, the pieces of lavender and citrus peels going down the drain, the scent lingering on her skin. After drying off, she changed into the comfortable trousers she'd been eyeing since their arrival. The lush gray fabric was soft to the touch and tight on her hips before gently billowing at the thigh. To finish the look, she slipped on a white tunic that clung to her body. The pain had yet to subside, but the clothes were at least cozy.

With the drapes shut and the door locked, Felicity called to her magic, letting it refract in the crystal beside the basin. There was an immediate relief in her muscles, and the nausea abated as she pulsed with the light before she forced it back. It was too dangerous to release fully. The chance of her magic being visible through a slit of a curtain or a crack of the door was too high. It had been difficult to keep such a secret at the Tower but it seemed impossible here without the regular use of her glamour. Hiding her heritage had been one thing, but her magic *needed* to be used. Each day she attempted to hold it in, the weakness spread and the chance of losing control would be heightened.

There was no doubt in her mind that she wasn't the only spy within these stone walls. Harrison had warned her about protecting herself. Her glamour needed to remain a secret, therefore her magic—especially from the king.

Felicity sighed and looked at the time. Dinner was at the seventh bell. She dreaded the possibility of being questioned on the island's culture by anyone, but especially by Miss Isleen who seemed to have read every book on the subject.

She needed to research the Oileán Territories if she didn't want to blow her cover.

After checking her appearance in the mirror—a new habit she was training herself into—Felicity walked across the hall and knocked on Ward's door. It opened rather swiftly, and his eyes narrowed upon finding her at his doorstep.

"Ward, who is it?" An unseen female, her voice vaguely familiar but hard to place, asked from within his quarters.

Ward's hair stuck up in different directions, his shirt untucked with the top button undone, but at least he was dressed. His jaw quivered before darting a gaze back to whoever he'd been with, not opening the door wide enough for Felicity to see in. "Just a moment."

He stepped into the hall as his gaze darted in both directions before closing the door. "What is it?" he hissed.

"Oileán?" Felicity snapped back, not appreciating his tone. "You're meant to give needed information."

His eyebrows drew together, then he huffed as he caught her meaning. "I'll meet you in the study in an hour."

"I doubt you need that long," she mumbled. She refused to feel guilty for interrupting whatever was going on within his room. He had previously walked in on her without an invitation after all. At least she waited for him to answer and didn't barge in.

"Trust me, you'll never find out." He seethed, a grimace appearing before the door shut in her face.

"Never said I wanted to," she countered before she strode down the hall. Instead of going to the study, she knew where she needed to go. The library. Now, to figure out where it was.

Chapter 8

It had taken some time, but after asking a few of the maids for assistance, Felicity found the library. Without drawing too much attention and feigning interest in the mainland's view of the islands, the librarian's assistant found a stack of books for her to peruse. All the trouble had been worthwhile when Ward arrived in a huff, face red.

"I said I would meet you in the study," he growled.

She shrugged. "Which one? Besides, everything I need is here. Guess I didn't need you after all."

He snapped his fingers, and the books levitated into the air. With a movement faster than she expected, he tore the book she was reading from her hands and stalked out of the library with the stack of books following him. She didn't try to hide her smirk as she did the same.

Once they reached a private study, he gently placed the books on the table before locking the door behind her. "Privacy is of the utmost importance within these walls."

"I'm a spy and assassin. I know all about privacy. Try granting me some." Felicity pointed to the stack of books. "These are harmless books and you're supposed to prepare me."

Ward snorted. "It's not just *me* interrupting your life. Will you ask the same of the other male I found within your quarters?"

"Oh yes, I fall right under the category of simpering female searching for high-profile males to keep her warm at night—if you're a prince, then you don't even have to knock." Her temper rose—her hand resting above the sheath at her thigh. Not to use as tempting as that might be but as a reminder of why she was there. It calmed the heat rising with her anger.

His jaw clenched as he regarded her, grip tightening on the back of the chair until his knuckles whitened. With a long exhale, his shoulders relaxed, and he waved to the empty chairs, which slid back as if on their own. When she crossed her arms, he released an exasperated sigh before taking a seat.

"Books are far from harmless." He picked up the second one from the stack. "Like this one here. Its title may be *The Geography of the Realms*, but did you know it also discusses each of the nine realms' magical properties and the abilities its descendants may inherit? Do you think that information could be formidable in the wrong hands?"

"Nine realms?" Her brow furrowed. "I thought there were only eight."

"Scáth means life. There is a realm, obviously not accessible to us, that is meant for the dead. Ankus is not discussed since it's considered a bad omen, even if it is an eternal rest for some and hell for others."

Information to consider but held a little of a fanatic's viewpoint. She filed it in the back of her mind nonetheless. Felicity cocked her head, considering the tome in his hands. "You like to read?"

"You don't?" He placed the book back on the pile, brushing a finger over the spines of the other titles.

Shrugging, she sat down in the nearest chair. "I've never had access to them in this way. We were taught to read and write but very little beyond that."

"Then even the Tower believed they were dangerous." He settled in the chair opposite her, pulling another from the stack to thumb through the pages.

She had never thought of it that way. "Maybe."

Ward pushed the open book towards her. "Here are the chapters regarding the islands. It's been decades since I've been so can't offer much personal insight." He ran a hand through his hair, brushing the dark strands from his eyes.

She looked down at the words. They jumbled together from the pain wracking within her head. It was getting worse. The little moments of releasing her magic wouldn't be enough for long. Closing her eyes, she massaged her temples before opening them again to dare a glance at the page. It helped a little. "Where have you been?"

The silence that edged through the room caused her to look up. His eyebrows were drawn together, jaw tense. "Aer a few times. Domhain and Visce once or twice. I've otherwise just passed through the other realms. Éardrom has always been my home. My father is light fae."

"Where is your father now?" Felicity dared to ask, wondering how much she could get from the male.

Ward shrugged and picked up another book, and she decided not to press.

The next hour was quiet as she read, and she didn't ask any more personal questions. On occasion, Ward would pass her a book to read a passage or interesting fact about the island territories. He never showed her anything of political or magical importance, keeping certain passages blocked with his hand. Since it was for the Tower, she didn't protest, although her curiosity rose.

After the bell tolled another hour, her head was in a fog. The ache caused her nausea to swell to life in her stomach.

"Are you feeling well?" Ward's gaze narrowed as he looked her over.

"A headache. Not used to all of this reading." The excuse seemed to pacify him since he began to stack the books on the table before snapping his fingers. At the command, the sconces dimmed to a mere tremor of light as a brush of air encircled the room, then diminished. "What type of magic is that?"

"Air," he grumbled, heading towards the door.

"You don't like me, do you?" Felicity blinked, surprised at her own question. Since when did she care what others thought of her? *Never*, she chastised silently.

He stopped at the door and turned to her. His eyes shined in the little light remaining. "It's not that simple..." He shrugged. "I didn't think you would care."

"I never said I did. If I'm stuck with you then don't be an ass and I'll make your life less miserable."

He chuckled. "You're just a crumb compared to my problems. Besides, you're a trained assassin and spy. Nothing personal but being in the same room as someone who extracts death or can uncover secrets if they dig far enough is a little unsettling."

The corners of her mouth lifted slightly. "That's true. If it makes you feel better, I'm more spy than assassin."

Ward snorted. "Well, at least the past few hours were bearable."

"Likewise." Felicity nodded towards the books. "Are there any other books you'd recommend?"

His eyes searched hers for a moment. "It depends. Are you returning to the Tower?"

"When this is all done, of course." It was such a ridiculous question that she had to stifle a laugh.

His voice turned to a whisper. "Are they going to take you back?"

"What do you mean? Why wouldn't they?" The pulse in her temples sped up, her head throbbing.

"It seemed they were sending you away. Is it often the guild agrees to these types of missions? Especially if you were to return with more information and insight than you left with."

Felicity could feel his stare even as she turned away to look over the stack of books. "They wouldn't do that. I've been there for almost fifteen years." Her skin flushed, feeling as though it was laid bare. Or maybe it was from her magic. "They raised me—I'm loyal to them."

"Fifteen years?" His gaze narrowed. "Are you sure?"

She began to rub her temples again, his words and questions causing pain to pulse through her. Irritation rose with the ache. "Why wouldn't I be?"

"Nothing." He reached for the door, ending the conversation that made her entire body feel like it would implode.

"You don't know me or how the Tower works," she said in an even tone. "They're my home. The closest thing to a family I've ever had."

He shuddered. Pausing to take a deep breath, his hand still on the doorknob as he expelled it. "I'll escort you to your room and call for dinner to be brought to you. I don't think you're well enough to join everyone in the dining room without causing a stir. Don't need them making assumptions. I'll blame it on exhaustion from traveling."

Felicity wanted to disagree with him, but the taste of bile coated her tongue. Instead, she brushed past him, heading straight to her room. To the privacy waiting.

Once inside her quarters and the door closed, she ran to the bathing room. She barely made it to the toilet in time.

***

Felicity hoped to sneak out before Ward could join for the training session, but he must have been prepared. Before she left, she repeatedly expelled a bit of magic to relieve the illness weakening her body.

"Are you well enough for this?" Ward's brow rose as she trailed after him into the training hall.

"Yes." The words were little more than a grumble.

Ward snapped his fingers and the dim lanterns stuttered then brightened—fed by his air. "I apologize for my assumptions earlier today. You know the Tower much better than I do."

She faltered. An apology wasn't what she expected. Felicity waved it away—even if it had been on her mind since he spoke the words. To admit such a thing, though, felt like a betrayal to those who raised her.

Ward took a seat, leaning against the pole near the bench. This portion of the training hall was small, and Felicity assumed the majority of training happened outside in the perfect Éardrom weather. Lanterns hung around the edges of the room, casting just enough light to see the wooden circles on the floor that outlined three separate rings. The circular room was covered by a thatched roof that arched upward to a center pole. The thatch was fastened to a pole that allowed a small opening to let in the ocean breeze while removing the stink of sweat and stale air. The twinkling night sky was visible, stars glittering down on them.

If Ward was going to be there, she might as well attempt to ascertain some information. "The gardens seem overgrown for a place often visited by the queen." Felicity removed her cloak, uncovering her tunic, leather vest, and training pants. It was comforting to be back in her usual attire. The dagger slipped easily into her hand as she gripped its hilt.

"It's an enchanted garden, originally planted by a previous queen of Éardrom." His voice was distant, and Felicity turned to find him looking out the hole in the roof he sat under. "When she died, it became unruly without her care. The gardeners worked meticulously in an attempt to keep ahead of it but were unable to gain control of the weeds."

"How did she die?" An ache settled in her chest at his words—the grief present on his face. An emotion she hadn't allowed herself to feel in years.

For a moment, she didn't think he would answer. "Childbirth. After giving birth to a prince, her body was too weak and couldn't heal after the trauma. Years later, the king remarried. His new wife took up where the previous queen had left off, doing her best to show her love to the garden. It accepted her even though she didn't have any magic of her own." He folded his hands behind his head.

"I assume it's not Queen Marquette or the current royal family?" After the first meeting, she had only seen the queen at dinner the previous night, leaving little opportunity for Felicity to observe her. From her rigid posture alone, Felicity did not believe the female warm enough to win over an enchanted garden.

"No, it's not the current family and definitely not Queen Marquette. She could never control it. No matter how hard she's tried, it doesn't accept her." A shadow of a grin appeared, then evaporated as he continued, "This prince's stepmother was murdered. The garden will not forgive what was taken from it."

Felicity felt the penetration of his gaze, similar to the one he gave her at the advisor's ball. "That is a sad story." She brushed off the feeling, beginning her training with a circuit of lunges, stabs and twists.

"You understand sadness?" There was a hint of a smile in his tone.

Without stopping the movements, Felicity considered his question. "I understand emotions. I just don't allow myself to feel them." She added a back kick after the twist.

There was silence for a moment. "How does it work?"

"In my line of work, emotions are a weakness. When you feel too much, it makes it harder to do what we're meant to do. Anger is allowed. It helps to block out the others. It's also why some find the social aspects of our training difficult. They've lost all understanding of emotion." Felicity's heartbeat quickened as she added a front roll into the rotation. "Therefore, many can't understand nuances in conversations." And jab. "So they're stuck to the shadows or used in other aspects of the missions."

"What makes you unique from the others?" The usual sourness wasn't present in his tone.

She rolled again then slid the dagger back into its scabbard at her thigh. "Besides my heritage?" Felicity peered over her shoulder at him. Ward just nodded. She contemplated his question. "I wouldn't say I'm unique. I've just excelled where others have more difficulty. There are different specialties for those within our guild: stealth, speed, strength, and social. Some have only one or two of these—I'm a part of the small group that has mastered them all."

He expelled a long breath. "The perfect weapon." He stood and entered the center of the training ring. "Show me."

"What?" Her shoulders tensed.

"I assume your heritage is partly to thank. From what I understand, the others didn't know about that side of you. Show me."

Felicity prickled at the observation—the partial truth. "Yes, it does have a little to do with being fae but that's not everything. I spent the majority of my life playing human, which has helped me hone my skills."

He smiled as he pulled a white handkerchief from his pocket. "Then this is your target. Get it from me."

"I don't need to pass any more tests." She had done enough in her short life. "Also, it's not much of an assessment when you expect it."

His smile lifted higher. "This isn't a test. It's for fun. If you can get this from me without being caught before you leave for Aer, then you win."

"Win what?" It was always risky to make a bargain with a fae.

"I'll show you the hidden passageways running throughout the palace." He stuffed the handkerchief into his pocket. "If I win—"

"Which won't happen."

"—then you have to train blindfolded for a week?"

She considered his proposition. "Why?"

He leaned against the center pole. "Because it would make things interesting for me while I sit here babysitting."

"I didn't ask you to come." Felicity snorted.

"Trust me, I doubt I need to be here either. Orders are orders, however, and you seem to be the type to follow them." He held out a hand. "Do we have a deal?"

"Shouldn't you show me the passageways anyway?" She rested her hands on her hips.

"No. I'm certain the king doesn't know about them." His hand extended further.

Felicity regarded him. Was there a reason behind his words or was he sincere? There was only one way to find out. She shook his hand. "Deal. But you're going to lose."

"We'll see."

She couldn't help but think this would be the first bit of fun she'd had in a long time. At least as far as she could remember. Her past had always been hazy, bits and pieces nothing more than what the council had told her. But her time at the Tower hadn't left much for fun and games. Maybe along the way, she could uncover a little more about the ward.

Chapter 9

Felicity used exhaustion as an excuse to get out of attending tea the following day. Ward told her where to find Lady Chartow's chamber, and Felicity knew her best opportunity to search her rooms would be while the female was engaged. The halls were busy with handmaidens carrying baskets of laundry, but none gave her more than a quick curtsy before continuing with their duties.

Her chosen attire was simple: a stark white gown that, if anything, only made her look paler. Wisps of hair wafted as she fluttered her fan from time to time. As far as any would believe, she was out for a short walk along the halls. Meira had wanted her to stay in bed but finally agreed that Felicity looked well enough to venture indoors.

Truthfully, Felicity was tired, so playing the part wasn't hard. After returning from the training session, she had spent most of the night sewing pockets into all her dresses with a special flap to make her daggers easily accessible.

She turned down the hall of suites and began to count the doors on the left-hand side until she reached the eighth one. The short hallway was deserted, so she hurried to the door, knocking twice. She remembered there was a Lord Chartow from the conversation at tea, but no one answered. She checked the handle first, unsurprised to find it locked before removing the pick she'd hidden within her hair. The familiar satisfying click sounded just as two handmaidens turned the corner. They were deep in conversation, huddled together and whispering to one another. Felicity didn't wait but slid into the room, locking it behind her.

This room had similar furnishings as her own, except the armoire was in the corner instead of against the wall. She willed the glamour into place and her features softened, her body relaxing at the use of magic. It was dangerous if anyone caught her, but if someone sensed another fae had entered their room or they connected it to her then she'd fail before she began.

She started at the writing desk, pulling open the drawers and searching for false bottoms. There were none, no hidden clasps or compartments, and the papers within were mainly blank. The one with writing was the beginning of a letter to a cousin in Aer. She moved onto the tables beside the bed with equal luck. Darting a glance under the furniture, she searched for loose floorboards. Another of her lessons from the Tower slid through her mind. *Look for the smallest hint of tampering in the least expected of places.*

Felicity thumbed over the books on a nearby shelf when she saw the edge of parchment peeking out from behind a cover. With deft fingers, she silently removed the book, popping it open. It was a crude drawing of a map of Talamh. Small numbers were written at different locations along the edges of Domhain and Aer. A few were crossed out with adjustments made to the amount. An X marked a spot near the border of Tine and Éardrom.

It didn't make sense and only confused her. These numbers, that mark, could mean anything. It didn't reek of conspiracy. She closed the book, glancing over the title. A book of children's stories.

Before she could give it a longer look, a knock sounded at the door. "Lord and Lady Chartow?"

Felicity stilled. *Damnit.* The sound of clanking keys put her into motion. She ran for the armoire and hid within, shutting the double doors behind her when the lock unclicked. Peeking through the slit of the armoire doors, a pixie handmaiden entered. She carried a wicker basket laden with clean sheets and started the process of unmaking the bed. A moment later, another handmaiden entered carrying a pail of water.

"Did they have any clothing sent to the laundress?" the pixie asked.

Felicity darted a look upward to see if she could hide within the compartment.

The pail of water sloshed as the second, a pale-skinned fae, wiped sweat from her forehead. "No, not today. After the bed, let's prepare the fireplace. I don't know why they prefer fires this time of year, but I don't want to receive the request at bedtime again."

The pixie nodded in agreement then they settled into their work. The handmaiden hummed while she changed the sheets. Both were efficient and done with their individual tasks in no time before turning their attention to the fireplace. If they had taken any longer, Felicity's patience might have worn thin. The pale fae brushed the old ash into a pile while the pixie made a pail appear from thin air. Then the fae levitated the pile into the pail as the pixie laid the fresh logs within the hearth.

"Done." The fae straightened, looking over the completed task. "Best be on our way. Lord Chartow should be back from his walk soon."

Felicity breathed a sigh of relief when she heard the door lock behind them. She slipped out of the armoire. There wasn't much time—not if the handmaidens had been correct about the lord's return. She searched corners and nooks but found nothing before slipping the book back into its place on the shelf. Daring a glance at the fireplace, Felicity cursed, frustrated that they had cleaned out the ashes before she had been able to search the remains for old parchment.

But that would have to wait until another time. Felicity trotted to the door and pressed her ear to it, listening for anyone within the hall. Removing the glamour once again, she opened the door and peered out, confirming no one was present. She used the pick to lock the door again and was walking away when a male with light brown shoulder-length hair stepped into the hall. He spared her a glance as he passed then headed towards the room Felicity had just vacated. Relief washed over her when his door closed behind him, and no exclamations or concern rose from his direction. It had been close for a moment. Although she hadn't found anything damning the female, Felicity filed the map in her mind and wasn't going to cross Lady Chartow off her list just yet.

***

Felicity vaulted off the balustrade and grabbed hold of the eaves. Pulling herself up, she stayed within the shadows, watching the royal guards patrolling past. After each training session, she spent hours out on the palace grounds spying. Not that it uncovered a single thing. No one was out except for dutiful soldiers and the occasional housemaid or servant doing late-night assignments. With only one more day until the remaining court members arrived, Felicity decided from that point on she would spy before training until she left with the prince for Aer. She was curious if Lady Chartow would be found in the dark hallways.

A loud gong sounded twice, signaling the hour. It was late, and there was no point for her to be out any longer. She climbed near the edge of the gabled roof, the darkness hiding her from view.

When she reached the balcony to her room, she stilled. There was someone inside—a bright candle burned on the table beside her bed. One she hadn't left lit. She held her dagger close. Near-silent, she opened the door and pointed the blade at the occupied chair, hidden in shadow in front of the extinguished hearth. When the scent of citrus swept past, she removed her mask. "Ward?"

The male leaned forward, the sliver of moonlight illuminating him enough for her to recognize his features. He stood. "Someone is here to see you."

She cocked her head at the tightness in his mouth. Her gaze flickered to his pocket—the location of the handkerchief. Probably not the time to be sidetracked by petty games. "Who is it?"

"Come with me." He didn't wait but swept past her. "I told him to wait in the study."

Him? "I need to change first. It won't go well if I am caught wearing this."

He nodded. "I'll wait in the hall. Hurry."

Her mind raced as she changed her clothes, slipping into a pair of dark pants with a tie at the waist, and a tunic—something more realistic for an evening traipse through the palace. She used the time to ponder on the reason for a visitor or the secrecy, but none came to mind. She slipped the dagger into place at her waist, pulling the tunic down to hide it from view. It wasn't much, but it would have to do.

Felicity met Ward in the hallway. Once they reached the study, he held the door open. Her eyes widened as she paused in the doorway.

"Hello, Felicity." Harrison tried to smile. Instead, it came out as more of a scowl. "I have brought something for you."

Chapter 10

Ward nudged Felicity into the room. Her body was stiff in shock at Harrison's presence that she almost tumbled over. Although this mission wasn't the norm for even a new graduate, there wasn't a time she was aware of a handler being sent out into the field. He always had others he dispatched for any concerns.

Harrison cocked his head, his attention on Ward, and Felicity noticed how his eyes narrowed on the male. "Could we speak in private?"

Ward's jaw tensed. "If she asks me to leave, I will."

Before either of them could continue, Felicity stepped forward. "What are you doing here? I'm not being called back, am I?"

Harrison's shoulders slumped and he spared a glance at Ward. "No, the opposite." He turned back to her and reached out a hand, an envelope within his grasp, the Tower's wax seal holding it shut. "I have brought you this, and I'm here to let you know that once you complete the mission, your compensation will be sent to you...but you cannot return to the Tower."

Not return?

Her knees nearly buckled, certain the ground had been pulled out from under her, the floor spinning. How she wasn't on the floor yet was a surprise in itself. She stumbled a step as her stomach rose to her throat. A brush of fingers grabbing her elbow pulled her out of her shock. She straightened. There were witnesses. Felicity couldn't have them think her weak. "Why?"

The handler gestured to a chair, but she ignored him and continued to stand at attention. Ward stepped back, pressing himself against the door.

Harrison also chose to remain standing and placed the envelope on the table. He cleared his throat. "Your presence at the tower has become too risky. The Countess had to make the call. The knowledge of your heritage has spread and created unrest within the initiates. She wasn't happy about it. Let me assure you, she's heartbroken with this decision." He spared a glance at Ward. "As am I."

Felicity noticed the rise of a breeze circling the perimeter of the room. She turned to Ward. "Could we have a moment, please?"

He nodded, pinning a glare on Harrison. "I'll watch the door."

In other words, he would remain nearby. Her brow drew together at the offer to watch her back. She didn't know if she trusted him there but couldn't bring herself to care right now. Not with her world turning upside down already.

She waited for the door to shut behind him. "The backup you sent saw that I'm fae." It wasn't a question.

"It took her a few days to return. According to her, she was being chased and didn't want to lead the guards to the Tower. She was under the impression she was blamed for the advisor's death."

Her hands clenched at her side. "You sent her there to help, didn't you? I used her as I saw fit."

She caught the smile that he quickly tried to hide, her attention drifting to the envelope between them. He followed her gaze. "It's a letter from the Countess." Another deep breath, "And it contains your memories."

Felicity's head snapped up. "Memories? What do you mean?" Her fingers went to the hilt of the dagger, fighting every urge to tear it from its scabbard. He was from the Tower—her home. Or it had been her home. Where did that leave her now? At the moment, it didn't matter. It took every ounce of her training to resist the desire to gut him and let her anger take over. She needed answers first.

Her hands were balled into fists and hung near the blade at her side. Harrison moved around the table to close the distance between them. He should be afraid of her right now, yet she saw no fear in his eyes. "It was for your safety." He reached towards her, then pulled back. "It was for our safety."

"You're confusing me more with each word you utter. I need you to explain before..." The dagger was in her palm, but Harrison's gaze didn't leave Felicity's even with the blade between them.

"The Countess was trying to protect you." Harrison rubbed the back of his neck. "You didn't age like the others at the Tower, which caused initiates to be transferred, things covered up—she wanted desperately to keep you safe within our walls. Only Bishop and I knew about this decision."

She continued to glare, waiting for him to go on as betrayal pulsed through her body. Her hand tightened on the hilt of the blade, grounding and forcing her to pay attention instead of falling into the abyss opening at her feet.

"Why did she trust you, trust the council, with this information?" Her arm shook from the tension of her grasp.

He dropped his arms to his sides. "She didn't. You did. You showed me who you were. So, the Countess chose to trust me as well."

"Why would I do that?" The edge in her voice was unfamiliar even to her own ears.

He inhaled deeply. "Because we loved each other. Once."

The dagger clattered to the floor. Ward knocked as Felicity clutched her stomach, trying to will air into her lungs. Harrison took a step forward until she raised her hand to stop him, and he froze in place. She took a few deep cleansing breaths.

"I'm fine. Go on," she lied. Her heart pulsed faster against her chest like it was ready to break free from a cage.

Harrison stepped back, his gaze softening. "When I had arrived as a recruit, there was an attraction between us. As far as I knew, you were almost twenty, but I watched you from afar." He blushed. "Until you kissed me, that is." Felicity worried at her bottom lip as he continued, "We kept it a secret for a while. Or so we thought. Nothing within the Tower is secret if the Countess is involved. Then you decided to share your true heritage with me. The Countess warned against it, but we were drawn to each other. So, she stepped aside to let us make our own choices. We loved each other very much."

She met his gaze. Felt the truth of his words as the reality of her hazy past settled yet didn't want to believe him. Even if the moments she'd felt drawn to him, or he'd looked at her with longing accounted for something. "I don't feel love."

"You did once." Tears began to form in the corner of his eyes. "I came to the Tower a few months after the first time you gave up your memories. I hadn't known at the time that this happened when our relationship began. When the option was given to you again, you told the Countess you wanted me a part of the decision, but it was ultimately yours. Somehow you came back to me after the second vial of memories was removed. That changed when I began to age beyond what would be considered an appropriate partner for you." He cleared his throat. "The third time, I was given the title of handler and brought on as a council member. When your memories were removed—" He swallowed. "This time, you didn't come back to me."

Felicity's grip tightened on the edge of the table as her head spun. It couldn't be true. They were her family—her home. Even if the initiates were not, the Countess had raised her. Harrison had observed each of her lessons, ensuring the trainers were doing their part. Even Bishop had a hand in her life if she wanted to admit such things.

Harrison wiped his cheeks with the back of his hand. "They trained the emotions out of you until it didn't matter anymore. You had become the ultimate weapon."

"How old am I really?" Felicity whispered.

"We can't be certain. The Tower could only assume your age at your arrival, but the Countess believes you are in your late fifties now. You were coming up to your fiftieth year at the Tower next Imbolc." Harrison pulled the chair out just as she fell into it. "She didn't do this to hurt you. Her words, this letter, will better explain her reasoning. It was your choice as well." He crouched in front of her, but she couldn't bring herself to meet his gaze. "I wanted to be the one to tell you, and she allowed me to come. Right now, you have been given a shock that could move mountains, but Felicity, when you have had time to process, I only hope you can understand."

"Why would I agree to this?"

Harrison searched her face. Instinct told her to erase all emotion, but she couldn't bring herself to do so. If what he said was true, he'd be able to see through her anyway. "I have my assumptions as to why, but only you can answer that. It was something you never shared with me."

Felicity shook her head as she got to her feet. "She took my memories." Her gaze met his. "And you went along with it." She stared at the floor. The white of the stone was too clean compared to the images in her head, red fury streaming into her vision. Magic beckoned at her fingertips, but she held it back. She whirled around on him. "You agreed with her. To even offer the option—"

His jaw tensed; the pain etched deep in his blue eyes. By his expression alone, she knew he had never agreed with it. She almost wished she could take back the words. Almost.

The facade she had worked hard to build all these years was crumbling—and she couldn't let it. Her chin lifted as she stood, inhaling a deep breath before leaning over to pick up her dagger. "Why do I have memories of the past fifteen years if what you say is true?"

"Because only ten years of your memories were removed at each interval. You still had the memories from before that period, when you had been a child at the Tower, to give you an ideal timeline," Harrison whispered as he straightened.

She slipped her dagger back into place and glanced at the envelope. Standing straight, she forced a cool countenance to fall over her expression. "There is nothing more to say. Goodbye, Harrison." Her questions were answered—for now. She was on the brink of falling apart and she couldn't let him see it.

Silence seemed to tick by as they both stood, neither moving.

"It was a choice, Felicity. To keep you safe. I always followed where you led and will till the end. I'm sorry." Harrison sighed—waited. But she couldn't forgive or look at him. Not now. Finally, he said, "Goodbye, Felicity. I hope you find happiness, and we see each other again under better circumstances."

When Harrison left, she pulled out the dagger and flung it. It landed hilt deep into the wood of the bookcase. It took all her will to hold back the magic. Gripping the edge of the table, she heard a small creak as she cracked the wood. She wanted to scream. Wanted to yell. Anger crashed through her as she tried to catch air in her lungs. She collapsed to the floor, gasping for breath.

A brush of a hand at her back and the scent of citrus encapsulated her. She stilled, her eyes widening. No one could see her like this—so close to losing control. Ward crouched down beside her. "Felicity?"

She gritted her teeth as his hand rested on her arm and heaved in deep gulps of air she couldn't hold.

"Count to ten," he ordered.

She pinched her eyes shut so hard tears formed at the corners. With her teeth still clenched, she started to count. "One."

"Breathe with each number," he added.

"One." Breath in. "Two." Breath out.

By the time she reached ten, her hold on the table loosened. She couldn't concentrate on one thought, let alone speak. The silence was deafening, and she was actually thankful when Ward spoke.

"Do you want to study? I can prepare you for the arriving courtiers?" Ward removed his hand from her arm and straightened. She searched his expression, relieved to not find pity in his gaze. She appreciated that more than anything else.

Felicity nodded. She couldn't fall asleep now.

He opened his mouth, but when she shot a glare in his direction, he shut it. She slumped into the nearest chair. "Let's get started."

When Ward stood in silence for a few moments, she grabbed the top book from the stack they had left behind at an earlier study session to flip through the pages. Even if there wasn't information about the courtiers within its pages, Ward took the hint.

The muffled sound of the clock in the hall chimed four times. Besides the magic thrumming under her skin, Felicity was beginning to feel the lateness of the hour. It wasn't surprising she had difficulty concentrating during the study session, and names were beginning to jumble together. "So, I'm to be wary around Lord Fiadh. Don't foresee a problem there since he won't be at any afternoon teas."

"No, it's Lady Fiadh." Ward rapped his fingers on a book. "I think we should call it for the night." He began to pile the study materials back onto the table, nothing private enough to be deemed worrisome to leave out. "Do you want to talk about it?"

Felicity eyed the envelope as her anger resurfaced. Instinctually, she wanted to hit something—hard. Instead, the words spilled out. "You were right. I'm not meant to return to the Tower." She grabbed the envelope, contemplating tearing it in half and shattering the thin vials on the floor. Her memories—judging by the multiple bulges of the envelope, there were three.

"Not that I would want to now. It seems they have been stealing my memories." Part of her wanted to have them all back. In reality, she was terrified of what she would discover. Why did they take them from her to begin with? Could she really have agreed with it? There was a chance the letter had an explanation, but she wanted to read it as much as she wanted to swallow her dagger. To chuck it in a fireplace and watch it burn seemed like a more satisfying option. Nothing the Countess could say would fix what they did to her. What they had allowed to be done.

A gust of air whooshed around the room, unsettling the papers on the desk. Felicity looked up to find a storm blazing in Ward's eyes. Her magic was beckoned forward by his wind, and it took sheer will to keep it back, her jaw tensing in concentration.

"Tomorrow after tea, meet me here." With a growl, the wind stopped, the room stilling. He took a deep breath and walked across the room to pull her dagger free from the bookcase.

Her brow furrowed as he handed it to her. "Why?"

"I want to show you something."

Chapter 11

The following day, she met Ward in the study. "What is it you were going to show me?" Felicity hated to admit that she was curious. But she was. More so, she wanted her mind to drift as far away from the memories and the letter she'd locked within her trunk.

"Study first. You need to be ready for the courtiers tomorrow." Ward laid out a map on the table. She grumbled under her breath but took a seat.

He began to go through the names of the new arrivals. "Lady Fiadh is the king and queen's closest friend and confidant. She's from Scáth."

Felicity glared as he pointed at the outline of the shadow realm. Did he really think she was as ignorant not to know the layout of the continent? They'd passed by it on their travels here. Despite her annoyance, she didn't interrupt though since she wanted this over quickly.

He continued, "You'll rarely see her without Marquette by her side. It's why the queen hasn't attended tea during your time here. Queen Marquette is very particular about the company she keeps."

"Why are they so close?" Felicity looked over the list of names. There were only two others she needed to remember. According to Ward, this group of courtiers would be more difficult to persuade into accepting her. Seeing as Lady Mistward still scowled whenever Felicity was in her presence, she would have her work cut out for her.

"That is something I cannot even begin to comprehend, but...it may have to do with Lady Fiadh's unique gift. She's a witch—human—and like most of her kind, she only has one specialty. Never underestimate her because she wouldn't have a close friendship with the queen without reason. I don't believe that any would doubt her relationship with the royal family, so don't expect her to be disloyal."

"What is her specialty?" Felicity blinked.

"Her magic—it's fickle. From my understanding, she can read the strongest thoughts within a room, but things can become jumbled and hard for her to decipher within a crowd or among a small group." He breathed a sigh, then frowned. "Don't be specific in what you're thinking in front of her, and you should be fine. This is all hearsay as she is a bit of an enigma. Don't expect to get much from her. She will be watching you—don't doubt it for a moment."

Speaking of enigma...

Felicity's brow rose, surprised at all the information he'd been willing to share. She watched Ward closely as the session continued, picking up on little nuances in an attempt to get a better understanding of the male. There wasn't much, however, beyond that when he was deep in thought, a crease appeared between his eyes, and he paced when he began to lecture.

When Ward deemed the session over, he led her through the garden past where she had tea earlier that afternoon. Gardeners clipped back at the vines growing through a particularly entangled rose bush with annoyed expressions on their faces. Felicity's brow rose at Ward's smile at their discontent.

A waist-height picket fence separated the gardens from the grass fields that led to the bluff overlooking the ocean. She inhaled the sweet scent of the sea, her body thrumming to life at the nearing sight of the turquoise waters.

He veered to the right and led her to a weeping willow, its long branches enclosing the earth surrounding its thick trunk. He held back the branches, allowing her entrance into the simple privacy of nature, the breeze rustling the leaves. Ward leaned against the trunk, crossing his arms. "I come here when I need to clear my mind." He looked at her for a moment. "And you needed to clear yours."

Felicity stood beneath the edge of the branches, letting the leaves brush against her body, feeling the touch of the ocean air. "Yes, I did," she breathed.

Self-consciousness tethered her to the moment. It had been so long since she had someone to speak to. To confide in. It had been

Garder for a short time—and apparently Harrison before him, although she didn't remember. It felt surreal, and she fought back the rising panic at having confessed so much already to this male she barely knew.

He cleared his throat. "I think you're looking at this opportunity all wrong. The Tower may have taken from you, but it is returning what wasn't theirs in the first place. They are offering you a chance to make your own life."

Feeling exposed, she wrapped her arms around herself. "It's the only life I've ever known. The life I was raised and trained to fulfill until death." She shook her head. "There was never a thought in my mind for something more."

"Or was there? You don't know yet." He moved beside her. "Have you read the letter?"

"No," she grumbled. Her frustration bubbled to the surface. It was better than the magic whispering to let it free. This was why she had waited. To read the letter, to return her memories—she was hurt by the fact the Tower didn't want her anymore and scared she wouldn't be able to control her response. What if those memories or that letter held more of a reason why, and she was to blame? The emotions that rose with those thoughts were unfamiliar after stamping them down for so long.

"If you want, I'll help you. I can teach you more about politics. About what is happening within the realms, which could help you to decide where your future may lead." He exhaled. "Your choice."

She glanced at him, his attention still on the horizon. "Why would you help me? You hate me."

He chuckled. "Maybe because I understand a little of what you're going through."

Before she could ask how, his nostrils flared. Felicity heard the footsteps before Ward turned.

Prince Alarian pushed aside the leaves and cocked his head at them, his lips a thin line. "You're wanted back at the castle, Ward."

Felicity was surprised to see him but kept her expression disinterested. Since the day he had barged into her room, he'd been absent beyond dinners in the dining hall. Not that she was complaining.

Ward sighed and nodded. "I'll escort Felicity back."

"No need." The prince's mouth parted as his attention was directed to her. "It's not like we're in any danger together. Besides, it's been a while since the two of us started a stir throughout the castle. Can't have that."

The way he said those words caused her shoulders to tense. Ward looked between them. She gave him a reassuring nod. The prince didn't unsettle her, and she didn't need Ward to deal with the arrogant male. "I don't need either of you to escort me anywhere."

Prince Alarian shrugged. "I never said you did. My father on the other hand—"

With a narrowed gaze, Ward parted the branches. "Don't make things difficult, Alarian." Ward glared at him before he left.

Prince Alarian chuckled and headed towards the bluff's edge. The desire to see the expanding sea pulled Felicity from the willow branches. The sun was already beginning its descent into the horizon and she marveled at the colors. An orange glow shifted from bright reds to subtle purples and finally the deep blue of impending night.

"Don't get too close to the edge." Prince Alarian grabbed her arm, causing her to step back a few steps. She hadn't realized she'd passed him. The ocean view beckoned.

"Are you frightened of the fall? I wasn't that close." She wiggled her arm free from his touch, ignoring the warmth left in its wake.

He sighed. "Maybe not, but there are stories about these bluffs—a great wind will pull those deserving to their deaths. The soldiers claim it's cursed by the previous king."

"You believe it?" This was the second curse she'd been told about. Between the gardens and this phantom wind, she was starting to wonder what these fae had been drinking. "Fae cannot initiate curses, only witch-kind can do so."

He shrugged. "When someone has a good reason, I don't doubt the power of a curse."

"And this king had a good reason?"

"His power was revered by many. When he was dethroned and forced from the lands, it is said he spoke a curse into the air and the wind responded." The corner of his mouth rose. "I don't know if you're deserving of death or not. I prefer not to find out."

With a roll of her eyes, she turned back to the view, taking in a deep breath of the summer air. All this talk of curses was becoming daunting. The breeze beat against her face, stinging her eyes. Yet, it felt as though it was giving life to her lungs, so she bared it. "If the king was respected, why was he cast out?"

Prince Alarian tensed beside her. It took him some time to answer. His eyes were alive today, and honestly, this was the first time in a while—or ever—Felicity hadn't seen him hungover or drunk. "Many believed he was going soft, and his leadership was under scrutiny. Some spread gossip and lies, promising the king's foes power to gain trust and then there was an uprising—a coup."

Felicity wondered if it was the same family as the murdered queen, the one who had tended the garden so carefully. No wonder the wind and earth wouldn't deem the new residents worthy. Had the current royal family been the ones to exile the previous king and kill his queen?

Maybe there was good reason for her to understand the realm's politics.

Of course, it also didn't guarantee Prince Alarian's family were at fault. There was a chance the exiled king had been guilty. Or previous leaders were to blame. There were too many unknowns for Felicity to pass judgments. Instead of delving further into those thoughts, she rolled her shoulders and folded her hands behind her back. "What is Ward's position here at the castle?"

Prince Alarian regarded her from the corner of his eye. "Why? Do you fancy him?"

She rolled her eyes. "Why would you assume my curiosity being of a romantic intent? It can't be jealousy. You have enough females begging for your admiration and attention."

Prince Alarian winked. "Because I like it when we play these games. I say something, you glare. It's our thing."

She smiled, turning on her heels to head back to the castle. As much as she didn't want to leave the view, the company was wearing. "You know"—she shot over her shoulder— "I could kill you in your sleep."

He had to jog to catch up. "You take all the fun out of flirting when you threaten my life." He smiled at himself. "Or maybe you don't. I haven't decided yet."

She remembered the letter locked away within a trunk. The private matters she had shared with the mysterious male in a time of weakness—something she didn't want to come to regret. Her stomach clenched. "Who is Ward, Prince?"

He took a step ahead and turned—walking backwards. "You should ask Ward. I don't feel it's my place to explain."

Felicity couldn't hide her grin as they neared the gate then shifted bright eyes to the male. His grin widened. Just as the back of his leg caught on the fence, almost falling over it, his hand caught on the picket's edge, cutting open his palm but keeping him upright. Her grin widened.

Before he could right himself, she unclipped the gate's hinge, and Prince Alarian stumbled. Unbalanced, he fell into the opening and onto the garden floor flat onto his back. He grunted.

"I'm not playing games." She made sure there was a hint of warning in her voice.

He winced, then began to laugh. Once she was further into the gardens, she couldn't stifle her own smile any longer.

Chapter
12

The courtiers arrived during the night and were introduced to court the following morning. Felicity sat next to Lady Solfire in the garden and analyzed the new faces in the circle of females. Lady Grandeur wore a grandiose hat with feathers and large purple dahlias decorating the brim while her sister Lady Trent sat across from Felicity, studying her as one might search for a spider in their shoe. Both were from Visce with dark bronze skin and hazelnut eyes. Their fingertips were dark gray and had scales in patches of different shades of blue and iridescent white along their skin. The infamous Lady Fiadh still had not arrived. She and the queen must have been held up.

The gardeners worked hard along the edges of the walkways, but the females took no notice of their presence. The curse of the garden seemed to be common knowledge, but Felicity couldn't help but watch as the workers moved through the rows, tearing at the base of the weeds; thin, wrinkled roots torn free from the earth.

They were working through vines that had overtaken hydrangeas, blossoms drifting to the ground as they unraveled the mischievous plants.

"I heard of your devastating introduction to our realms, Lady Dwauer." Lady Grandeur's puckered lips looked ready to kiss at any moment. "Such a heartbreaking story. To be by the advisor's side at the end. When my husband told me of his passing, I couldn't eat for days."

Felicity gave a simpered smile. "It was not the way I had hoped to be welcomed to the mainland, but I was glad to have known him for a short time." This was a dangerous subject to linger on. "I heard you were unable to attend court earlier due to traveling conditions."

Lady Trent grunted, and Lady Chartow patted her arm. The former flicked open her fan. "It's hard times on the roads as of late. Travel is not nearly as safe as it used to be."

Miss Isleen slumped in her chair, looking more like a child than a young female on the cusp of adulthood. Her mother gave her leg a nudge, causing her to sit up—although slowly.

Lady Chartow snorted. "Safe times are gone. I was surprised when this one"—she pointed her fan at Felicity— "arrived without any difficulty and with such few guards. Especially with the prince as one of her escorts. Seemed like the perfect chance for the rebels to take a chance."

Lady Grandeur shook her head. "The rebels are growing daring. If the king doesn't do something, we will have a war on our hands."

She reached for a sandwich. "But I'm certain King Roald will crush them soon. None other have the might of the king's guard."

"No one can stand against our rule." As the queen's voice rang clear through the gardens, each lady rushed to their feet—Felicity included—and dipped into a low curtsy. "Please sit, my friends. I apologize for my absence as of late, but it was necessary. I've missed our afternoons together."

Queen Marquette met Felicity's gaze, her thin mouth reaching into a smile. "Lady Dwauer, to you, I offer my deepest apologies. I've ignored my duties of making you feel welcome within my home."

"No apologies necessary, Queen Marquette. Everyone has been most welcoming." Felicity dipped lower, but the queen gestured for her to take a seat with the others.

Queen Marquette's smile widened. "Of course they were." She gestured to a young woman behind her. She looked only a little older than Miss Isleen—and Felicity was forced to remind herself of her age as well—this woman had an air of regal maturity about her. With her chin held high, dark hair tied atop her head, and a long neck on a stocky body, her proportions seemed slightly off. She wore a fitted tunic and pants similar to those Felicity had donned during Harrison's unexpected visit.

"I see you've met the others. May I introduce Lady Fiadh of the Shadow Realm." The queen settled into the high back chair that had been left vacant at each tea session prior. Lady Fiadh sat beside her, a bland expression on her simple face.

Felicity's skin prickled when the witch looked her way, a strangeness settled, but she was unable to pinpoint why her piercing gaze felt as if she was tearing away the layers of Felicity's skull to see the contents within her mind. It was only when Felicity remembered Ward's warning that she cleared her thoughts, settling her attention on the queen as a light conversation began. It took all her willpower not to wince at the claw-like sensation that dragged up her neck.

Felicity hoped to veer the topic back to travel and the rebels, but the queen intercepted her plan. "I hear you and my son are getting along well." Queen Marquette folded her hands in her lap primly. "He spoke of you just yesterday."

Cursing the prince under her breath, Felicity made sure her smile showed more excitement than she felt. "He's been kind to me."

Lady Grandeur's brow rose. "I haven't seen the prince ever keen on one fae before. It could be quite an advantageous match for one from Oileán." Felicity heard the quip in her remark but chose to ignore it.

"No ill will towards the prince, but he tires quickly, so only time will tell," Lady Mistward said. "I do hope he chooses a bride soon." She reached over to squeeze her daughter's hand. "One that would benefit all of the realms."

The queen's demure facade faltered. "He's a stubborn male, resisting his marriage rights as long as he can." Lady Solfire gestured to the queen and offered to fill her cup. Queen Marquette held up her saucer. "I may have to step in." She peered at Felicity, her brow rising. "If things don't work out between the two of you, of course."

"What of Ward?" Miss Isleen offered. "Has he bonded with anyone?" The question earned her a glare from her mother.

Questions settled on the tip of Felicity's tongue. A bond was something she'd only ever heard in passing. She made a mental note to discuss this with Ward.

The queen's mouth twitched. "The king will decide when and if the time is right for Ward to step into any relationship."

The male was still a mystery—one that no one seemed to want to clarify for Felicity, gossip or not. She hadn't asked Ward yet. The understanding they had didn't extend to personal matters. Not that she blamed him—there was plenty she kept from him.

The subject was dropped, and for a moment, silence spread through the group.

"What are you planning for the king's upcoming birthday?" Lady Trent asked before she took a sip of her tea.

The rest of the conversation remained on the upcoming celebration. Lady Fiadh said nothing, but Felicity could sense her penetrating gaze slipping from each of them from time to time. Yet, it always seemed to come back to rest on her.

When tea came to an end, Felicity watched Lady Chartow. This was as good a chance as any. If she could follow the female—

Lady Grandeur stepped in Felicity's path. "My dear, I hope I didn't offend you. It was no ill will towards you, of course, just more of a warning as to the prince's demeanor."

It was anything but, and Felicity knew it. She wondered if the female had a daughter pining over the prince. Either way, she was going to lose Lady Chartow if she didn't end this conversation.

"I assure you, Lady Grandeur, no offense was taken. The prince and I are merely getting to know each other. I, for one, wouldn't rush into anything with a male of such stature." Felicity gave her best smile before she side-stepped alongside Lady Grandeur, moving parallel to her as the female moved with her. Once on the other side, Felicity gave a slight curtsy. "I really must go." She turned on her heel, watching her steps over the cobbled path to ensure her exit looked as poised as possible. "It was an honor to meet you," she said over her shoulder then left Lady Grandeur, eyes wide and sputtering, in the garden.

It didn't take long to find Lady Chartow within the halls walking alongside Lady Solfire. Felicity kept her distance and a steady pace.

Lady Solfire said her farewells before turning down a separate hallway in the direction of her own room, but Lady Chartow continued, not sparing a glance in Felicity's direction.

When Lady Chartow made a sudden left—the remaining guest quarters were to the right—a spark of excitement rushed along Felicity's spine. She wished she had worn the pants, the skirts wrapping around her legs as she hurried. Sure, there was a time and place for proper attire—and tea was it—but the dress could get in the way of any attempt for proper spying.

Felicity didn't follow her around the corner right away but only stole a glance from time to time to see where Chartow ventured.

When the female reached a door towards the middle of the hall, she stopped to search the hall from left to right. Content the coast was clear, she opened the door and slipped inside before closing it behind her with a resounding click.

Felicity entered the hall and walked to the door. She first pressed her ear against it. During her searches of the castle at night, she knew these rooms were similar to the study she and Ward read in—the perfect meeting room.

If she went back to her quarters to change her clothes into proper attire to spy through the windows, it could waste time or Felicity could lose Lady Chartow completely. There was no guarantee there was a balcony off the room as only a few studies had one. She listened for a moment. No voices—the only sounds were the rustling of fabric or chairs being moved. If she could, at the very least, see who Chartow was meeting, then it would be better than nothing and give her another individual to trail.

With a gentle twist, she tried the door. It had been left unlocked. Slowly, so it didn't creak, she opened the door and peeked through the crack. Felicity froze, the handle gripped in her palm as she met Lady Chartow's gaze. The female was pressed against the wall by a male with shoulder-length brown hair who fondled her breast as he kissed her neck. Lady Chartow stilled, her eyes widened, a mirror to Felicity's.

"What?" Lord Chartow, the same male she'd passed in the hall of their room, started to turn around, but Felicity didn't wait. Flushed a deep red, she snapped the door shut. Her feet tapped on the floor in rapid succession as she attempted to put as much distance between herself and the couple as she could.

***

Felicity sat in her chambers, staring at the letter from the Countess. She turned the envelope over, still sealed and now creased from being stuffed in her trunk. Even though she tried to forget it, it was never far from her mind. Grazing the envelope, the parchment now smooth from her touch.

After the blunder with Lady Chartow two days prior, Felicity went back to spying in the safety of the night. Lady Chartow and Felicity pretended nothing had happened, averting each other's gazes. Although the older female smirked from time to time. She could only assume the female was proud of her sexual prowess.

Felicity had never remembered being embarrassed in such a way—which led her back to that damn letter and vials of memories.

The temptation becoming too much, she stood to toss the envelope in the trunk. The vials moved within the envelope, the coolness bleeding through the paper to her skin. Deliberate and slow, she snapped the seal and the wolf's head was cut clean in half. Felicity held the opened envelope over her waiting palm until the three vials fell into it. A murky liquid filled all three, misting against the glass. A reminder that her memories were just a shadow of what they once were.

It was her own version of torture to have them within her grasp while not knowing the truths they contained. Her truths. Since Harrison's visit, she'd felt lost. As if she was going through the motions but uncertain of her destination. Maybe these memories could guide her.

She thumbed the glass canisters as she sat again, placing the envelope still containing the letter and two of the vials on the table beside her. The tip of her nail cut through the wax seal along the edge of the cork and it popped free. She inhaled the scent of mildew, pine trees with the metallic tang of blood, and steel. If this was the scent of her memories, Felicity didn't know if she wanted them.

Was it worth resisting the temptation any longer? Each day she denied the truth, she also denied herself. That was what these memories were—who she was—and the past that led her to where she was now. Homeless—within a court of games and curses.

Before she could second guess herself further, she pressed the vial to her lips, tossed her head back, and emptied the contents into her mouth. Felicity almost gagged the liquid all over her dress. It didn't go down easy as it tasted twice as bad as it smelled. As she finished swallowing, her body convulsed, and her muscles went rigid. Then she went suddenly slack, unable to carry her own weight as she slumped against the chair. Her head throbbed as she surged forward, falling onto the floor to her knees, clutching her skull in her hands. Images danced in her mind. The memories were a jumbled mess that made her pulse throb against her fingertips. Grabbing fistfuls of hair, her grip tightened, pulling at her scalp.

Felicity opened her mouth to scream but nothing came out. As she gasped for air, her hand searched the table beside her, batting the letter aside to find the remaining vials.

For a moment, she considered stopping and if it was worth all of this. But it was now or never. She wasn't one to back down when she started something.

Felicity unfastened the other two containers with shaking fingers and tipped one after the other into her mouth. As her body reacted, she gripped the arm of the chair, her eyes unseeing, the room around her no longer present as the memories convulsed within her mind. Felicity curled up in the fetal position on the floor as her body spasmed. When the darkness took her, she was thankful.

Chapter 13

The fire was low when Felicity came to. Vomit was on the floor beside where she lay, chunks stuck in her hair and splattered on her cheek. Her head ached as she tried to concentrate. The memories were only glimpses flittering within her mind—out of reach. With the pounding in her head though, she wasn't surprised. She forced herself off the floor by grabbing the chair beside her and dragged herself into it.

The scent of burnt fabric caught her attention. Felicity noted her clothes were singed along her neckline where her pendant rested, and she had no clue how that had happened. The ache of her magic wasn't beckoning as it usually did. Her only consolation was her room was as it had been. Everything was in its place, and she doubted Meira would have left her on the floor.

Just the thought of the handmaiden must have been enough of a summons because there was a knock before Meira entered, carrying a tray of cookies with a pot of tea.

As soon as she saw Felicity, she dropped the tray on the nearest table, teacup unsettled onto its side. "My lady, oh my. What happened?" She rushed to Felicity, careful to avoid the vomit stinking up the room. "Here, let me help you to the bathing chambers."

Meira's lean form held more strength than expected as she easily supported Felicity's weight. The handmaiden assisted Felicity to the bathing room, and after sitting her on a stool, Meira turned on the faucet.

"Thank you, Meira." Felicity's throat was scratchy—her voice hoarse, resting her hands at her neckline to hide the burnt garment. "I apologize for the mess."

"There's no need." Meira helped her out of her clothes. "We can get rid of this. I didn't much care for that dress anyway. Doesn't match your coloring."

If the handmaiden noted the singed neckline, she didn't comment, and Felicity wouldn't draw attention to it. The dress was in a pile, rolled in upon itself, against the floor. The vomit and stench should be enough to keep eyes from searching it further. Or Felicity hoped.

With a damp towel, Meira cleaned what she could from Felicity's face and hair and combed out any sick that remained. "There now. Let's get you in the bath. I will send word that you're unable to attend dinner this evening."

"I can manage, I assure you." But Felicity's protests came out weak, and she didn't have the energy to bicker. Her head still ached, and although her stomach grumbled, the thought of eating anything caused bile to rise.

Once Felicity was settled within the tub, Meira placed a warm compress over Felicity's forehead. With a moan of relief, she closed her eyes and leaned her head back.

Meira patted her arm. "I'll return with a towel. Is there anything else I can get you?"

"No, Meira. Thank you." Felicity didn't attempt to open her eyes, even as the handmaiden added lavender-scented salts to the bath. Her body slumped deeper into the water and began to relax in the warmth.

Felicity waited for the door to shut behind Meira before she released a long sigh. Taking the moment of quiet, she tried to piece together the puzzle of her memories. Although they were there, they weren't in any particular pattern or timeline. They were jumbled as stilled images without a story. Felicity felt more lost now than she had been without them. Ignorance may have been a better alternative.

***

The following morning, Felicity had nothing to do. She and the prince were meant to leave the next day for Aer's summer festivities. Due to the importance of the visit, Meira had canceled all of Felicity's previously accepted invitations, informing the queen and the others that it was important she continued to rest.

In all honesty, it only gave Felicity more time to repent on her desire to know about her past. It felt like the biggest mistake Felicity had made—well, of the mistakes she could recall. Her memories were still nothing more than jagged pieces floating about, incognizant and scattered. Besides the continuous throbbing in her head, nothing had changed.

Due to her plans being cancelled, Felicity couldn't even walk the grounds without causing suspicion, so she was sequestered in her chambers. To help with the discomfort of her magic, she would call on her glamour within the privacy of her room. At least it helped while the books Ward lent her only led her mind to wander.

The knock at her door was a welcome reprieve from the mundane day. Felicity waited until her glamour was gone before she answered the door. She hadn't expected Ward to be the one to visit. "May I come in?"

She pulled her shawl tighter over her shoulders, stepping to the side to allow him to enter. As he passed, she dropped her hand, and the side of his body brushed against it. She couldn't hide her initial smile but by the time she had closed the door, it was gone.

As she faced him, he gave her a once over and nodded. "Meira said you were very sick. I'm glad to see you're doing better."

"Meira seems to be on the side of dramatic or over-cautious. I haven't decided which yet." She took a seat, resting her head against the chair's stuffed back.

"You gave her a fright." His words were quiet, barely a whisper. "Do you know what caused your illness?"

"I have returned my memories to their rightful place," Felicity said. The words came easier than they should have. She still barely knew him, and yet he was easy to speak to. It caught her off guard. Went against her instincts.

Ward inhaled and took the other seat across from hers. "What do you remember?"

"Nothing yet." She shook her head. "It's like a giant puzzle my mind is trying to make right again. I almost wish I hadn't done it." The envelope caught her eye, the one still waiting on the table, ignored in all of the activity.

"Have you read it yet?"

She jerked her head in his direction. "Maybe once I return from Aer I'll be ready for that step."

"It could give you an idea of how to make sense of your memories."

Felicity shrugged. "Maybe." Her frustration, the sense of betrayal—she wasn't ready to let go of those emotions yet. She knew she'd made the Tower the scapegoat and wasn't sure she wanted the truth. Until she was ready for it, she couldn't allow herself to open that letter.

He leaned back and cracked a smile. "You leave tomorrow. You still haven't gotten the handkerchief from me."

She grinned. "Is that so? Have you checked?"

His gaze narrowed, eyebrows furrowing as he dipped his hand into his pocket. Then the next.

Felicity held up the handkerchief, waving it gently between her fingers. "When you came in the room. You made it too easy."

Ward chuckled. "You took advantage of my concern."

"It's not my fault you were preoccupied." She thumbed the title of the closest book. "Now you have to show me where the secret passages are."

His only response was to smile. She met his gaze, surprised at how relaxed he looked. In the short time they had known each other, she had never seen him lean back, shoulders slack with a thoughtful expression on his face. Her head ached at the observation, and Felicity turned away.

"I have a question about fae. What is the bond?" She tilted her head in consideration.

He cleared his throat, thumping his chest as if something had lodged itself there. It only made her brow rise further and he waved off her concern. "Why do you ask?"

"Because it seems that you and the prince's marriage and bonds are being considered and I can't look like the ignorant fool to these females." Her mouth pursed.

Ward grumbled under his breath. "Well, when two individuals fall in love—"

She rolled her eyes. "I don't need a lesson in sex."

His cheeks shimmered, a flush rising.

Felicity gawked. "Are you blushing?" She wadded up and tossed the handkerchief in his face. He didn't attempt to catch it as the fabric met its mark, then fell in his lap.

He rubbed the back of his neck with a grimace. "This is awkward to discuss with you."

"Why?"

Ward sighed. "It just—" He shook his head, his expression shifting into a frown. "It just is. We're getting off track."

"Only because you're acting like your explaining intercourse to a youngling. If you ever have children, your partner should initiate this conversation."

He stilled for a moment, and a look she didn't recognize crossed his features. As quickly as it appeared it was gone. "I'll keep that in mind."

He cleared his throat, his attention on the handkerchief now threaded between his fingers. "The bond is more than sex and stronger than love. It's a connection that forms between two individuals that is offered by the magic of the earth and can be denied or chosen."

Felicity considered his words. "How does magic offer it?"

"I honestly don't know. It's not offered to everyone. And how it comes to fruition changes for each individual."

Felicity pondered what he said, trying to ascertain if she had any further questions.

Ward didn't wait though, cutting the silence. "I came here to warn you about the prince."

The ache in her head expanded. "I can take care of myself."

Ward leaned forward, resting his elbows on his thighs. "I wasn't doubting your resolve. But the prince is known for putting others in *uncomfortable* situations. His reputation isn't held in the highest regard between the countless females, the drinking..." He sighed. "It's best you're on your guard for whatever he might try to pull while he's with you. The king has probably banned him from attempting anything, but he's known to ignore his father's direct orders."

"There's nothing the prince could make me feel beyond annoyance and anger." She held back her frustration. "But I appreciate the warning. Even if it's unnecessary."

He tapped his finger against his crossed forearm. "How are things going with the mission? Any leads?"

Her chin lifted. "Not yet."

"Be careful, Felicity. You don't want to find out how short the king's temper is."

She didn't respond, unable to dismiss the warning. Already she was feeling the pressure, and the lack of results was only aggravating her too. She thought she'd be further along by now.

Ward searched her face, a frown forming his lips. "I cannot train with you tonight. There is another matter I must attend to." He stood and patted her shoulder. "One of the guards who escorted us from Saol will be there to take my place."

The relief she began to feel evaporated. Felicity had almost been allowed freedom. "You'll be missed."

Ward headed towards the door. "I didn't think that was an emotion you allowed."

She shrugged, pushing to her feet. "Maybe not. But I have my doubts that the guard will be an interesting conversationist."

"You have a low bar of what counts as intriguing conversation if I'm how you measure such things." He laughed, and she couldn't help but smile at the sound.

Ward stopped short, looking at her face. "Was that a genuine smile?"

"Don't flatter yourself." She pushed his shoulder, and he side-stepped to catch his balance.

"My mistake." But she caught the grin plastered on his own lips as he left the room.

***

The guard was more statue than a male. He didn't move, keeping his position by the door and his expression vacant. If this hadn't been her last chance to train for three nights, Felicity would have found a way to make him break his composure. Instead, she got right to work, moving through the paces of her usual warm-up.

"Leave us."

The order interrupted her exercises. She rolled to her feet, dagger pointed at the door.

Prince Alarian grinned as the guard strode from the room, leaving them alone. "Well, look at you. I wondered what constituted a training session for a spy."

At the sight of him, her annoyance swelled. Her gaze slid over his broad shoulders, the vest hanging open over a rumpled tunic, before settling on that damn grin he flashed her way. "I have three days of your presence to deal with. You can see yourself out now." She turned, starting the circuit again. Lunge, stab, twist, back kick then a front roll.

"You know, no one else would talk that way to me. Well, if you don't count Ward. He's been that way since we met." The prince stalked forward, his shoes dragging through the sawdust, raising dust.

"No wonder you think you can walk all over them." She jabbed again then added a wide arching slash into the circuit. He continued to watch, his gaze prickling the hairs on the back of her neck.

"Do you know I had multiple reasons to ensure you attended the party at my side?" His voice drawled out slow and steady. She found him leaning against the pole Ward usually sat under, one foot cocked over the other and his arms crossed. His biceps were defined, hard lines visible through his tunic. With his shirt opened at the neck, a peek of his collarbone revealed toned muscle that disappeared under his clothing. She wondered how far those muscles extended. Would she find hardened abdominals, strong legs, the V that pivoted downward from his waist—she turned away to expel those thoughts, not wanting him to catch her staring.

Why would a drunken prince train? Maybe a requirement. Her teeth gritted together, annoyed at herself for noticing such things. "What were your motives?"

He cocked his head, that mischievous smile rising. Felicity wanted to throw her dagger at him and see how much smiling he would do between the metal of her blade. He waved his hand, and a paper appeared in a wisp of shadow, hanging in the air until he grabbed it. "I made a list just in case you asked."

Felicity turned back to her movements, sweat clinging to her brow and running down her temple. "If you had to write it down then it's too long, and I'm already bored."

"What is it that you don't like about me?" His annoying smile was still on his face as he stuffed the list into his pocket. "Compared to Ward, I welcomed you so warmly."

"Ward isn't obnoxious," she snapped. "And your reputation precedes you, Prince. From what I've heard, there is nothing to respect. So far, Ward hasn't proven to be unworthy."

Prince Alarian's back straightened as he stiffened. His gaze darkened and the room with it. Shadows brushed the outline of his body—emitting from him. Her mouth parted in wonder at the sight. Did he have a little of his mother's magic after all?

Then the shadows disappeared, and the lights snapped back to life. "My reputation has proven me unworthy? That I can understand." He sighed as he took a seat on the bench. A muscle in his jaw tightened. "By the way, my father is getting impatient. He'll want a report once we return from Aer."

"I'm working on it." Her heart sped up and she blamed it on the exertion.

Prince Alarian's gaze thinned. "It's my ass on the line too, you know? I brought you here for a reason."

"Why me?" She spun around and glared at him. "Out of all the spies in all of Talamh, why me?"

His shoulders drew back, his mouth tight. The prince cleared his throat and looked away. "Your guild came highly recommended. The Tower chose you and I assume it's because of your skillset and what you could offer the kingdom."

"I won't make you regret it." Even after everything that happened between her and the Tower, she still needed to complete this mission. It was the key to becoming one of the Dearmadta—and that title would guarantee she had a future to look forward to. The only future that was still an option for her.

"I know I won't. I have high hopes for you. But I'm not the one you need to convince." He closed his eyes, resting his head against the pole behind him.

The prince was silent for the remainder of the time. As she worked through her movements, he sat, watching the lantern's flickering lights or the dancing flames from the lit braziers. His attention never moved towards her.

Felicity continued her circuits, adding more moves as she went, switching hands and positions until her muscles ached. But something from their conversation tickled the back of her mind. Like everything else within her jumbled thoughts, Felicity couldn't put her finger on it.

Chapter
14

The carriage traveled along the road, an occasional bump the only thing that jostled Felicity and the prince from their brooding. He was quieter than usual, but she didn't mind the silence. The headache from her retrieved memories had abated, but the aches from withholding her magic after having to limit her use of the glamour had returned. The prince's jaw quivered. Felicity blinked and looked away, realizing she was staring at him, his attention on the passing landscape. With the dangers of travel, a handful of guards escorted their group of three carriages, other members of the court joining for the festivities.

Felicity was disappointed that Lady Fiadh had chosen to stay behind with the remainder of the royal family though she was relieved not to have the female's beady gaze following her every move. Even if Fiadh was in the king and queen's confidence, Felicity didn't want the truth to be widespread knowledge. The fewer who were aware, the better.

"We're staying at Cnoc, a town just past the border in Aer." The prince's voice broke through her thoughts. "It's one of my favorite stops to visit. Would you care to join me in town?"

Felicity's teeth ground together. Ward's warning, as much as it was unnecessary, rang in her head. "No, thank you."

"Fine." He turned away again. "Just so you're aware, I'm not forcing you to be civil or even attempting to make others think we're engaged in any type of relationship. If you choose, we can ensure the end of this charade at the next stop. I think Lady Mistward would love it if I extended an invite to her daughter."

"Would that be fair to Miss Isleen?" Her head sliced in his direction, eyes narrowing. "Are you attempting to make me jealous?"

He sighed. "Never mind. Whatever I say to you is the wrong thing." His lips thinned and he stared straight ahead.

"I don't think your father would be thrilled if we ended it too soon. Some might question my reason for staying in the court. After all, I think it was you who said to let them make their own assumptions," Felicity said.

In her own annoyance, Felicity's attention diverted to the window as the town came into view. The gate was wide open, and their traveling procession continued beside traders pulling carts towards their homes for the evening. They passed in slow succession over cobbled streets along a row of storefronts. Different castes of faeries and humans milled the streets. A púca with their telltale pitch black eyes waved to a nymph with turquoise scales before stopping to engage in a lively conversation.

When the carriage came to a steady stop in front of an inn, the door popped open, and a hand reached out to assist them from the carriage. Felicity's eyes widened as she emerged. Gears and cranks made up one side of the nearest tower and built near the top were mechanisms for a clock face. Two hands, one longer than the other, moved with precision by the machinery below that gave off an audible click-clack. A smell of oil, leather, and grease filled the town, seeping from the industrious buildings and its inhabitants.

Felicity spent more time looking at the attire than at the individuals themselves. Many wore pants and white ruffled tunics peeking out from under leather vests. Atop their heads were tall hats adorned with feathers or thin wires twisted in different patterns. Some held walking sticks with bronze handles.

Then there were those with leather satchels on their hips, harnesses filled with tools, and a few wore glasses similar to those worn by Lady Chartow. Most had smears of grease on some portion of their bodies or attire. A fae stopped at the base of the clock and pulled a tool from her harness. It had two long handles that pivoted open. She used it to grip a metal bolt then twisted it twice, tightening it.

Felicity stepped off the road as a sweeper passed by with a wheeled cart grinding against gears, causing a bristled end of a broom to brush dirt to the side of the road. Another man followed behind pushing a machine with multiple trowels that spun on a wheel, picking up the dirt to drop it into a metal bucket.

The prince led her by the arm, pace slow, allowing her to take in this new world around her. The town they had stayed in upon their original journey through Aer to Éardrom had been nothing like this. Here was proof that Aer was made of inventors. Everything around them spoke of industry and ideas. Through a window, she witnessed a shop owner preparing to close for the night. He rolled large blueprints and tied them closed with twine. The prince stood quietly beside her, allowing her to watch. When finished, the proprietor exited, locking the door with a thick key before pulling out another key that he inserted into a box by the door.

"What does that do?" Felicity asked, surprising herself. She hadn't realized she spoke aloud.

Prince Alarian leaned in towards her. "An alarm system. He just turned it on to ensure no one can get into his shop unless they have that specific key. Otherwise, an alarm will sound that will alert the guards."

"Why isn't this technology everywhere?" She blinked. It was a good thing she didn't have any jobs in this area prior or she would have been oblivious—and in a shit load of trouble. Maybe this was why the Tower had never sent her this far north before.

The prince shrugged. "They use air magic—wind—to produce many of their instruments and tools. Most of the resources they need are found in other realms and cost enough money on their own to have transported. They cost too much to build, let alone outsource to other realms to adapt their own towns for such technology. Even the palace has trouble affording Aer inventions. But we have adapted in some areas. That is why we have plumbing for water within the palace and many outlying villages. Éardrom had to choose what was worth the price."

When they reached the door to the inn it creaked open by another set of gears and wheels. Felicity tilted her head to watch in awe. Inside, the inn itself was made up of different metals—except iron. It was the one metal that weakened the faeries, but somehow, Felicity was immune. The bar was made of thick bronze, judging by the color. A row of stools made of steel and wood were settled in front of it. Next to a winding set of stairs with bronze railings sat a table with a burly man leaning over a notebook, quill in hand.

"How many rooms do you need?" he asked without looking up.

Prince Alarian opened his mouth, but a male from their party stepped forward before he could speak. Felicity lowered her head to hide the blush as Lord Chartow pulled his wife beside him and bowed to the prince. "Excuse me, Your Highness. Please let me see to these matters."

The innkeeper looked up, his balding head catching the limited light. "Ah, we've been expecting your party." He gave a half-bow, then snapped his thick fingers and a clurichaun appeared from a door beside the staircase, his long nails clicking together. The innkeeper nodded towards Lord Chartow. "These are our special guests, Lidwick. Have Galvon assist you in getting them settled in their rooms. Second floor is all theirs."

The prince stopped Felicity, allowing the others to file past. He gestured for her to follow as he passed a few tables and the bar, towards a side door. For a moment, she hesitated, darting a glance after the others but gave in with a sigh and followed. When they entered a back alleyway, she stopped at the stoop and examined her surroundings, trying to decipher their destination. Nothing gave a hint of where they were going.

"What are we doing here?" She took a step down onto the graveled alley.

Alarian smirked over his shoulder. "Ye of little trust. It won't take long. Figured you smuggled those apples at lunch for a reason."

Felicity stopped in her tracks. "For a snack later."

"Just like you would save them for the horses when we traveled to Éardrom from Saol?" He didn't slow, and with her curiosity peaked, she quickly caught up.

Alarian turned the corner and entered a small barn, the scent of leather and horses mixing with hay. She bit back a bubble of excitement at the familiarity. A longing tickled her fingertips to pet the nose of the nearest horse that nickered a welcome. The others poked their heads over their barn door with curiosity.

"They work hard." Felicity stepped inside; her arms taut at her side to ward off her temptation. "They deserve something for hauling our lazy asses around."

A stable hand passed by, nodding as he went. Alarian glanced into stalls then stopped in front of a gray horse who peered over the half door. "There you go then. Thank them."

Felicity glanced at him, then back to the gelding. The horse shook his head then stretched it out, as if aware she had something waiting. Damn, how could she resist? She fished the apples from her skirt she had stuffed into the pocket opposite the one concealing her dagger.

Alarian held out a hand. For a moment, she considered giving him one or not, but his green eyes shined eagerly. She handed over the red apple, and he went across to the second horse from the carriage team. Felicity watched as he fed the chestnut and scratched the horse behind his ears. She moved in beside the gray, holding the apple out on a flat palm. The gray nibbled it up, sending juice and apple bits flying. Felicity patted the horse's neck, closing her eyes as the horse's large head curled over her shoulder to nuzzle her.

"Who would have thought that someone so deadly had a soft spot for animals."

Her moment of peace vanished. Felicity gritted her teeth and stepped aside. The gray snorted, bobbing his head up and down. "Want to know how many animals I've been contracted to kill? Zero. You know why? They aren't completely horrid to others."

Alarian leaned against the stall next to the chestnut. "How do you know that every mission you've been sent on was for the better good? Maybe some of them were innocent or in the wrong place at the wrong time. Or maybe what you've taken from them was theirs to begin with? Do you get the specifics for your missions?"

No. Her jaw tensed. And she had never asked questions because her loyalty had always been to the Tower. She was their weapon. For the first time, she didn't know how to respond to shut the male up.

His lips parted before closing, shoulders lowering, a frown forming. "I'm sorry. I sounded judgmental, which wasn't what I was going for. I shouldn't have said anything."

Felicity patted the gray on the neck again and headed back the way they came. "I'm ready to go back to the inn."

"Of course."

Once they reached the second floor, the prince dropped Felicity off at her doorway and then walked down the stairs without looking back.

Felicity settled within her room—the space sparse but comfortable. There was no sign of the inventions or gears here—just a four-poster bed, nightstands on either side and a warm fire in a fireplace with a lone chair settled in front of it. A partition stood next to a sink. Moving around it, she found a bathtub with the plumbing she'd grown to love.

Removing a block and dagger from her pack, she settled in the chair. She spat on the whetstone, starting the sliding movement, attempting to lose herself in the simplicity of the slash and slick of metal against stone. The attempts to remove the residual effects of the prince's words from her mind weren't working. Because he was right. But admitting it out loud, even to herself, went against everything she worked so hard for. She yearned for the normalcy of the Tower and the life she lived there. But now, she didn't know if she would go back even if she had the choice.

Chapter
15

*T*he wind blew, the tall grass brushing against her skin. Felicity spread the grass open between her two palms. Her heart quickened. She dropped to the ground as his scent swept past her. Covering her mouth, Felicity closed her eyes tight, hoping he wouldn't find her.

Two large hands wrapped around her middle and tickled her sides. "Gotcha."

She fell, giggling as she kicked her feet, trying to get away.

"All right, all ri—"

In an attempt to free herself, she rolled, but his tickles persisted. Felicity wiggled loose, and he crouched over her, hair falling over his eyes. It was impossible to make out his features—the sun surrounding his head like a halo and blocking them from view. "You're getting better at hide and go seek."

Felicity knew there should be a mouth, and it would be shaped into a smile. There should be eyes, warm and calm, but there was *nothing—a blank canvas to be filled in.* "*Where did you go?*" *she asked.*

He held out his hand. "*Now it's your turn to find me.*"

The crash of the door opening woke Felicity with a start. The dream—memory—left a residual haze in her mind.

With a shake of her head, she grabbed the dagger from the table, ignoring the ache in her neck from sleeping in the chair. She stumbled to her feet, ready for an attack and listening for any sounds. But it didn't come. Her grip tightened on the blade's handle, and she adjusted her body, still ready to move if necessary.

Never put your guard down. She was beginning to hate that the Tower's lessons echoed in Harrison's voice. Tasted of the Countess's secrets. Yet they still came to mind as easily as she breathed.

The scent of ale and smoke made her nose crinkle. Her eyes adjusted to the light surrounding the intruder's silhouette. Shadows danced off of him, creating wisps of movement. "Prince Alarian?"

He grunted, and Felicity realized he was leaning against the doorframe. "I couldn't find my room," he grumbled.

She stormed across the distance and reached out to bar him from entering further. He stumbled, and she caught him before he fell, his weight almost taking her down with him until she adjusted her hold. With him so close, a new scent entered her senses. Her eyes narrowed.

Blood.

"Who did this to you?" She shut the door behind him, and with a grunt, she hefted his body, half holding him up, half dragging him across the floor to the bed. She began to search his body for the injury, the prince only grumbling intoxicated words she couldn't decipher. When her hands slid over his stomach, it came away sticky and murky gray.

Shit. *His* blood—Scáth blood. She tore open his shirt and gasped.

He chuckled, the sound raspy.

The gray-tinted fluid wept down his skin from a knife wound to his abdomen. Instincts took over as she ran to her pack and removed the suture pouch she always kept with her. It held the necessities: needle, thread, tweezers, a vial of antiseptic, and a few remedies for poisons. She'd only ever used it once on herself. But that once had saved her life. He should heal quickly, his fae blood giving him that ability alone, but the wound was deep and smelled off.

She leaned in and sniffed. "The blade was laced with something. Why are you getting knifed in a tavern?"

Felicity's jaw tensed as she searched the room for supplies. Scurrying to the sink, she grabbed a towel, drenched it then wrung it out before racing back to him.

"Cards." He hissed as she wiped away the blood to inspect the injury. "They thought I was cheating."

"Were you?" she asked to keep him talking. Judging by the location of the wound, there was a chance a major organ may have been hit. She wasn't a surgeon, and he may need one. Some fae were able to heal threatening internal injuries, but she didn't know if he could.

The medical training she'd received flashed through her mind: clean the area, get any grime or debris clear, check for swelling, and how deep it was. Then sew it up. It wasn't methodical—if there was internal bleeding, she knew little of what she could do.

Sensing her thoughts, he shook his head. "No surgeon. It's merely a flesh wound. Just close me up." He winced as Felicity pressed the towel against the injury to stifle the blood flow.

"I can't be certain it didn't hit an organ..." Using her forearm to apply pressure, she used her other hand to wipe off her hands enough to open the vial of ointment. "I think whatever was on the blade is slowing your ability to heal. It doesn't smell like any poison I'm familiar with." She pulled out a small satchel of herbs from her pouch and shoved them in his mouth. "Chew on this."

He chewed, his face scrunching up in distaste. "I knew if I came here, you wouldn't let me die."

With a growl, she dipped the needle into the antiseptic and threaded it, blood sticking to the instrument. "After I get you settled, I'll track them down."

"Don't go after them. Long gone." He swallowed. "Can't leave a trail. Not important."

Felicity pulled the rag away and inhaled. The piercing of the needle into his skin caused a growl to escape, the shadows expanding further into the room. "While shadows are interesting, they make it damn near impossible to see," she mumbled.

His brows knitted together. "I'll try."

Her request gave him something to concentrate on, the shadows retreating as she worked. Her own magic thrummed under her fingertips, and it took concentration on each stitch for it not to break free.

She glanced up as his eyes fluttered closed. Felicity pursed her lips, attention back on her work. By the time she finished the last stitch, the prince was unconscious, body sprawled across the bed. Felicity shuddered at the residue sticking to her arms, the soaked remnants of his shirt and the pools of blood on the floor. At least the wound had stopped bleeding. She pressed her eyes closed, willing her heart's rapid pace to slow and the foreign emotions to quell.

This was why she had always bitten back anything other than anger. Every other emotion got in the way. Made her weak. She had been a weapon long enough to know death intimately. But seeing Prince Alarian laying in his own blood sparked something within her. Memories fought for purchase, rearranging in her mind, causing Felicity's head to ache. Not a single one connected to this particular moment. The dream he'd interrupted lay unclear—but now wasn't the time to concentrate on the faceless male.

With numb fingers, she began to clean up the mess. The methodical act was familiar. Her missions often weren't this sloppy, but sometimes she was caught, or targets fought back. The fighters were the ones she most often cleaned up after. At least enough so their loved ones wouldn't find their remains scattered about. She left enough of the chaos—fallen over chairs, broken baubles, something to prove they had died with dignity and honor—with some fight in them.

"Maybe you're not so apathetic after all." He chuckled.

Felicity turned in the prince's direction. His eyes dulled by pain and alcohol, watched as she sopped up the puddle near the door. "What does that mean?"

"It was in your expression. There was something there." His voice changed to a whisper, eyes fluttering closed again. "Even if it was only for a moment."

He must be delirious.

***

Felicity leaned against the headboard. It was almost morning—a dim light peeked in between the wooden slats of the window. Exhaustion settled between her shoulder blades. Had the dream been a distant memory? Another one she couldn't yet piece together. Nothing had felt familiar in that moment except she knew she'd been the young female at one point in her life. It wasn't the Tower—or had it been? Those fields could be found anywhere within the realms. She wondered what would have happened if it hadn't been interrupted by the damn prince. Why did he always arrive at the worst moment?

With her thoughts going in the wrong direction, she was careful not to jostle the bed. More than once she'd considered hunting down those who did this to him. Make them suffer for it. Only because the prince had disrupted her night. Or at least that's what she told herself. But when he'd spiked a fever, her plan went to shit.

She rolled her shoulders and then her neck and spotted the lip of the tub sticking out from the end of the partition. Maybe that was what she needed—a nice warm bath.

The prince stirred beside her, and she sighed. A bath would have to wait.

Long lashes fluttered before opening. "What happened?" His voice was raspy. Felicity handed him the glass of water from the bedside.

He took it but didn't drink. "Please tell me I'm not losing my mind or worse yet, that I forgot something as wonderful as last night."

With a roll of her eyes, Felicity adjusted the pillow she leaned against. "I was tired but had to make sure you didn't have an infection."

"To do so, you laid right next to me? Isn't body heat the worst thing for a fever?" Felicity could hear the smile in his tone. "Or was there another reason you wanted to be close to me?"

"Don't make me regret suturing you up. I can easily cut that wound open again."

"Too bad. I think it's healed now." He sat up with an groan. "All right, so mostly healed."

"Either way, I could give you a new one." She attempted to re-fluff the pillow again. Once she had been certain the fever had subsided, sleep hadn't been easy to come by. With every move or grunt he made, she'd wake. Not that it had been peaceful when she was able to fall deep enough into sleep—the memories disorienting her.

"And I'm shirtless too. Bet you couldn't keep your hands off me."

She bit her bottom lip to stop the retort, but it came anyway. "No wonder you were stabbed over cards."

He shrugged then stretched, and her gaze followed the defined lines of his arms down his chest to—

"Like what you see?" There was a hint of laughter in his voice.

"I was deciding how to inflict the slowest death with the easiest cleanup since I don't want to scrub your blood from the floorboards again." She pushed up from the bed, knowing she wasn't going to get any more sleep. And to resist the desire to ask about the tattoo curving over a shoulder from his back. She hadn't allowed herself a closer look despite her curiosity. To ask him now would only provide him with more reason to pester her. "You need to get out of here before there is talk against my character."

He moved behind her. She stilled as he reached around her and grabbed the bloody shirt off the nightstand.

"Thank you for your help."

The sincerity in his voice made her shift until she was face-to-face with him. She lifted her chin so she could look into his eyes, thinning her own to slits. "Next time, maybe stick to your room instead of a tavern. It seems the locals are not keen on cheats."

His bare arm brushed against her own. He tossed the blood-stained shirt over his head as he moved past. "Noted." He headed toward the door. "Lock up behind me. You don't want just anyone stumbling in."

Felicity sputtered a few choice words but did as he recommended. Not that she wouldn't have anyway. In fact, she was certain she had locked it last night. In his state could he have picked the lock? She unlocked the door and opened it. There was no blood on the handle. Did she forget to lock the door after all?

She knew one thing: Ward was right—she needed to be wary around the prince.

Chapter
16

Their arrival at the beautiful stone manor was welcomed by a summer breeze and singing birds. Nestled in the middle of a copse beyond a field, it was a few short miles from the nearest town. Felicity's jaw dropped when she exited the carriage and a shadow forced her eyes upward. A group of what looked to be large, winged lynx were coming in for a landing.

Alarian chuckled softly beside her. "Careful, someone might see."

"What are those?" Three of the cats landed softly on padded feet. They had thick grayish- white coats with a short little stub of a tail, tufts of black fur at their pointed ears, and what could be described as a mustache that hung from both sides of their mouths. Their powerful feathered wings folded in at their sides as their riders dismounted.

"They're cailleach. Loyal to their riders, lithe and quick. They are the main form of transportation for the residents of Dorcha."

Alarian stopped for a moment. "Between the snow and mountains, they needed something that could scale the heights as well as survive the weather."

"They're magnificent." She blinked, realizing she was staring and turned her attention towards the prince.

He smiled at her. "Maybe someday you'll have the chance to ride them. Do you want to meet them now?"

She weighed the offer but shook her head, butterflies fluttering in her stomach. "No but thank you."

"So polite today." He steered them towards the manor and in a low voice asked, "Does it take near-fatal injuries to receive your kindness?"

If there hadn't been anyone present, she would've elbowed him. "Why do you keep making me regret it?"

His only answer was another chuckle as they headed up the few steps toward the manor's entrance. From the outside, it looked like a small cottage, but once you walked in, it was massive. The entry was warm and inviting with wood flooring, decorative panels up the inner walls, and massive rugs layered the floor in hues of reds and browns. Despite its splendor, there was only a taste of the eclectic inventions found within the cities. A grand fireplace had a spit rotating by the now-familiar gears, moving all on its own. On the spit was a slow-roasting chunk of meat that emitted a savory scent that made her mouth water. Felicity took it all in with the best passive glance she could muster.

The prince asked to be shown to their quarters and a butler led them down richly decorated halls.

When they were taken to the same room, Felicity's eyebrows pinched together. She hadn't expected to be sharing a room, and as though he could decipher her expression, he laughed. "If you haven't noticed, we're not staying at a palace. Most of the other guests are at a nearby inn. Doubling up isn't out of the ordinary, especially when we traveled together."

She surveyed the room—a plush sofa at the end of the bed, an armoire beside a door she hoped led to a private bathing room, and a desk settled under the large picture window.

She grabbed a pillow and the throw blanket from the bed and stuffed them against his chest. "You're sleeping on the floor." His laughter made her bristle. Felicity busied herself by removing her dress from the trunk to loosen any wrinkles from it for the evening's festivities.

The prince laid the pillow and blanket on the sofa. He sat to remove his boots and emitted a low groan followed by a hiss. His hand rested over the bandaged injury she had hoped would be healed by now.

"Is it still bothering you?" Felicity crossed the room, hands on her hips with a quizzical brow. "It was deep. Maybe we should check with a healer."

He met her gaze. "The stitches are pulling."

"Let's remove them." She pushed his shoulders back against the seat. Pulling the corner of his tunic up, she felt a warmth move through him, his skin flushing under her touch.

"I can manage." He pulled his tunic from her fingers and held it up just enough to show the injury.

Felicity peeled away the bandage, and he winced, the gauze sticking to one of the stitches. She concentrated as she checked the skin around the wound, ignoring the prickle of her own temptation to brush her fingers over his muscled flesh, her eyes grazing over his defined body. With a silent curse, she reprimanded herself. How long had it been since she had been with another? This was not the time, and certainly not something she should be thinking about with her current company. Without a word, she went to her pack to grab her suture kit.

"Well?" His breathing had heightened but she didn't dare meet his gaze.

"It's healed. Doesn't seem to be infected or swollen so there shouldn't be internal bleeding." She held up a pair of small scissors and tweezers. "This will do it."

"How do you know any of this? I wouldn't think an assassin or spy would be taught the art of healing."

Felicity picked her words carefully. "We were taught to use it on ourselves and our compatriots in the field. They send backup on some missions when necessary—to ensure success. It isn't always a possibility with more discreet missions, so we were taught how to deal with our own wounds. Sometimes, it can be the difference between life and death." Felicity settled herself on her knees in front of him. "You need to lay back so I can see the stitches."

"Are my muscles getting in the way?" He grinned.

She poked the tweezers into his skin. He jumped with a yelp and she smiled.

"All right, I got it. No fun and games." He laid down on the sofa, the side with the injury towards her.

For a sweet, incandescent moment she was able to work in silence. It was over quickly. "When Ward and I met you at the Tower, you were in your human form. Judging by the stares we received, I didn't think the fae were welcome within the Tower." Prince Alarian hissed as she pulled the first stitch up to cut the knot.

She sighed, contemplating what to tell him. "In my time at the Tower, I don't think a single fae had ever entered. I don't think they aren't welcomed, but a guild of humans isn't a commodity often used by faeries. None other than the council knew of my true heritage. Not until now."

"Then you taking the mission—"

"Test," she interrupted, tone flat.

Felicity could feel the penetration of his gaze but kept her attention on her task.

He was silent for a moment and then, "You gave up your secret when you were given the test?"

Her jaw clenched as she stilled, the stitch held between the point of the tweezers. "I did. I trusted the Tower and I wanted to be the best."

"Wanted?"

She hated the way he said the word. As though he knew every single emotion attempting to coerce its way to the surface of her mind. She wouldn't tell him that they didn't want her to return. There was no way she was giving up this mission. Instead, she forced the words back and met his gaze. "The Countess informed me before I left that I had reached Graduate status."

"Then what next?"

The warmth in his tone, the way his eyes held a sparkle of concern and curiosity made Felicity want to...well she didn't know what she wanted to do. It wouldn't do to dwell on deciphering her own wants right now. They certainly didn't involve him.

"Now, I fulfill my mission for the Tower." Before she pulled the stitch loose, she sighed a deep breath, trying to concentrate on the task at hand. It was easier now that she had a much clearer view of the stitches. And his muscled chest. *Damn it.* "After that, maybe I'll achieve the title of Dearmadta and be integrated into a class of a guild that many strive for but never meet."

"You want to become one of the Forgotten?" His brow inched higher.

She ignored his reaction and his knowledge of the group. There were whispers of the Dearmadta and she assumed he knew of them because of his search for a spy for hire. A nod was her response.

"What does that title grant you?"

It was hard to concentrate on his questions. Not when the answers weighed on her own mind. "Options." It was the truth, after all. She just didn't know what her options were now.

He didn't press further, and she appreciated it as her fingers grazed his skin, and warmth ran up her torso into her chest. A vision of hands wrapped around her naked body flashed through her mind. She pinched her eyes shut to push it away. Now wasn't the time to piece her memories together. With a few snips and tugs, the last of the stitches came free. The prince remained quiet except for an occasional hiss.

"Done." She stood to clean her instruments.

He grasped her arm, the touch firm but gentle. "Thank you."

Felicity froze in place, but his expression was sincere, the usual sarcastic smile gone. She nodded and slid free from his grasp. "This doesn't mean you can sleep in the bed."

He laughed as she walked towards the bathing room. A bath—maybe a cold one—was needed.

The rest of the time they spent within the room was in preparation for the party and moving around each other in a silent dance. The sun was nearing the horizon when Felicity emerged from the bathing room, ready for the celebration. Prince Alarian stilled as she walked steadily to a mirrored vanity to sit.

"What is it?" she asked, peering at him through the mirror.

He snapped his mouth shut before he took a seat to slip on his boots. "Nothing."

Felicity looked at her own reflection. Meira had packed the perfect outfit to wear for such an occasion. A long skirt in three layers—thankfully sans ruffles as they would have gotten in the way—sat high on her waist. It was tapered in the front to reach just below her knees, lengthening along the sides until the back of the skirts reached her ankles. It was made of black satin, soft to the touch. A contrast to the cream tunic under a sable corset with silver fastenings tucking into the skirt.

Felicity styled her hair and pinned it in place, letting the strands of curls hang over her shoulder. It was simple, but all she could pull off without the Tower's stylists. She slid on the fingerless lace gloves before adding the final piece—her dagger strapped to her upper thigh.

"Do you have a plan for tonight?" Alarian cleared his throat, and Felicity's mouth flickered in amusement. She knew he was watching her, even if indirectly. It was interesting to have this effect on him, even if she would never allow it to escalate.

"See if anyone stands out. Observe." It wasn't a diabolical plan, but when inhibitions were low, it was all that mattered.

Chapter 17

The main dining hall was smaller than Felicity had expected, making the event intimate. Even so, their hosts had outdone themselves. Doors were wide open to a view of a beautiful garden and a cool breeze spread the scent of roses while cooling the guests and fluttering skirts. It was a casual affair compared to Felicity's expectations. All the same, it was well attended.

Prince Alarian led her straight to the entrance to introduce her to their hosts, Lord Dimitri and Lord Lian. Lord Dimitri's skin was translucent with purple and blue veins that ran upward until they hid under clothes and revealed themselves again in his neck and hands. His blond shoulder-length hair seemed to move on its own personal breeze. Dimitri's wide girth and height made Lian look small beside him. Lord Lian's skin was brown with hints of orange like the changing of an autumn leaf. His deep, purple-tint-ed hair was cut short to his scalp. Rings that pierced his nose and ears tinkled together like wind chimes unsettled by the smiling

Lord Dimitri's magic. Both took turns clasping hands with the prince and pulling him in for tight hugs. There was a familiarity she hadn't been prepared for between the three males.

"Who is your companion?" Lord Dimitri regarded her with a warm smile. "It takes a special female to snag the prince's attention."

"Let alone his heart," Lord Lian finished.

Felicity opened her mouth to object, but Prince Alarian chuckled, stopping her words at the tip of her tongue. "She has agreed to join me, but I think that's as far as it goes in her mind, my friends."

Lord Dimitri cocked his head in her direction. "Then she's worthy of you." Their hosts broke into a fit of laughter that forced a long sigh from her.

"Must make sharing one room awkward." Lord Lian snorted and gave her a plaintive nod. "Would you like us to have him sleep in the stables?"

"Not this time," the prince grumbled.

"I told him he could sleep on the sofa," she added.

Both Lords glanced at each other. Lord Dimitri's eyes sparkled with mischief. "We like you, Lady Dwauer. Put him in his place."

Lian nudged the prince with a wink. "It's about time you brought someone worthwhile around. More than an accessory to annoy your parents."

The prince grimaced, opening his mouth to respond, but Dimitri interrupted. "Now, my Ciadh. Let's behave." Felicity hid her smile as Prince Alarian glared.

Demitri gave a short bow and gestured to the party. "Please enjoy our summer celebration and don't stab his royal highness just yet." With a wink, he turned to the next guest and the prince led them deeper into the party.

"Are they close friends of yours?" Her brow lifted in curiosity.

"Must be if I let them get away with that." He sniffed, his features rearranging into a crooked grin and shining eyes. "Ignore them. Their favorite thing to do is poke fun. Usually at me."

"Oh, then let's go back. That sounds like more fun." She started to turn.

Alarian's grip tightened on her arm and she faced him, that damn grin flashing. "If that's your idea of fun, we need to broaden your horizons."

His emerald gaze slid over her body before meeting hers. A flush worked its way up her neck, and she took a small step away from him, ignoring the draw to get closer instead. The prince cleared his throat and a nearby laugh from a guest broke the moment further. The mission. Her goal. This—he, was not her priority. She glanced about the room. "We should walk around. Maybe introduce me to some of the guests?"

Alarian straightened and he gave a small bow, his hand dropping from her arm, the other arm extending in an exaggerated offer. "After you."

They walked deeper into the celebration, and Felicity took in the crowd. A stout Clurichaun with a pointed chin and spindly fingers stood among pixies and a nymph as they conversed with a few fae.

Felicity also caught sight of a púca, the fae turning from a stubby male to a tall, lanky female within a blink.

The main space itself was comfortable—homely. Thick stacked stones made up the wall until it led to a planked wood-gabled ceiling. A long table sat upon one side with a spread for an abundant feast. On the other side of the room, near the open doors to the garden and beyond, were covered tables set for everyone to eat. Built against the back wall was a stack of large gears, some overlapping the other. They cranked together with an audible click and groan, the base building up to a large clock, the face settled over the top set of gears. Large hands pivoted from the center, the hour hand as long as Felicity's arm, ticking with each passing second. While it was impressive to Felicity, most guests barely noted the prominent piece.

"Would you like to dance?"

She whirled around on the prince, his body in a mock bow. He looked up expectantly, gaze piercing from under thick lashes.

"You're meant to introduce me to the guests. Remember?" She peered about the room, recognizing a few from the palace.

"I will. But if we cause a bit of a stir, then they will come to you." He winked as he held out his hand to her.

"Maybe I don't want their attention following my every move." She took his palm into hers as he grinned.

The prince pulled her close and whispered in her ear. "You've poisoned a man in front of a room full of people. I think you can manage a dance. You survived plenty with the advisor."

A musky scent of a damp forest and the mint he'd chewed before their arrival, filled her senses, drawing her closer to him.

"But then I was able to kill him," she reminded with a smirk.

He chuckled, the sound reverberating against her neck. His hand slid along her side, resting finally on her hip, a gentle tug and her leg brushed his as they danced.

Prince Alarian cleared his throat. "There are other stories I've heard whispered in small circles about a spy as fast and lithe as a cat. I can only assume they're about you."

"Many stories are exaggerated." And while some may be about her, there was a chance they weren't. She wasn't the only spy—and certainly doubted her expertise had made it to the northern shores when she'd never been here prior to this mission.

His green eyes met hers as he smiled. "They may be exaggerated, milady, but I have no doubt they're about you."

They moved steadily on white tiles that were laid in a pattern that mimicked a tornado. The prince spun her to the center, twirling her from him before pulling her close to his body with her hand resting on his shoulder, his on her waist. She could feel the beat of his heart, his scent becoming too familiar at their close proximity. The music shifted, a crescendo rising, and the temptation in her body doing the same. Just a small step and she'd be flush to him, and for a moment, she thought he was thinking the same as his eyes darkened, his throat bobbed.

Then the large clock chimed the hour, the sound collided with the moment, drawing Felicity back to reality.

"You need to stop drawing attention towards us." She could feel the crowd watching and with a pivot, her suspicions were confirmed. Forget an introduction to the guests, he was making her more visible when she needed to disappear. No one would take chances if they noticed her observing. "Otherwise, I'll never be able to do what I came here to do. You're the distraction so I can do my job."

Prince Alarian's mouth tightened, and he stepped back. "You have your mission."

"I do." She caught his gaze again, the music seemed to shift with his expression as the mischief left his eyes. A pang of guilt coursed through her. Damn him—trying to make her feel things. She didn't have time for his games.

They finished the dance, but when the next song started, he led her off to the side of the room. This time he didn't take her along when he went to speak with another guest.

Felicity took the moment to slip behind the table ladened with platters of food. She grabbed one of the plates, scooping some potatoes, green beans, two still-warm rolls, and a leg of some type of fowl. She moved around to another corner of the room, aware of the eyes following her, before settling in a seat.

The one benefit of arriving with the prince was that none dared to ask her for a dance or attempt a conversation. With the newly available prince to draw them in, she was free to peruse the room. After some time, any curiosity in her direction was dispelled, forgotten. Already Lady Mistward had Miss Isleen at the prince's side along with a few other maidens. Without any doubt, many females hoped to take her place on his arm or in his mind.

Felicity knew the only thought centered on her was how to come up with his next way to annoy her, but the easy-going smile he spared to one of the available females made her chest tighten. *Mind on the mission. No distractions.* She had a goal for tonight.

She walked along the edge of the room, pretending to analyze the tapestries and wall art as she observed the guests. Most mingled together in small groups, laughing or chattering about whatever pleased them. Others danced, the band playing relaxing jigs that slowed or sped up from one melody to the next, keeping people on their feet. Servers took empty plates, walking the room with trays of wine goblets or bite-sized morsels.

This was probably her type of party. She frowned. Why had the thought even crossed her mind? As far as she recollected, she had only ever attended these affairs on a job. Shifting through her memories, she tried to ascertain if there was one to connect this moment, but none stood out. As she scanned the room, the prince seized her gaze and gave a pointed look to a side door. Following his attention, Felicity caught the swish of skirts rustling behind someone just as the door closed.

Moving slowly but purposeful, Felicity searched the guests once more and ensured no one watched her before opening the door and slipping through. As quiet as Felicity was, her target was too. The individual was already out of sight. Felicity walked down the dim corridor lined with statues and a few doors—this wasn't a hallway meant to be traipsed through this evening. When silence met her, no sign of her target, Felicity thought she had lost them. Or maybe it was just a couple looking for a private place to meet. Then a scent caught Felicity's nose—a familiar one. She stopped at one of the many doorways where the trail ended and pressed her ear against it.

"It needs to be soon. If the king keeps rounding up everyone, we won't have a following strong enough to strike. These small attacks aren't enough to raise others to our call or weaken the king's forces."

"If we do it too soon, we could lose the war before it's even begun."

Felicity didn't recognize either voice. Their words came through the door muffled and hushed.

"The people are suffering. For all we know, those who have been abducted are being killed or tortured. It doesn't matter what caste they are from—fae, human, fairies...if they have two working legs, they're at risk. Younglings and children are being left to fend for themselves. Many have moved to the streets and rely on begging to survive. They don't know what happened to their parents or caregivers. The king is creating orphans every day." There was an edge evident in the male's tone.

"We know now." Felicity barely could discern the second's words, the female's voice lowering. "They're being forced to work in the canyon."

Felicity heard the distinct thump of something tumbling to the floor—books maybe. "Enslaved? What are they being forced to do?"

There was an inaudible response.

The female continued, "Then that should be our first priority. Free them and recruit those who'll join us."

"I'll send out a few for intel."

There was a sound of swishing skirts and—was that wings? "Send word when you have it. We need to make our move."

"Autumn is just mere weeks away. How can we construct a rebellion strong enough before winter?"

The female snorted. "Trust me. He'll send word. A plan is beginning to form."

Footsteps headed towards the door, and she scrambled for a hiding place. A statue of armor was positioned across from her. She lowered herself to the floor, leaning against the wall to hide within its shadow.

The door opened and Lady Chartow exited. On her heels was a pixie with green skin and translucent wings that fluttered as quickly as a hummingbird and kept him a few inches above the ground. Felicity didn't recognize him from the palace.

The two disappeared down the hall, but she stayed in her hiding spot, considering what she overheard.

The king was rounding up faeries and humans? What was the canyon? Why were they being enslaved to work within it? There had never been a need for her to learn and understand more than who were the traitors. There was little doubt now that Lady Chartow was aligned with the rebels, and she believed an attack against the palace was inevitable. Maybe that map had meant more than she thought. Without direct information, she couldn't begin to decipher it.

Felicity shook her head to clear her thoughts. There was a mission to complete, and with or without the Tower, she had a goal. Except there were the truths the prince had spoken in the stable that danced around in the back of her mind. Even if she was to complete the missions she had been set out for, her loyalty was no longer to the Tower once it was complete. And what if the king was part of the problem...or was the problem?

Felicity headed back to the party where a toast was being made. All eyes were on the hosts who were in the midst of thanking their guests for coming. She searched the crowd until she found the prince, his own glass raised towards the two lords, and his rapt attention hanging on to every word. The group of females were no longer by his side—many looked to be pouting. Felicity crossed the room, watching her escort. His hand was steady, his glass full. She was surprised he wasn't inebriated with all the alcohol available, although she appreciated that she wouldn't have to drag him back to the room.

"To the remainder of summer and preparations for a bountiful autumn, we hope it produces enough to sustain us through winter." Lord Dimitri smiled while the others cheered their agreement.

Felicity slipped in beside the prince. He handed her a glass as if he knew she would be there. She met his gaze for a brief moment before he turned his attention back to their hosts. But she couldn't concentrate on their words. The Tower had been her guide in the past, but now it didn't feel right. They had never steered her wrong, but they hadn't always been truthful either. As much as she despised admitting it, the prince was right—she hadn't known the reason behind all the missions she completed. Maybe keeping herself in the dark about politics was no longer an option. Not only for herself but for the choice she would be forced to make.

She had been hired to discover the operatives—Felicity had found one. Then...why was she hesitating to turn in Lady Chartow's name? If she did, if Felicity fulfilled her mission, could she live with herself for enabling the king to imprison his people and leave children behind? Orphans who, like her, didn't know what had happened to their parents. If that was what the king was doing, then could she allow that and assist him? Was there even another choice? And why did she care? It was always about the job—proving to them she was worth the effort. Maybe there would be other guilds willing to take her in.

Alarian leaned in close to her, interrupting her thoughts. "Everything alright?"

Out of instinct, her expression went blank. She looked up at him, plastering a fake smile on her face. His brow rose—could he tell? "Yes, everything is fine."

Chapter 18

Two days later, they were back in the carriage, heading to Éardrom. After an uneventful night at the same inn at the town of Cnoc, they were scheduled to arrive at the palace around nightfall.

"Glad you stayed out of trouble last night," Felicity mumbled to Prince Alarian who leaned against the carriage wall.

He shrugged. "Staying in my room makes it a lot easier."

"Then did you pay the barman to bring you drinks? You smell horrible." It was true. The scent of alcohol seeped from the prince's pores.

He snorted and closed his eyes. "Well, you ordered me not to crawl into your room last night—even if I did prove that I'm a wonderful roommate. Besides, I had the coin to spend. It's a smart move to pay a little extra for delivery."

He ran a hand through his hair. The movement made Felicity's head spiral and the image of the prince blurred as a memory pieced together.

He brushed his hair away from his face as he lay beside her, his head resting on his other arm. Harrison leaned forward, his kisses were sweet against her lips. A finger lingered on her jaw, another fluttering against her cheek.

He pulled back, his eyes searching Felicity's face, slow and steady. "You're beautiful," he whispered.

Harrison wrapped an arm around her body. As he leaned back, he pulled her to him until her skin was flush with his side. She sighed, closing her eyes as she laid her head upon his bare chest. "I bet you say that to all the women who could slit your throat."

His chuckle vibrated against her, causing her body to yearn for more of him. "There is only one I know who can."

While probably true, a few were starting to worry her. The training had become more grueling, and Felicity's size was not the most foreboding. "The initiates don't think I belong."

"They are just afraid. You've lived here since you were a young child. They've only been here a few months. Besides, I didn't think you cared what they thought of you."

She kissed his cheek, the beginning of stubble on his young face rough against her lips. "They like you though."

He laughed. "Of course they like me. Unlike you, I don't look like I know hundreds of ways to kill them. Maybe try a smile." He grinned at her. "See, it looks like this. Can be quite effective."

She pushed his chest, feigning annoyance. "We're supposed to let go of our emotions."

"It depends on how you look at it, Felicity. You can let go of your emotions, but then you wouldn't feel anything when I did this." He kissed the hollow of her neck then nipped her shoulder with gentle teeth. Her toes curled at the touch. "Or you could compartmentalize your emotions—allow them out when the time is right." His kisses trailed lower. "Then you can still enjoy life a little."

As his kisses trailed below her breasts, she groaned.

"Felicity?"

Her eyes fluttered open at her name, shoulders drawing back as reality surfaced.

"Where did you go?" There was a flash of interest in the prince's gaze and she turned away. There was no way he could know where her mind had led her. Had she groaned out loud?

With her mouth set, she settled her attention out the window. "Are we close to the palace?"

"Not quite."

There was something in his tone that drew her attention back to him. A tension had fallen over his expression. Then she felt it—a thrum in the air. A horse snorted outside as a guard moved in closer to the carriage. They had left earlier than the rest of their traveling party. Some of the guests had remained in Aer a day longer. Only the driver and two of the guards accompanied them back.

"What is it?" She shuffled aside her skirts to unsheathe the dagger from her thigh.

The prince's hand gripped tight on the door handle. "I don't know." His gaze met hers. "You can sense it too?"

She nodded, holding out her dagger. If it came to it, she wanted him armed. He shook his head and sat up. "Don't worry about me." His tone low.

"I have others." She assured him. His gaze raked over her body, but this time there was nothing suggestive in his examination. It was an attempt to uncover her weapon's hiding places.

A horse whinnied as the carriage came to an abrupt stop. She caught herself on the window ledge before smashing headfirst into the prince. He reached out an arm to steady her.

"Sorry, Your Highness, there's a tree down in the road." The driver then called to the guards, "Clear it out."

One of the guards beside them urged his horse forward as Felicity peered out the window into the gathering darkness of the woods surrounding them. She felt them before she saw them.

"No. Stop," she yelled.

Her alert came too late. The horse screamed, and the guard's body toppled to the ground, an arrow jutting from his neck. The guard's mount galloped as though a pack of wolves were on its heels, leaving his rider choking on his own blood. Felicity's grip tightened on the hilt of her blade, teeth gritted.

Lights glistened in the distance, brightening as their attackers stepped into view. They began to take shape—three of them. When they reached the road, Felicity inhaled, air whistling between clenched teeth as the attackers raised their weapons. She loosened her skirts and slipped out of them easily, thankful she'd thought to wear pants underneath.

Prince Alarian's eyes widened as she jumped from the carriage, dagger held at the ready. *Use the anger...*

Now, she would.

The carriage jostled as the horses pranced in place, fighting for control from the driver. They must have felt the anxiousness in the air.

"Get the prince out of here," Felicity ordered. "Turn the carriage around."

"No, Felicity—" The prince attempted to exit, but she forced the door shut.

"If you move the carriage, we'll shoot." Their attackers snickered, each held a weapon aimed at her, the driver, and the remaining guard. There was a fourth. She could smell him, his scent intermingling with memories. But she kept herself focused on those in front of her. The spokesperson pointed his sword at her. "Step aside and we'll let you live."

The remaining guard lifted his weapon. The subtle movement was enough. The demi-fae highwayman aiming at him loosened his arrow. It hit the guard between the opening in his armor at his neck. He slumped forward, and his horse took off down the road with his rider clinging to his back.

"I won't ask twice," the closest attacker warned.

Felicity dropped her dagger and raised her hands into the air.

"Good, now step away from the door."

Her heart raced, but she took a deep breath in. These highwaymen may have decent aim but weren't well trained. All three of them were stiff as they held their weapons up. With a step back, as instructed, and a pivot, she kicked up the dagger and grabbed the handle. She hurled it at the closest attacker. It embedded into the demi-fae's side. The highwayman beside him threw his spear. Felicity sidestepped, dodging its point and grabbing the shaft before it hit the carriage. Arcing it around, she sent it back at the male, impaling him.

She took a moment to catch her breath, adrenaline coursing through her. They always underestimated her. A lesson they wouldn't learn fast enough.

The fourth came onto the road, and she recognized the familiar assassin's clothing. He wore a mask, only his eyes visible. Questions racked her brain, but she didn't have time to ask them, his attacks fluid and swift. The moves were familiar as he jabbed and then kicked. Felicity blocked and dodged both, pulling free another dagger. Metal met metal, the assassin wielding his own blade.

"Felicity," he hissed. "I've waited for this."

"Garder." There was no question, only understanding. Anger pulsed to the surface. If he was sent, then it was for a reason. Unless he chose to walk away from the Tower. To act alone. Either way, he wouldn't leave her alive. She recognized that glint in his eye, a change she had noted in their sparring sessions right before he turned his back on their friendship all those months ago.

He pushed her with his free hand, Felicity's back hit the carriage and the horses shrieked as the impact jostled the shafts. The driver tried and failed to hold them back, but the two horses took off, heading straight for the fallen log. Without the carriage to hold her up, she staggered, falling to the ground. Garder was on her in a breath, his dagger flashing with the sudden appearance of the moon from behind the clouds.

This wouldn't be her end. It had been a while since they sparred, but she still knew his moves. She grabbed for the hilt, stopping him before the dagger could meet skin. He pressed down, and with effort, she kept it back—but she didn't have the leverage he had. It nicked her throat when a crash sounded.

Both looked in time to see the horses clear the tree and the carriage shattered against the trunk. *No!* The driver flew through the air and the deafening snap of his neck echoed through the clearing. She took advantage of the distraction, twisting one leg around Garder's and just as quickly pushed off with her other until she was above him. He kicked her off, her move enough to get the upper hand, but not to keep it. They both rushed to their feet.

"Get the carriage," Garder ordered through gritted teeth. "The prince."

His last accomplice ran towards the carriage, and Felicity allowed her anger to consume her. *Use your anger...* She wanted to run to Prince Alarian—he had to be alive. Garder intercepted her, his next attack swift, but she dodged it with a pivot. *Don't let your anger use you.*

Felicity sent a knee to his groin, and he yelped. She wrenched his body around, pinned him to the earth and punched him in the face. He groaned, eyes fluttering as she pulled him up by his tunic and punched him again, mask hanging haphazardly. Clawing off of him, she grabbed his dagger as she ran for the prince. For all she knew, he was injured or worse. If only she had let him out of the damn carriage.

The injured attacker grabbed her ankle as she passed and yanked her off her feet. She landed face first—hard. She turned onto her back, wiggling free from his grasp. With a tight hold on his wounded abdomen, he kicked her then reached for one of the daggers, pinning her arms with one knee and grabbing hold of her other with his free hand so Felicity couldn't stab him. He'd pay for that.

Garder's laughter echoed. He hobbled over her, his smile rising. "It wasn't exactly how I envisioned taking down a weapon. I guess it will have to do." He raised his hand in the air, another dagger at the ready.

There wasn't time for fear. Second guessing. Having let it build, she grabbed the pendant at her neck and let her magic free. Her light hit the crystal and sent waves cascading around the clearing. This time she didn't hold back the intensity as much as she had in the privacy of her room. The rebel hissed as he was swallowed by the shimmering silver rays. He stepped back, stumbling into Garder. Both raised their arms, attempting to block their eyes as she and the crystal became a beacon. Felicity stood, letting her magic expand, prepping for her final move.

She stabbed the first highwayman, this time a killing blow, and he crumbled, hands falling away from blinded white eyes. Garder, eyes closed, attempted an attack, but she was ready. Felicity's dagger dug into his gut, his own slipping from his fingers to clatter against rock and dirt. She pulled him in close, dropping the pendant that bounced against her chest, his blood pouring over her hand. She called the magic back, her light dimming. "You didn't know all my secrets."

Crimson dripped from his mouth. His eyes widened, looking her straight in the eye even as he coughed up blood and spittle. "Whore."

Felicity twisted deeper, her hands sinking into his abdomen. How had they ever been friends? She couldn't recall as the life dimmed from his gaze. Remembering the prince, she stepped back, pushed Garder's lifeless body to the ground and turned to run.

But Prince Alarian stood nearby, facing her with the other attacker on the ground at his feet. He stepped over the body. They walked to each other, meeting in the middle. Her chest rose and fell in succession to her steps.

"Did you two know each other?" He nodded towards Garder. "Seemed personal."

She considered how much to tell him, but maybe there was a chance he hadn't noticed the use of magic. "He's from the Tower."

"They wouldn't have sent someone for you, would they? Or was I the target?"

She'd wondered the same thing, adding to the doubts that already plagued her mind. "I honestly don't know. It seems I have some questions for the Countess."

"You have magic," he breathed, his expression softening.

Obviously, her hope was misled. Felicity's mouth grew taut, her hand tightening on the hilt of the dagger, blood dripping from the blade. It would be easy to kill him and blame it on the attack. It would be easy to leave the prince here—to keep that secret close—hidden from others.

"That's why you've been ill. You've suppressed it all this time." As if knowing her thoughts, he reached across and placed a calm grip over her hand that clutched the dagger. It wasn't enough to stop her if she wanted him dead. She was as fast as her light. But it was a touch of trust and understanding. "You're safe. I won't tell anyone."

Felicity's jaw quivered, her grasp loosened, blood flowing back into her limbs—her magic sputtering under her skin. "How can I trust you? Or you trust me? I've deceived you."

He shook his head. "You've protected your true identity alone for too long. This I can assist with. Have you ever had training?" He looked behind her at the carnage she'd left.

"How could I? I was at a Tower of humans who thought me one of them." It had been the only thing that was her own. If they reacted this way about her heritage and learned she had magic, it would incite more than hatred—she'd be a power they'd want to break. But she had proven more than once she was strong enough so why did the Tower now consider her a burden?

The prince interrupted her thoughts. "I can train you—allow you to use your magic. Otherwise, it could destroy you." He had her dagger in his hand.

Her empty hand clenched. *How had he done that?*

"There is no reason for you to help me." She took a step back, annoyed with herself for letting him take the dagger away. For showing weakness.

"We can help each other. Allow me to train you. Trust me with this secret. You can repay me by making the others believe there might be something between us."

"Why?" She shook her head with a snort. She had dealt with the courtier's reaction to her and the prince's supposed relationship long enough as it was. If the others assumed there was more...

"This a secret from your father. I can accept my punishment. Leave." To where she would figure out later.

Prince Alarian shook his head. "No, my father cannot know. Sending you away would be the furthest thing from his mind. And as for why—I'm tired of being considered the most eligible bachelor. I don't care that my parents want me to choose a wife. By agreeing to this, you will force their hands to still. At least for a little while."

Felicity looked away, uncertain if she should agree, her eyes lingering on the dead highwayman behind him. She frowned as she noticed his clean hands had no visible wounds. "How did you kill him?"

He looked behind him. "I'll tell you if you agree."

"A bribe?" She glared.

A ghost of a smile played at his lips. "If it is how I get you to trust me, yes."

She considered his proposition and then held out her hand. "A blood oath then?"

It was a dangerous agreement. One that could hurt her as much as it hurt him, but a pact she could agree upon. The blood oath meant that if either member deemed that the other broke it, they would fall under a pain that grows over time until they admit their transgression or die from it. But the mission, even with all her questions, had to come first.

He cocked his head as he contemplated the request. With a nod, he handed the blade to her.

She'd never done this before, only ever heard of it. What she did know was that the wording was important, so she ran through the phrasing in her mind before she sliced her palm. "With my blood, I agree that you will not speak to anyone of my magic, will assist in my training for a chance to use it, and in return I will smile and say kind words for others to witness. This I promise until the oath has been met."

He took the dagger and cut open his own palm. Their hands met, blood melding while he repeated their agreement. Before he let go of her hand, he added, "And two more dances between us at any time of my choosing. This I promise until the oath has been met."

There was a rush of magic at where their palms met. Felicity's gaze narrowed and she tore her grip from his, wiping her palm against her pant leg. "Ass."

He shrugged, his hands sliding into the pockets of his trousers. "Can't blame me, can you? At least I didn't include a kiss. Though it was tempting."

With a curse under her breath, she looked down at her palm. The bleeding had stopped, a scar already appeared as a reminder of the deal they made. Except, instead of red and puckered, it was a smooth line of silver and pink.

"Our blood."

She looked up to find him watching her. "Silver for Scáth," he finished.

Pink for—her brow furrowed, a thought triggered then gone just as quick. She turned towards the destroyed carriage. "We should probably start walking."

Prince Alarian cleared his throat. "Your magic wasn't like anything I've seen before. It isn't orange and bright like the sun. It's—"

"Like starlight," she finished, a memory tickling in her mind. Someone else had described it that way before.

He grinned. "Yes—white and bright like the moon and stars."

She flung the door of the carriage open with force then slid inside. When she re-emerged, she had slipped on her skirt. "How did you kill him?" Felicity hadn't forgotten the bargain even if she hadn't included it in the oath.

"Your magic is light. I can wield shadows to do my bidding." A hint of a smile rose at the corner of his mouth. "I wish you let me out of the carriage even if you did have control of the situation." He stuffed his hands in his pockets. "Their death would have been much faster. We still might have had a carriage too."

Felicity wondered how long he had stood by and watched before he acted. "How was I to know? All I've ever seen are shadow wisps.

I didn't know what you could do." She rolled back her shoulders. "It's my duty to protect you."

He chuckled. "A little trust can go a long way." He kicked a stone. "And it was never your duty to protect me. I'm honestly shocked you wanted to."

She bit her lip, tasting blood from a gash she hadn't known was there. "Well, I don't think it would look good if you ended up dead."

He cocked his head in her direction. "You considered my death yourself."

She knew it was no use denying it. "Don't make me regret not killing you."

"I won't," he chuckled.

Night fell as they walked, thick and all-encompassing. Exhaustion had begun to settle as her adrenaline faded, her body drained from the fight. For the first time in a long time, the burden of her magic was gone, a lightness in her chest spreading through her body.

The moon was hidden again behind mist and clouds. When an occasional patch of clear sky broke through, starlight glittered their path for a moment.

"You could use your light to lead us."

She protested under her breath, not daring to call upon her magic. To make her point, she pushed the pendant under the neckline of her bodice.

"It's not a weakness," he said, guessing her thoughts. "Besides, you can just kill anyone who crosses our path to keep your secret."

"Do you think it's fun for me to kill?" Felicity grumbled.

Seriousness edged his tone. "No, I don't think that. I was trying to make light of the situation."

She glared at him. He raised his hands in mock surrender. "What?"

"You weren't using puns on purpose?" Her gaze narrowed. "It's like you to use humor to bring down one's defenses. Haven't you learned yet that it doesn't work on me?"

His brow furrowed before a smile spread. "I didn't even try. I guess I'm just witty." His chest puffed up and she rolled her eyes. It was silent for a few steps. "If you don't like being an assassin or spy, then why be one?"

She wished she had grabbed her cloak, goosebumps running over her skin. It was starting to get chilly, so she rubbed her arms to warm them. "Because I'm good at it."

"I think you could be good at a lot of things." The playfulness was gone. "If you hadn't been at the Tower, was there something else you would have chosen for yourself?" he asked, removing his coat, settling it over her shoulders.

She contemplated his question, deciding to ignore the gesture. To bring notice to it would only cause him to preen. An ache settled in her chest. In her entire existence, Felicity couldn't remember ever wanting something else. It had been her only aspiration, a goal to prove herself and her worth. In the end she just shrugged. When he didn't push her, they walked in silence.

They reached the top of a ridge and looked down upon a village with dim streetlamps and pointed rooftops. Just beyond it, the castle's bright lights were visible from the distance. At least they would make it before morning.

Prince Alarian stretched his arms up and folded them behind his head. "I forgot to ask. Did you hear anything of importance the other night? Find a lead?"

Felicity hadn't made a decision on what to divulge from Lady Chartow's conversation—if anything. Too many questions had kept her up the past two nights and she had breathed a sigh of relief when he hadn't mentioned it. She'd hoped he wouldn't ask. Of course, she had hoped too soon.

"Nothing pertinent unless you want to discuss your marriage options."

The topic of marriage shut him up, and they trekked along in silence for the remainder of the walk leaving her to stew more on what the Tower had to do with the attack. And the many questions that remained unanswered.

Chapter
19

They arrived at the castle as the sun was beginning to peek from the horizon. Before she was able to do more than bathe, a missive arrived demanding Felicity's attendance at a meeting with the king. Meira was gentle in dressing and styling her hair, careful not to inflame the injuries that hadn't yet healed. Ward came to collect her with an apologetic expression at having to interrupt any chance of sleep, then led her to the same room as the previous meeting.

Prince Alarian stood beside his father's empty chair, tall and erect. He didn't meet her gaze as they waited.

The door closed behind the king, his guards waiting on the other side. He glared at Felicity as he strolled towards his chair. "Sámhach."

The room went silent, only a buzz audible, like an annoying fly in her ear. Her gaze dropped to a spot on the table. On her last visit, she had decided the knot of the wood resembled an eye trimmed with thick lines of kohl.

The table shook, the king's fist marking a groove into the wood where he'd punched it. She'd resisted the flinch and kept her attention on that knot. The eye began to expand, a pupil forming, and then an iris the color of deep cherrywood. It peered at her, watching with keen interest. Her brow furrowed and it did the same. She wondered why she would create a mirror of her frustrations within the grooves.

Because that was what she was—frustrated. The concept seemed foreign. She stood in front of the king, silenced. Anger at him and the Tower boiled under her skin.

"Felicity."

At the sound of her name, her head snapped to attention. The king's voice ran through the small study, stern and dangerous. "Have you found anything?"

Felicity met the king's gaze. "Your subjects are loyal, Majesty. And if they are not, they do not trust me enough yet to let their guard down." It was easier to lie to the king than she expected. In the past, she would never have kept anything from the one she served. "None have traipsed the halls at night and there have been no notable rendezvous besides the occasional dalliances between couples." King Roald's gaze only narrowed so she continued, "If the courtiers are informants, I've yet to find anything damning against anyone. They must be too smart to conduct anything disparaging on the palace grounds."

"Need I remind you that you haven't proven your worth to *me*?" The king's jaw tensed as he thrummed his fingers on the table. His nails grew into long talons, and he slid them over the wood, leaving scrapes on the surface. "Because you protected my son during the attack, I'll be patient for a little longer. Know this—my patience is dwindling.

"Yes, King Roald." Silence spread through the room. She wondered if he wanted her to continue, but she remained quiet. It was always best to say little when trying to keep information hidden.

When he spoke again, his tone held a bite. "You have ten days to bring me a name. If you fail in this, you'll be punished and sent back to whatever cursed hole you crawled out of."

She curtsied. "As you command."

He waved his hand, excusing her. Ward led her out, his back stiff as she walked a few steps behind him. It hadn't been a surprise, after all. The king had hired her for results. If he meant to frighten her, he hadn't.

But her unknown future—that was something else entirely. Felicity felt like she was standing above a precipice, and there were only two ways to cross. One was a bridge with handholds and a taut certainty while the other was a rickety log teetering on the edge. Her path had always been clear, but now she wasn't so sure.

Ward didn't speak as they walked. A breeze streamed off him in gentle gusts, ruffling her skirts. He'd always seemed reserved with his magic. Something had bothered him during the discussion with the king. Was he one of the reasons for the king's punch to the table?

Once they reached her quarters, Ward entered first. After she passed the entryway, he shut the door and turned to her. "I hate the control they have over you." His hands fisted and that line appeared in the center of his brow.

He began to pace, only relaxing enough to run a hand through his hair. "Is there a way to stop it? Will it end the spell if you remove the clasp from your ear?"

Felicity considered and straightened to her full height. "The king has been given the power to control it. Would you deny your king the choice to use it?" A question—a test.

Ward shuddered, standing still while his eyes raged. "Can you find your way to the gardens this afternoon?"

"Of course." Felicity folded her hands behind her back, her own fury beckoning. Not just at the king's callousness, but at Ward's unsolicited concern. She could take care of herself.

"I will see you in the study hall after." He strode to the door and looked back before opening it. "Do you want to know what was said?"

She shook her head, her fingernails digging into her palms. Although she appreciated the offer, what would it mean if she said yes? There was trust between her and Ward, but she wasn't willing to cross that line. Not yet. Not when she was still trying to find out what was on each side. And where he stood.

His jaw quivered. "See you then." The door slammed shut behind him.

***

Felicity woke from a short nap, her eyelids heavy from the need for sleep. Between her mission, the decision now laid before her, and the fitful dreams or memories—unable to comprehend which was which—her mind felt ready to burst. Exhaustion settled within her body.

And now it was time for tea. Chartow would be present unless she had remained in Aer another day. Felicity wanted to keep an extra eye on the female until she made her decision.

After checking her reflection, ensuring her hair was in place and her cosmetics weren't smudged, she breathed a heavy sigh before she exited—then stopped dead in her tracks.

From the hallway, she could hear voices. She spared a glance in each direction and the words quieted as she closed the space between her and Ward's door.

It was silent for a moment. This time when the male continued, his voice was lower. "Why couldn't you have listened when I said to pick someone else? Anyone else? She doesn't even know about our ways or the realms."

Doubt. Ward's words were laced in it.

"I have my reasons. Besides, you're around to help her out. Are you not up for the task?" Felicity's chest constricted at the sound of Prince Alarian's voice.

Ward ignored the prince's question. "I never asked anything from you until this. You're acting irresponsibly, as always. There was a reason only two guards were present—because you were part of the traveling party. They didn't think they needed to be there with a *Shadow* around. You're lucky those who attacked didn't have magic."

"She handled it. And she wouldn't let me out of the carriage or I'd have done my part sooner," Prince Alarian snapped back. "Stop coddling her and maybe trust that even if our attackers had magic, she could take care of herself. Trust me."

Felicity silently inhaled. Even with the blood oath, he could still share her secret. But with such information, would the prince care if it hurt to break their agreement?

"Trust you? After what you did? The promises you've made me, then broke? Never." Ward's voice heightened. "They were attacking the traveling party because of you. They thought the lazy, drunken prince would be an easy target."

Her brow crinkled. The prince had smelled of alcohol, but now that she thought about it, his eyes had been clear, his mind sharp. It took a lot to get a fae drunk, yet with the smell he'd emitted, there would have been a lot consumed.

"Just stay away from her. Stop trying to drag her into whatever shit you roll through. Remember, you brought her here to perform a job not to fulfill whatever fantasy with death you imagined." Felicity heard a whirl of air rush through the room, rustling papers and toppling things.

When everything stilled, Prince Alarian's voice held a note of warning. "If you won't trust me then trust her. I'm not looking for anything risqué with anyone who can slit my throat." She heard the sound of something being placed back on a table and wondered which of the males was cleaning up. "I came here to tell you my father has asked me to accompany you both when you head into town. He wants extra eyes to see if she is up to par. I think we should go—"

Another gust of air, a crash of something, and Felicity stepped away from the door. If either male came out soon, she didn't want to be caught. Besides, she was going to be late for tea.

The discussion of town, the warnings from Ward, and even the prince's accolades were enough to cause her own magic to simmer to the surface. It boiled with anger while also providing comfort and warmth—emotions battling within her. Emotions she couldn't grasp and wanted nothing to do with.

***

Felicity wished she could do almost anything except for attend tea. To make things worse, the topic of conversation had everything to do with her and the prince's attack.

"We were happy to hear you're both safe," Lady Solfire said after Lady Mistward told the group about coming upon the remains of the damaged carriage.

Lady Chartow had chosen to remain in Aer for a few extra days with her husband. Only the second carriage with the Mistward family had followed a few hours behind.

"Not only safe but up and around. Glad you could join us today." Lady Fiadh's voice was unemotional, her expression blank. "I had expected you would need rest after such an ordeal. It's not every day a lady is attacked on the road."

"It's becoming more of a common occurrence as of late." Lady Mistward shivered. "It was terrifying to think the worst. All those bodies." She squeezed her daughter's hand. "I wish we caught up to you on the road. If only we had driven together, then the prince wouldn't have had to walk such a distance." The female sniffed. "And you too, of course, Lady Dwauer."

"Yes, how did you escape?" The queen's brow rose. "My son gave little details."

Felicity and the prince had agreed upon a story on the trek back to the palace. The queen knew Felicity's true identity, so it surprised her that the monarch would ask. Was she testing her quick thinking?

"It was terrifying. I was in the carriage during the crash." The perfect excuse for her injuries. "The driver gave his life to kill one attacker, and a guard gave his to kill another." And in case there was any chance of question, she added, "The prince killed the last two." It irked her to look like the maiden in distress, but it would be best if others didn't question her further.

"I'm thankful to the guards who gave their lives and for the prince's presence. Otherwise, I might not be here now." She shuddered, wrapping her arms around herself.

Concern was obvious on all of their faces. Even the queen played along. All, that is, but Lady Fiadh. Her lips pursed together, gaze flat.

"Do you mind if we change the subject?" Felicity whispered.

"Oh, of course." Lady Solfire patted Felicity's hand. "We shouldn't discuss such dark things at tea. Not when they are fresh in your mind." The female picked up Felicity's saucer, cup rattling slightly and held it out. Felicity took it, giving Lady Solfire a warm smile as she sipped.

"Has the king had any luck discovering who's behind all of these attacks? Certainly, he must have an idea?" Lady Grandeur faced the queen.

Queen Marquette cocked her head, sending Felicity a pointed glance out of the corner of her eye. "Do you assume my husband isn't doing everything in his power to find the culprits? He could have lost his son."

The sound of shears snapping vines, and the fresh scent of dug-up dirt had Felicity's senses turning towards the gardeners' direction. There were a few more today, spread out over a wide expanse, trying their luck at the overgrown shrubs.

"Of course not, Your Majesty. I was only hoping he had some luck in the matter." Lady Grandeur studied the ground at her feet.

Queen Marquette's gaze searched each of their faces. "There is hope that the attack on my son and Lady Dwauer will lead us to more information. The rebels' bodies have been recovered and are being analyzed for clues." Her shoulders drifted back, making her already foreboding appearance more frightening—for some. Felicity met her gaze, unafraid. The queen continued, "It would be best not to question your king's urgency on this matter. Your safety and the safety of the realms are of the highest importance."

"I apologize, Your Majesty," Lady Grandeur said.

Felicity felt Lady Fiadh's gaze but didn't meet it. The woman's attention remained on her as she tried to peel each of Felicity's layers to view what lay beneath.

"Will the gardens be ready for the king's birthday celebration?" Miss Isleen had remained silent until now, her own attention on the finger sandwiches or sipping primly at her tea.

The queen's expression softened, and she smiled at the youngling. "We can hope, but after so many years, the weeds have taken control. I attempted to have the entire garden removed years ago to start anew, but it grew right back. A group of spellbinders have been called in and will arrive tomorrow. We hope they can return some semblance of order."

Lady Trent sniffed. "I, for one, hope you have luck. These gardens hold such promise."

"That they do." Lady Fiadh tilted her head as she picked up her tea. "Such promise." But the woman's gaze never left Felicity.

***

The study lights were dimmer than usual. Ward sat, staring over books, and upon Felicity's entrance, handed her a rather large text. He pointed to a paragraph regarding the geography within the southwest corner where the fire, light, and stone realms met. His mood was palpable, and as much as Felicity wanted to rage at his over-protectiveness, to ask him about what she had overheard, she kept her mouth shut. She didn't know why he thought she needed to be coddled or what it was about her that he deemed unfit for the mission.

After reading other minuscule facts regarding the way the realms were separated, she snapped the book shut. "I need to know more."

Ward's head jerked up. "More about what?"

She swallowed, steadying her voice. Trusting Ward could be a mistake. "Politics. After this mission, the Tower is not my home anymore and has no hold over me."

Ward folded his hands in front of him, regarding her for a moment. "All right. I should ask though...do you want books the king would deem appropriate or books that allow you to form your own opinion?"

She rubbed a finger over the smooth surface of the table, feeling the minute indentations of the wood. The crack she had made when Harrison arrived was just to the left. Staring at it, she considered his question. "Is there a difference?"

He inhaled. "There is. The king would have you believe certain things. You might not agree with him."

"Then I guess it depends if King Roald will know I'm studying politics." It was a dangerous comment. She still didn't know what or who Ward was. To the king, to this palace. He was an enigma—untitled and undefined. But it seemed wrong to spy on him—like she would be breaking the tentative truce between them. Instead, she collected pieces of information through these sessions. Felicity wouldn't call it friendship. It was dangerous to assume such things. Yet, it felt right. Safe.

"I've been given the task to prepare you for court." A corner of his mouth lifted as he piled the geology and geography books atop one another. "The king requested it, and that is what I plan to do. I'll bring the books tomorrow."

"Thank you," she whispered. Then, before she could second-guess herself she, she added, "You shared the list of advisors, but I noticed something. Are there no other Scáth representatives in court beyond the queen and prince?"

Ward's brow furrowed. "Fiadh is from the Shadow Realm. Or do you mean advisors?"

"Yes. I didn't think Fiadh discussed political matters."

He shook his head. "No. At least not with an official title. Scáth separated from the advisory committee years ago. Most believe it is because the queen and prince are considered enough of a representation for the realm."

"Do you agree?" She might as well test her theory a bit.

Silence spread, his gaze pinned on the table between them. "No. I don't."

She considered asking him to expand on his response, but instead just nodded, standing and pushing in her chair.

Ward's shoulders bunched as he exhaled. "I'm sorry I missed taking you to tea. Did it go well?"

It was the perfect opportunity to ask him about the conversation she overheard, but she bit her tongue and nodded her head. Too many questions and he might start to think her a threat. No need for that just yet.

He cleared his throat. "The prince and I are going into town tomorrow night. It's been decided you should join us to see the people and observe the nightlife. Because you only have six more days, you might need to venture into the village since being within the castle walls is not enough to find the rebel's contact."

"I don't think it will do me any good to attend a drinking fest with the prince while you babysit." The words came out harsher than she planned, but Ward smiled. One of the rare smiles that reached his eyes. Part of her frustration with him faded away.

"I'm glad to see his charms haven't worked on you. So many others have fallen for it in the past." He snapped his fingers, the books levitating beside him. "It shouldn't be like that, however. If it is, we can leave him behind at a tavern for someone else to drag back to the palace. His father would love that."

Felicity smiled. "Deal. Also, when will you keep your bargain and show me the passageways?"

"Soon." He headed towards the door, mood improved. "Very soon."

Chapter
20

She sat on the ground against the trunk of the willow tree. The glittering waters shifted in and out of view with the wave of its branches. The scent of grass and salty ocean mixed and filled her with a nostalgic complacency. In her hand she twisted a reed of grass around a finger, trying to gain a grasp of the many thoughts in her mind. The mixed memories, the unknown future, the decision she needed to make. The use of her magic during the attack two days prior had assisted with her body aches, but the stress of the choices she had to make brought on a new heaviness.

A fox darted into view, pouncing and leaping over the tall reeds and batting at pussy willow, forcing tufts of the plant to flutter into the wind. Felicity couldn't resist the smile, a small laugh escaping. The gray fox came to a standstill, grass flat under its feet as it stared at Felicity with wide eyes.

"Looks like you're having fun," she called to the animal, her grin widening when it tilted its head at her. "I don't remember fun."

Her voice lowered, and she rested her head against the tree. "In fact, I don't remember much of anything."

The fox took a few tentative steps forward, watching her carefully from the outskirts of the willow branches.

"What is it like to be carefree? To play within the grass and run about?" She sighed, and the fox darted back a few steps at the unexpected sound.

Now it was her turn to tilt her head. Felicity had seen few foxes in her lifetime but even fewer gray ones. "I have some big decisions to make. Not only are they life and death, but they are lifechanging. Is there a way to become a fox and hide away from such responsibilities? Or maybe become a cailleach and fly into the snow and mountains of Dorcha?"

The fox raised its head a little higher. When she was about to continue the one-sided conversation, it crouched down and leaped into a tuft of grass. It continued to run away until it was no longer visible. She closed her eyes and hoped when she opened them, all her troubles would too be gone.

But that was a dream world—where foxes didn't run away but talked back. There was a time when Felicity had wanted the freedom to make her own decisions—to choose the next mission. Now she just wished to return to the Tower and have them tell her what to do next.

Someone cleared their throat from behind and Felicity winced. She got to her feet and turned to face Ward. He chuckled, "Do you often talk to wild animals?"

She brushed her hair behind her ear. "Do you often listen in on private conversations?"

Ward didn't comment, a smile edging across his face as he turned to where the fox had run off to. "Surprise you didn't follow. The stories say that they are cunning and seductive creatures that can help you adapt to new situations."

"I've also read that their presence means you need to be aware of your surroundings. Obviously, that was the point of this interaction." She started towards the palace, Ward walking alongside her.

He snickered. "I thought that you didn't read much?"

Felicity blinked in surprise, her brow furrowing. "I—" She cleared her throat, trying to recall where the memory had come from. "I don't know how I knew that."

"It seems you're starting to remember things after all." The warmth in his expression made her pause.

He ran a hand through his hair, and she turned her attention towards her destination.

"Where are you headed?" Such a loaded question. She heard the grin in his tone but didn't look at him.

"I should prepare for the trip to the town. Were you out here for a reason, or just to spy on me?" A breeze, a touch of magic within it, brushed her shoulders and she remembered the stories of the curse the king had left behind.

"I have no need to spy on you, Felicity. That's your job."

How right he was. And maybe tonight, she would learn a little more about this enigmatic fae.

***

A carriage pulled into the curved drive by two horses prancing excitedly as the gravel crunched under their hooves. Although she wished to pet them, it was bad enough that Alarian had witnessed her attention to the horses. She hoped Ward wouldn't notice it too. Even if she wasn't to return to the Tower, she was still a weapon—weapons didn't get caught fawning over animals. Ward and Felicity stood together while they waited for the prince. He was late, but it didn't surprise either of them.

"Are we ready?"

Prince Alarian's lilting voice caused both to turn. Ward inhaled deeply.

The prince stood beside Lady Solfire and at the sight of Ward and Felicity, her smile widened. "I hope you don't mind me tagging along. He insisted."

The prince walked down the steps in his usual lazy saunter, hands in his pocket. "It seemed proper to invite another female along on this little escapade." The corner of his mouth rose as he winked at Felicity. "Didn't want you to be stuck all alone with us stubborn males."

Ward growled, his upper lip rising, a warning in his gaze. Felicity cleared her throat, and his expression softened, but his eyes still held a glint of annoyance.

Prince Alarian brushed past to step into the carriage. He poked his head out the doorway. "Are you coming?"

Lady Solfire flushed and cocked her head at Felicity. "After you, Lady Dwauer."

"Thank you." Felicity followed the prince into the carriage, taking a seat across from him. Lady Solfire sat beside her, leaving Ward to sit next to the prince. It seemed like a precarious situation to have the two males beside each other. The carriage had already felt cramped and suffocating before Ward stepped in.

"You look lovely, Lady Dwauer." Lady Solfire beamed.

Felicity returned the smile. "Thank you. As do you."

Prince Alarian folded his hands behind his head. "You both look beautiful. Now be truthful, how do we look?"

Ward rolled his eyes and crossed his arms over his chest as he leaned into the corner to keep distance between the two of them.

Lady Solfire cleared her throat as the carriage started down the curved drive. "Where are we going tonight? The prince said little except that we would be heading into town. It's been a while since I've ventured into Koselig. Seems wrong since it's so close." She spoke hastily, her eyes darting between the two males.

The prince broke eye contact first. "I thought we would take an evening tour of the town for Lady Dwauer's benefit. Maybe stop at the city center for dinner, listen to the minstrels, then end with a stroll through the *Solas* District."

Ward's jaw fluttered, and he rolled back a shoulder. "No tavern to drink your life away?"

If the question bothered him, the prince didn't show it. Instead, he shrugged. "It's not about me tonight but thank you for your consideration. Maybe next time. Although if that was your plan for the evening, I would be happy to oblige. Would love to see the stoic Ward cut loose and inhibitions low."

Before Ward could respond, the prince's attention turned towards Felicity. "You're quiet this evening."

"Not certain if I want to deal with male egos and pissing matches tonight." Felicity smoothed out her dark green skirt. Lady Solfire's eyes widened as she covered her mouth. Felicity was almost certain it was to stifle a giggle. Felicity might like this female. Maybe.

Prince Alarian chuckled. "I knew I could count on you to lighten the mood."

Ward groaned as he looked out the window. Felicity followed his gaze, her mouth falling open. The town was alight with different hues of color, the buildings aglow.

The prince leaned across the space between them. "Just wait. It gets better." His green eyes sparkled with mischief.

The driver slowed the carriage as the crowd thickened. The prince pointed out different shops and restaurants as they passed. With their doors still open, the fresh scent of bread and sugar from the bakery wafted into the carriage. A herbalist's shop with dried bushels hanging in their windows had shoppers exiting with bouquets of thyme and lavender while others held open a door to go in. They passed a library where Felicity could see the outline of bookcases, the darkness holding the promise of parchment and ink.

The horse's hooves clip-clopped on the cobblestone road as they passed more shops leading them towards the center of town. Once they arrived outside the town center, the driver stopped, and a footman opened the door, offering his hand to assist them from the carriage.

Felicity shivered, the summer breeze running along the nape of her neck chilling her skin. The sights were intoxicating and pulled her attention away from the weather. The center was filled with humans and faeries. At least for tonight, they had no worries, only caring about the perfect weather and enjoyable atmosphere. Even Felicity's shoulders relaxed, although her attention darted from one corner to the next, aware of every body and movement around her. But it wasn't her instincts taking over as much as her desire to see everything.

Some chatted while others sat at little tables outside of small cafes or waited near doorways to restaurants and taverns. In the center of the roundabout was a grass field with benches, bushes laden with roses of different colors, and a band of minstrels playing stringed instruments that filled the area with a beautiful melody.

"Do you like it?" Prince Alarian's warm smile surprised her.

She had never seen anything like this before. Any time she had ventured within the nearby towns of the Tower it was for training or to complete a mission. When every corner had a memory laced with blood, it was hard to find the beauty underneath. After a while, Felicity stopped trying. With a nod, her own smile grew. "It's exquisite."

The prince held out his elbow, offering it to her. She spared a glance behind to find Ward's gaze narrowed on the prince's back. Felicity stepped away, starting to walk the circular path. Alarian chuckled. Her rejection was against the blood oath, and if he chose to take offense, she would find herself writhing in pain. Luckily, he accepted her choice. Besides, he had been the one to ask Lady Solfire along in the first place.

The female in question caught up with her, leaving Ward to saunter behind with the prince, and pointed out a few of her favorite places to visit. "That shop there has the best seamstress in all of Éardrom. I mention it mostly because I've seen you wear a few of the trousers she designed."

Felicity couldn't help the smile. "The pants with the ties? They're comfortable."

"Is anyone hungry?" Ward interrupted, coming up alongside Lady Solfire.

Prince Alarian strode with his hands in his pockets until he passed them, then stopped to create a circle of their group. "I had a place in mind. Unless there is something that has caught your attention, Lady Dwauer?"

She considered the restaurant with the smell of the fresh rolls drifting from the window or the one with homemade pasta packaged in brown bags. "What do you recommend?"

"Don't assume the worst—follow me." Prince Alarian started down one of the small alleys off the center. Wisteria grew along the stone walls and wrapped around wires that hung over the expanse above.

He led them to a pine door with a small sign that read 'Godrey's Pub' and opened it. Ward and Felicity shared a glance as they ducked inside after the others.

A man led them to a table in the back. He rattled off the menu for the night before bustling away with the promise to return to take their order.

As far as she could remember, Felicity had never gone to a restaurant with others before. To sit at a table and find a target or collect information—yes. Usually that involved a cup of tea or an ale but nothing more and never with another.

When their food arrived, everyone tried a different dish and shared a bite, and Felicity had to admit the meal was superb. The prince ordered a bottle of wine for the table, and Felicity noted he only consumed one glass. With the warmth of the alcohol and a full stomach, they headed back to the town center. The music had taken on a new liveliness as couples danced in the streets. Prince Alarian led them to the outskirts of spectators to watch as dancers laughed and pranced about to the music in unfamiliar steps. Some made up their own movements while others seemed to have a routine prepared.

A dancer came by and waved to their group to join in. Felicity shook her head, stepping back. An unfamiliar pressure settled on her chest. There was no way she was going out there. She clapped along with the others to the beat, trying to blend in with the crowd. Another dancer grabbed Lady Solfire's hand. The female laughed and reached for the prince's arm as she was pulled away. He didn't fight it as the couple was pulled to an open spot. The dancer showed them a complicated jig, and although they failed miserably, both laughed good-naturedly at their missteps. The two came closer, their movements bringing them back toward Ward and Felicity.

Noting the glint in Lady Solfire's eye, Felicity positioned herself behind Ward. He wasn't prepared when the female grabbed his hand to pull him into the center. Wide-eyed, he tried to fumble back, but she held tight with both hands. Prince Alarian stopped beside Felicity. She looked up, noticing the color on his cheeks wasn't too many shades away from his fiery red hair.

He met her stare, and she turned away. Prince Alarian chuckled and held out a hand. "Dance with me?" It wasn't an order—a hint of a plea in his tone.

Felicity cleared her throat as she watched the dancers move in unfamiliar patterns. She was aware of how many were watching the festivities. "No."

"Do you mean to tell me I found something you're frightened of?" Prince Alarian leaned in. "Didn't think that was possible."

She recognized the challenge and yearned to prove herself despite his manipulations. "I've already demonstrated that I'm an extraordinary dance partner."

The prince took her hand, catching her off guard, and maneuvered through the couples into the center. He twirled Felicity, and although she tried to wiggle free from his hold, he held tight, pulling her back to him. She smacked into his body, her head almost knocking into his shoulder. Prince Alarian straightened, and Felicity stilled, the scent of a forest filling her senses. Then he stepped back, the smell abandoning her as he attempted a complicated move.

She almost walked away. Should have left him there alone—it would serve him right. But he looked up, his gaze a shimmering green with that damn grin. The words of the blood oath trickled in the back of her mind.

She didn't want to question why, but she stayed. "This counts as one of your dances."

"Deal." His smile widened, beckoning her to try—to join him.

Biting her bottom lip, Felicity concentrated on the steps. With a deep sigh, she mimicked his movements, a broken mirror to his attempts. The dance came out more like a jagged array than anything resembling what the more advanced dancers could do.

With each fumble, a smile began to form on her own lips. When the prince almost toppled over, she laughed, a sound unfamiliar to her own ears. It was a little rough, but it felt good as well, a lightness spreading in her chest. Tears glistened in the corner of her eyes as Felicity tried to control the fit of giggles that broke free, her usually sure feet turning into a tangled mess.

When the song ended, the prince clapped along with the others, but his gaze never left hers. His smile was contagious—all toothy grin and male charm.

So, she smiled back.

The group found each other again after a few more songs. Prince Alarian took the lead down another alley, leading them this way and that way, in directions most would find confusing, but Felicity's training kicked in as she tracked each left and right turn they made. He turned right once more before stopping, leading them into an alley wider than the previous ones. Once they entered, she let out a long breath in awe.

The narrow road was covered in bulbs of string lights. They dangled between buildings while others hung from balconies and balustrades, the lights dancing within the glass lanterns in all colors of the rainbow. Bougainvillea in shades of pink grew along the left side. Branches curved around the lantern wires, making a canopy of flowers, their scent intoxicating. Wisteria spread on the opposite side, the purples adding new shades of colors to the surroundings made visible by the glowing lanterns.

"Welcome to the *Solas* District," Prince Alarian whispered to her.

Felicity's attention darted from one minuscule detail to the next as they strolled down the alley. Lady Solfire pointed out a sculpture of steel shaped into vines, the lights in shades of purples and blues created a blossoming effect.

Felicity felt prickles against her and peeked from the corner of her eye, finding the prince's expectant gaze.

"It's stunning," Felicity said, realizing she hadn't spoken a word. "I've never seen anything like it."

He nodded. "I hoped you would like it."

Prince Alarian took a tentative step beside her. "The two of them would be good together. If my father would allow it."

Felicity followed his gaze.

Ward was leaning in close to Lady Solfire as he pointed out another sculpture of miniature lights, shaped like little stars, peeking around clouds made from tinted white glass.

Felicity tilted her head. "I've—"

A scream echoed down the alley, and her head jerked in its direction. Another followed and she was already running by the time the third pierced the air.

Holding her skirt up so she didn't trip, she sensed the other three on her heels as she ran. At the end of the alley, a fae raced by with others close behind. Sliding to a halt, Felicity assessed her surroundings and reached for a pipe that led up to the rooftop. Someone grabbed her shoulder, twisting her around and pinned her to the wall.

"Don't," Prince Alarian hissed.

More screams. Yells for help. The sounds of chaos and rushing feet. Chains and the draw of swords. The wall she was against shook and out of her peripheral there was a flash of light.

Felicity fought against him, trying to wrench herself free from his grasp. She was about to knee him in the groin when Ward pressed himself to the wall beside her to keep from view, his mouth taut. He held Lady Solfire close. The female faced Felicity, eyes brimmed with tears.

"Be still," Prince Alarian ordered.

More ran past, screams and shouts disrupting what had once been a lovely night. The ground shook and vines broke through cobblestone, grabbing hold of a man's leg, tripping him.

"Grab them," a gargled voice called. "Get them in there."

Felicity jerked again, trying to free herself but the prince's grip tightened. "It's not safe, Lady Dwauer," he whispered sharply.

At the sound of the title, she stilled and looked behind him at Lady Solfire's petrified expression.

Felicity faced the prince. "What are they doing?"

He tensed and loosened his hold, one hand still gripping her arm as he peered around the corner.

The sounds of metal banging shut and the pleas and cries that followed made her head want to burst. She shuddered under the prince's touch.

Ward leaned in close. "Let her go, Alarian."

The prince didn't listen but met her gaze, his chest rising and falling. "We need to go."

"Not until I know what's happening," Felicity shot back in a harsh whisper, frustration rising with each of the prince's breaths. "What are they doing to them?"

"Rounding them up. It's a raid." Prince Alarian turned her back the way they came but his grip didn't loosen.

"They need our help." Bile rose in her throat. These were the same people who were just dancing, enjoying an evening with their neighbors and friends.

Prince Alarian shuddered, his hold loosening.

Ward called behind them. "We should intervene. This isn't right..."

The prince stopped, turning quickly to square off with Ward. Lady Solfire's expression hardened as she pinned him with a glare, a protective stance beside Ward. Prince Alarian ignored it. "We can't. I doubt I need to tell you what that would mean if we interfered."

Ward cowered slightly and although Felicity had a feeling she knew why the prince was forcing her to leave, she didn't care. "I can help." She hated to beg. More so, she hated that she felt the need to do so.

"No." He shot her a glare, then began moving, heading back towards the town center. "I order you to desist."

She faltered, almost falling as he pulled her along. "They are your people. I have training," she whispered.

"And those who were rounding them up are my parent's guards," he ground out. His green eyes darkened as the shadows outlining him grazed against her skin.

The fight left her. Felicity stopped pulling, and although he didn't drag her, the prince held tight.

Ward and Lady Solfire caught up to them. "I told you to let go of her, Alarian." Ward grabbed the prince's forearm. "Now."

Prince Alarian stopped, noticing the hold he still had on her. He let go and stepped back. "I'm sorry. I was concerned for your safety."

Felicity rubbed at the spot now free from his touch. She stepped forward, the slap across his face echoed in the alley. He stood by and did nothing. Watched as his people were taken and acted as though it was a normal evening. She wanted to thrash at him, magic pulsing against her skin and it wasn't just anger that consumed her—but something foreign. Something... Disappointment. At herself. At him.

No one said anything. The surprise of the others hung in the air, but Prince Alarian lowered his gaze to the ground.

Lady Solfire sniffed as she wiped at the tear streaking her cheeks. "We should go."

Felicity led this time, the prince a step behind, her senses heightened by her magic. After memorizing the route, it took no time for them to reach the city center. It was empty now, with no soldiers or patrons in sight. The doors were shut, the lights extinguished—deserted. The merriment of the evening forgotten.

Sticking within the shadows, they rounded a corner to find the carriage waiting in the darkness under the balcony of an inn.

"Glad you're back, Prince Alarian. I was getting concerned." The driver climbed up onto his seat as the footmen helped them in.

No one spoke on the way back to the palace.

Chapter
21

Afternoon tea was a waste of time. Spying in the corridors in hopes of hearing late-night whispers or secret conversations behind closed doors had led to nothing. If anyone else sided with the rebels, they were careful. Felicity had a name—one name—but protected it, not uttering it to anyone. After the visit to town two days prior, Felicity was less willing to turn in Lady Chartow. But the countdown was running short and a decision needed to be made.

She had never felt such uncertainty in her entire life. Her dreams were filled with pieces of memories that floated in orbs she needed to catch—but only in a particular order or they would break into smaller bubbles and float away. Besides the dream of playing hide and seek with an indistinct figure and the memory of Harrison, none had held much substance. Or deemed important enough to be considered groundbreaking.

Her life was in disarray, unchartered territory. She never had to rely upon herself to make such decisions. It weighed on her. Heavily.

And so did her magic. She had skipped training, avoiding the prince, and her body was protesting. The use of her magic in Prince Alarian's presence had been the last time she had fully called upon it. The little bursts she dared in private were not enough. There were times she was certain she was being watched. The king didn't trust her yet, even with Ward as her babysitter. She was certain someone watched her while she spent her nights spying, but it was usually easy to evade them. But during the day, it was more difficult with others around and a schedule to keep.

Instead of training, she spent her evenings searching the other buildings on the castle grounds. So far, she'd been to the stables, the armory, the blacksmith's hut and even the crockery in the hope of finding anything to help make her decision easier. She was a spy. A weapon hired for one purpose. Now she knew why the Tower had kept them sheltered from the outside world.

Felicity wished to return to that way of life—to make her choice easier. She didn't fear for her own life. The king may punish, torture, or throw her out, but none of that would matter if she couldn't live with the decision she had to make. Which surprised her more than she was willing to admit. It had never crossed her mind to turn away from her mission before. Who was she if she wasn't the spy she had been trained and raised to be?

What would Bishop say about her now? *A spy with morals isn't a weapon.* His snarl would extend the 's' in each word.

Felicity slid the last knife into place at her calf. She planned to search the gardens and meeting rooms that night. Although she doubted there would be anything worth finding, it was something more than sitting in her room. Her hand grasped the door handle leading to her balcony when a knock sounded at the door. It would be easy to ignore. Meira had already completed her duties—whoever it was could wait. But with an inhale, citrus filled her senses.

She let Ward in. He examined her from head to toe, hesitating on the mask she held in her hand. "Going somewhere?"

"Only have a few days left. I'm checking the grounds to see if anything is going on." She slid a finger over her daggers, finding comfort in touching each hidden location.

He cleared his throat. "I wanted to check on you. You haven't come for training or spoken to me when I've escorted you to the gardens for tea." He paused, glancing at the door to the balcony behind her. "I wanted to show you the passageways and had the books waiting in the study as well."

Doing anything that wasn't tied to her mission seemed like a reward—something she didn't deserve at the moment. She hated hearing the hint of understanding in his voice.

"Didn't feel like it." Her lips pursed as she headed towards the balcony doors again.

"Felicity. I haven't known you long, but that night—" He hesitated for a moment. "I understand. I saw so many emotions from you." He trailed after her, his presence like that damn cloak again. "And it wasn't just anger."

"You won't see it again." The chime of the clock in the distance marked the twelfth hour.

Ward was beside her now, resting his shoulder against the doorway. "How are your memories coming along?"

Felicity snorted, her anger surfacing. As far as she was concerned, he was as guilty as Prince Alarian. Then again, so was she. "Why does it matter? You have your issues and I have mine. At some point, I'll figure out my memories, and maybe you'll get over whatever it is that is between you and the prince. In other words, I'll take care of my shit and you take care of yours." She twisted the handle, but his hand covered hers.

"What do you mean between the prince and I?" Ward's eyes brightened to a deeper blue. "You can't think...what is it you think?"

She yanked her hand free from his grasp. "You call him by his name, no title. You were upset he brought along Lady Solfire and have spoken ill of his drinking habits. Lady Solfire is obviously interested in you, but you don't return the sentiment."

Ward fought off a smile, his mouth contorting in different directions. "I don't call him by his title unless I have to because I don't respect him. He's a drunk, addicted to females and cards, and has never done a single worthwhile thing in his entire existence. I don't have an ounce of feelings for him and wouldn't waste any." He bit his lip. "As for Lady Solfire, she is none of your concern. Besides, I wasn't the one dancing with *him* all night."

"What, were you jealous?" She growled.

He straightened, features darkening. "No, Felicity. I wasn't jealous."

Her brow bunched. "Then why are you here? Who are you?"

Ward stepped back, his hands dropping to his side. His gaze fell to the floor, and she could see by his expression that he wasn't going to talk.

"Fine." She opened the door. "Don't ask about my memories. I have it covered."

"All right then. What about the mission? With only a few days—"

"I'm well aware of the timeline." She disappeared into the darkness, leaving his pestering behind.

She couldn't deny her frustration with him for not standing against the prince the other night. Maybe if the two of them had stood their ground they could have gotten to the bottom of things regarding the king's plan for the people of Koselig—or maybe they would have been imprisoned and tortured for their choices.

Even so, it would have been the first choice that she had made on her own. Yet, she had hesitated. Meeting Ward felt like her own uncertainty was being thrown in her face. A reminder of her lack of freewill. The Tower's influence still led her after they abandoned her.

The moon was high overhead as Felicity overlooked the grounds from her perch in the niche of the pinnacle inlay along the castle wall. She tightened the straps to the mask covering her face. The guards would change shifts soon and she planned to use the chance to climb down to the next level of meeting rooms. The gardens had uncovered nothing, which hadn't been surprising. Even with the overabundance of weeds, there wasn't enough opportunity for privacy within the open space. From here, Felicity could see the guards walking through the paths surrounded by overgrown hedges.

The clang of the bell announced the hour, and the guards began their shift change. Because the king didn't know who to trust, her identity was kept secret from them, and they became another obstacle for her to plan around. After the many spying attempts, she at least had learned the guards' routes and schedule.

Using the grooves sculpted into the smooth stone walls, Felicity climbed down until she reached the first balcony of meeting rooms. Only a few had them, but they were connected to smaller, more intimate spaces. If someone had the audacity to meet, it would be in one of the smaller spaces—well, at this point, it was the last idea she had since every other attempt had been unsuccessful.

She stood outside the doorway of the first room and pressed her ear to it. As far as she could discern, it was empty. Picking the lock, she entered and searched it and then the three rooms following it.

Nothing.

It was becoming more difficult to deny that Felicity's choice was limited. Either she turned in Lady Chartow or she failed. Felicity had always completed every mission given to her. Not doing so now wasn't an option.

The thoughts caused her chest to ache and she blamed it on the thought of defeat. But deep down knew it had to do with the choice laid before her.

Back on a balcony, she considered her next move, her own thoughts a distraction. At the twang of a bowstring, Felicity dodged too late. The arrow sliced her arm, taking a chunk of muscle with it. Shit, she'd been found.

She hissed as she curled into a protective roll, her body jarring at the impact of the stone. With a firm grip over her injury to apply pressure, she jumped to her feet. The sound of near-silent boots approached from all directions. She was surrounded. There was only one way to go.

With a glance upward, she released a quick breath before she leaped, grabbing hold of a gable. It took sheer will not only to pull herself up but to resist the scream at the mounting pain shooting up her arm. Her injured arm seared, and for a moment, she hung by one hand, taking the chance to search her surroundings before another arrow flew past.

She was up a level by the time the guards were under her, and she heard the whispered command to send others inside to head her off. Blood trailed down her arm, and tears stung her eyes as she painstakingly made it back to the niche where she had begun. *Don't leave a trail others can follow.* Another lesson—useless right now—echoed in Harrison's voice. Ragged breaths tore at her throat. Her heart raced as she clung to the blood-stained white stone. Staying here wasn't an option. They may have levels of stairs to climb, but she wouldn't have much of a lead if she didn't keep moving. Arrows were shot again but just missed, hitting the stone near her body. The soldiers were spread out on the balcony below, keeping their eyes on her.

When they began to prep the next round of arrows, reinforcements came in, and the reality of her position sunk in. She gritted her teeth and pulled herself upward to the next level, nausea rolling through her. The shock from her injury was beginning to wear off, and with it, a new level of discomfort—and weakness—would come.

Guards started climbing the wall after her. They weren't as lithe as she was, but even with their bulk, they were gaining on her fast. She reached around the side of the building, each step a potential slip to her death as she tried not to use the injured appendage. Sweat made it harder for her to get a grip, her palms now soaked not only with blood but mixed with salty perspiration.

Two more rooms and she would arrive at her destination. It was one of the last places she wanted to go. The only choices otherwise were being captured or death. Likely both.

Landing on the balcony, her legs were like lead. Dragging herself across the stone, she fumbled with her lock pick, almost dropping it.

"Over here," a guard called to his compatriot. "They're getting inside."

She didn't dare look to see where the guard was. The click of the unlocking door had never been so satisfying. Before she could open it and bolt inside, the guard grabbed her shoulder and pulled her back. She cried out at the pain lancing through her arm but zeroed her attention on him. If he was here, another would be right behind, and she needed to get inside quickly—without him following her.

Jamming the elbow of her uninjured arm upwards, she heard the gratifying snap of a broken nose. The soldier growled, but Felicity didn't slow. With a swipe of her leg, she caught him off balance, and he fell, his head giving a resounding crack against the stone. He tried to get up, settling on all fours before he crumbled to the floor. This was her chance.

She bound around him, swiping the dripping blood from her shoulder. Then with a leap over the railing to the next balcony, she flung open the door and slammed it shut behind her, locking it. Hopefully, it would be enough to keep them guessing which direction she'd gone long enough until—

A dagger forced her to duck. "Ward," she hissed. "It's me."

He stepped into the moonlight, eyes wide. "Curses, Felicity?"

Ward inhaled and his attention fell to her arm. Without a word, he pointed to the bedroom door. "Open it, drip blood down the hall a few steps then get back in here. Give them a trail to follow first."

When she came back, he had the armoire pivoted away from the wall, and behind it, a door was open. "Get inside. Quick."

Even with the questions rising to the surface, now wasn't the time. Another set of boots landed on the stones of the balcony.

She darted through the opening and Ward shut it, blocking her from view. The sound of wood scraping stone informed her that he was moving the armoire back in place. Then she was surrounded by a deafening silence. Whatever was happening on the other side of the door was a mystery. Darkness encompassed her and she couldn't make out where she was, even with her fae instincts. With the rising pain, the racing of her heart, and the blood sliding down her arm, she leaned back against the stone wall, trying to ground herself. What could have been mere seconds felt like hours.

Stay awake. She willed herself, the pressure she tried to hold on her wound weakening.

Felicity jumped when the door creaked open before she recognized Ward as he dropped down beside her. "Felicity?"

She groaned. It was the only sound she could muster. With shaking hands, she tore the mask off her face, feeling safe enough to do so.

His hands felt like ice against her skin. The smell of antiseptic stung her nose, and she bit her lip to hold back the scream as Ward cleaned the wound, muttering to himself.

The stitches were next. She squeezed her eye shut against the sting of the needle. It took everything in her to concentrate on each of the steps Ward took to clean and treat the wound, using it as an anchor to consciousness. Her head lolled against the stone, the coolness of the rock a crutch against the hardness. When he was bandaging her arm, his mutters turned to discernible words. "What the fuck, Felicity?"

She peeked through one eye, his face contorted in concern illuminated by the crack of the doorway and the light of his room. His brow was drawn together, a little imprint in the center creating a worry line she knew meant he was concentrating.

"Thank you." It was all she could think to say.

He fit the bandage in place and then sat down across from her, catching his own breath. "It wasn't my best job. I didn't want to bring you out in case they came back tomorrow to search for more clues."

"Where are we?" She blinked a few times. Ward held out an ewer and she took it, water sloshing within it was comforting as the cool liquid met her lips.

Ward ran a hand through his hair. "The passageway. Maybe now you'll meet me for that tour."

Felicity handed him back the ewer, water down her front as much as she had consumed, then stumbled to her feet. Ward darted up, assisting her. At first, she recoiled at his touch. In the past, needing help would have been a sign of weakness. It would have meant she had failed her mission because she hadn't been able to complete it on her own. The only thing she felt now was relief that Ward had been there. And that confused her. "Maybe it would mean less chance of late-night medical visits."

Ward chuckled as he pushed open the door. "Don't want to find you dead or imprisoned one day."

Now within the moonlight of his room, she swallowed as what he said sunk in. "I'm fine. All part of the job."

He nodded, an indifferent expression falling into place—one she knew all too well. It was what she wore so often. A pang of guilt ran through her. "Sorry about this. I didn't have anywhere else to go."

"You don't need to apologize." A smirk rose at the corner of his mouth. "I don't know if it means much, but you can count on me."

Her expression softened and her shoulders relaxed. "Again, thank you."

"Anytime."

She ducked towards the door, needing an escape. It was too much, too fast. He seemed to realize it because Ward cut her off. "Let me check to make sure it's clear first."

After he deemed it safe, Felicity crossed the hall to her room. A long sigh passed her lips as she leaned against the closed door. It hurt to strip out of the attire that she hid until she would have a chance to deal with it properly. Now she needed sleep. After she cleaned the blood from her skin, she slipped into a long sleeve nightgown. It would be warm, but it would be worse if Meira happened to see the bandage on her arm in the morning. As soon as Felicity's head hit the pillow, she fell asleep.

Chapter
22

S he'd slept soundly and even rose a few hours late. No dreams or memories had jolted her awake. They may have been a mess still within her mind, but she appreciated the reprieve of a full night's rest. It wouldn't do her any good to miss tea—not with the guards out in full force looking for any suspicious activity. According to Meira, who took the chance to inform Felicity to be careful around the halls, the guards believed it was a male who had scaled the walls. Probably because they wouldn't want to admit that a female could escape them. Let their egos cloud their judgment—it only helped Felicity, after all.

Everyone was present at tea, and the upcoming celebration for the king's birthday was the main topic of conversation. While the females tittered about decor and the guest list, Felicity's head pulsed—her magic becoming a living thing within her, testing her resolve. Her arm was nearly healed, the muscle uncomfortable and bruised, but by tomorrow, she should be able to remove the stitches. She wouldn't have a choice but to train tonight, no matter how much she wanted to stay away from the prince. The thought of him had her magic spreading under her skin, and Felicity closed her eyes, willing a calmness.

"You had some luck with portions of the garden, it seems. Does that mean the king's birthday celebration will take place here? I bet the weather that evening will be divine." Lady Mistward fluttered her fan.

Why they still chose to sit out here, Felicity didn't understand. The ocean breeze helped keep the bugs at bay, but it was doing little for the thickening heat—the last bit of summer trying to take its hold. The stubborn females wouldn't budge though, no matter how quickly they fanned themselves or that warm tea was less than ideal. The benefit was the experience was shorter, so everyone could be inside before they passed out from the sun's heat.

"The weather may be wonderful, but unfortunately, I do not think we will be able to. By tonight the gardens will once again be a mess. That's not acceptable for our guests." Queen Marquette sighed. "The ballroom will be a beautiful alternative with the view of the sea."

Lady Grandeur nodded her agreement. "It will be wonderful no matter where it's held, Your Majesty. Your events are always the envy of all the realms."

Lady Chartow's fan sped up, her lips a thin line. Felicity was certain word was spreading about the abductions, but none spoke of them at tea, and she wasn't going to be the one to bring it up.

Tea ended shortly after. As everyone stood to head indoors, Queen Marquette brushed Felicity's arm. "Will you walk with me, Lady Dwauer?"

Her head pounded, but Felicity knew she couldn't deny the queen's request. "Of course, Majesty." The queen pulled Felicity's arm through the crook of hers.

Lady Fiadh tilted her head in their direction, but the queen waved her away. It would be just the two of them then. A sense of relief washed over Felicity but being within the queen's clutches didn't allow it to settle.

The queen steered Felicity away from the palace and deeper into the gardens. The growth became wilder here, the gardeners not even attempting to touch the vines and bushes that grew in haphazard antics. Thistles tore through shrubs, burrs poked out over the walkway. "You remind me a little of myself, my dear."

Felicity almost balked but kept a stoic grace in her step. "I do?"

The queen smiled. "Yes. My parents wielded the shadows—I was born and raised in Scáth. Have you ever been there?" When Felicity shook her head, the queen continued, "It is a primitive place where homes are built within the trees, and the people are considered more barbaric than *some* of their surrounding neighbors. All the same, my time there held some important lessons for me."

Although she nodded along, Felicity had no idea where the queen was going with this conversation.

"You see, when I was young, my parents were killed by members of Visce." Felicity knew the shadow and water realms were neighbors. The queen continued, "The faeries wanted to claim some of our land—cut down the trees and let their waters spread. I was left an orphan, a youngling without a family. Then, my magic hadn't fully developed, just a figment of what it is now. And just like you, I was thrown into a world unlike the one I had only ever known." She patted Felicity's hand. "And I know that this may feel that way right now. You play a part, are asked to fulfill what seems like an impossible task, and the way of life is unfamiliar."

The queen sat down on a bench and gestured for Felicity to do the same. "I went from being a part of a well-respected family to an orphan overnight. My people didn't know what to do with me. I was passed around from one family to the next, but mostly I slept on doorsteps or within tree branches. Until they forgot about me. I was abandoned and alone." She paused for a moment, and Felicity remained still, patient. Uncertain.

"Then there was another attack, I was abducted by a group of humans that wanted the veil torn open again. They spoke lies about the realms, spreading disdain and rumors about our rulers. You see the veil had been closed just a decade before and there was unrest with many of the humans gone. With the veil closed, that didn't stop the fact that our continent wasn't the same. Magic had shifted. The earth had changed. And I was sold to faerie and human rebels where I cleaned, did chores...was abused and tortured."

The queen took a deep breath, her attention on the plants. "You're sold from one job to the next. But know this, my dear girl—you're worth more than they may be willing to pay someday. King Roald found me after I slaughtered every member of the last family that would ever own me. My magic had finally developed and I showed them just how powerful I could be."

Felicity could understand the retribution the queen felt but the way she spoke of it, as though she enjoyed reliving their deaths, caused Felicity's stomach to churn.

Queen Marquette didn't seem to notice. "But I hadn't learned how to control it, and I drained myself. My sweet Roald took me in and showed me what strength and power could look like. When I returned to Scáth, I showed them what I could do in a way they'll never forget." Queen Marquette's tone steeled—the words clear and precise.

"What you're doing here, for our people, is giving them the knowledge that their royal family is strong and secure. I know my husband has asked of you what seems to be an impossible task, but I see a flicker of promise in you." She looked at Felicity from under her long lashes. "My husband needs you. Our people need you. The realms need you. Don't become someone easily forgotten."

She stood again, but Felicity stayed seated. The queen looked down at her. "I think you want to be remembered. Just like me."

As Felicity watched the queen walk away, a corner of her mouth piqued. The queen didn't understand her at all. Her entire purpose was to complete the mission—and make sure she was forgotten.

***

Felicity sat in the study, alone, except for the pile of books and a particularly large tome opened in front of her. The lights cast shadows around the room, enhanced by the dim sunlight from a cloudy afternoon. She pinched her eyes closed, trying to resist the pull of her magic.

At the sound of scraping on the floor, she twisted in the chair, dagger pointed at the intruder.

The bookcase against the wall was wedged open, and Ward peeked from the opening. "Want to explore some passageways?" A smirk played at the corner of his mouth. Part of her was still frustrated with him, even after he had saved her life last night. His over-protectiveness wasn't forgotten, nor that he hadn't stepped in on behalf of those being rounded up. But if she showed these feelings, she worried he would withhold this opportunity a little longer. If last night taught her anything—she needed these passages.

She sheathed the blade and met his gaze, her own narrowing at the speculation in his eyes.

"What? Don't blame me for being curious where you hide those." He gestured to her full skirts and bodice of pale blue. "Especially in all of that. I would think it would get lost."

"While I don't mind these skirts, they are a bit fuller than my usual taste. It's your kind that prefers the opulent number of layers and frill." She walked to the bookcase, touching the edges and feeling for the release mechanism. Just that morning, she had asked Meira for more pants, but the female had only puckered her lips and furrowed her brow. Felicity didn't know if that would mean she would receive what she requested or not.

"My kind? I'm a male of a simple mind. Wear what you want."

Too bad his opinion mattered little with the company she was meant to keep—the part she was to play. She scrunched up her nose as she ran a hand over the doorway, finding the mechanism within the wall.

He crossed his arms. "What are you doing?"

"Figuring out how it works." With a push of a latch, a book popped out a mere inch. "And now I know." She released the latch and analyzed the title.

"*The History of Locks.*" With a chuckle, she pushed the door closed and pulled on the book—with a faint click, the bookcase slid against the stone. "I assume only the royals know of these passageways?"

Ward shrugged. "Honestly, I don't think they do. I discovered them years ago and haven't shared them with anyone."

"So, I should feel special?" She cocked her head.

"You should." He walked into the darkness. "You coming or not?"

Of course she was.

They walked to a torch that Ward had waiting. He led her down one passageway to the next. The dank space smelled musty—the air stagnant. Except for the small flame, they were shrouded in darkness. Ward pointed out doorways he didn't dare open, but they snuck a peek into the ballroom, the entrance hidden behind a tapestry that hung near a sculpture of a past king. After showing her a few more locations, he led her to the doorway out of the palace grounds. This one veered off in two directions. The first led to the stable yard, but he took her down the one heading to the outskirts of the gardens that exited into a root cellar near the outer walls.

Once in the root cellar, he pointed to the floor where a rectangular grate was built into the ground. "That leads to the sewers. There is a pathway to walk along to keep out of the muck." He gave explicit instructions on how to get to a blacksmith's house. "No one lives there now and the road from the house leads to Koselig."

As they headed back through the passageways, Felicity created a map in her mind, and he peppered her with questions, testing her. After hours of exploring, he leaned against the wall, the door to his own chambers on the other side. "I blocked it with my armoire as soon as I found it. Since I don't know who else is aware, I felt it was safest."

He sat down, his back against the wall and the torch glowing in its holder above. Felicity sat down on the opposite wall, a healthy sweat cooling her skin. "Smart."

"The one to your room is also behind your armoire. I made sure it was covered."

There was a vague memory of the armoire being relocated after her new attire had arrived, but she had thought it had been due to Meira's preferences. "Why would you do that? When I first arrived, I thought you wanted me gone immediately."

He shrugged, leaning his head against the wall and closed his eyes. "You ask who I am, but like you, Felicity, there is a part of me missing." There was silence for a moment. One she felt the need to respect. "My name isn't Ward—as I assume you're aware. It is just a title that has become my name."

"But why?" She drew her legs up, wrapping her arms around her knees.

"The garden isn't the only thing cursed. I failed, and for my punishment, my name was taken from me and wiped from everyone's memory." He opened his eyes, concentrating on the dark ceiling.

"Then who were you? Not your name, but who were you?"

He sighed. "If I could answer, I would. It's strong and worsens with every year that passes."

"In other words, you can't answer that question." Felicity tried to think of anything else to manipulate the curse. "I feel—" Her mind went blank.

"Feel what?" Ward's jaw feathered.

Felicity shook her head. "I can't remember."

Ward leaned his head back again, his mouth a thin line. "For all that I have failed, maybe it's I who is the real curse to these lands."

She reached across and squeezing his hand. The touch felt instinctual. "I don't believe that. Neither should you. Every curse can be broken, and mistakes can be mended."

His gaze fell to her hand. She pulled back, uncomfortable. He cleared his throat. "How is your reading coming?" Just that morning he'd dropped off books to her room.

"Slow." It didn't make sense to lie, and by the distant look in his eyes, he needed a change of topic. "There is a lot of information to try to understand. I miss my old life and being kept in the dark."

He chuckled and a bit of the heaviness lifted. "It will only become more confusing. Have you started the history book I gave you? Might want to start there."

She remembered the thick spine with letters painted in gold against a leather cover. "No, but I will."

With a heavy sigh, Ward stood and brushed off his pants. "Come. It's getting late."

They headed back towards the way they came, and Ward had her lead to test what she remembered. With only a few mistakes, they made it to the study. She pulled on the latch beside the back end of the bookcase and the door popped open, a minuscule light visible. Inhaling to check for the scent of any individuals in the room, she pushed the bookcase open once she knew it was safe.

Before Ward left, he peered at her. "The prince has been at the training hall. I thought you should know that he's been waiting for you."

She bit the inside of her mouth, trying to dispel the rise of frustration. "Thank you."

"Be careful with him, Felicity." He dropped his gaze. "I know I've warned you before, but sometimes I feel he carries the biggest secrets within these walls."

Without waiting for her response, he left. Felicity considered his words and wondered what secrets Prince Alarian kept. But right now, he was the least of her concerns. Ward's confession had shaken her. The truth of his identity, who he was, was gone. She closed her eyes. King Roald had done this to Ward. Even if he hadn't said it directly, she knew it as fact. But why? What was he being punished for? After the conversation with the queen, Felicity knew which way she was leaning—what path she was being pulled towards. And it wasn't the easy one.

***

Felicity's body ached from her magic. After the events of the previous night, spying seemed like the worst possible choice as there was no doubt the guards would be on high alert, so she made her way to the training hall. As soon as she entered, she noticed the braziers were lit, their warmth spreading through the hall that removed the last of the evening ocean breeze from her skin.

"Took you long enough."

She spun around. The prince stood in the middle of the sawdust training ring in a location he hadn't been upon her entering. "How did you do that?"

He chuckled, then took a step into the shadows around the dim brazier light—and disappeared.

Shadows. He could travel in the shadows.

"You've never shown me what your magic could do," she breathed. Despite herself, she couldn't help to be in awe of the ability he showed.

When he appeared to her right, she whirled around to face him.

"I figured since you showed me yours, I'd show you mine." Prince Alarian strutted back towards the center of the ring. "Now you need to learn how to use your magic properly."

Felicity blinked in surprise as she took tentative steps in his direction. That he knew her secret was hard enough for her to grasp. "Why? I'm handling it just fine on my own."

"Because you never had formal training—or so I assume. Since I'm the only living being who knows of your magic, who else would train you?"

Crossing her arms, Felicity glared. "I don't want you to train me." She was mad at him, not intrigued by his magic. By him. He'd lost the chance to be those things when he didn't help those people. Yet, they had an agreement—and she was here for a reason.

Prince Alarian snorted. "That may be the case, but your magic needs to be used, and if the past few weeks have been any indication, you become ill when you hide it. Unless you choose to tell Ward your secret, I don't know who else you trust enough."

She attempted to ignore the fact he noticed when she was sick. That was a detail she wanted to remove from his mind. "What makes you think I trust you?"

He shrugged. "Fine—the blood oath then. Besides, I promised I would never tell a soul. I also brought you here. I feel a sense of obligation for your wellbeing and your success."

Her hands grew clammy.

Prince Alarian smiled. "First things first...drop and give me twenty."

Felicity cocked her head and narrowed her gaze.

"No? Not going to fall for that, I see." He snickered to himself and strutted closer, stopping in front of her. "All right then, let's see what you can do." Laying his hands out and his palms up, he gestured for her to do the same.

Hesitating, she stared at his palms and then stole a glance at her own hands. "That's not how it works. I need the pendant to reflect the light."

"I'm not asking you to do much. I saw you glow. I just want to see what control you have for now."

She didn't move, biting her bottom lip. Control wasn't her problem. If she didn't have it, then knowledge of her magic wouldn't still be hidden.

His brow furrowed. "I'll tell you a secret if you tell me one."

She snapped her mouth shut, and he chuckled. He nodded to his hands and Felicity laid hers above his, careful not to touch his skin, uncomfortable with him knowing hers were sweaty.

Alarian smiled. "Now draw the magic to the tips of your fingers. Let them warm and embrace the light, but don't try to burn me."

"I can only burn you if I use the pendant," she grumbled.

He ignored her tone. "Allow it to come to the surface and fill you. I'm curious about something." His shadows began to build, surrounding them as they brushed against her skin.

"What exactly?" She pursed her lips, her brow creasing. "I've done that many times—my light doesn't do much in this form."

"That's the point. I'm curious if you can use it in close range and how much authority you have over it without the pendant." He stood still, and she couldn't help but think he was aware that one wrong move would send her out the door. "I want you to allow your light to flow within you. Not just a portion of you, but your entire being."

She called her magic and it came willingly to her fingertips, as if it had been withheld by a dam and now flowed free.

"Slow—too fast and you can hurt yourself." Prince Alarian didn't flinch as beads of sweat formed at his temples. That's when she noted that his palms were singed. She pulled her hands away from his, the magic receding within. He didn't move, his own magic already beginning to heal the small burns she'd created.

"I didn't mean to." She hadn't done this with someone so close before. Hadn't realized that without the crystal she couldn't control the temperature—or was it him? "Are you sure about this?"

"You've never physically touched anyone with your magic, have you?" When she shook her head, his gaze met hers. "Don't worry. I'll tell you if you need to stop. I trust you, Felicity."

Another comment she chose to ignore. "I've never used it except to distract someone. That night with the highwaymen was the first time I've used it for something more." Or as far as she remembered anyway, but he didn't need to know that. "Just in case, I've always worn the pendant but have used it for nothing more than private training sessions and to dispel my magic." She glanced down at her palms, wondering what else she could do with practice. If she spent the time and attention on the power that was always a thought away.

"It must have taken a lot of time to gain the ability to keep such a secret for so long," he whispered.

Felicity stilled, frozen for a moment as a memory tickled, not coming to fruition. She shook her head, clearing her mind. "Secrets can be carried on a breeze."

"We're alone." His emerald eyes reflected the light of the braziers.

With a deep breath, she lifted her hands again and placed them over his. The magic spread slower this time, her own will fighting to dampen the light and warmth that came with it. This close to him, she remembered the feel of his hands on her hips as they danced. The way he'd laughed and smiled at her. She cleared her throat.

"Good, now let it spread from your arms and down into your torso and legs. Try to control the temperature as you do."

She nodded, attempting to ignore the way he made her mind wander and concentrated on the movement of her magic, feeling it inch up into her elbows and then towards her shoulders.

"While I might look like my father, my mother's magic is the strongest of my abilities. My father's magic is from Domhain."

She listened, concentrating on his calm voice.

"Not many know that I have little glimpses of his earth magic. Besides my parents and the trainer I had as a child—who is long dead—less than a handful have been trusted with its existence."

Her muscles tensed at his declaration.

"Healing is usually controlled by water, fire, and the earth realm. With my earth ability, I can heal myself."

"I didn't tell you a secret," she whispered.

His hands lowered slowly, and she looked up to meet his gaze again. "You already did." Prince Alarian's smile widened. "You're glowing, Felicity."

She looked at her hands and arms and could feel the magic to the tips of her toes. It wasn't like the small bursts of light she allowed within her room. Instead, she remained a beacon within the shadows. There wasn't heat now, just a light that had spread through her entire body.

"And you're exquisite."

The light vanished, sputtering to a stop and disintegrated into nothing at his words. Felicity dropped her arms to her side and stepped away, her gaze falling to the empty space between them.

Silence echoed through the room. She could sense his gaze, felt it penetrating her skin. The prince's shadows had wrapped around them, hiding them from view. With the expanding distance between them, his shadows dispersed into tendrils of mist. The memory of Koselig—her anger. She grasped for it.

"That's enough for today," he whispered. "Maybe tomorrow?"

Felicity cleared her throat. "Maybe."

His footsteps sounded as he walked away and halted near the door. "Ward."

She jerked her head up, the prince nodding to Ward as he entered.

Ward watched him leave before he stalked over to her. "What is going on between you two?" His jaw tightened as he came to a stop. "I've warned you to steer clear of him."

Her awe at her magic and discomfort with the prince's words vanished. "Stop treating me like a child." Her hands turned to fists at her side. "He was just helping with my training regimen." Or was that it? Felicity didn't trust the prince, but he knew her deepest secret.

Ward growled. "His only goal is to bed females considered impossible to get."

"I'm not a simpering female. Besides, why would you care if I bed him? Maybe I would be the one to initiate it." She didn't mean it, of course. As she stomped past him, her shoulder rammed into his. She stopped at the door. "Or maybe I don't want anything to do with you stupid males and your bullshit."

She slammed the door, and the walls rattled.

Chapter 23

The ballroom was decorated in ivory, sparkling gold, and a shimmering pale blue for the king's birthday celebration. Although the garden had been deemed a lost cause, the doors were opened for guests to enjoy the patio area and fountain with fragrant flowers floating on the surface of the water.

Felicity was in no mood to be here. Her history readings of the land were more intriguing and eye-opening than she had been prepared for. Late into the previous night, she had found herself still awake, skimming through stories of past leaders and realm dynamics.

The realms had once all been separate, led by their own governing leader. Depending on the realm, the ruler was either named by birthright—such as in the light realm, an individual who fought their way to the position—Domhain, or elected—Saol. When there was an attack from an outside continent, the realms were brought together under one banner to fight for their freedom.

They all turned to the queen of the light realm to lead, and she created rule and order among their armies. She had done so with such bravery and strength that the others exalted her name, and she had been crowned queen over the eight realms. After their enemies were vanquished, the queen ruled for another twenty years before she died, and the role was handed to her son, King Bastien.

That was where Felicity had left off, her eyes drifting to sleep, the words blurry when she had finally put the book aside.

Now she was dressed in an elegant gown of dark shimmery silver that clung to her body. The original long-sleeve lace overlay had itched profusely, so Meira assisted with shucking it off once Felicity's annoyance had gotten through the female's stubborn ears. The handmaiden had muttered curses about fashion and respecting good clothing as she left the room.

When she returned a few minutes later, Felicity allowed Meira to do as she wished with her hair and cosmetics to pacify the handmaiden. Thankfully, it had been deemed enough of an apology. Felicity didn't regret the decision since Meira had outdone herself. Her hair now cascaded in loose curls, covering her exposed back where the dress slipped low to her waist. Kohl rimmed her eyes with a dramatic air.

Upon entering the ballroom, Felicity bowed to King Roald and Queen Marquette before moving through the crowd, her eyes on the guests. The ballroom's tall white stone ceilings had arcs curving from each corner of the room to meet at the center point of the domed ceiling where an extravagant chandelier double the size of the one in the throne room hung. Pearls, diamonds, and crystals dangled from it, and the prisms cast shimmering light around the room.

Felicity inspected the statue in front of the tapestry that hid the passageway. It was of a regal fae, standing tall with a crown upon his head. On the opposite side of the ballroom was another statue of a female fae with a similar crown.

"You know, many of these males would like to ask you to dance." Lady Solfire stopped beside Felicity. "Have you considered relaxing a bit? I think they fear you might bite their heads off."

As it should be. "I'm quite content not dancing, thank you."

They hadn't spoken beyond pleasantries since that evening in town. At tea, Koselig's attack was never brought up. Felicity had wondered if anyone knew about the whereabouts of the abducted townsfolk—of the children now living on the streets, starving, uncertain where to go and who would care for them. The truth of how lucky she had been to have a roof over her head wasn't lost on her.

"When you danced the other night, I believe that was the most relaxed I'd ever seen you." Lady Solfire folded her hands in front of her. She looked elegant in her full skirt and bodice of ivory and gold. She was one of many who had planned her outfit around the décor.

With a step closer, her voice lowered and she glanced around before meeting Felicity's gaze. "I don't like what happened either. But what are we to do? We are mere females waiting for the right male to ask for our hand. And we just hope it's a good one."

Her tone was thick with sarcasm. She stepped back. "Enjoy your evening, Lady Dwauer."

Felicity grasped her hand, stopping Lady Solfire in her tracks. "Call me Felicity."

She smiled over her shoulder. "Then you must call me Avyanna."

And Felicity knew that, if anything, she had found a kindred spirit. One smart enough to keep her mouth shut.

She continued her rounds, listening in on other conversations as she did. Guests from other realms were present, but the dignitaries and high-ranking officials didn't speak a word of attacks or difficulties within their realms. Most kept the discussion light, dodging such subjects, but the reason as to why could vary from ignorance and avoidance to uncertainty within their current surroundings.

"Lady Dwauer?"

A familiar voice came from behind. Felicity's back stiffened.

"Is that you?" Lady Molyle moved around the pillar, her smile enveloping her entire face. "It is you!" she squealed as she reached for Felicity's hand. "I have thought of you often and wondered whether you remained within the realms or headed home."

Felicity fought the urge to nibble at her lip. "Lady Molyle, what a pleasant surprise. I hadn't expected to see you here."

"This is the place for everyone to be, is it not?" The female brushed a pearlescent finger along Felicity's arm. "How lucky we are to see each other again."

"Who is your friend?" Lady Fiadh seemed to have appeared from thin air.

Felicity's chin rose slightly. "Lady Fiadh, this is Lady Molyle. We had a brief meeting earlier this summer."

"Yes, when poor Advisor Boister met his end. I wonder if anyone has ever found that server who killed him?" Lady Molyle inched a bit closer to Felicity.

With a shake of her head, Felicity frowned. "It seems they escaped."

Lady Fiadh cocked her head, her long neck elongating like a serpent as she shot a glance in Felicity's direction. "I heard of the advisor's unfortunate demise. It was a painful loss for Domhain. I know the king was quite displeased."

The way Lady Fiadh spoke, Felicity believed that her words were true regarding the king's feelings. But if that was the case, why would he have targeted the advisor? Unless Lady Fiadh was good at playing this game—which Felicity didn't doubt.

Lady Fiadh raised an eyebrow. "Tell me, what did happen to the advisor? I have only heard hearsay. It never seemed polite to bring it up, but since we're on the subject..."

Before Felicity could respond, Lady Molyle began a long tirade of the entire evening. The story must have been well practiced as she even described some of the guest's dresses and quoted other attendees about Felicity and the advisor's short love affair. From the way she spoke of the evening, Felicity had become a widow who had lost the love of her life.

"But how did the advisor get poisoned?" Lady Fiadh had hung onto every word, her eyes in rapt attention while her tone remained bored and separate.

"It was in his drink." Lady Molyle shook her head. "But poor Lady Dwauer. She and I both were caught up with our introduction to each other. Neither of us noticed who did it. Someone even tried to blame her but directly after, they discovered a server had disappeared." Lady Molyle snapped open her fan and fluttered it in her face to cool the heat rising in her cheeks.

"Interesting." Lady Fiadh's mouth pursed as she regarded Felicity from the corner of her eye. "I wonder how the server knew which glass the advisor would receive."

Felicity opened her mouth to respond but Lady Molyle interrupted. "I wouldn't know. That heathen must have either been lucky or well-trained. I couldn't even imagine what was going through their mind." Lady Molyle's fan sped up.

Felicity's brow knotted together as she nodded in agreement. "It was such a traumatic ordeal. I cannot believe it happened. It was all so fast."

This conversation was dangerous. The way Lady Fiadh's beady eyes seemed to hover over Felicity made her feel that every one of her completed missions was on display to be critiqued for flaws.

Lady Molyle wrapped her arm through the crook of Felicity's. "It was wonderful to meet you, Lady Fiadh, but would you please excuse us? I want desperately to catch up with Lady Dwauer." She steered Felicity away, and although she yearned to keep her distance from Lady Fiadh, it wasn't any safer beside Lady Molyle.

"That was odd. She wanted so many specifics. What a dark subject for a lady." Lady Molyle led her around the edge of the room. "Now, where have you been all this time?"

Felicity gave her best smile and patted the female's hand. "Here, actually. After all that took place, the prince asked me to be his guest. He didn't want my experience on the mainland to be about death."

Lady Molyle's mouth widened in surprise as she closed her fan and pointed it at Felicity accusingly. "Are you the one the courtiers are whispering about? It's the gossip through all the realms—the female who stole the prince's heart."

"I don't know about that..." Felicity feigned a blush.

"Oh! You are, aren't you? Everyone is bursting at the seams, saying that he has never spent this much time with one female before." Lady Molyle rested her hand on Felicity's. "You must tell me everything." She leaned in closer. "But be careful with that one. He's been known to have females on the side. A friend of mine fell hard—unfortunately, one of her other close friends did as well. He didn't mind the drama that unfolded when they found out about each other."

As though he knew he was being spoken about, Prince Alarian intercepted their path. "Lady Molyle, it's been a while."

The female stopped short, her eyes widening. Even with the warning, Felicity noticed the flush that crept up Lady Molyle's neck and rose to her cheeks. "Oh yes, it has. Hello." She dipped into a staggered curtsy and flung her fan over her face as she rose.

The prince's mouth quirked, and he turned his gaze towards Felicity. "If you don't mind, I've been looking for this one the whole evening. I had hoped she wasn't eluding me on purpose, but I see she is catching up with an acquaintance."

Lady Molyle's grip tightened on Felicity's arm. Felicity wasn't certain which of them was the least of the two evils, but it wasn't a choice she could make. She had to deal with the prince. They had an agreement.

"And what can I do for you, Prince Alarian?" She made sure to add a hint of mock curiosity in her voice.

With a chuckle, he stuffed his hands in his pockets. "I was hoping for a dance but would even accept a walk through the garden."

Lady Molyle's shoulders slumped, and Felicity almost felt sorry for the female. Maybe she should introduce her to someone so she wouldn't be alone. Yet, Felicity was certain she would be fine on her own. If her ability to tell a story could intrigue the indifferent Lady Fiadh, the female would have no trouble finding another interested party to listen to the tales she could weave.

Lady Molyle dropped her hold of Felicity's arm. "Of course, Your Highness. Lady Dwauer, I will hopefully see you later this evening."

Queen Marquette walked by then, causing Lady Molyle to dip into a low curtsy. The queen didn't pay them any attention as she began introducing Lady Fiadh to a group of delegates. Lady Fiadh kept a vacant expression, her gaze seeming to see right through each individual. Felicity needed to keep a closer eye on her. At that same moment, Lady Fiadh shot a glance in their direction before it was redirected to the delegates. A more important reminder to watch her thoughts.

Prince Alarian held out the crook of his arm. With a long sigh, Felicity took it. Once they were out of earshot, she leaned closer to the prince. "I'm over this. Just escort me towards the door and get me out of here." If anything, it would be the perfect excuse to slip out of these clothes and spy on the guests from afar.

He leaned in and whispered into her ear. "If you're serious…I can arrange that."

"Seize her." The queen's roar caused every guest to come to a standstill as the music stopped with an abrupt twang.

The queen stood on the dais beside her husband, a thin finger pointed directly towards the center of the ballroom. The king gestured to his guards who rushed forward. Felicity released the prince's arm to give herself a clear view as others started to search the crowd for the interruption's culprit.

A pixie—fluorescent wings vibrating against her pale purple back—launched upward into the air. Her thin body and short height had made her almost inconspicuous.

Before the pixie could reach a safe height, a guard jumped and grabbed her ankle, forcing her to the ground. The pixie searched the crowd, pleading loud enough for all to hear. "Please. Help me."

Another guard pinned her wings to her arms, and they carried her from the room. "Help…" echoed as the doors shut behind them.

Bile coated Felicity's throat as anger pulsed against her skin. The music started again. The crowd began to drink and dance as before. Even those who had just been speaking to the pixie closed their circle and continued their conversation as if she had never been there.

Felicity looked back at the prince. His expression was unreadable in response to her accusatory glare. With a deep swallow, he broke the stare first. She took another step away from him.

The bells tolled the hour as her anger became a living thing. Before she could react, a boom echoed and the walls rattled as the guests screamed.

Chapter 24

Another crash reverberated against the far wall, and the room shook from the impact, her arms flinging outwards, others grasping neighbors or furniture to remain upright.

Guests crouched down and clutched each other in fear. Felicity was one of the few who remained standing, searching over the heads of the guests. Lady Chartow clutched her husband's arm. The pair were huddled together near the outskirts of the crowd along with Lady Mistward. Knowing where her first target was, Felicity looked for him but didn't find the second one within the crowd. No whisp of dark hair to prove his innocence or that her suspicions were incorrect. Her jaw clenched—she hoped she was wrong. She didn't know what she would do otherwise. In the meantime, she inched her way closer to the king and queen.

The king stood when the castle stilled. "Guards, go."

The soldiers fell into line. All released swords from scabbards and half of them stormed out the doors. A few surrounded the king and queen, while the remaining spread around the room guarding windows and entryways.

"Where is our son?" Queen Marquette searched the crowd but there wasn't a hint of concern in her voice.

"Here, Mother." Prince Alarian made his way towards them, stopping at the bottom step of the dais.

King Roald pointed towards the door. "You know what you're to do. Serve us well."

"Of course, Father." Prince Alarian faced Felicity again. With a heavy breath, he stepped into a nearby shadow and disappeared.

Felicity diverted her attention towards the king and queen, heat simmering under her skin.

Another boom and dust broke free from the ceiling and pillars, falling upon the guests cowering with wide eyes. Some whimpered, others cried, but many looked to their king in fear. A few stood, ready to run for the door, but the king's booming voice halted them in their tracks.

"Stay here. We're safe." He met Felicity's gaze, his eyes narrow slits.

She knew the unspoken order and slipped out a side door at the next bang, running towards the hall to her room. Her daggers warmed in the sheaths strapped to her legs, but the dress didn't allow for easy access or for pants to be worn underneath. When she reached her room, she threw open her trunk and pulled out what she needed. Screams from the staff splintered the silence when another impact caused the castle walls to shudder.

Felicity cursed under her breath.

Once she was dressed in the proper attire, Felicity pushed the armoire aside, muscles aching from the strain. Her fae strength opened it enough for her to slide through the hidden doorway. There was no torch, only darkness. She placed the pendant in her hand, called a flicker of her magic to light her arm, and concentrated on keeping it within her palm as she ventured deeper within the passages.

Part of her hoped she was wrong. That she wouldn't find what she expected. But the newly awakened part of her, the one that witnessed the faerie arrested with no explanation, wished she would.

After many turns, a scrape of steel and a whiff of a familiar scent—citrus—Felicity extinguished her light. Out of habit, her dagger slid into her palm. Felicity turned the corner and stopped short. A figure stood two steps ahead. The point of her dagger was at the back of Ward's neck before he had time to react.

"What are you doing?"

Wind rushed around him, his torch went from flame to embers. He took a step forward and turned slowly, his eyes widened, and his jaw flickered. "Felicity?" The gust immediately stopped.

A small gasp sounded down the passageway and Felicity was certain pixie wings disappeared around the corner.

On instinct, she swung her leg out, knocking Ward's feet out from under him. Pressing a knee to his chest, she held the dagger to his throat. A spot of blood pooled under the steel. In the darkness, the torch lying on the ground beside him glowed before it dimmed again. She could barely make out Ward's face.

He cleared his throat. "I was checking the passageways."

"You let her go. The pixie?" She kept the dagger at his throat. Her magic crawled to the tips of her fingers, ready to be used.

He raised his head but didn't speak.

She only released a minute amount of pressure. "You're a part of the rebellion. I already know, so you might as well admit it."

His chest rose and fell, and she could hear the thump of his heart. Or was that hers?

He stilled. "I am. But this wasn't me." Ward's chin rose slightly, giving her better access to his throat. "Not the attack anyway. As for her, I couldn't allow another to be used." He met her gaze, his eyes sharp in the darkness.

She'd anticipated this. But his admission still pierced her chest.

"What are you going to do with that information, Felicity?" He swallowed, his throat bobbing. "I saw your reaction to what happened in Koselig. Do you know what they are doing to them?"

"He imprisoned them." She drew the blade back a little, keeping it at the ready. Her body thrummed, heat rushing up her back into her neck.

His eyes widened. "You knew? But then that means you have a name, doesn't it?"

She nodded. "Yes, I have a name. Now I have two." The passageway was getting smaller, the walls crowding in on her.

"But you didn't turn the other in." Ward regarded her as he leaned upon his forearm, nearing the blade she held at the ready. "You can't decide, can you? If you should do your duty or follow your gut?"

"I have a job." She pricked the knife into his skin. "And I have never failed a mission."

"I don't blame you for turning me in—it will save your own neck. Let the other one free and give my name instead." His jaw tightened. "Take me to Roald."

She grabbed his withheld arm and with a twist, turned and forced him facedown into the stone. "You would do that?"

Her muscles ached as her magic pulsed. She shuddered—now wasn't the time to lose control. A scream clawed at her throat as the walls pressed against her, darkness creeping in.

She should take him in. It was the easiest choice. He'd given himself up.

It was her mission.

A calmness came over Ward, present in his voice and the way his body relaxed. "For the cause and to save you? Yes."

The sound of her dagger clattering on the floor reverberated in her ears. Felicity released her hold as she slumped against the wall. The words—his words an undoing. Her entire body shook as she gasped for air. With each ragged rise and fall of her chest, a sob built, but she fought it and pushed it away as her lungs raged for breath.

"Felicity." Ward crawled across the space. "Put your head between your legs." He tried to position her as her body fought for control—from him and from her. With some work, Ward maneuvered and pressed her head between her knees, rubbing her back in slow circles.

"Breathe in." His voice pulsed against her temples. "Breathe out."

She gasped for another breath, the world caving in.

"Breathe in, Felicity. Do it with me," he ordered.

She concentrated on his words, trying to do as he said. Just like she had when they had been at the study. When Harrison had told her she couldn't return home. A new wave of panic rushed to the surface.

"Breathe out, Felicity," Ward ordered.

She pinched her eyes shut as memories flooded over her.

The first time she had alcohol and felt the regret of a hangover. Her first kiss with Harrison. The first time she had climbed the Tower's wall to the window ledge outside her room.

Everything ached. Everything felt like it was crashing down around her.

"Remember to count," Ward called to her. "One and breathe."

Running through a field, sunlight illuminating her skin. The Countess sitting in the meeting room. Harrison standing by her side. A flash of light followed by a scream.

Her throat stung with each breath, but the memories slowed.

"Two and breathe." Ward's voice grew louder.

The faceless boy's echoing laughter in a field of tall grass.

"Three and breathe."

The memories dissipated. The smell of the dank passageway returned. Her body shuddered, but Ward's hand on her back continued to move in those damn circles.

"Four and breathe."

She began to relax under his touch. Felicity breathed in with each of his inhales and did the same as he breathed out, the pain slowly dissipating from her chest.

"I can't." She shook her head, inhaling the last breath as he counted to ten. "I can't take you in."

Ward slumped against the wall beside her, his own breathing labored. "I'm sorry. Sorry to make you choose."

"No." With a shake of her head, she was slow to rise, her muscles and limbs heavy, and then faced him. "I needed to decide. I knew what was right, but it went against everything I've been taught to believe and trust." Felicity stared at the corner where the wall met the ceiling. "I can't turn you in. But I don't know what to do."

Ward's gaze rested on her, she could sense it, but she didn't turn to him.

He sighed. "There is one thing. But it will be tricky." Ward moved around until he stood in front of her. "I meant it. I didn't plan this attack, but I had to free her—to give the pixie a chance. I also came to check if anyone was in the passageways but I found no one. I think it was only a warning. The rebels are getting restless." He shook his head. "From the beginning, because of my status within the palace, I've told the rebels I'll only divulge the information they *need*, but I never wanted to know a thing. There are ways for the king to uncover the truth, and I didn't want him to use such magic against me and ruin their entire operation."

Felicity ran her hand over her face. "Then who orchestrated this attack?"

He reached over and picked up her dagger. "I've been told there are other contacts within the castle." Ward's gaze sliced towards her as he handed her the blade. "But we want to steer the king away from the rebels as much as we can. We need to protect the other name you hold."

"Then what do you propose?" They started back down the darkened passageway. As much as she wanted to share her own secret with Ward, Felicity couldn't bring herself to do so and left her magic unused. He had said so himself—he could be a danger with such knowledge. She leaned over and picked up the torch. It was barely lit, not enough to do more than ensure they didn't run into a wall.

Ward created a small breeze with a twist of his pointer finger and the embers flickered. With another gentler brush of wind, it sparked back to life. Since her hands were still shaking, Felicity handed him the torch.

"I can feed you names. There are some influential supporters the king has little interest in beyond their resources and most of them are vile in their own right. They are weak points with strong backings. If we work it properly, we can take away the king's strength and some of his advisors. We just need to find something that makes them appear guilty within the king's eyes. He has a short temper. We should use that to our benefit."

Felicity nodded. "Give me the list and during the next few days, I'll see what I can put together."

"If you are running short on time, turn me in. The king won't kill me. If he controls his temper, he'll just throw me into prison."

She eyed him from the darkness. "That will be the last resort."

Ward sighed a breath of what Felicity had to believe was relief. "Deal."

"I need to walk the grounds. I don't want to return too soon." Felicity veered towards the exit that led to an underground door near their side of the palace walls.

Ward nodded. "I'll join you."

Once finished, no rebels in sight, Felicity slipped back into her room unseen before pushing the armoire into place. With a quick change, she stuffed her garb back into the trunk, locked it, and put on the dress. After a quick glance in the mirror to fix her cosmetics, she ran back into the hall where Ward met her. He'd changed his tunic and cleaned up the nick at his neck. The attack had stopped, forcing the celebration to an end. When they reached the main foyer, the guests were trickling out of the ballroom into the hall.

Felicity and Ward slipped in with the others undetected due to the hubbub of activity.

Prince Alarian pushed through the crowd. "Everything all right?" His gaze darted between the two of them, his face an unpleasant scowl. It was an expression Felicity never remembered seeing on his face before. His pants were dusty, and a twig stuck to the hem of his shirt. He must have been with the guards.

"We went to search for anything amiss within the halls and grounds," Ward whispered. "I assume no one got in here?"

The prince's jaw feathered. "No, I returned a moment ago. They were quick with their attack. By the time I reached beyond the wall,

the rebels were already fleeing. It seems to have been a warning."
He turned his attention towards Felicity. "Anything to report?"

She shook her head. "The guards were searching the grounds, so I stayed near the wall. I agree that they didn't want to enter—just to send a message."

Prince Alarian sighed and ran a hand through his hair. "At least everyone is safe."

"What is happening here?" Felicity looked over the crowd as families clustered together, and many held others in comforting embraces.

"They're frightened. Once the guards complete their rounds, they will escort guests to quarters for the night." Prince Alarian gave a worried glance at the space between her and Ward.

Avyanna broke free from the crowd and almost fell into Ward. "Oh, sorry." Her eyes widened as recognition settled. She gripped Felicity's arm but spoke to Ward. "Here you are. I was worried about you both."

"Must have gotten lost in the crowd with everything happening." Felicity inhaled as a deep shudder ran along her spine. Lady Solfire's grip tightened and Prince Alarian fought off a smirk.

The female reached for Ward's hand. He took it instinctively, eyes widening when he realized. He gently tried to release it, but Lady Solfire didn't allow him a chance to reconsider. "Would you escort me to my room, please?"

Ward nodded, then tucked her arm into his and led her away as he spoke reassuring words in a low tone. Lady Solfire seemed to be hanging on every word and by the smirk she gave Felicity as the two disappeared, this was all a part of her own game.

Felicity was impressed.

Prince Alarian held out an arm for her and with a hesitant sigh, she took it.

"I'm sorry," he whispered.

She sliced a look his way. "For?"

He leaned in, his lips close to her ear. Felicity softened her expression for those watching, playing her part as the simpering lady. His breath warmed her skin, and the hair on her neck rose in response. "The pixie."

Felicity's toes curled as her anger rose. It seemed ridiculous to have both reactions at the same time.

Everything in her wanted to push him away. At least, that's what she told herself. Felicity batted her eyelashes and smiled. "Think nothing of it."

A blush rose to her cheeks when he leaned away. She definitely didn't want to consider how much of her body's reaction to his proximity was a part of her act. And how much was not. She hated that she had to smile at him, blush at his words, and act as if there was something between them. When, in reality, she just wanted to beat him to the ground for standing by as his parents tormented others. There was no reason for her to feel anything but frustration in his presence.

When they arrived at her quarters, Prince Alarian stopped at the door. "Goodnight, Lady Dwauer."

He released her arm and gave her a short bow.

"Thank you for escorting me to my room." She curtsied as a couple passed, both fae watching them from the corner of their eyes as they continued down the hall.

The prince walked in the opposite direction, away from the direction they had come. Felicity closed the door and leaned against it.

The only reason she was doing this was because of the blood oath. No other reason. That had to be why her heart hammered within her chest. Why she missed his scent. There was no other rationality to yearn for his touch.

***

She smelled like a garden of roses. Felicity nuzzled into the female's neck, her small frame held tight in their grasp. Felicity was slowing her down. No matter how fast she ran, those after them would catch up. Their pursuers were on horseback, and they weren't carrying a load. With a whimper, Felicity wiggled, trying to break free from her hold.

"No, my darling. Be still."

The female's long legs lengthened their stride. She darted from the brush and spared a glance behind her, lights dotting the distance. For days they had stayed ahead. They had thought they had made it. But they had been wrong.

The female gulped a breath of air and ran faster. They were nearing a road, visible from where Felicity peeked out from under the female's arm. A metallic sting hit her nose and Felicity looked at the lace of her sleeve, stained pink from an unknown injury.

She stifled a sob. "Momma."

"Shhhh, my Light." She kissed the top of her daughter's head as they came to a fork in the road and stopped, searching in each direction. To the right, a building rose in the distance, a few lights illuminating stained windows. She broke into a run, veering off the road but heading towards the tower. Grass tickled Felicity's legs. Citrus-scented flowers fell from branches that grabbed at their clothes. The tears streamed down the young girl's face as she heard the distant sound of a horse's snort. They weren't on them yet. Maybe they had a chance.

They were almost there.

Her mother tripped with a grunt. Felicity slipped from her grasp, rolling in dirt and grass.

Her head hit something hard. And it all went black.

Chapter
25

The dream left Felicity drained. Or was it a memory? Again, it was hard to be sure since it had come while she had been sleeping. She perked up when she found a letter slipped under her door with four names and an arrow pointing to the one at the top. Lord Marthlow, a delegate from Tine, who she remembered meeting at the summer celebration in Aer. He had proved to have a little brain and a big mouth—a helpful combination. After her studies, Felicity knew the Fire Realm was the largest resource of coal, and in turn, diamonds. Most jewelry came from their horologists. They also forged many of the weapons that armed the royal soldiers. A dangerous asset to lose.

And the perfect target to hurt the king's standing with the realm. Even more helpful, Marthlow was staying in a manor on the outskirts of the palace walls. After sitting at tea under Lady Fiadh's critical gaze and a dinner that had her sensing the king's glare on more than one occasion, she was ready to stretch her legs and get outside. Two days. That's all she had left to prove her worth in the king's eyes. To turn in a name.

Felicity took the passageway and exited at the old hut Ward had mentioned once belonged to the blacksmith. Her breath misted in the cool night, heartbeat steady as she stuck to the shadows, following the wall in the direction of the lord's manor. It didn't take her long to reach the outer gate and slip through an opening.

Upkeep was kept to a minimum. Long vines and old barrels littered the side of a pebble walkway. It looked like the manor had been in disarray for some time. Darkness enveloped the home, except for a dim light that flickered from the back corner of the house.

Staying low, she traipsed through the grass, the ends of the stalks brushing against her skin. Once Felicity reached the walls of the manor, she edged towards the light and settled herself under the window. With a deep inhale, she slid slowly until just her eyes peeked over the windowsill.

The fae lord was sitting, swirling his glass of wine, eyeing a woman dusting the knickknacks along the mantle. His mouth was moving but Felicity couldn't understand a word. Trusting herself to read his lips was too far-fetched an idea. Not if she wanted to ensure his condemnation.

She stepped back and searched the side of the stone building. With luck, a window was open above. She needed to be wary of others in the home as she searched for a way to climb up. Felicity stretched out her arms, loosening her muscles, and began the climb. Her biceps strained as she found handholds and ledges to put her feet. Peering inside, the room was dark but held no scent of occupants.

Carefully, she pushed the window up enough to fit through. It creaked and she froze, listening for any indication that the two below had heard. Once she entered, Felicity walked on tiptoe to the door and down the hall. Reaching the top of the stairs, their words became more distinct. By the time she reached the first landing, she could see and hear the two of them perfectly.

Lord Marthlow was no longer sitting. He stood behind the woman, his hands resting on her hips as she reached up to dust a bust on a pedestal in the corner of the room. The glass of wine was left abandoned on the table beside the sofa. "You know I would've taken you if I could have."

The woman harumphed. "Don't give me excuses." The shoulder of her white ruffled top slid down her arm, revealing pale skin. The male behind her pressed his lips to her exposed neck. She kept dusting, ignoring him. "I missed all the excitement. I heard there was an attack and everything. While you were out dancing and consorting with who knows what, I was here."

The lord twisted her around to face him. "You missed nothing. The attack was minimal with the might of the king's army at its back and his son at its front."

This didn't sound good for Felicity. She needed something to pin on him, and an affair with his maid wouldn't be enough.

"What did the king do? Did he stay with his people or rush to defend them?" The way she spoke the words, a hint of seduction in her voice, the corner of Felicity's mouth lifted into a smirk. Maybe there was something here after all.

"He stayed with his people. The ballroom was well protected." The lord pressed her against the wall, unsettling the pedestal. He stilled it with one hand while the other braced his body mere inches from hers. "The rebels didn't stand a chance." A huskiness entered his voice.

"Where did the soldiers head first?" She arched her back, pressing her body into him and he growled.

"The grounds. To check the wall." He nipped her neck. "But enough of this talk."

"And the prince, where did he go?" The woman ground her body into his.

"I don't know. He disappeared. I don't want to talk about him." Marthlow lifted her, her legs wrapping around him. His hair ignited into a darker shade of red, wisps of flames along the tendrils left a trail of smoke. He ripped her blouse, exposing her breasts as he dipped his mouth to her nipple, and began to carry her towards the stairs. By then, Felicity had heard and *seen* enough. She tiptoed back towards the room and slipped through the window, not bothering to lower it much since she doubted they would notice the few extra inches it was open.

Felicity lowered herself from the window ledge and began the climb down. Marthlow wasn't guilty in the technical sense, but he was inadvertently feeding information to what she could only assume was a rebel spy. And if she could spin it just right, it would be enough to convict a lord.

When she returned to the palace grounds Felicity headed straight to the training hall to release some of the feelings bottled within. It was strange how her emotions were harder to expel and ignore now that her memories were returning and no matter how much she tried to concentrate on her anger and use it, other sensations came through. Sadness. Disappointment. Loneliness. All of it was confusing and made it all the more daunting to keep her priorities straight.

When she entered, she found one of the reasons for her turbulent emotions sitting on the bench, leaning against the pole in the center with his head propped up toward the sky through the opening. Prince Alarian didn't look her way. "Busy night? You're later than usual."

"Had something to do." Her jaw twitched and her magic pulsed. He was the enemy. Felicity had made her choice on whose side she was on, and it wasn't his. "Where's Ward?"

"I sent him back to the castle." Prince Alarian rose from his seat and stuffed his hands in his pockets. His usually styled hair hung lazily over his brow. "I think we need to talk."

"That's not why I come here." She wished he would leave. But mostly, she wanted to let out her suppressed aggression and she grasped hold of the familiarity of it.

Felicity brushed past him towards the ring of sawdust and sand. Instead of arming herself with her daggers, she loosened the straps to the different holsters and dropped them on the side of the ring. "If you want to make yourself useful, then do so or get out. But I came to train, not talk."

The prince eyed the pile of weapons and breathed a deep sigh. "Are you sure about this?"

"Rules." She ignored his question. "No magic and no weapons."

"Where is the fun in that?" He grinned, but she didn't return it.

With a tentative step, Alarian dropped his weapons beside hers, then removed a few more blades—one from his boot that she hadn't noted before—alongside it. She remembered Ward's warning about the secrets he believed the prince kept. But now wasn't the time to try to unravel all that this male was. Not when he was the vein feeding so much of her anger.

He rolled back his shoulders and entered the ring. "If this is what you need, then I'll oblige you."

With a smirk, she settled into a fighting stance, her arms held up at the ready. "It is."

She attacked without warning. Her fist met his chin, but he dodged her next move—a left hook aimed for his opposite cheek.

She sent a high kick to his gut, too fast for him to block, and he stumbled a few steps back. "Come on. Or are you nothing without your magic?" she taunted, letting her anger consume her. It needed an outlet.

He blocked her next punch and pivoted on his heel before her knee went for his gut. Instead, it connected with his hip. Her leg quaked at the impact, and she stepped back, catching her footing and testing its tolerance. A bruised bone—nothing more.

But he didn't come at her. He stood waiting, his expression placid, and her anger exploded. She lunged forward, a fury of fists and legs, and he blocked or dodged each, few connecting with her actual target. Her heart raced, sweat dripping from every pore. Stepping back, she inhaled a deep breath. She shouldn't be tired this fast.

A few bruises bloomed purple on the prince's arms and face, but most had already begun to heal.

"Why won't you fight me?" she growled and lifted her fists again in the ready stance.

His shoulders drew back. "Because I deserve it."

"Fight back." It came out more order than request.

"Why?" It was a simple question with a much too complicated answer.

Her magic swelled to life, her body overcome as it pulsed from her feet to the top of her head. She had never felt free—capable of what she was meant to be. Fae, but most importantly, herself.

Alarian pinched his eyes shut and his shadows expanded, surrounding them—to hide her magic from outside view. At that act, that offer of protection, her magic sputtered, flickering. But he didn't react. Even if she was a blinding light. And she hated the weakness. Hated that she reacted to his protection as her anger beckoned for more. *Use the anger...*

"My father and mother want to rule over all with an iron fist—be the most prominent figures within the entire continent. Any other sign of power is considered something to destroy. If only they knew the truth." He breathed a heavy sigh. "That so much power can come from the unexpected."

Her magic extinguished, her light gone, and she crumbled to the floor. She grasped at sand and sawdust, her hands tightening into fists. One hit after the other, she beat the ground. A roar, one she didn't recognize, tore at her throat as she lifted her head and bellowed.

Prince Alarian bent down in front of her, and she dropped the sawdust held in her grasp and hit his chest. Not hard, the fight leaving her. He pulled her close as her breathing became ragged, sweat mixed with the dust coating her skin.

"Why?" Her voice was haggard against his chest. "Why don't you stop them?"

"What does anyone expect me to do?" he whispered.

She shuddered in his arms, then stilled. What was it she wanted from him? He had made it perfectly clear what type of male he was. No one expected more from him, and she shouldn't either. But she let him hold her, her arms dangling at her side.

"When was the last time you lost control like that? Really raged." He brushed her hair behind her shoulder with one hand while the other held tight.

She blinked. "I don't remember." And that was the truth.

Slow and deliberate, he leaned back and looked at her. "It's surprising you didn't drain. That was a lot of magic."

"Drain?" She heard the word before but never asked its meaning.

"It can happen when you use too much too fast. If you call your magic, let it grow before using it, then it doesn't happen. But, if you just force it out, then it can make you very ill and weak. And, depending on the situation, it can kill you."

If she was honest with herself, she felt drained—but not in the way he meant. Her magic still pulsed under her skin and beckoned for use. Felicity shrugged off his hold and pushed herself to her feet.

"Sorry." She brushed the sawdust from her clothes.

He reached across the expanding space between them and removed a wood chip from her hair. "You have nothing to apologize for." His shadows were gone, but she didn't know when that had happened.

"I beat on you like you were a training dummy." She shook her head. "And thank you...for hiding my magic."

He rubbed the back of his neck. "We all have those days. But I deserved each and every hit you gave me. Probably more." The prince shook his head. "I don't agree with my parents. But I hope that you can at least accept me and once this is all over, you can do whatever you deem necessary and I won't say a word."

"I have a mission to fulfill first." Felicity stepped from the ring and picked up one dagger and sheath at a time, placing them in their proper location. "Then I can leave this all behind."

"Yes, you do and you can." His voice was distant.

She peeked over her shoulder to find him looking back up at the opening in the ceiling. A star flew across the night sky, tickling at a memory that wouldn't form—that she couldn't grasp onto and hold. It disappeared—as the star did, into darkness.

She stalked across the room. That had been more than she expected tonight. Training now seemed unnecessary.

"But will you be able to turn your back on it? Can you leave behind those who deserve to be punished? Or maybe you are the retribution we all deserve."

Felicity froze at the exit. She considered his words as she straightened and without looking back, she left.

***

The next morning Felicity delivered the name to the king. She had heard nothing except that King Roald had brought in Lord Marthlow for questioning. After last night's training session, she had to admit that her frustration had dissipated. Holding onto her anger had been as much of a weakness as the other emotions she worked hard to dispel.

That evening a heaviness followed Felicity as she walked toward the dining hall. There was a sense of foreboding palpable by the staff's hurried footsteps as they disappeared from view and then from the silence that welcomed her arrival. There weren't the usual boisterous sounds of eating and talking. Even the meal smelled of stale bread and unseasoned meats. And blood.

Felicity came to a slow halt at the sight that welcomed her. Chained in iron manacles in the center of the room crouched Lord Marthlow, his shirt removed with welts covering his back and orange-tinted blood that dripped down his pants to the heels of his boots. With his head hung low, his thin shoulders shuddered as the whip cracked, breaking the silence of the room.

No one spoke—no one gasped. The only sound was the snap of the whip against skin. The lord was weak enough now that his body wasn't healing anymore—if he had the ability in the first place. Those who had been walking with Felicity stopped in utter shock, mouths agape.

The queen sat beside her husband at the head table, the corner of her mouth lifted at the spectacle before her. They enjoyed this, Felicity thought. They relished the idea of torturing a male for his crimes in the dining room for all their guests to witness.

"Answer the question." The king's voice held the same crack of the leather switch in the soldier's hand.

"I never..." Lord Marthlow spit as blood dripped from his chin.

Felicity came to stand beside Ward. They had been a part of this. The lord wasn't a good man. She knew this. He had sided with King Roald.

Was this remorse she felt? For someone vile? No. She wouldn't allow it.

With a lift of her chin, her expression grew cold. Prince Alarian met her gaze and his cloaked eyes made her wonder if he knew the truth. The prince's jaw tensed, and Felicity returned his hardened expression with a steely one of her own—until he diverted his gaze.

"There is proof of your wrongdoing. Just admit your crimes and this all can be over."

Tears and sweat fell down the lord's face and mixed with flecks of blood. "My loyalty has always been to the crown. I would never work against you, Your Majesty." He shuddered again as the whip cracked against his back. Layers of skin and sinew hung in shredded strings.

King Roald stood and sauntered across the room. He stopped in front of the fallen lord. "Have you been having relations with a rebel?"

A woman was dragged into the room. A female guard held her by a chunk of the woman's brown hair and tossed her on the ground beside Lord Marthlow. Felicity stilled, her heart beating harder against her chest.

Marthlow's eyes widened. "I didn't know she worked with the rebels, My King. I swear it."

The maid pushed herself to her feet. "He didn't need to know. He swore his heart to me. That he belonged to me." The woman had no injuries. Whatever she had told the guards, it had been without torture.

Felicity sliced a look at Ward, his own expression tight. This was lucky for her. The king would be pleased—but it wouldn't be for the rebels. If what the woman said was true, an asset for the rebellion would be lost.

King Roald didn't seem thrilled that the woman spoke openly. His eyes narrowed to slits as he considered her. "Did he speak to you of secrets of our kingdom?"

"He told me stories and whispered secrets as sweet nothings." This woman knew what she was doing. She wouldn't leave alive and wanted to ensure the fae male beside her would share her fate.

Lord Marthlow tried to push to his own feet. "Never, My King. I didn't tell her anything. She speaks out of turn." He shot the woman a pained look. Was that actual adoration and sadness in his eyes? Had he truly loved her?

The king mutated right before their eyes. Horns protruded from his head, his feet transformed into hooves, and his hands grew long talons. Long tufts of hair sprouted from beneath the seams of his clothes. A roar echoed in the room as the king's transformation ended. With a growl, he locked eyes with the lord.

"My King, I sw—" Lord Marthlow's throat was torn out before he could say more, blood gushing from the gaping wound. The woman beside him screamed. The king lifted her by her neck, his grip cutting off the sound of her fear.

For a brief moment, Felicity could see the consideration in King Roald's eyes. She'd seen it with many of her fellow recruits, especially those who were trained specifically for assassinations. If he tightened his grip just a bit, he could snap her neck. Kill her right there. As the woman clawed at his hold, he loosened just enough and threw her to the ground. "Take her to a cell for questioning."

The rebel didn't even have time to find her voice to beg. The soldiers grabbed her and dragged her from the room.

Death and Felicity were close friends. They had long been well acquainted. But what she had witnessed hadn't been the death of the guilty. Marthlow had been butchered and the rebel woman's fate would be much worse. And it was Felicity's fault.

Just as quickly as he had transformed into a beast, the king became the fae male again. It looked painful, his mouth in a half howl as his body contorted and shrunk into itself. His torn clothes hung from his body with rips and holes where the bestial attributes had just been. King Roald shook the sinew from his hand, droplets landing on terrified courtiers as he stalked back to his seat. One fae stood with wide eyes, his mouth open in the middle of a scream, blood dripping down his forehead.

"Clean this up." The king's voice was guttural, more of a growl.

Queen Marquette sat with her back erect in her chair, a small grin on her face as King Roald took his seat beside her. While Felicity considered the queen's expression, she noted no one else paid her attention—everyone looked at the king, unsure what would happen next. Soldiers rushed forward to remove the bodies.

"Let this be a warning to those who would consider working against our cause." The king picked up a napkin and wiped his hands, the once white linen now stained deep orange. "It's time to eat."

Servers rushed in to distribute plates of meats and vegetables to the tables. The food was plain and looked like charred cold remains served on fine china. It took only a few seconds for the courtiers to begin to move towards their waiting seats. Many diverted their gazes from the dead but a few couldn't turn away, eyes wide and staring. Then there were those who looked at the king and queen with a sense of awe and esteem.

The queen cleared her throat. "Your king has and will continue to protect us all from the rebels. We should drink in his honor."

Those who had been staring were suddenly moving—rushing to their seats. Felicity sat down beside Ward, her grip on the arms of the chair so tight her knuckles were white. She considered all the ways she could attempt to rescue the woman. Guilt. It had been years since she had felt such a thing. A memory tickled but didn't rise to the surface. A scream echoed in her mind without breaking through to remind her of when.

The queen raised her glass, and everyone mimicked her movements. "To King Roald, the savior of the eight realms." None spoke, the silence that followed was deafening.

The king looked from each face to the next until he landed on hers. He lifted his glass a little higher before they all took a drink.

Thankful of her ability to hide her emotions, Felicity nodded, and a corner of his mouth rose slightly as the cup met her lips. She could play along. It was one game Felicity was well versed in. Another gaze penetrated her skin, but she wouldn't allow herself to look towards the prince. Not now. Not when he seemed to be able to glean more from her than anyone else. Felicity couldn't give herself away. Lives depended on it.

It was too bad the prince hadn't chosen the right side.

Chapter
26

Lady Chartow sipped her tea, her mouth in a thin line. Lady Solfire and the others sat with grave expressions. The queen and Lady Fiadh hadn't yet arrived, late as usual. If the rumors were true, the king hadn't uncovered what he had hoped from the rebel before she had died.

After the spectacle the previous day, there was a stifling heaviness that went beyond the courtiers and to the staff. Even here in the outdoors, it felt uncomfortable despite the fresh air. None knew what to discuss. Instead, they concentrated on their tea or held their cross stitch in hand.

The usual bustle of activity continued in the garden as workers sawed at strong branches and clipped thick vines. There seemed to be more of them now as if doubling their efforts would give them a better chance to appease the queen.

"Good afternoon, everyone." Queen Marquette broke the group's silence, and everyone jumped to their feet to curtsy.

Felicity inhaled a deep breath as Lady Molyle took a step out from behind Lady Fiadh. The witch took Lady Molyle's arm and led her to a chair beside hers. Lady Fiadh's gaze rested on Felicity as the queen took her seat, everyone else settling in their own chairs. Hiding her surprise, Felicity smiled at Lady Molyle.

Queen Marquette gestured to their new guest. "This young female is Lady Molyle of Visce." Her brow furrowed and the beginning of a frown showed the queen wasn't happy with this unexpected addition. For once, Felicity had to agree—any more questions deeper into Advisor Boister's death could possibly bring unfortunate things to light. This must have been Lady Fiadh's idea. But if that was the case, the queen had no need to agree unless she found a good reason for the female's presence.

The queen rolled back her shoulders. "She will be visiting with us for some time. I believe you are already acquainted with Lady Dwauer but let me introduce you to the others."

Felicity ran through all the reasons for the Visce's presence as Queen Marquette made the round of introductions. Lady Molyle sat, back straight and hands fidgeting in her lap. Felicity was certain it was due to the anticipation and excitement of being asked to tea with the queen. As the introductions continued, Felicity analyzed the female and gauged the others' reactions. By the time the queen had finished, Felicity already knew what to use to steer the conversation if it became a necessity.

"How did you and Lady Dwauer meet?" Lady Mistward asked, a sharp gaze stealing towards Felicity before returning to the new guest. Of course the female would bring up the one conversation topic Felicity had hoped to ignore.

"We met upon Lady Dwauer's arrival from the islands at our dearly departed Advisor Boister's midsummer ball." Lady Molyle spared a quick, warm glance in Felicity's direction. "The advisor had been entranced by her all evening and I was introduced when there was a little fumble over a glass of wine." Her cheeks reddened.

Lady Mistward snorted behind lace gloves. "It seems Lady Dwauer has caught the eye of many males upon her arrival to the mainland."

"It's quite by accident, I assure you." Felicity studied her hands in her lap, keeping her voice low.

"Let's hope the prince doesn't meet the same end. What was it that happened to the advisor again?" Lady Mistward pestered like a fly Felicity wanted to crush.

"He was poisoned by a server," Felicity murmured, looking up through her lashes.

Lady Solfire reached over and took Felicity's hand. "All the things you've been through on our shores. Between the advisor's assassination, the warning at the ball, last—" Avyanna froze, the words stuck in her throat. Lady Solfire shook her head. "Were the islands this *adventurous*?"

Felicity shrugged. "Every place has its own adventures, I suppose."

Lady Molyle's eyes lingered where Felicity and Lady Solfire's hands were joined but shot her gaze up to Felicity's face. Avyanna leaned back, her hands moving to her own lap.

"How long do you plan to stay, Lady Dwauer?" Lady Molyle asked tentatively.

"I plan to return before winter. It would be best for traveling." Felicity opened her fan and waved it in front of her face.

Lady Fiadh leaned against the arm of her chair. "What keeps you here? I know many who would have returned home by now after what you've been through."

Felicity blushed, the heat running up her neck into her cheeks. "I would rather not say." She fluttered her fan a little faster like any of the gossiping females would do.

"The prince?" Lady Molyle gushed, and Felicity knew she had her.

Felicity dropped her gaze to the cobbled floor and shrugged.

Queen Marquette's gaze went cold as steel. "My son has informed me he will be traveling for some time. I hope you two haven't tired of each other."

Felicity was caught off guard but kept her expression relaxed. The others quieted, and by their eager looks, awaited her response. "Nothing has been outright stated, Queen Marquette. And yes, Prince Alarian has informed me of his upcoming absence. He requested that I stay through to Lughnasadh and asked if he could be my escort."

Lady Mistward's eyes narrowed to thin slits. Miss Isleen looked as though her greatest wish had been fulfilled. The contrast between the mother and daughter brought a hint of a grin to Felicity's lips.

Queen Marquette sighed and gave a deceptive smile, the way her gaze sliced to Felicity enough to show her true intentions. "I'm glad to hear. My son's happiness is important to the future of the realms."

Lady Fiadh poured herself some tea. "I heard the recount of the late advisor's story. It all seems so curious, don't you think?"

Felicity resisted a glance towards the queen. Did she know her friend was attempting to uncover Felicity's identity or was it something else that brought about this line of questioning? She couldn't fall into the spider's trap. "Since I haven't been here long, I wouldn't know what you mean."

The courtiers shared a glance and Lady Grandeur cleared her throat. "It does seem odd that the server wasn't caught. I wondered if it was an inside job. The lord wasn't well-liked by his staff as far as I've heard."

The witch shrugged. "Or if not an inside job, I do wonder if someone was hired to get close enough to kill the advisor."

Felicity knew tears wouldn't be effective in this instance. To object would only keep the others, especially the buzzing fly that was Lady Mistward digging deeper into the story. "There are many speculations, I'm sure. It's probably best to leave it to the professionals."

Queen Marquette groaned. "Enough of this chatter. Come, let's discuss much less somber things. We uncovered a rebel and a traitor yesterday. Today we are one step closer to ensuring not only the citizen's safety but also the future of our people."

One step? Felicity hoped it was all for show because she wouldn't want to weaken a rebellion that needed to succeed. Not only for the citizens but for the entire continent.

***

Ward leaned back in his chair, feet crossed on the table. "The king says I don't need to escort you to training, tea, or for your daily walks anymore."

"I never needed you for daily..." Felicity snapped shut the book she'd been reading and glared at him. "How does it make you feel—not to have to be my nanny any longer? Besides, you haven't been at the past few sessions anyway."

"But you hadn't been alone either," he pointed out. "Is there a reason the prince feels the need to attend your training?"

"Nothing more but to ensure I'm doing my part to fulfill my role." Felicity rolled her eyes and opened the book again. With her decision made, she continued to read to better understand politics—and the world. As far as Felicity could ascertain, she'd had been living in a cave her entire life. However long that had been. She still hadn't forced herself to read the Countess's letter although she knew, after the dreams and glimpses of further memories, she would soon need to face her own barriers.

Ward snorted. "Well, at least you've been granted some trust."

She had already known it was true and was certain she had the prince to thank.

"I'm available to train if you would like a sparring partner." Ward looked at her thoughtfully, the corner of his mouth extending into a playful grin.

"I might take you up on that offer soon." Just not when she needed the chance to train in the use her magic. Although there were moments she wished to tell Ward the truth, she held back.

Felicity pulled another book into her lap and mimicked his position, crossing her legs on the table as she stuffed her skirts between her calves to keep some sense of decency. All it did was earn a chuckle from her study mate.

This had become, more or less, routine. After every afternoon tea they would meet in the room, read through books, and Felicity would ask questions while he tested her on political figures, laws, and histories.

"I have somewhere I want to take you soon. I know last night didn't sit well with you."

Felicity shuddered. The death of the woman had burrowed in her chest in a way no other death had.

Or as far as she remembered. The memory that kept attempting to form was still a figment in her mind. And guilt—another emotion supposedly dampened to non-existence—kept rearing its ugly head.

"When and where?" Felicity pushed his feet off the table using her foot and they crashed to the ground, unsettling him.

His gaze narrowed, and he grabbed her feet and flung them to the ground. She'd been prepared though and stopped them midair. With a grin, she propped them back on the table.

He glared. "In a week or two, and I would rather not say where. I need to finalize a few things first. But training—you just let me know when."

"Fine. But I already have a training dummy, so I don't know if you would be of any use to me. When was the last time you've been in a practice ring?" Felicity hid her smile behind the book.

Ward snorted and with a swipe of his hand, a gust of wind flew under her chair and tipped it back. Her legs fumbled high, arms flailing, the book dropping onto her chest as she tried to grab for purchase while also covering her underthings.

As she lay sprawled out on the floor, Ward laughed so hard that tears streamed down his face.

***

The training room was empty when Felicity arrived at midnight. She wondered if Prince Alarian had already left on his journey without telling her. She hated that she expected him... Maybe he knew Lord Marthlow hadn't been as guilty as he seemed and the prince was attempting to punish her. Either way, she wasn't going to waste the peace and quiet. Pushing herself through the usual movements and positions, there was a sheer layer of sweat on her skin when the lights dimmed. Felicity whirled around.

Whispers of smoky gray tendrils spread across the edges of the room. She turned in a slow circle as her surroundings darkened. It beckoned her, a sense of familiarity and a hint of the scent of spring rain within the magic. A smile crept upon her face. She was light. Letting her magic run along her limbs, Felicity glowed, her skin illuminating the center of the training circle as the darkness gathered, a mere body length between herself and those shadows.

Closing her eyes, she removed the pendant from under her tunic. She felt the distance between the shadow magic and reflected her light against the crystal, stretching the rays beyond her. When she opened her eyes, the warmth and white glow of her magic filled the space. It wasn't blinding like it had been many times before but comforting and glimmering.

With a yip, a fox trotted out of the shadows and into the center, its tail curling the expanding shadows. It settled on its haunches near the edge of her light and tilted its head, watching her.

It seemed to dare her to try. She positioned her crystal, controlling the brightness as her light shifted through the tendrils of shadow, letting her magic brush against them and slide off in waves. Goosebumps pimpled upon her flesh as the fox's magic touched the warmth of hers. It cooled her, taking away the heat from her light, and as their magic began to intertwine, she closed her eyes again.

Instead of attempting to overpower the dark shadows, she envisioned her magic dancing with it, swirling like the crest of a wave, caressing the mist as it took the shape of the serpentine tendrils. When she opened her eyes again, she gasped—the fox was gone and the prince stood in its place. His torso was bare, firm muscles visible, and he held her gaze as he pulled a shirt over his head, shadows around his waist hid his lower half from view.

Another secret he entrusted her with after how badly she had treated him. It seemed he had more from his earth heritage than a glimpse of healing magic. Heat, not her magic, ran through her body. She forced her attention to the visual display their magic created and away from him.

The starlight and darkness were a beautiful juxtaposition, like the moon creating a glimmering trail dancing along waves. The colors of her light reacted within his shadows, and his magic formed to the rays of her own. It felt like their skin was touching when still so much space stood between them. Felicity met the prince's gaze, now clothed as he stepped beyond the shadows. A heaviness settled in her chest. Ached.

No. This wasn't right. Then, just as suddenly, the memories of the fox snapped into place.

Her eyebrows drew together, and she dropped the pendant, her light breaking free from his shadows and dispersing the darkness altogether.

Prince Alarian's shoulders slumped. Or was that a trick of the light?

"Was that you? Out on the bluff that day?"

"It was but let me explain."

She turned to walk away, her body crackling with power, sweat coating her skin. How could he? The things she said, what she'd admitted. Those words had been meant for only herself and a woodland animal—not the prince.

"Felicity," he whispered, longing in his voice.

The tone alone made her stop. "What?"

"I hadn't expected to come across anyone on the bluff. When it was you, I was curious, of course, but didn't think you'd say anything to me. As soon as it became personal, I left because I didn't want to break your trust. It's also why I showed you my other form now."

She couldn't look at him. If she did, Felicity didn't know what she would do. The self-imposed warnings in her head sounded an alarm she hadn't heard since training at the Tower. A session in the training ring, faces undefined. It could have been any moment in her time at the guild.

He sighed. "You're still glowing."

Felicity tried to call the magic back in, but it didn't listen. Instead, it stretched outward, moving towards the prince. It wanted to play that little game again. She would call it a game—even if it felt like one of the most intimate things she had ever done in her life. The attempt to replace the *need* with anger wasn't working. She tried to snuff out the rays but her skin didn't dim.

"The ability you have with the prism as a conduit is impressive. Is that how you blinded the attackers on our return trip?"

Words failed her, so she nodded.

"Can you light the lanterns with it?"

They were all extinguished, her magic the only light in the room. "It doesn't work like that."

"Why not?"

Her gaze thinned, her patience with it. "Because I don't have that type of control over such a distance. It's hard to shift the rays with the crystal."

"You didn't have a problem doing that just a moment ago."

She met his gaze, the shine of his green eyes unsettling her, and she bit her lip. "I have blinded and burned people with my light. I've never tried to use it that way before."

"Try," he repeated. "This time the distance is the challenge."

She wanted to put as much *distance* between herself and the prince as possible. But she knew she couldn't leave glowing—a torch in the night.

Facing a set of lanterns along the wall, she pointed her crystal, reached out her magic, and concentrated.

The first one shattered as her magic met glass.

"Try again."

Felicity's teeth clenched. She looked at the second lantern and extended her magic, using the pendant in an attempt to control the way it traveled, how hot it was, and the wave it created. Rainbows illuminated the distance between herself and the lantern. This time she didn't shatter it, but the light engulfed the wick and it blazed to life only to burst into flames. She didn't see how he did it, but the prince sputtered the fire to wisps of shadow.

"Again."

"If I continue this, there won't be any lanterns left," she grumbled.

She knew he heard her, but he didn't respond. His previous request was not meant to be ignored. "Damn Prince, always needing to get your way."

"If I got my way, then we would be doing something else entirely right now." His voice was guttural.

She faced him, the snide remark on the tip of her tongue dissipating as she took one look at the shadows edging around him. He looked exquisite. He had his hands in the pockets of his black pants. The tunic he wore was cut to fit his frame perfectly and showcased muscles and fine lines. His green eyes shone with their usual mischief through the strands of fiery auburn hair that hung over his sun-kissed brow. But the usual playfulness in his smile was gone, replaced by a straight mouth and furrowed brow.

She'd never allowed herself to look at him this way. Or maybe it was the way the darkness seemed to enhance his features, shadows causing a sense of intrigue as they curled around him. A bushy tail made of those shadows had formed and wrapped around his back and lazily brushed upward to his shoulder.

It nearly took her breath away.

But she didn't fawn over others. She sent her magic towards the lantern, one after another, and they blazed to life—only two more cracking under the pressure—the room brightening with an almost blinding white light before dimming to sizzling embers. With an intake of air, the flames settled and the lanterns remained lit.

"I knew you could do it." A hint of a smile rose at the corner of his mouth.

"I did what you *asked*. Now we're done for the night." Her skin no longer glowed. She turned, nearly bumping into the prince. He must have used the shadows to move in behind her.

Looking up into his face, his hooded expression halted her. Her lips parted slightly as his eyes roamed her face. She bit her bottom lip and his gaze rested there.

His deep inhale broke the moment and she turned away. "I heard you were leaving. You should make sure I know these things so I'm not caught off guard at tea. Otherwise, they'll never believe there is something between us."

"I decided this morning. Planned to tell you tonight." Prince Alarian sighed and he shook his head. "Felicity—"

"I told her you'll be escorting me to the Lughnasadh ball. I don't think your mother appreciates our escapades." She faced him, and he stilled. He was too close. Too...everything. She wanted to touch him, brush the hair from his face. Instead, she cleared her throat. "Goodnight."

"I didn't take you as one to run away." He rubbed the back of his neck, his freckles standing out in the lamplight. "What are you running from?"

She straightened and raised her chin. "Nothing." He was about to interject, but she continued. "I've heard about your many females, and I've seen what type of prince you are. We may have a working relationship, and I appreciate you keeping my secret for me, but I cannot be more than what I'm meant to be within these walls. I'm here, *Prince* Alarian" —she added emphasis to his title— "because I'm meant to discover your father's enemies."

"You're quite observant." A twinge of sarcasm laced his words.

Felicity took the cloak she had hanging by the door. "Have you ever given me, or anyone for that matter, anything else to believe?"

He nodded as he took a step back, his hands slipping back into his pockets. "Goodnight then, Lady Dwauer."

She brushed past him, and he called after her. "I know who I am, Felicity. The question is, do you know who you are?"

Turning on her heel, her hands formed fists at her side, but before she could respond, shadows wrapped around him and he was gone. What had she just done? She knew it was necessary, but he knew her deepest secret. Saw more than she wanted him too.

But he wouldn't break their oath. She knew that. He'd bared too many secrets on his own—without any question or pressure. He trusted her. The biggest problem was that she couldn't move—couldn't run anymore. Instead, she stood, staring at the place he had just disappeared from and hated to admit that she yearned for him to come back. Wished that he stood against his parents for *his* people. If only...

Chapter 27

It shouldn't have been a surprise when King Roald summoned her the following day. He was already waiting when she entered the meeting room. Felicity sent a quick glance around the space. She knew he wasn't there, but still, it felt strange that the prince was absent.

Ward stood at attention a step behind her, his eyes on nothing in particular. Felicity waited for the order, for the silencing spell to be engaged as she lowered into a curtsy. But it didn't come. Even as she straightened, she didn't know where to settle her gaze, unprepared for the king's full attention.

"You have done well. But I feel there are other, more prominent figures within my court conspiring against me." King Roald's gray eyes pierced the distance between them. "Your job is not yet complete."

"Yes, Majesty." Felicity nodded.

He cocked his head, regarding her for a moment. "You have proven a minuscule amount of your worth. In appreciation, you'll benefit from a bit more trust. As you're aware, you no longer need an escort to train. If you choose to go into town, the stables are for your use. But this is a reminder that only the two guards who journeyed upon your arrival here are still aware of your true identity. You've already seen what happens when they consider you a threat."

Those words alone told Felicity he must have ascertained that she was the thief who'd escaped.

His jaw twitched as he stood, then leaned on his hands over the table. "My wife is tiring of your *relationship* with our son. Whatever you two have created for the others to see has frustrated many of the courtiers and the queen's plans for his future. It wouldn't make sense to have you stay here beyond any separation between you and Alarian. Therefore, the ruse must continue. Your queen will only allow her consent to your attendance as long as you continue to prove your worth. But your time is limited—she will not accept your presence much longer. Neither will I."

Felicity felt Ward stiffen behind her. She kept her own expression neutral and lifted her chin. "Understood."

"Good. Your mission must be completed prior to the winter solstice. We'll determine who will break whose heart then." King Roald's lips broke into a toothy grin, his canines extending. "You're dismissed."

***

It had been seven nights since her interaction with the prince—since he left. Felicity left her room at night to practice controlling her magic in the confines of the training hall. There had been two sessions where she invited Ward to join her. Both ended up with her kicking his ass. All the same, he proved that he was a formidable sparring partner. The other nights she had needed the space—the privacy. Not only to use her magic but to think. Each time she entered the training hall, she hated that she looked for Prince Alarian's presence.

There was no desire to venture out past the walls, to search for the next name on her list. The blood-stained face of the rebel woman had settled within her, keeping her up at night. It was abnormal. She didn't remember the last time death had kept her awake.

Even with the king's warning—she trained. But this evening was different. Ward met her at the door of the training hall, dressed in riding breeches. "It's time. Come with me."

He didn't wait for her response as he brushed past her, heading along the base of the outer wall until they came to the stables. "The king thinks I'm joining you on a mission. With your current standing not in question, I doubt he'll feel the need to have someone trail us."

She grinned. "Because we're trustworthy?"

Ward chuckled.

Although it had started with the training sessions—which she had initially thought Prince Alarian had orchestrated—she realized there hadn't been eyes on her at every turn. She felt more comfortable now using the passageways. Before she had been concerned about using anything other than the entrance from her room, worried that someone would see her and learn of them. There was still the question of whether anyone else knew of their existence, which had Felicity on high alert.

Felicity patted the bay mare's neck and wished she had a treat for the horse. Ward was in a hurry and even with their growing trust, she didn't need him mocking her love of animals. They mounted, and Ward led them out a side gate, a guard waving them off. After some time had passed, Ward slowed his horse to a trot. Felicity did the same, keeping her own mount at an even pace. "We'll leave the horses up ahead. There are some crags and brush to hide them in."

They arrived at his designated location and hobbled the horses, who began to munch on the dry grass, content. Ward removed his pack from the saddle. "Stay close. We need to remain quiet. Stealth is key."

Felicity crouched down and followed him, her feet silent even with the dead grass and twigs under each step. Ward lost track of her twice and would turn abruptly, concern etched in his expression. His entire body relaxed as soon as he realized she was still there.

After some time, her legs aching from remaining low, they came to a rock outcropping that reached into the sky and leaned over a deep precipice. Two trees hung over on each side, covering the rock from immediate view. He signaled for her to go ahead, and Felicity inched herself on her stomach and crawled onto the rock, stepping into indentations in the stone to keep her footing. Once she reached the top, her stomach dropped, and her heart followed suit.

In a long and deep canyon, torches were lit every few feet, lighting a trail into a cave. Humans and faeries of all castes were chained with heavy manacles of iron. Soldiers held long whips that cracked against the ground in warning while others crashed against skin, flaying backs and legs open. There was a pile of dead bodies, the stench reaching her on the ledge, mixed with the smell of bile and sweat. Flies buzzed around the dead, feasting upon their bodies—a reminder to those chained of their fate.

Ward moved alongside her and crouched until his stomach was pressed against the rock.

Felicity wanted to leave. But even more so, she wanted to rage, fight and free as many as she could until her dying breath. Instead, she laid there, watching as they struggled—as those imprisoned souls stumbled into a cave and others came out wheeling carts of rock and dirt.

When her heart felt like it would burst from her chest, she climbed down and stalked away, hands in tight fists gripped at her side. Once they were far enough away, she fell to her knees. Felicity opened her mouth, a silent wail fleeing from her lips. Every part of her body wanted to scream, but the danger was too great this close. Her magic brimmed to the surface but with the last ounce of self-control she had, Felicity pulled it back. She stood, whirling to pummel the nearest tree. With each punch, her arms moved in a rhythm of left to right and back again. Chunks of bark flew, some hitting her face, other pieces clinging to her hair. Ward tried to pull her away, but she broke free from his hold.

It was beyond her control. Punch.

The Tower abandoned her. Punch.

Her memories were a jumbled mess. Punch

Children were orphaned. Punch. *Left to suffer.* Punch, punch.

Imprisoned for nothing, and she couldn't do anything to stop it. Punch, punch, punch.

The scent of sap intermixed with blood. But she didn't care. This she could control. Ward tried again, pinning her arms and pulling her back in a tight hold. She wanted to cry, a thought that Felicity didn't remember having in her lifetime.

But tears didn't come. Only anger. She fought against his brace-like hold, thrashing, but he didn't relent. By the time she stilled, sweat clung to her skin and her breath was ragged.

When he deemed it safe, Ward wrapped an arm around her shoulder, holding her close. Neither spoke. Felicity appreciated the silence.

After some time, she peeled herself away from his embrace and continued walking to the place where they had left the horses. When they reached the animals, Felicity's mount gave them a careful glance before continuing to graze. Ward stopped beside her and looked at her fists. "I should treat your hands."

Felicity stretched her fingers. The appendages stung from the movement. "No."

Ward opened his pack. "Let me see them at least."

She held her hands out, splinters and blood coating her knuckles. He analyzed them, turning them gently. Removing his canteen from the saddlebag, she pulled her hands away. "I said no."

"Why?" His mouth set as he opened the pouch.

"It will be a reminder that what I'm doing is little compared to how much they're suffering. They must be freed." Her body shuddered.

Ward inhaled and ran his free hand through his hair, that indentation appearing between his brows. "Then let me at least get the wood pieces out and wash it off. No salve or bandages."

She gritted her teeth and he growled, his canines gleaming.

"Fine," she agreed.

Once cleaned enough to keep Ward content, they mounted and steered the horses back to the palace. "What are they searching for?"

Ward shrugged. "I don't know. I've never seen anything but dirt and rock removed. Even the rebel spies have nothing to report. Some are beginning to think it's just the king's way to enslave them. But I don't know. It seems connected to something—a purpose, but I can't pinpoint what it is."

Felicity's teeth ground together. "He should be the one down there." Her grip tightened on the reins, the pain searing to life. "How does this end, Ward? What are we doing?" She turned in the saddle to see him better. "What am I doing?"

"The rebels are growing." His mount shook his head. "Soon enough, they'll be able to stand against the king. I wish I was at my full power. That I could help more."

"Would it help to find your name?" Felicity bit her bottom lip in thought.

He nodded. "It's part of the curse. Without my name, I don't have my magic. It's dimmed to carrying books and toppling chairs." He gave her a lazy grin that she didn't return.

"We need to search for your name. Maybe in the archives or—"

Ward grunted. "That was the first place I looked. The curse is powerful. It's gone." He urged his horse to take the road towards the palace. "There is something important we need to discuss. I need you to promise me something."

"Promise what?" The tone of his voice put her on edge.

"If I'm caught, if anything happens to me..." He didn't look her way. "No matter what, you must promise me you won't try to rescue me. Don't send any suspicion in your direction. Keep helping the rebels."

Felicity shook her head. "I can't promise that."

"You must. If you get caught—" His body went rigid. "Then I won't be able to forgive myself for dragging you into this."

"Ward, you already said there were other informants within the castle. There is little I can do." Anger flared in her chest at the stupidity of his words.

"There is plenty you can do. Another assassin will take your place if the king doesn't deem the mission fulfilled. The informants could be found, the rebellion broken piece by piece. Every ally is important in these times and your role is just as vital." He inhaled. "If I'm caught, allow me that honor. To die for them is all I can offer right now."

Magic prickled against her skin, called by her frustration—by emotion. She held it at bay, trying to concentrate on his words. "I hate you."

He chuckled. "No, you don't. And do I take that as a yes?"

Felicity sliced her gaze in his direction and frowned. "You better do everything within your power not to get caught. If I'm to agree to this, it's not permission for you to do something stupid."

"On my honor." He crossed his arm over his chest, fist resting against his heart.

"Then I agree. I won't step in."

The corner of his mouth piqued but disappeared quickly. "It shouldn't be hard for you. You don't get attached—no emotion, remember?"

Felicity's gaze narrowed, and she maneuvered her horse until she was close enough to reach across and push his shoulder, almost unseating him. He laughed, pulling himself upright. She smiled back.

They rode in silence for some time until he broke it. "There is one final thing."

"No. I won't save your illegitimate children and raise them."

He groaned and it took some effort for him to hold in the laughter she could see dancing in his eyes. His hand rubbed over his face. "Every five days, I meet with my contact. My next meeting is tomorrow night at the second bell. Keep track of the days, so you don't miss them if I'm gone. We meet in the back of the dilapidated blacksmith shop outside the walls. Use the passageways to reach it. I'll tell him tomorrow and if necessary, I'll arrange a meeting."

Felicity nodded her agreement, unable to speak.

"Who is your next target?" Ward asked. She could tell it was his attempt to change the subject since he was the one who had given her the list.

"Lord Karmor from Aer."

"Oh yes. He should be easy to pin. Just get him drunk and he talks about anything. He isn't vital enough to hurt the kingdom too much, but his influence over the realms will be difficult for the royal family to overcome." Ward urged his mount into a trot.

"Does he deserve to die?" As much as she wanted to hurt the king, she didn't want to kill a decent male.

"He doesn't treat his staff well—most are starved and beaten." Ward's jaw tightened. "And what he does to the children in servitude to him..."

The last bit of information reminded her of the queen's story. Although Felicity knew that the female was the last person Felicity should trust, her words still rang in the back of Felicity's mind. The glint of anger in Ward's eye told her she didn't need him to finish the sentence. "Then he'll pay."

Chapter
28

*L*ong ago, Felicity had decided the table in the study had divots and rings that made it look like a great horned owl. A knoll in the wood looked like its beak. Rings expanded out from the center of two dark circles, the colors in the wood lightening as the rings grew wider, giving the impression of the owl's eyes. Although off centered above the eyes, the horns were caused by the grain of the wood peaking upward before straightening.

"Felicity."

She jerked her head and met the Countess's gaze, the spell broken. Her eyes held a warmth that Felicity had rarely seen. It had been strange enough when she had been asked to sit at the table instead of standing.

"Yes, Countess. I live to serve." She bit her tongue. On more than one account, Felicity had come off as being too energetic and had been working to pull back the flattery.

Harrison reached a hand under the table and grasped tight onto her thigh. He'd never done this before in front of the Countess. Although the woman was more than aware of their relationship, for him to physically touch her now made Felicity's senses rise with the hair on the back of her neck.

"The time has come for us to discuss the option of the ritual. The dangers have become too great and as much as it hurts for me to do this to you again, the choice is yours."

"Ritual, Countess?" Felicity felt Harrison's grip tighten on her leg.

The Countess met Harrison's gaze and nodded. He started to speak, tears settled in the corners of his eyes. "You have a choice, Felicity. You can stay here and continue to be a part of the Tower—be the weapon. Or you can leave."

"Why would I leave?" She pulled her leg from his touch. "Why would you send me away?" With each breath, her chest tightened.

Harrison pulled his hand back and rested them on the table. "It's your choice. They aren't sending you away," Harrison whispered. All Felicity heard was yet.

He continued, "If you choose to remain, the recruits will be sent to other guilds. We won't allow any to remain to keep your identity a secret. Some have begun to note you haven't aged, and questions have been brought up. Because of your heritage, it's too dangerous for you to be here with the knowledge you have. You need to start over again, and the ritual allows you a fresh start as a new recruit. You've made that choice in the past."

"What does the ritual do?" Felicity's heart hammered away within her chest, so loud she was certain everyone heard it.

The Countess's eyes brimmed with tears. "It removes your memories. You've made the choice to complete the ritual two other times."

Felicity's own eyes stung, but she inhaled a deep breath as Harrison interjected. "It will remove your memories for the past ten years—the point of time from the last ritual."

Felicity sliced her gaze to the Countess. The woman nodded and continued where Harrison left off. "It's for your protection. With the abilities you have, it's unsafe to have you stay without drawing attention to yourself. We'll start a new group of trainees alongside you." The Countess lifted her chin, any hint of tears gone.

"I won't become an initiate?" Felicity's brow furrowed.

"No." Bishop cleared his throat. It was strange he had been quiet for as long as he had been. "You're still young and brash due to your other heritage. This gives you an opportunity to learn and expand your abilities. Hone your craft, you might say."

Felicity bit her lip. She hated when he added his opinion. When it came to her, he was always negative. "Why do we have to remove them if you're bringing in new initiates?" By the way Harrison gripped her hand, she knew this choice—her choice—was about them more than anything.

Bishop snorted. "We tried that before. It didn't end well and caused more work for us. This is the choice you have to make."

She faced Harrison. "But what about us?"

The corner of his mouth rose and quickly fell. "We've found each other before."

"This time will be different, though?" She asked the question she knew he didn't want to answer. He turned away. He had aged in these years of training—gray beginning to dust his hair.

"Yes," he inhaled the word. "This time, I won't be allowed to train you. I'll be joining the Council."

"And if I choose to leave?" Felicity asked the Countess.

The Countess seemed to know Felicity was going to ask the question, her answer prepared. "Then Harrison has offered to leave with you. He will live his mortal life alongside you. If you want him to—and you'll find your own way in this world."

It wasn't the proposal one dreams about, but Felicity knew what it meant that Harrison was willing to give up everything he had worked so hard for to be with her. Tears, unfamiliar, began to stream down her face. She reached a hand across to Harrison and found his, gripping it. Felicity couldn't look at him. Not yet. "How long do I have to decide?"

The Countess nodded and Harrison answered for her, a rasp in his voice. "Tomorrow."

***

Felicity had woken and before she could consider sitting up, the memory had bombarded her. The after effects left her chest hollow, bared open to the point where it ached. The previous day, the Aer advisor had been executed, another name off her list. She had another ready, but it would have been suspicious to turn in one so soon.

Meira, who always seemed to know when she woke, knocked on the door and slipped inside, interrupting her thoughts. "Good morning, milady. I'll bring you some breakfast. Tea or coffee today?" She crossed the room and slid open the large drapes, letting in bright sunlight that illuminated the room but not Felicity's dreary mood.

"Coffee please." Felicity pulled her legs up to her chest. "Could you close the drapes a bit?"

Meira stopped her usual morning routine. She looked Felicity up and down, shoulders hunched together. "Is it because the prince hasn't been by to visit in a while, milady? I hear he's back. I assume he'll want to see you."

It had been twelve days since her training session with the prince. Goosebumps prickled on Felicity's skin. She didn't know if they were from Meira's assumption that she was lovesick or the thought of seeing him again. "I'm not feeling well today. Will you send word to the queen that I'll not be able to attend tea?"

"Of course, milady. Should I call for a healer?" She was by Felicity's bedside in a breath, a cool moss-covered hand pressed to her forehead. Felicity sighed under her touch.

"No, thank you. Just cramps." She pulled her legs in closer to her stomach for effect.

"Is it your cycle? I could get some herbs to help clear the discomfort right up." Meira started to pull up the sheets to check, but Felicity tightened her hold. The Tower had prepared them for such instances of cycles and cramping. The tonic was in her bedside table and her fae heritage also helped by only ovulating twice a year.

"I have what I need but thank you, Meira. Breakfast would be nice." Felicity gave a weak smile.

The handmaiden patted Felicity's hand before closing the drapes a fraction, allowing just enough light within the room to go about one's business. "Maybe all you need is something to eat. I'll send a note to the queen, however, and check in around noon."

Once the door clicked shut, Felicity slipped from the warmth of the bed and stared down at her trunk. With a deep breath, she opened it and removed the letter from the Countess. It was wrinkled from being stuffed away and the occasional moments when she had taken it out to stare at it, attempting to talk herself into reading the words.

After the memory, now was the time. She couldn't hide from the Countess or the Tower forever. With leaden steps, she made her way to the chair and took a seat. Her stomach clenched, the anxiety within her chest tightening as she unfolded the missive.

Dear Felicity,

This won't be easy. Not on your part or mine. Included with this letter are memories that I withheld from you, some for your own protection and some for the protection of others. The choices we have made, many of them together, regarding your past and your life have never been easy. While I will understand your disdain, I promise you that I didn't make the decision lightly when I chose to remove parts of who you were. And I don't think you did either.

Neither of us wanted you to leave the Tower. We tried not to remove your memories, but your instincts were too quick for the new initiates. You had to learn to be human—to rely on that part of your body to keep your identity safe. To start as a clean slate. While, in most instances, you made the final choice, I always felt responsible. You were young—the Tower was all you had. Why would you ever choose to leave when you had known nothing else?

And now you can't return. I know it's your home but it's time for you to find your path and I ask that you trust that I have reasons for this decision. Many of which you won't see or understand right now.

You need to make your own decisions and take your proper place in this world. Because as much as it pains me, that place is not here, Felicity. The world has far bigger plans for you. Maybe someday our paths shall cross again. When you're ready, when the time comes, I know you will have many questions to ask, and I'll be here to answer them. Perhaps then you will be able to forgive me, or you will hate me still. But know, sweet child, that this life we have given you was the best we could do with what we had.

In your debt and love,

The Countess

P.S. Make sure to take each vial in small sips, not gulps, or the influx of memories will make you terribly ill and take longer to unjumble. Things may be a bit hazy for a while but should piece together. Be patient. And do take them, as much as I know you won't want to.

At those last lines, she almost tore the paper at her own stupidity. Of course, if she had read the letter first instead of being a stubborn ass, she would have bypassed all the pain and confusion.

The choice hadn't just been the Countess's, her memory had been proof enough, but seeing it in writing eased the heaviness inside her.

Felicity was still hurt that she wasn't meant to return—that they had kicked her out and worse, that a Tower's assassin had come after her and the prince. And yet, a bitter relief settled within. There were many questions she still needed answered. Was there more behind their reason to take her memories? Why did they send Garder? Why was it so important to keep so much of who she was a secret? Maybe one day she would be able to return and ask those questions but until then, she let go a little of the anger she held so close.

After breakfast, Felicity took a nap and read one of the books piled beside the bed. Before Meira could check on her, she slid into the pair of loose pants and flung a linen tunic over her head. Was this what it was like for high-bred ladies? If this was her day-to-day, she would grow bored, but she appreciated the moment of quiet for now. Ward came to visit for a bit, and they sat on the balcony, chatting as they overlooked the plains and in the far distance, the ocean glistened in the afternoon light.

When he left, she took advantage of her freedom and ventured past the gardens and into the fields until she reached the willow tree. So much had changed since her last visit with the fox—or should she say, Prince Alarian. The long reeds had lightened to a soft brown, the stalks bending in the breeze as the sun beat down on them.

She sat against the trunk for a while, watching the ocean waves dance in between the hanging branches of the willow. With a deep inhale, the scent of the sea called to her. She put her chin up as she neared the bluff's edge, the wind brushing against her skin and hair flying behind her. Felicity closed her eyes, spreading her senses out.

She felt him before she heard him and snapped to attention. "What are you doing here?"

Prince Alarian stopped beside her. "I heard you weren't feeling well. Meira told me you were taking a walk and I saw you head this way."

His voice was distant, and she stilled, regretting her harsh tone. "I heard you were back."

Prince Alarian sniffed. "Checking up on me?"

She cocked her head in his direction. "Everyone thinks I want to know about your whereabouts."

He shrugged and crossed his arms. She noted he was dressed in training gear and sweat interlaced with his usual forest scent. "Why did you follow me?"

Prince Alarian's mouth grew taut and his gaze distant. "The fresh air. And I can always rely on you to be a quiet companion. Though today you're extra chatty."

Her brows furrowed, and she turned her attention back to the sea.

After some time of silence, just the crashing waves below interrupting, he breathed a heavy sigh. "Tell me something. Tell me a secret or a lie. I don't care which. Just tell me something."

Her brow crinkled together and she bit her lip. "You just said I was too chatty."

The smile he attempted was forced, his hands dropping to fists at his side. "I guess I need chatty," he whispered.

She scanned the ocean view, another gust of wind cooling the heat spreading through her skin. Felicity grazed the clasp on her ear. "The Tower has let me go. I'm not meant to return."

"Why?" He faced her. "My father hasn't complained as far as I'm aware. He has no reason to when you've been successful."

She shook her head and walked back towards the tree. "No. It has nothing to do with that." There were some things she was willing to share. Others, not so much. He strolled beside her as she ducked into the coverage of the branches. "I just read a letter from the Countess. The others know the truth about me—it would be more trouble if I returned."

With a snap at the hinge, she released the clasp from her ear and held it in her hand. "I guess I don't need this anymore." Her chest ached, and she met his gaze. "Unless your father demands it. It's what holds the spell that allows him to silence conversations." She looked back at the gold jewelry in her hand and tightened her hold. "Maybe I should wear it until the mission is over."

Prince Alarian's hand covered hers. "Felicity, don't. Don't wear this for him or anyone."

A wave of emotions rushed through her, many she didn't comprehend, and her body heated. The prince stepped back, releasing his hold and his eyes widened. He scanned their surroundings before turning back. "Felicity, your magic. You're glowing."

Chapter
29

Fear consumed her chest as she attempted to call in her magic, but it surged through her to the pendant on her neck and spread out around them. The prince shielded his eyes with his arm just in time.

"A dampener." Prince Alarian's voice grounded her. "You need it back on, Felicity. Now."

She looked down at her hand, attempting to put his words together. Felicity opened her grip and stared at the little golden clasp in her palm. The power this little thing must contain. A thrum of her magic rushed through her body.

She fumbled, almost dropping the clasp as she slipped it back on her ear and the magic dimmed, receding within her body. She gasped for air and fell to the ground on her hands and knees, weak and exhausted. "I..." She tried to catch her breath. "I feel sick."

"That was too much too fast." Prince Alarian squatted down beside her. "You must practice without it to learn to control it. You're almost drained."

Bile coated her tongue and she vomited, just missing the prince. He held back her hair as she heaved again, and her morning meal splattered the stalks of grass.

She sat, wiping her mouth with her hand as he rubbed slow circles along her back.

"Thank you," she croaked.

"Did you know she spelled the clasp to dampen your magic? I thought no one knew about it." He scanned their surroundings again.

She inwardly thanked him for his concern of who may have seen. "I guess I was wrong." What other memories were still missing?

Strong arms wrapped under her legs and behind her back as the prince scooped her up and pressed her to his chest. Her first instinct was to fight him, but her body ached, spent from the magic it used.

Prince Alarian leaned close to her ear. "We need to get you water and some food. That will help. As far as I can tell, no one saw you. But until you have gained control within the training ring, if you want to keep your secret, I recommend refraining from removing that thing until you have practiced. If you ever want to know what is said within those meetings, just ask."

She quirked her head toward him. "Why?"

"I told you. I brought you here. Therefore, I'm responsible for you." He gave her a quick grin before concentrating on opening the gate to the garden. Guards ran to meet them as they entered the castle halls. He growled and ordered them away.

The prince took her straight to her room, pulled the cord beside the bed and a gentle chime sounded to alert Meira. Felicity had never needed it before. The handmaiden always seemed to arrive whenever it was necessary.

Meira bustled in with a smile which quickly turned to a frown. "What happened?" Her gaze met the prince's, and Felicity noticed the shadows rise along the wall behind him.

"She'd ventured too far it seems. Her illness caught up with her." Prince Alarian didn't move from his spot, still holding her in his arms.

"It isn't an illness, Prince." Concern etched across the handmaiden's face, and Felicity felt the rush of guilt for deceiving her. "Set her down. I can't treat her from there."

His grip tightened for a moment, a primal fae expression crossing over his features, but with a pursed mouth, he set Felicity down in a chair. "She needs food and water."

"She needs rest." Meira's nose crinkled as she stepped closer. "And clean clothes." She waved at the prince. "Out with you, so I can do my job."

He nodded. "I'll wait outside."

Before either she or Meira could protest, he stalked from the room. Meira clicked her tongue as she began to remove the tunic. "I've never seen him that way before." But Meira didn't venture further on the subject. She started filling the tub and magicked the stone floor to roll Felicity's soiled clothes into a pile by the door.

"Fae rarely become ill." Meira hesitated for a moment, peering at Felicity through the corner of her eye. "Is there something I should know?"

At first, Felicity didn't piece the question together. Oh shit, did she think Felicity was pregnant? There was no way she wanted Meira to believe she was having anyone's child—least of all the princes. The rumors that would ensue—

"No, I think something I ate didn't agree with me. Unfortunately, between that and cramping, it didn't end well."

Meira glanced at Felicity's clothes—possibly searching for them to be tinged with blood—then patted her arm.

After a while, Felicity was settled in bed, clean and wearing a nightgown with a brewed pot of tea settled beside her. "I'll bring back some broth and update the prince." Meira patted her hand. "You look better, milady. Your pallor is already improved."

Once alone, Felicity sighed and leaned her head back into the pillows. Still physically drained, she closed her eyes before they flew open as a movement caught her attention. The shadows in the corner by the bed began to twist and extend before taking form as the prince stepped out, still wrapped in its mist.

She blinked in surprise. "You could've knocked."

"It was the only option." He rubbed the back of his neck. "Meira told me I couldn't see you."

"I'm all right. It's nothing to worry over." Felicity held up the cup of tea. "See—already having something to drink."

He stuffed his hands into his pockets. "You need to be careful. If my father finds out about your magic, he *will* kill you. To lie would be considered punishable, but your light magic—that would ensure your death."

"I didn't know it would happen. The Countess kept more from me than I thought." Thankfully he didn't ask for more specifics. She thought of that letter stuffed back in the drawer. Part of her wanted to watch it burn, while the other part wanted to curl up with it and inhale the scent of the Tower—or what was left of it—instilled in the parchment.

He pulled a chair closer to the bed and took a seat. "I hadn't seen that much power at once in a long time." His gaze pierced her from under his full lashes. "You worried me."

"Don't think that simpering male look works for you." Felicity put her teacup down on the table.

Prince Alarian chuckled. "Maybe not."

"How does it work? Your magic? I know you mentioned that you could travel through shadows—but through walls?" Felicity folded her hands and rested them in her lap.

He shrugged. "It's a little complicated to explain. Maybe someday I can show you. Basically, if I know where I'm traveling and where the shadows are in that location, I can travel through them. It's similar to those from Dorcha with their dark magic. Except shadows can be found throughout the day and night. Most Dorcha faeries can only travel at night."

Felicity's brow furrowed. "You could travel anywhere, no matter the distance, as long as you're familiar with the location?"

"Yes and no. The distance does matter. Especially if I want to return quickly. Long distances deplete my magic, and I can only go so far. For instance, I wouldn't be able to reach Saol from here, but I could reach Aer. Although...I would need to ride back or wait a few days before I could return."

"Do you use the shadows to fight?" Felicity had accepted his half-answer then but now, when he was opening up, she had questions she wanted answered.

Prince Alarian's face grew taut as his eyes searched hers for a moment. "I mentioned before that my father wants to be the most formidable within a room?"

Felicity nodded when he paused, listening intently.

"My mother is far more dangerous than he is. Her magic, like mine, can not only expand already existent shadows—using them for our own purpose—but can also be used as an extension of ourselves." He inhaled deeply. "They are a weapon that can be used to cut off the air of someone from the inside, drowning them in their own bodies."

She blinked. "I should have let you out of that carriage." Felicity gave a small smile.

He chuckled, the corner of his mouth lifting slightly. "Yes, you should have. Truth is, I could have gotten out sooner if I had wanted to."

"Why didn't you?" She worried her bottom lip.

The prince snorted. "You didn't need me. Like I said then, it seemed personal."

Silence stretched between them for a moment, and his gaze grew distant again. She sat up, making sure to keep the blankets taut. "What's bothering you?"

He sliced a look in her direction. He opened his mouth to speak then his head jerked towards the door. "I better leave. Last thing I want is one of Meira's lectures."

He stood, pushed the chair against the wall and circled in place before he disappeared into the shadows.

The shadow waved before it dissipated. Felicity couldn't help the smile as the door opened and Meira walked in carrying a tray with bread slathered in fresh butter and a bowl of steaming broth. "Eat slow." She searched the room and her nose wrinkled. "Did that male come in here?" Her gaze narrowed on Felicity.

"What male?" Felicity took a bite of bread and moaned in delight, her stomach gurgling from hunger while attempting to hide the laugh brewing. She couldn't believe sweet Meira had made a grown male run away.

Meira shook her head, took a seat, and made herself comfortable as she pulled a knitting project from her wide apron pocket. It seemed she was planning to stay, her eyes darting in Felicity's direction from time to time. "Would you like to hear a story?"

Felicity thought it strange that the handmaiden would ask such a thing. "I—"

Meira blushed. "I shouldn't have asked. It was silly."

"No." Felicity curled up under the covers and looked towards the matronly female. "Please."

Meria's voice was a smooth cadence like honey as she spoke of a young male who went on adventures in search of the truth. Before Felicity could concentrate too deeply, a memory tumbled to the surface of her mind.

The Countess brushed the hair from Felicity's sweat-soaked forehead. "A story to help you sleep. One of myth and truth. Finality and uncertainty."

Felicity shivered, clutching the scratchy wool blanket tighter around herself. The Countess peered over her shoulder. "While we wait for this bout to pass. Water and food are on the way."

Felicity could only nod.

"A gentle reminder, my dear, you need to wear the clasp. If you take it off, then your magic will overcome you. We must maintain a strict schedule for a little longer. Magic training must only be at night. Understood?"

"I..." Felicity swallowed deep. "Yes, Countess. I didn't mean to."

The Countess tutted. "Of course. Mistakes happen. Now that story while we wait." She cleared her throat as she dipped a cloth into a bowl of water and wiped Felicity's face. "Before the veil was closed, humans congregated throughout the realms. One young girl lived with her mother, her father long gone, in Domhain. It was just the two of them, attempting to survive alone. But soon tragedy hit, and the mother became very ill. The girl did everything she could to save her mother, but no matter the spell, the healer...there was nothing anyone could do. That was until the girl heard of the heartstones.

"Each realm needed their stone to feed the magic to the earth—and to those born of it. The girl was told that the heartstone may help her mother. But where to get it and how? She traveled far, finally able to locate the stone in the center of a deep cavern. The girl brought the heartstone back to her mother who was healed within days just by the stone's close proximity.

"Soon others heard of the power of the heartstone and came to take it from them. But when the girl went to return the stone, someone from her town came running to catch up, informing her that her mother had made a turn for the worse. Without the stone nearby, the girl was certain her mother would die.

"This forced the mother and daughter to run, and they soon found themselves in Saol. Others followed and the stone was lost along with the girl's mother, its whereabouts still a mystery. It wasn't until years later that the effects of the heartstones absence were seen for what it was. Domhain began to weaken, the earth shifting and changing..."

The image disappeared, the Countess's voice shifting into Meira's as she continued her own story about the young male's shenanigans. Exhausted, her head ached not only from draining but from the memory, Felicity bit back the sting of emotions that rolled through her. She forced herself to listen to the handmaiden's voice, concentrate on her words and not on the confirmation that the Countess knew of her magic. It only made her wonder what other parts of her past were forgotten.

Under Meira's watchful eye, Felicity slipped off to sleep, accompanied by dreams of shadows and warm arms.

Chapter
30

Even though it was no longer a requirement, Ward had continued the duty of escorting her to tea but today was different. Felicity was surprised when she arrived to find the females standing outside of their usual seating area, heads down studying fidgeting hands.

"You know this is unacceptable. They are *your* people." Prince Alarian's voice rose from the clearing where they usually sat.

"This isn't the time. Go. We'll discuss this later." The queen's voice held a dangerous amount of venom.

The prince snorted. "Everyone knows how we feel about each other, Mother. There is no reason to pretend. Besides, you have ignored my request to speak with you. If you hadn't, we wouldn't be here now."

"Fine. Your father and I will meet you after tea. He's discussing the fomorian raids with your uncle. But if you continue to make a scene—"

Felicity considered her lessons with Ward. He'd told her how the fomorians, a hostile and battle-hungry race of faeries, had slowly been expanding their area of control in Domhain. The stone terrain had forced the humans and other faeries to spread to the perimeter of the realm leaving it an easy target for the monstrous fomorians.

Prince Alarian grunted his agreement, then left in the direction towards the bluff. Felicity felt a pull to follow him but ignored it.

None of the females moved. Lady Grandeur's fear was palpable in her expression as she gripped her sister's hand. Lady Mistward had her daughter in the corner, covering her ears as she held Miss Isleen close to her chest. When Avyanna's gaze met Felicity's, the female swallowed. Lady Fiadh turned the corner and nodded to the group. "Come, sit with us. It's time for tea."

No one spoke of the incident. They weren't stupid enough to broach the subject, but Felicity wondered what it was the prince had needed to discuss that he would disrupt tea.

Even so, Lady Chartow's mood was sour, pursed lips and a furrowed brow settled on her face. The others began to chat about the upcoming Lughnasadh celebration—anything to find familiarity in the situation. Felicity had grown tired of discussing one event to the next, and the cold steel at her thigh beckoned her to leave—to train. Something she wouldn't be allowed to do until much later.

Meira had sat with her the entire previous evening, not allowing her to even attempt to leave her room. Upon waking that morning, she found the handmaiden asleep in the same chair.

Lady Fiadh sliced a glance in Felicity's direction, bringing her back to the conversation at hand. Felicity had attempted to follow Fiadh a few times, but it had always led nowhere. On one occasion, Lady Fiadh had gone into a study and sat there looking out a window. Once the second set of bells sounded the hour, she left and returned to her room. After two similar instances, Felicity had given up. Either she wasn't up to something, or Lady Fiadh was a step ahead of her. There had been a moment of hope that she could find something to blame on the queen's confidant—to turn suspicion in her direction and break up their little triangle. Besides, it felt dangerous to openly watch the woman the queen held in such high esteem.

"How is everyone today?" Queen Marquette looked up from her tea, her gaze settling on each of them in turn as though daring them to mention the overheard conversation.

"It is a sad day, Queen Marquette," Lady Chartow grumbled. "Not a day for celebrating."

Queen Marquette tried to fight a smile but it slipped through. "And why is it not a day of celebrating? I've only heard good news. The king told me last night."

Lady Trent hands fidgeted in her lap. "The roads should be safer."

Felicity wanted to ask, unsure what they were discussing, but Lady Mistward sat straighter. "Our king has provided protection for us. The rebels were becoming more of a hindrance to the people. It was time he did something about it."

With practiced poise, Felicity kept her expression unreadable and her mouth shut.

"But to slaughter all those young ones," Lady Chartow hissed. "They didn't know better."

It took *all* of Felicity's training not to react.

Lady Fiadh cocked her head and with a serpentine grin, her attention settled on Lady Chartow. It went eerily quiet.

Queen Marquette lifted her chin. "Watch yourself, Lady Chartow. You wouldn't speak ill of my husband, would you?"

Chartow swallowed. "Of course not, Queen Marquette. I speak ill of the unnecessary death of younglings who were in the wrong place at the wrong time." Everyone averted their gaze from the female.

The queen straightened her maroon skirt. "Then the rebels shouldn't have their families with them. They shouldn't have chosen to betray their king—the one who protects them—with their younglings at their side."

Lady Chartow's gaze fell to the pebbled stone under their feet. "I apologize, Queen Marquette."

The queen considered her for a moment. "We shall drink to my husband's success in weakening those who poison our lands." Queen Marquette lifted her teacup, waiting for everyone to do the same.

Felicity wasn't the only one to hesitate.

"To the king," everyone repeated before they took a sip.

"Now, let's talk of other things." Lady Solfire took a finger sandwich from the tray.

Miss Isleen, who had remained quiet and poised during the entire conversation, grinned. She darted her gaze about the gardens. There were more gardeners today in their attempt to battle back the weeds. "The garden looks lovely in parts today." She pointed towards Felicity. "Look at the rosebuds behind Lady Dwauer and Lady Solfire. They are quite healthy." A safe conversation topic. The young female was a quick study.

Queen Marquette's gaze narrowed on the spot. "You're right. Look at that." The warmth returned to her expression, and she took another sip of her tea before placing the cup back on its saucer. "Maybe we're finally overcoming this curse."

Lady Solfire cocked her head in Felicity's direction before peering behind them at the flowers budding on the bush. Felicity hadn't noticed them, used to the gnarled branches and thick weeds.

The queen picked up a strawberry. "It will add to the celebration of Lughnasadh. By then, maybe all these gardeners and enchanters will have paid off." She took a bite as red juice from the strawberry stained her lips. "Lady Fiadh will be leaving tomorrow for a short time. She'll return in time for the ball." She eyed each of them. "We'll miss her, won't we?"

Everyone gave a fervent nod—a few added exclamations of feigned sadness.

When tea came to an end, Queen Marquette asked Felicity to join her again for a walk in the gardens. This time, the female didn't speak about her past. In fact, she was quiet until they were deep within the tangled mess of overgrowth where no gardener was present.

"I was wondering, my dear, if you had looked closer into Lady Chartow?" The queen swept dry leaves and pushed a vine off a bench almost hidden within the brush.

She gestured for Felicity to sit beside her and kept a solemn expression of disinterest. Felicity acquiesced to the invitation. "I have, Majesty. After multiple observations, I've seen nothing amiss and didn't uncover anything of note in her rooms."

The queen considered her words. "But here within our own afternoon tea, I've heard plenty that would make her guilty of disloyalty to the king."

"I've been tasked with uncovering those who are feeding information to the rebels. Not uncovering that which is spoken plainly." Felicity's mind raced in an attempt to protect Lady Chartow. But it was true the female had spoken clearly enough for all to hear and on more than multiple occasions. "I don't think she is any danger to you or the throne—if that is your concern."

Queen Marquette grinned. "Maybe not. Thank you for your input on the matter, Lady Dwauer. I'll consider your words."

Felicity was dismissed. There was nothing she could do. If she spoke for Lady Chartow further, her own loyalties might be questioned. If she tried to protect the female by stowing her away, then it would be obvious Felicity was working against the king. It would take some work, some thought, and a lot of manipulation to get Lady Chartow out of this mess. Felicity just hoped she had enough time to figure out how. If not for the female herself, but for the rebels who relied upon her.

***

Usually, the morning was quiet. But the following morning was eerily silent. Felicity had finished a nice breakfast in her room, but Meira had been distracted and unwilling to discuss the shift in her mood. The staff dodged anyone they came across in the halls. Before tea, Felicity found out why. She had been on her way to the gardens when Meira rushed to her, tears streaming down her face. "The king has requested everyone to the ballroom immediately."

Felicity walked with the handmaiden as staff ran from one room to the next, letting the occupants know of the summons. Others walked a step behind the fae, their heads bowed, a few trembling. When Felicity entered the ballroom, she stilled.

A floor that had been filled with dancing and celebration not long ago was now covered with splatters of murky water. No—Aer blood—clear except for wisps of gray and red. Lady Chartow was on her knees with chains connected to iron manacles snapped around the female's neck and limbs. Welts bloomed on her body. Open gashes slashed down her back, leaving skin laying open, chunks of bone visible beneath the blood and stripped sinew.

Once again, Felicity was appalled at what lay before her. The king was in his bestial form, pacing back and forth on clopping hooves that echoed with the female's painful sobs. Tattoos of a goat and lion Felicity had never seen before were illuminated on his arms between tufts of fur. Chartow must have been there for some time, but why the king had chosen a public place for such torture was sadistic.

The king looked at all who entered. Many stood frozen at the door, unable to pass the threshold. "This is what happens to those who speak ill of their king." He bared his teeth, green-tinged blood dripping from his maw. "This is what happens when you don't show the respect necessary to the one who protects and houses you." He spat on the floor beside the female.

Ward's scent informed Felicity of his arrival by her side, but she didn't look his way. Instead, she looked up at the dais to where Queen Marquette sat on her throne, her putrid smile of pride making Felicity's magic pulse—her anger come to life. As if she knew Felicity was looking at her, the queen tilted her head in Felicity's direction. She made sure to check her expression before their gazes locked.

Shadows erupted in the corner, and Prince Alarian stepped out of them. He stuttered to a stop at the sight. "Is this what I was summoned to witness, Father? Another rebel caught? Seems dramatic to host a blood bath in the ballroom."

King Roald roared, the sound reverberating against the pillars. The whimpers of his prisoner faltered, and Felicity's gaze fell to the female at his feet. Ward grabbed Felicity's arm and she stopped, not even realizing she had been moving towards Lady Chartow. She glared at his hand and then shot a venomous snarl his way. But he only shook his head.

"Well, get it over with, Father. We were all called here to witness her death, were we not? Another rebel killed—another victory for the king." Prince Alarian sounded bored, his hands in the pockets of his pants. He leaned against a pillar and cocked one leg over the other.

"She isn't a rebel," the king bellowed. "But she isn't loyal—she spoke falsehoods openly about the kingdom and therefore is just as vile as a traitor."

Felicity was impressed that the female hadn't broken and told everything she'd known judging by the torture she'd been put through. It was a testament to her resolve. Unbidden tears threatened to fall, but for Lady Chartow, Felicity forced them back and lifted her chin. If the female on the floor could die to protect others, Felicity could do her part to respect the female's sacrifice.

The king's gaze scanned the crowd, but no one spoke until a male stepped forward, a sneer across his face. "Then, by all means, your Majesty, punish her for her crimes." Canines elongated from the male's mouth, and Felicity recognized him as a general of Tine.

The king returned the smile. Others started to cheer for her death, a chant beginning through the crowd. "Kill her. Kill her."

Felicity remained silent, her expression neutral while her blood boiled. She searched the crowd until she found Lord Chartow. The male stood stock still, tears in his eyes as he was forced to watch as the king ordered guards to raise his wife to her feet, one holding her up on each side. Her husband didn't respond, his gaze boring into Lady Chartow's, the female meeting his stare. Felicity could feel the understanding within it. The pain Lord Chartow felt—evident in that shared look. There was an agreement, similar to the one between Ward and herself.

The king spread his hand out wide, his talons extended from inhuman fingers, and he clawed her down the front. Her stomach tore open, blood gushing, intestines hanging, and ribs visible. A silent scream etched across her face.

The guards stood there, arms quaking, as Lady Chartow's body jerked and bled all over the ballroom floor.

Someone retched as the king shook the blood from his talons, his body slowly contorting back to his human form. Felicity ignored him though, her attention on the female, promising to watch her least breath. To remember her. It was quick, but Felicity swore she saw a shadow slither away from Lady Chartow as her body stilled.

Chapter 31

Felicity begrudgingly fell back into a routine in the weeks leading up to Lughnasadh. Quiet mornings, tea, a study session with Ward, training, and spying at night. The prince hadn't shown again, and she had looked more than once for him within the shadows.

With Lady Fiadh gone, Queen Marquette only joined for tea every few days, her absence almost a welcomed reprieve for the ladies. No one spoke out of turn, too frightened, so all conversation stayed on subject matters of dresses, gossip, and seamstresses the females had commissioned to create their Lughnasadh gowns. Topics never strayed towards talk of rebels or politics—or Lady Chartow.

In other words, Felicity was bored. Even though the female's death weighed heavily on Felicity's shoulders, she jumped back into her mission with a new fervor—to weaken the king.

The rebels had quieted, and King Roald was starting to believe that with the executions and their dwindling numbers after the king's attack, Felicity soon would no longer be necessary. But Felicity heard the words whispered within halls and quiet conversations of more townsfolk disappearing. She also knew one thing to be true: the rebels weren't gone. This was just the calm before the storm.

Her list was shortening. Two others had been quite easy to pin, and Felicity had spread their deaths just enough to not cause suspicion from the king on a sudden influx of activity. But it had been at least a week since the last name was delivered. She had remained quiet, giving King Roald a false sense of security—that it was more difficult to find someone working against him. Since the king hadn't threatened her recently, she could only assume it was working.

It was early evening when Felicity reached the end of the passageway, letting out behind the old blacksmith's hut. She poked her head through the door and scanned her surroundings. Remaining low, she inched along the building until she was far enough from her original location and headed towards the walking path to Koselig.

There were three individuals that Felicity struggled to spin guilt against. Therefore, they continued to breathe. But Felicity didn't stop watching them. Advisor Gallist of Domhain had been the most elusive thus far—until she discovered he frequented a local brothel. The once intriguing fae had become nothing more than a portly male with a sad attempt at a mustache. His build held the promise of a once battle-savvy fae who had grown accustomed to a life of leisure. Of all the locations she'd followed him to, this by far was her best chance at finding cause for guilt.

The sign to the *Rose & Wisteria* hung over the door, swinging daintily back and forth with the ocean breeze. A brothel was a place of kept secrets. None spoke of who they saw or what they over-heard—the perfect location for finding reasons to turn in another name. Felicity took the back entrance. Getting a job there hadn't been too difficult. A past mission had put her in a similar position, and she knew what the Mistress was looking for.

Felicity ducked inside the kitchen and nodded to a young girl stirring a pot of thick stew over a fire. With matted hair falling over her face, the little girl bit her bottom lip in concentration, blood welling at the spot.

When the girl saw Felicity, her eyes blazed to life, and she began to stir in a hurry. "Missus is waiting for you." She turned back to the stew.

"Thank you." Felicity slipped into a side door to Mistress Ho-laps' office. The thick smell of roses engulfed her, and her nose twitched. By just stepping in here, Felicity became a rose lady.

"Right on time." A thin, short bauchan—Mistress Holaps wel-comed her with a toothy grin. "I like that about a girl. Now take off your cloak, let me look at you."

Felicity undid the tie at her neck and removed her cloak. Mistress Holaps' grin widened. "That's much better than those scraps you showed up in." She grabbed Felicity's bare shoulders and held her at arm's length, looking up and down at the black lace that lay over a merlot satin corset. Felicity had wrapped a lace shawl around the low dip of her waist, tassels grazing her bare legs.

The mistress pivoted Felicity in a circle until she saw the tattoo on her thigh, and her gaze thinned to near slits. "You didn't mention the markings."

Felicity swallowed. She had glamoured her scars but hadn't thought to cover the moon and stars. If the tattoo cost her this job...

"Some males like them, others not." Mistress Holaps took the shawl wrap and twisted it till the knot was over Felicity's opposite hip and the tattoo was mostly covered. "This way, it will peek out just enough to create curiosity."

Mistress Holaps analyzed Felicity's hair and cosmetics. "It will do." She stepped back. "You'll start in the Wisteria Room tonight. If you do good, we'll see about getting you into the rotation for the Rose Room."

Felicity's jaw clenched but she nodded. "Yes, Mistress." The Wisteria Room was for the middle-class clientele. If they had the money to pay, they were allowed access to the Wisteria Room. But Felicity knew without any doubt that Lord Gullist frequented the Rose Room—the place reserved for the high-class.

Felicity was dismissed with a shove towards the door. Mistress Holaps took to her seat, a quill flittering in her hand.

The previous night's tour had been quick, Mistress Holaps not wanting Felicity seen in the soiled clothes she had arrived in. Laying claims as a street urchin on hard times, at first, the mistress was tempted to throw Felicity back into the alleyway. It had just taken a wet rag for the mistress to see her face for her to change her mind.

Felicity glanced at the doorway of her desired destination as they passed. One night. She had done a similar job before and could do it again. With a deep breath, she slid into the door on the left and went straight to a bar tabletop and grabbed a tray of drinks. Nothing drew the attention of a male better than a drink and a scantily clad female. The room was furnished with enough seating for the entire court to sit.

Felicity moved through the small crowd. Four males sat at a table playing a game of cards. A Water Sprite sitting on one's lap as he held his cards and she nibbled at his neck.

Another two patrons sat on a deep-cushioned bench along the wall. The first male wore a mask made of porcelain that stood out against his black skin. A male sat on the back of the bench with his legs straddling either side of Porcelain Mask and rubbed his shoulder. A female sat beside him, lazily grazed her fingers over the masked male's skin as he spoke to another patron. The second wore a hat and a copper mask covering the upper half of his face from the tip of his nose to forehead. A female—with glossy hair that fell to her ass and a bushy brown tail similar to a wolf's—sat beside the male in the copper mask twirling his hair between her fingers, and went mostly ignored.

Felicity passed by the card players and attempted to draw their attention, slowing to offer them a drink. The players were too involved in their game, so she moved on to take her chances with the already preoccupied males on the bench. She leaned over and placed a glass of sweet-smelling drinks on the table in front of them. The one with the hat and copper mask nodded in her direction, still engrossed in his conversation with the porcelain-masked male. Copper Mask picked up the drink and slammed it back with one gulp. He inhaled, and his body stilled before he looked up at Felicity from under the brim of his hat.

Porcelain Mask made a joke, but Copper Mask only cocked his head in Felicity's direction. "New?" His voice was guttural—terse.

She nodded as the male on the other's lap leaned in closer to take the chance to draw his conquest's full attention. The female playing with Copper Mask's hair slid closer to him, giving Felicity a warning glare.

Felicity didn't want to get on anyone's bad side, so she turned to leave but was interrupted when Copper Mask cleared his throat and stood. He looked Felicity up and down then nodded towards a door. "Come."

The long-haired fae hoisted herself off the bench. "But Bruin, I had wonderful plans of how we were going to spend tonight." She moved between Bruin and Felicity.

Felicity knew this was a dangerous position if she wanted to get into the Rose Room. There was a chance that taking another's conquest would only cause her to be stuck here longer. Yet the others weren't begging for attention. None had even lifted their heads from their game.

"I'm the one paying." Bruin brushed a finger along the female's chin. "Next time, maybe."

Then his hand slid up Felicity's arm and goosebumps trailed under his touch. A grin flashed from under his mask.

Bruin pulled her close, wrapping a claiming arm around her shoulder and led her towards a room. He closed the door and then pressed her up against it. *Well, he got right to the point.* He leaned into her neck, tracing his lips against her skin. The smell of alcohol was thick around him, and Felicity compartmentalized her emotions, shoving back the anger and desire to slice this male's mouth off versus finishing the job. Sacrifice. Perfection. She needed him to get into the Rose Room.

He nipped at her neck, and she flinched, her reaction as unexpected as the nibble. His scent brushed her nose, and she inhaled deep—it was familiar under the pungent smell of alcohol and warmth spread through her body.

The male stepped back and pulled her towards the center of the room. Two candelabras in the far corners of the room emitted a soft glow, illuminating the space to show the four-poster against the wall, a nightstand, and a chaise at the end of the bed. Felicity allowed the mission to take over, and she pressed her body into his. Tearing the hat from his head, Felicity purred as she traced the line of his jaw to the point of the mask, her eyes finding his.

And then the dam broke free—his scent and those damn eyes.

"Alarian," she hissed, her anger boiling. "What the fuck?" She tore the copper mask off his face.

He chuckled, stepping back. "Wanted to see how committed you are to your job."

She slapped him hard, his head jerking sideways from the impact. When he faced her, he was still smiling. When she raised her hand to slap him again, he grabbed her wrist and held it still. "Once was enough. I wouldn't have taken it too far, but can you blame me for having a little fun?" He released his hold. "Didn't expect to find you here."

"What in the hell are you doing here?"

The prince sat on the bed and leaned back on his elbow. "Do you really have to ask that question?"

Felicity stilled. It felt, for a brief moment, like her heart had stopped beating. Frozen in place, she inhaled a deep breath, and relaxed her shoulders as her jaw feathered. "I'd think with a court of females fawning over you, this would be the last place you would need to be."

"Not if I am with the beautiful Lady Dwauer. It would be impolite and a fast way to get my mother on my back again." Prince Alarian wiggled his fingers at the mask in Felicity's hand. "Who's the target? I hope it wasn't a fae named Bruin?"

Felicity pushed the mask into his waiting grasp. "It's only a hunch, so I don't want to say." Felicity crossed her arms over her chest.

He looked her up and down, his gaze taking its time. "You're committed, that's for certain. Anything for the job?"

Felicity shrugged. "You think this is my first time in a brothel? It's often the most common place we're sent to complete a mission—depending on the client. Territorial males aren't nearly as bad as bitter females and there are many opportunities for secret meetings that a spy may need to overhear."

The prince chuckled. "Well, I guess it's a good thing I'm here then."

"Why is that?" She had a hundred reasons running through her head why it wasn't.

He pushed himself up and came around the chaise until he was standing in front of her. "Because I can keep some of your dignity intact." His grin returned. "And if you choose to trust me, I could help."

"What makes you think I have any dignity?" she growled.

"If you didn't, you wouldn't have stopped me." He winked while she considered his offer.

Although currently, she just wanted to slap him again. With a deep sigh, she waved her hand at the door. "I need to get into the Rose Room by tomorrow night. My target is in there, not here."

His gaze narrowed and he cocked his head. "That part will be easy. I can sing your praises in the morning. Of course, things may be a bit uncomfortable in the meantime."

"Why?"

"The sounds you need to make..." He tsked. "They need to be believable. I have a reputation to keep."

"There's no way—"

He grabbed his hat and jammed it on his head. "Then good luck with whoever is left out there."

Felicity cut him off before he reached the door. "You're despicable," she hissed.

She tore the hat off his head again. Tossing it to the ground, she let out a high-pitched moan that silenced those on the other side of the door and froze the prince in place. Every inch of his body stiffened—some more obvious than others—and his eyes darkened. The smile that stretched on his lips was bestial.

She pushed him away, annoyed he won. But two could play that game. "It won't be believable if you don't join in." She stepped towards him until she was a mere inch from his body and looked up into his eyes. "Otherwise, they might send you to the Rose Room instead of me."

He met her gaze, that corner of his mouth inching upward into his mischievous smirk. For a moment, she considered closing that gap...to find out what his lips tasted like. To form her body to his and feel his skin against hers. It could be just for the night—let that part of her *want* take over. Then it would be out of her system, and she could ignore whatever part of her that was drawn to him. The part that searched for him in the training room.

Before she could act on it, he blinked and stepped back, letting out a moan that forced a warm shudder to rush through her body and pool in her core. He continued to put distance between them, and Felicity grinned, hiding any thoughts from her expression.

The next few hours—because he ensured that his stamina was up for the task—they each let out interspersed sounds and added in the occasional tumble with falling furniture and baubles clattering to the floor. What the others didn't see was that both she and the prince sat in different locations, neither of them on the bed. Felicity felt it was dangerous ground to be anywhere near that particular piece of furniture. Especially by the way her senses were heightened by each sound he made. Even looking at him at times made her want to prowl across the room and...

She wasn't willing to go there. It would be a mistake.

When it was well past midnight and the two large candelabras dimmed, Prince Alarian stood and stretched with a wide yawn. "It's time for sleep." He trudged a few steps then fell face-first onto the large four-poster bed, upsetting the pillows that still remained.

Felicity stood over his silent body, crossing her arms. "Who said you get the bed?"

He reached an arm out and patted the empty space beside him. Turning to his side, he looked up at her. "There's plenty of room."

"Or you could sleep in the corner on a bed of pillows like a good fox." She tossed a few pillows against the wall to make a point.

He pushed himself onto his forearms, and Felicity ridiculed herself for noting the strain of his muscles as he looked at the spot she designated for him. "No. You were going to share a bed with a strange male. You can handle this."

She hated the truth in his words almost as much as she hated him at that moment. With a huff, Felicity tore back the blanket and tucked herself under, pulling it up to her chin. Curling on her side, she turned her back to him.

"Why the Wisteria Room?" Felicity asked.

He was silent for a moment. Her gaze wandered through the darkness, settling on the shape of shadows. She wondered if he had fallen asleep when he cleared his throat. "It's less likely I'll be recognized."

"Seems like a lot of thought for a vague answer. Besides, you wear a mask." Felicity faced him, making sure to keep the blankets over her. The lack of clothing had never bothered her before, but she felt self-conscious with her current bedmate.

He searched her face. "You've heard the rumors about me. Do you really want me to elaborate on my reasons for being here?"

"Only the most interesting people have stories about them." She grinned and he returned it.

He adjusted his pillow, stuffing his arm under it to lift his head slightly. "What was it like growing up in a guild of spies and assassins?"

"Why would I tell you?"

Prince Alarian stared at the ceiling. "Hope, I guess, that there was an ounce of trust. I wasn't asking for their secrets. It's something to pass the time."

She kept her mouth shut and by the way he chuckled, he had made her uncomfortable on purpose. *Damn him.*

He continued, "I spent many years of my youth in Scáth. Have you been?"

She peered at him, knowing by the smile across his face that he knew the answer to his question. "No, I have not. It isn't a place usually visited by outsiders."

"They are not the warmest of folk, that is true. Well, unless you prove you deserve their respect—but not beforehand."

"I've heard many have entered the forest never to leave it again." It felt blasé to discuss children's stories, but if it kept him away from pestering about her past...

"Here's a little secret." He turned onto his side to face her. "That's what they want you to believe. I spent most of my time climbing trees, trying to capture will-o'-the-wisps, getting in trouble with pranks, and playing hide-n-go-seek."

"None of that is hard to believe." She wouldn't admit she was entranced by the images he was creating in her mind.

He adjusted the pillow under his head. "The Shadows believed it was the best way for us to learn. Not only to control our magic but to control ourselves. When you have elders who can catch you within a beat of your heart, you have to learn fast or be faster."

"That wasn't how I was taught." She bit her bottom lip, surprised she'd spoken the words aloud. *When had she turned to face him?*

His eyes searched her face, landing on her mouth. "I would assume not."

Her jaw ticked. "From the first time I saw the initiates training I wanted to be one of them, moving through the positions..." She trailed off, remembering the feeling of the first staff in her hands. The memories she had been allowed to keep from her early years at the Tower now felt long ago. "There wasn't a chance for games. Not if I wanted to prove myself."

Alarian sighed. "We'll have to be sure to remedy that. Games and fun are important in life."

"Tell me about them."

He smiled and his emerald eyes shined. "Imagine trees that cover the sky. They are the perfect height for branches to climb, crevices to hide in."

As he spoke, she closed her eyes, tall trees growing in her mind, extending from the earth strewn with leaves and shrubs.

She didn't know how long she listened to his childhood stories. More than one occasion had her laughing, and then a moment later, she was entranced by the memories he shared. "The heartstones of Scáth were sometimes a point of our games. The importance of their protection is our main focus."

When the clock chimed thrice it signaled a yawn for her.

"Did I tire you out?" Then his mouth widened, and he covered it, trying to stifle his own yawn.

Felicity smiled and closed her eyes. "Don't flatter yourself."

"Felicity?" Prince Alarian whispered.

She didn't open her eyes. "Hmmm."

"What is that mark on your hip?"

Felicity blinked and then stared at him. "It's a tattoo. A moon—the stars surrounding it have been added for each completed mission."

His mouth twitched. "How many?"

"This is my thirtieth mission." She curled her fingers into fists around the blanket. "When I graduated to initiate, they began to mark my completed missions with a star." Had they chosen when she was able to move to the next rank and her memories would no longer be taken? Is that why she always stayed as a trainee or apprentice when they took bits of her past so the marks weren't necessary? More questions she needed answers to.

"Will you return to the Tower when this is done to have it added to the tattoo?"

Her brow furrowed. "I... I don't know. I hadn't thought about it. Is there a tattoo on your back?" The last words were out of her mouth before she could stop them.

"It's a fox." He winked at her. "I knew you looked."

She almost smacked him, but he closed his eyes before she could. "Good night, Starlight."

For a moment she considered asking about the nickname. To demand he never speak it again. But not tonight—tonight she enjoyed the way it sounded and that it was the last thing she heard before falling into a dreamless sleep.

Chapter 32

He was gone before Felicity woke. The place where his body had been still warm to the touch. It surprised her that he could slip from the room without notice—that had never happened in the past. But then again, he could use the shadows.

After fixing her appearance, she headed back to the Wisteria Room to find Mistress Holaps waiting.

"Bruin said you were worth every cent he paid. And he paid handsomely." Her smile lengthened. "I don't know how you did it. It's been weeks since he's taken a girl." She gestured for Felicity to follow her. "You get one night in the Rose Room. I expect the same performance, or you'll be right back where you started."

Felicity wouldn't need more than one night. As long as the advisor arrived...

She wouldn't allow herself to think like that.

Mistress Holaps didn't wait for her as she tittered down the hall. Felicity caught up with quick steps. Once they reached a doorway, the mistress snapped a few times before a young girl hurried from the kitchen, carrying a bag of cosmetics. The girl reapplied kohl to Felicity's eyes and painted her lips deep crimson.

When the mistress considered her appropriate, she opened the door and Felicity strutted in, the door snapping shut behind her. Three females, a male, and a human sat at a table. Each looked up from their breakfast at her arrival.

"Fresh blood," a fae hissed as she licked each of her pointed teeth.

"Don't expect it to be easy in here," added another with a bushy tail. "We're in this room for a reason. You gotta prove yourself."

The warnings weren't necessary—Felicity wasn't meant to stay.

For most of the day, she gave the others space, observing as they sauntered by patrons and whispered in their ears. Thankfully business was slow, so she was able to keep her distance. Some used magic, air brushing around necks, water to fill a tub in the corner and bathe, and fire to light candles were just a few of the tricks up their sleeves. A female with a tail wrapped it around arms and brushed it along thighs as she passed. They gave Felicity a wide berth at first but began to relax when she proved she wasn't there to force them out. She just hoped Advisor Gullist didn't have a favorite because she needed his attention tonight. Or at least preoccupied enough to spill secrets.

When Lord Gullist finally arrived in the early evening, he wore a thin mask covering the left half of his face that did nothing to hide his identity.

He and Felicity hadn't interacted in court. She was confident he wouldn't recognize her with the dark makeup and sleek hair. He looked her up and down with a leering smile then ordered a drink as he took a seat at the table where a card game had begun.

The door opened again, but Felicity kept her attention on the lord as she considered her next move. That was until the becoming all too familiar scent of misty spruce and pine wrapped around her. Felicity whirled and this time there was no denying it was the prince with those piercing green eyes that immediately settled on her. His hair was painted black, and he wore pristine clothes, high boots, and a mask made of thin black metal with an intricate feather engraved into it.

She'd never seen him dress this way at the castle. Even his royal attire didn't hold the same striking air as his current ensemble—except when he had been present at any of the celebrations.

"Master Harlin," one of the fae purred. "It's been a while. Where've you been?"

Of course, he had another identity. Felicity almost hit her own forehead but instead gritted her teeth.

"Business has kept me away." Even his voice had an air of social numbness that made Felicity want to shudder in disgust.

Harlin sauntered across the room, but the first female grabbed his arm and pulled him onto a settee. The human woman ran to get him a drink and returned, settling herself on his other side. "We've missed you." The woman traced her thumb along his jaw and Felicity ignored the desire to break each one of her dainty fingers.

With the others entertained by the prince's arrival, Felicity grabbed a drink from the bar and took it over to the lord. *He* wasn't her concern—Gullist was. She hoped she wouldn't need to take the portly male to a room and would just need to be close enough to hear where conversations turned. Or if, by chance, he said or did something she could use against him.

"Drink, milord?" She bent over as she set it in front of him, making sure her assets were in full view.

Advisor Gullist's gaze brushed over her skin, causing her stomach to turn. "Thank you. Keep them coming."

The prince cleared his throat, and the patrons playing cards turned. "Is there a seat for me?"

The female and woman inched closer to him, obvious in their attempt to keep him to themselves.

"Sure," answered a female patron with multi-colored twigs and flowers sticking from her hair. Pulling out the chair beside her, she looked back at her cards. "When this game's done, join us." Her smile widened. "Or if you want to take care of other needs first…"

The prince stood and pulled the chair back farther. Felicity's eyes narrowed as he tugged the human onto his lap. "Needs can wait. Deal me in on the next game."

The bell tolled on two separate occasions while they played cards. Felicity was kept to the outskirts. She'd never been unsuccessful in such a position, and she couldn't help but blame the prince's presence for her bad luck. It was hard to concentrate on the task at hand when her stomach churned whenever the human curled his fake black hair or nuzzled his neck.

Felicity attempted her luck with the other males to remain busy and not draw suspicion, but it was obvious they were in no mood for the females yet—or at least not her. One of the men had left the table a few hands before, taking one of the prominent fae to a room.

"New girl." Alarian's voice drew her attention. The woman had moved behind his chair, her hand on his shoulder as she watched the game. The prince waved two fingers at her, and although Felicity would rather throw the drink she was holding in his face, she sauntered across the room.

He looked her up and down, and Felicity almost slapped him when his grin extended to a mischievous leer.

He patted his other thigh. "There is room for you here."

Felicity made a show of biting her lip as her insides battled. He was offering her a chance to listen in—one she couldn't pass up. She sat on the edge of his knee, and he wrapped a hand around her waist. Her mind and body were in a battle of wills, her back reveling in his touch while she internally lectured herself.

"Gullist, how has trade been going?" The prince asked, and Felicity's desire to hit him diminished internally thanking him for steering the conversation.

The advisor lowered his cards. "Difficult with the new laws in effect. The king has strong input on who we can hire now." He shook his head. "You'd think he'd be happy with whomever I used to drag stone from one location to the next. It's for the best, though. Tough times will lead to a better future."

Prince Alarian leaned a little closer to Felicity and inhaled. "You smell like flowers." He buried his head into her neck, and she arched her back, bearing into him.

The human's shoulders slumped, and the prince faced her. "Could you get me another drink?"

The woman knew her time was up, and once she was gone, the prince maneuvered Felicity fully onto his lap, his arms wrapped around her to hold his cards. This part she could play. Resting her head into the apex of his neck, she breathed gently onto his skin. She tried to ignore the shiver that ran through him, but Felicity's body reacted, pressing closer into him. While one hand held cards, the other began a lulling pattern of circles on her thigh and Felicity's body warmed.

Gullist was pushed into the back of her mind, the prince to the front. His touch brought her alive. A graze of his hand forced a moan from her lips. Suddenly the night before, the talks and stories told were not enough. On instinct, her body ground into his lap. She grazed her mouth over the crook of his neck as his hand gripped her thigh.

"Careful," he whispered as her fingers twisted the hair at his nape.

"Or what?" She purred, nuzzling his ear.

His heartbeat quickened under her hand that rested against his firm chest. Felicity smiled to herself. She liked making him react this way, the evidence of his own want pressing against her. Her skin tingled, her body reacting to the feel of him—his scent—everything that made this male.

She breathed a gentle sigh against his skin and Alarian purred, the prince's breath tickling her skin. With a nip to the lobe of his ear, she was about to invite him to the nearest room when—

"Aer and Visce have a new round of inventions coming to the fair this autumn. Sounds like they may finally be able to expand some of their ideas beyond their own borders."

Gullist's voice brought Felicity from her reverie, and she pulled back from Alarian's touch. It almost ached when the prince's hold loosened, and she hated the lord for interrupting the moment.

And yet...*what had come over her*? She sat up straighter. It was going to be near impossible to break Lord Gullist in his current state. All she needed was just one slip-up, one-minute detail that could be used against the male. That was what she needed—not the distraction of the prince's touch.

When the cards were shuffled for the next game, Felicity turned and slid across the center of the table, drawing all of the seated patron's attention. A fae across from Gullist grinned at the view she displayed. She met the lord's gaze. "Can I get something else for you to drink?"

Gullist smiled. "Yes, make yourself more useful than warming that male's lap." He nodded towards the prince.

Prince Alarian leaned forward. "I like my lap warm."

Lord Gullist and the others chuckled as Felicity walked away from the table towards the bar.

The prince continued, "Don't you remember how it is on the ships for a month? Or longer? When was the last time you rolled in a ship's cargo hold with anyone other than your wife?"

Felicity froze at the bar, worried the prince had taken it too far, relaxing only when Gullist chuckled.

"Too long. But when you're married to the king's sister, the dangers of being caught make it intriguing enough. Although, I like to go to sleep knowing I'll have my head still attached in the morning. With the king's current mood, I don't want to test his resolve."

He is the king's brother-in-law? Shit. It was a long shot, but Felicity noted the male's adultery. If anything, it could be the nail that sealed his coffin.

"And what about you, Harlin?" Gullist picked up the cards dealt to him from the table and organized his hand. "It's been weeks since I've seen you here and even longer at the docks?"

Why would *Harlin* be at the docks? Felicity carried the tray of drinks across the room, sashaying her hips as she did.

Prince Alarian's gaze had settled on her. With a jerk, he looked at his cards and Felicity couldn't help but smile as he answered, his voice thick. "Busy finagling the new laws. I considered getting another crew but with the upcoming change in season, I think we'll plan for a spring sailing to the islands." He cleared his throat. "We have enough to hold things over until then. In the meantime, we're working to extend trade routes to the farther continents."

Felicity stopped across from Gullist and bent over subtly while she passed drinks to the others. When the advisor looked up, his eyes rested on her breasts and slowly inched up to meet her gaze. At Prince Alarian's growl, Gullist blinked and turned back to his cards. Felicity shot a quick glare at the prince, but he shrugged it off.

Prince Alarian played a card. "As for my absence here, I've had other things keeping me busy."

Gullist chuckled. "And what is her name? Or his, perhaps? Would I know who it is entertaining the second most eligible bachelor in Éardrom?" The advisor peered at *Harlin* over his hand of cards. "Never seen you at any parties. You keep most things private, so give us a little taste of your secret life."

Felicity slowly worked around the table, dropping a goblet down beside each player. While entertaining and eye-opening, Felicity didn't need gossip centered around the prince—or any of his personas. She slowed as she passed Gullist, a finger brushing along his shoulder blades, and he gave her a half-smile as she took the tray to the bar.

"I like my privacy, Gullist. You should consider it yourself. It can keep you out of trouble."

The players snorted or chuckled in response. When Felicity returned to the table, Prince Alarian leaned back to allow room for her, but she ignored him and stood at the advisor's shoulder. She needed the male to be sidetracked enough to not concentrate on what he divulged to the group. Since the alcohol hadn't been working, it might take a little more to preoccupy him. And if the prince was willing to help, she would let him keep asking questions while she did her part.

Resting a hand on Gullist's shoulder, she purred, "Tense, milord. May I?"

Gullist looked at her and his mouth pursed. After some consideration, he turned back to the game. "Please."

"So polite," she whispered as she moved around him to place both hands on either side and began to massage his shoulders. The advisor groaned and sank into her touch.

The rest of the game continued and the two others at the table ignored Felicity. But it was too quiet. She shot a glance at the prince, attempting to beckon him to continue his line of questioning but the male was scowling. Not at her, but at the point where her hands rested on the advisor's shoulders.

"Master Harlin," she purred in an attempt to get his attention. "Why all the secrecy? My cousin works at the dock and said that trade was doing well. Sends off on a new ship every chance he gets."

He shook his head, looking back at his cards. "Secrets are made for dark corners and sleepless beds. Not to be shared over a game of cards."

Gullist chuckled, leaning across the table to place his bet. "Seems we have a smart one in our mists. She's right. You might want to consider getting in one or two more trips before the winter months. More money to spend here."

The prince didn't deign to respond, a grunt the only hint he even heard them. Felicity continued her massage, and the lord groaned in pleasure. His game was going horribly—which meant she was doing her job. But if he caught on to the fact that he was doing badly too soon, he could pull out and drag her to a room. Or ignore her again. Trying to draw him into a conversation was not what she was meant to do within these walls. Not in her current position.

"With the king's rules tightening, I just hope we can make it to the border continents. I was close to getting some promising contacts out there." The prince played another card, staring hard at his hand as though it would jump from his grip.

Gullist closed his eyes, resting his head on her hand for a moment. When she stopped, he sat up and looked down at his cards, throwing out the wrong one. Felicity leaned over and blew a slow breath in the male's ear. He shuddered.

The advisor's eyes flickered open, and he sat up, clearing his throat. "What did you say?"

Prince Alarian repeated the comment, his body tense.

Gullist nodded in agreement. "Well, yes. The king's rules have been more difficult to work with as of late. He's been moody and I've heard rumors it might get worse before it becomes better. With the continued issues of the rebels, things seem to be out of His Majesty's control. We're losing numbers to properly crew the boats. No one wants the job of swabbing decks and cleaning up grease and piss except for the orphans being left behind. If he continues the shit he's doing with the adults, we aren't going to have anyone left."

Felicity began her massage again, working on one side of his shoulder. *Keep talking.*

"Does he plan to send them to the border colonies?" the prince asked, his jaw feathering.

Gullist shrugged. "Possibly. I don't know what he's planning, but I swear that queen of his is whispering evil things in his ear. My wife has been concerned about her from the beginning."

As if the mention of his wife was enough, Gullist jerked his shoulder from out under Felicity's touch. "That's enough."

And it was enough.

He had spoken ill against a member of the royal family, which had been enough to condemn Lady Chartow. Felicity stepped away at the same time the prince's chair was pushed back, and he blocked her path. She met the prince's gaze, and she could almost hear the anger in the rush of his blood. *But why was he upset?*

With his eyes, he gestured towards the door. "Let's go." Felicity froze in place, her heart pounding against her chest, a flutter and heat emitting from her center. He brushed past her towards an oak door.

Gullist chuckled as she followed. "Have fun," the lord called. "Make sure to save some of her for the rest of us."

Chapter
33

Felicity entered the room, not certain what she'd find. The prince closed the door behind her, and his shadows enveloped the space, the candelabras extinguished into darkness.

She whirled around and ran into his solid form. Their gaze met and everything else disappeared. The mission, the sounds on the other side of the door, any thoughts of why she was here. She knew she could get lost in his emerald eyes and be happy about it. That heat in her core spread lower. It had been too long. Since she'd been touched. Kissed—

He didn't move as Felicity tilted her head up, invading the minuscule distance between them. His gaze slid to her lips and all she would need to do was lean into him. Let the confusion of every emotion he elicited from her go and allow the moment to take over. Get him out of her system for good. Maybe all it would take is one kiss. One touch. One night.

But he didn't close that distance, even with the want evident in his expression. The feel of his need brushed below her waist as she reached up to touch his face.

For a moment she wondered if he even breathed—but that moment was gone when he inhaled. Her thumb brushed his cheek and Alarian didn't need any further invitation. His arm wrapped around her, pressing their bodies together and his mouth was on hers. It began gentle. A taste. She bit back a moan at the feel of him. Then she brushed her tongue against his lips, asking for entrance. And gentle was gone.

A growl emitted from his throat. His arms tightened their hold, one at her neck, the other around her waist. Hell—she could feel all of him. Wanted all of him. Clothing, even as little as she wore, was in the way. Desire, heat—lust. It all came together. Her hand tugged the hair at the nape of his neck to raise his chin and her lips trailed to his throat.

She stepped back, towards the bed, pulling him along. There was no hesitation as his mouth found hers again.

Alarian buried his hand into her hair, and he nipped at her earlobe, forcing that resisted moan from her lips. She wanted this. Needed this.

The back of her legs met the edge of the bed, and she fell back, taking him with her. He braced himself over her, that grin she loved to hate playing at the corner of his lips. As she reached for him, the need to explore him overpowering any sense of self, his expression changed—brows drawn together, his smile wavered.

The prince froze. He swallowed as his body shuddered. Felicity's brow furrowed but before she could decipher that look, the shadows coalesced, and he was gone.

She sat up as he reappeared against the far wall, his outline visible in the darkness. Although tempted to touch her magic and light the room, she resisted the call. It wasn't safe here.

Even with the distance between them, she could see his chest rose and fell with deep breaths, his gaze settled sharply on her.

As Felicity stood, he raised a hand. "Stop." He shook his head. "Stay there..."

With a cock of her head, she crossed her arms over her chest. Her lips were bruised from their kiss. Confusion mixed with reality. Not only at his response but what they had just done. Damn it all, she'd kissed the prince. "Did something—"

"Quiet. For just a moment." Frustration laced his tone, his hands forming fists at his sides. The shadows leaked from him, the room darkening. "Please," he breathed, and she noted the pleading note in his tone.

She blinked, giving him the requested space and quiet. With each of his cleansing breaths, the darkness receded, the shadows leaving the room. And with it, reality settled. Where they were. Why she was here. For a moment she'd forgotten who she was and who he was. *Don't let yourself become distracted in moments.* This time the lesson was in the Countess's voice.

He slumped against the wall, falling to the floor in a crouch, and covered his face with his hands.

On silent feet, she trotted towards him then lowered herself to his level and reached a hand out, grazing a finger over his. It was good they had stopped. For both their sakes. She couldn't be mad at him for it even if a sense of embarrassment momentarily awoke. There was no reason to be ashamed about what just happened. "What is it?"

He pulled his hands away from her touch, and Felicity noticed sweat glistening at his temples. "Alarian?" She kneeled on the floor, sitting back on her legs.

With his head in his hands, he shuddered again. "I don't like the idea of you being here—what you might have to do for my father. You should have a choice, Felicity. Even now." He breathed a heavy sigh. "I know you were struggling with it, but maybe it's for the best you cannot return to the Tower."

Felicity bit her lip—emotions clinging to her. None familiar. None made sense. Except for anger. She gripped hold of it as an anchor. "I can handle myself." She pushed herself off the floor and kept her voice low though she wanted to yell. "I'm a weapon. You don't need to come traipsing into my life as if you're some prince to save me." Her blood boiled. "Because it's too late. I am what I am—and it wouldn't have been the first or the last time someone used me while sealing their own fate."

The prince was in her face within a breath. "Then fucking change *your* fate," he growled.

This is how he acted after a kiss? A kiss she thought he wanted too. She stood and he did the same. Before he looked at her again, she schooled her expression to indifference. Let the mission come to the forefront of her mind. He—this shouldn't matter. "What is this? You could have cost me all the hard work I've done. Made this entire escapade useless."

"It was useless. There isn't enough to prove Gullist's in league with the rebels. I don't like the male, but not even I can find reason for his death." Prince Alarian shook his head. "Come, I'm taking you back." He held out a hand, palm up, waiting.

"Don't worry—I can handle the lord myself. And we can't just traipse out of here. This is a brothel, not a place where a harlot runs off with a trader. By the way, who is *Harlin*, Prince?"

He growled. "You ask a lot of questions. I'm not the one on trial here." Prince Alarian nodded to his waiting hand. "I'm taking you by shadow, now hold on."

Felicity opened her mouth to contradict him, but common sense took over. It would be the easiest way. "But how do you plan to return here after stealing the new girl?"

"Harlin won't be necessary soon." His patience was spent, obvious by the darkness that enveloped them. He pulled her close until her body was flush with his. She attempted to resist his hold, but she stilled as the shadows pressed in around her. It was cold, especially in the little clothing she was wearing. The tendrils of mist and gray rushing past her felt like ice sliding across her skin. But the prince was warm, his arm tight around her back. She found herself settling into his touch until there was a sudden impact and her knees buckled.

Alarian held her up as the shadows slowly dissipated and she recognized the stone walls. "How? I would think there would be enchantments against using magic to enter the palace."

"There are. Those who can travel through shadow or darkness can do so within the grounds but not past the wards. The enchantment only deems entrance to members and those loyal to the royal family."

The familiarity of her bed, the chairs in front of the fire, began to come into view as the last of the shadows disappeared. "My room."

"Yes, your room." He inhaled as their eyes met. Felicity's heart raced, and it took her a moment to realize she wasn't moving away from him.

She touched his black hair. "I prefer it red."

The corner of his mouth lifted. "I didn't think you would prefer me in any way." His hold loosened but Felicity didn't move. Absentmindedly, she bit her bottom lip.

His gaze traced her face, his expression hardening. "Promise me something, Felicity."

She blinked. "What?"

"After all of this is over, don't ever let anyone ever use you again."

Her lips parted as she breathed in deeply. "Alarian—"

But before she could continue, he stepped away from her and the shadows enveloped him. When they dissipated, he was gone.

"I promise," she whispered.

Chapter
34

Two days later, Lord Gullist was bound in iron chains in the center of the ballroom. It had become the norm that everyone's presence was required for those public executions. With the way things were going, Felicity wondered when they would be taken into the town itself. But she was certain that the king didn't want the weakness of his court on display. Felicity stood with the other courtiers, waving her fan to cover her face, the heat penetrating through the tall windows. With the number of bodies surrounding her, it was stifling. Ward moved through the crowd until he was nearby.

"Did you speak out against your queen? Side with others against us?" King Roald's teeth had elongated, his broad shoulders squared to the male bound and crouching before him.

"Never, your Majesty. Whatever allegations you've heard against me are false." Lord Gullist stuck out his chin in defiance. Although he had been beaten, his solid expression was resilient—evident in his set mouth and fierce gaze. "And I demand proof be brought forth before you tear me apart."

The king's teeth clenched. None had asked for proof in the past. Not a one had questioned the king's motives. Of course, there had been enough witnesses or small truths to the accusations. This one was based on hearsay and the 'witnesses' had been too drunk to remember a thing. And no one could find *Harlin* to question him. Felicity half expected the king to find her in the crowd and force her into the center of the room beside the lord.

"Father." The prince sauntered in with his hands in his pockets, his dark auburn hair freshly trimmed. Many gazes turned to him in surprise at his arrival. His on and off absences had been noted by many as of late. "What fun have I been missing now?" He stopped beside the lord, cocking his head in his uncle's direction.

King Roald's face turned a shade of crimson. "I'm glad you deemed it important enough to arrive." He growled at the man crouched before him. "Accusations have been made against Lord Gullist. Now my traitorous brother-in-law demands proof."

The prince chuckled. "Didn't Lady Fiadh arrive today? It seems this could be cleared up quite easily."

King Roald smiled. "Of course." He pointed to the nearest guard. "Find her."

Felicity's fan sped up, unnoticed by others between the heat and the show before them. She found Ward's gaze and his jaw clenched. Lady Fiadh hadn't been due to return for a few more days.

The king was pacing by the time Lady Fiadh arrived. She seemed to float in, her dress unmoving with each step. With a blank expression and her hands folded in front of her, she stopped and bowed before the king. The queen stood, taking her place beside the king, suddenly alert at the arrival of the witch.

King Roald beckoned her closer. "We need your expertise, Lady Fiadh. There have been allegations regarding Lord Gullist's allegiance to the crown."

The witch's head sliced towards the lord as she passed him, a steely look of malcontent resting on her sharp features.

She stopped before the king, her gaze never leaving the lord. Prince Alarian stood at attention beside Lord Gullist, his hands clasped behind his back.

Lady Fiadh's expression transformed into a dangerous sneer, her eyes piercing. "He's not worth the time to slice his throat, My King. The lord has worked against you with the rebels. He's shared many secrets. In fact, he met with one rebel yesterday morning."

Lord Gullist's eyes widened, and his mouth dropped. "Never."

"Who?" King Roald bellowed. "Who is his contact?"

Before Gullist could expel any words, the king transformed. Lady Fiadh shook her head. "His thoughts are scattered. Too many." She gripped her head, cowering. "No, too many. Make it stop," she screamed.

With sharp talons, the king ripped out the male's throat, tearing flesh and organ. Green blood splattered and gushed all over the prince who stood, unflinching, as gore dripped from his attire.

King Roald's chest heaved. Some cheered at the guilty being slain, while others averted their gaze to anywhere else. Lady Fiadh gasped for breath, shuddering as she fell to the floor. Queen Marquette gestured for a guard to lift her and with a stoic calm, walked out alongside the guard. The crowd parted to let them pass.

The prince bowed to his father. "I think my deed is done for today." He moved to leave. His gaze found hers, his mouth set, the lord's blood dripping down his temple.

Felicity couldn't ignore the pang that pulsed through her body. And she hated that she recognized the emotion—guilt. Again.

Shortly after the execution, before Felicity could make it to tea, the king demanded her presence. With gore still staining his clothes, face and hands, he watched as she entered the room. Ward stood behind her, his arms crossed as he leaned against the wall. The prince wasn't present, which caused that damn guilt to settle deeper.

"You have done well. But I need the rebels," King Roald snapped.

Ward snorted. "Maybe if you asked more questions instead of killing so quick, you could have had them."

The king's nails lengthened into talons, and he pointed one at the male. "Don't speak out of turn, boy. Or I'll have you punished."

Ward didn't flinch. His expression remained unreadable, lips pursed together.

The king regarded Felicity for a moment. "I need a direct lead, their contact, and when and where they meet."

Felicity nodded. "As you wish, King Roald."

The king's mouth was a thin line. "Others will demand proof prior to their sentences being filled, so from this point forward, you need to have it prepared. I don't want to rely on Lady Fiadh's presence. They won't be brought forward and used as an example until they have been questioned and confirmed guilty. I do not want to be made a laughingstock or my motives questioned."

"Understood." Felicity bit the inside of her mouth too hard, a metallic tang coated her tongue.

King Roald turned to Ward. "Give her what she needs. Carriages, clothes, weapons, whatever is necessary. She's taking initiative by going to the town, but I want more information sooner rather than later."

Ward nodded, and they were dismissed. Neither spoke until they reached her room.

"That was a close one." Ward breathed deeply after he shut the door. "I thought for sure there was no way that would work out."

"It still doesn't make sense." She smoothed out the pleats in her dress as she sat, her mind drifting in an attempt to put the pieces together. "It was a stretch, Ward. Something isn't right." Felicity shook her head. "I shouldn't have turned him in. I pushed it too far."

Ward looked at her from the corner of his eye. "We'll be more careful. We must have got lucky. Or Lady Fiadh made a mistake for our benefit."

"Could Lady Fiadh be another contact?" Felicity kept her voice low and her senses on high alert. Her eyes widened. "Or was Lord Gullist?" The past events were making her question herself.

"It definitely wasn't the lord. To him, anyone below his title is considered nothing more than grunt workers, so there is no way he would side with them against the king." Ward shook his head. "As for Lady Fiadh, her ability is hard to understand. She can read a person—their thoughts, memories—but as I mentioned they can be convoluted and incorrect depending on the circumstances and the crowd. Either way, I don't think she would ever side against the queen—or the king for that matter. There is too much strength in that triad."

His gaze hardened, and he ran a hand through his hair. "The king is getting nervous. As much as the attacks and the rebels seem to be quieting, I think he senses more is to come. He just doesn't know when. We have to keep him guessing." Ward's brow scrunched together.

"There is only so much I can do." Felicity's jaw clenched. "And I don't like that." Prince Alarian's words rang in her ear. *Change your fate.* "What is our plan here? To frame the king's connections until we are caught?"

He shook his head. "You're weakening his trust in who he considered his closest allies. Things will start to unravel from there."

It wasn't enough. "The rebels need to make a move."

Ward nodded. "Soon, Felicity. I guarantee it will be soon."

The memory came unbidden. *"Soon."*

Felicity blinked and stretched her legs into a fighting stance. "You say that every time."

A laugh flitted across the room, and she shot a glare at the boy. His smile lengthened as he lifted his arms, fists forming.

Harrison pointed to the center of the ring. "Begin."

Felicity ducked, expecting the boy's right hook and as usual, it was too high. Felicity did an uppercut with her left hand. The impact of his chin cut open her knuckles. He stepped back, off balanced but raised his hands again, rocking back and forth.

"But I'm ready and you know it," Felicity bickered, sending a swinging right kick at her opponent's legs, but this time he was ready and blocked it.

"That may be the case, but it isn't time. The Countess will call upon you when you're ready to be an initiate." Harrison crossed his arms over his chest, the movement catching Felicity off guard. The boy took the distraction and punched low in her gut, one after the other.

Felicity groaned but lowered one arm, blocking his next punch, then sent a right hook that was meant for his temple. He dodged, a grin stretching from his bloody mouth. Her own vision was shaky at best. Her teeth grit together, trying to concentrate as the boy rushed her.

Her magic pulsed, then expanded from her skin, unbeckoned. The boy squealed as he hit her then cowered, dropping to the ground at her feet, covering his eyes.

"Felicity," Harrison yelled, but she couldn't see him, her magic uncontrollable. Nothing she did could call it back.

Her opponent screamed louder, and Felicity brightened again, her eyes pinched shut. The heat at her chest told her the magic had found the pendant, but she didn't know what to do. How to stop it. So new and untrained. Then all light disappeared, and she fell to the floor. The boy still screamed, and she saw his white eyes, blinded, and his body charred—a sickening burn covering his torso, face, and appendages. Guilt burned at her gut and through her chest. Tears fell down her face as her vision grew distorted and oblivion took her.

"Felicity?"

With her head held in her hands, she waited for the memory to fizzle. She looked up—now she was on the floor—and found Ward staring down at her, a hand on her shoulder. "What the hell was that?" He assisted her into a sitting position.

"A memory." She massaged her temples. "From the Tower—a training session." Tears remained stagnant in her eyes at the pain she'd inflicted on that boy. The truth of her past uncovered. It hadn't only been the Countess who had known about her magic.

"Is this happening often?" Ward's jaw tensed. "You can't just drop like that. If you do that in public..."

She shook her head, trying to clear the emotion from her throat. "No. None of the others have caused that." Felicity pushed herself up. "This one was triggered though."

Ward's brow furrowed. "You need to be careful."

With a groan, she stretched and swore she saw something move in the corner of the room but ignored it. "I'm quite aware that I need to be careful, Ward."

"Anything you need to discuss?" The crease appeared in the center of his brow. She wasn't doing well at hiding her emotion, it seemed. He held out his arms prepared to catch her in case she fell again.

Felicity sighed and stalked across the room. "I'm fine now."

It took him some time to deem her well enough to be left alone. After the door closed behind him, Felicity turned to the place where she had seen the movement and found a piece of parchment on the floor. She unfolded it to discover a note in a sharp, elegant script:

Are you alright? -A

Felicity rushed to the small table and pulled a quill and ink from the drawer.

I will be. But how did you know? -F

It didn't seem right to lie. She didn't ask anything more specific, uncertain what to say. She dropped the parchment back in the same spot she had found it. Then it disappeared. She waited.

When nothing happened, she went about her business but after a few moments, movement caught her eye again. Felicity rushed to the spot and crouched down, unfolding the parchment.

Good.

Felicity considered writing back to ask for more specifics—to get anything from Prince Alarian beyond one word. Anger pulsed, his silent accusations coming to the forefront of her mind.

But mostly she was frustrated at herself. Even without the rest of the memory, she knew the boy had died from his injuries. Was this why the Tower had hidden her past? To protect her from this? She recognized that version of Harrison. It had been when he had become an initiate and she was still a recruit.

It wouldn't do her any good to hold onto the guilt alongside the anger. Not now. Not after all these years, but it felt like a fresh wound cut open.

She stuffed the letter from the prince in the drawer with the ink and quill, slamming it shut. The way he had looked at her in the ballroom had made her ill. How he had reacted at the brothel, the words he said—she wasn't being used.

But she knew she was lying to herself even if she didn't want to admit it. Otherwise, why else would the Tower keep such a liability within their walls?

It probably hadn't been her best decision. But Felicity needed the release. Somewhere to put all the pent-up frustration surging to the surface when she was supposed to be asleep. Fury was what fueled her ability to do her job. It was a fire within. One she fed and used to separate from everything else that attempted to draw her in. Spies needed to be cool, collected, ready for anything. And right now, she was flailing.

While training alone, she had been practicing without the cuff on her ear. Simple things so far. Enough to keep control and call on the influx of magic slowly. Not only to not burn out, but also to call it to the pendant and hold it steady and at the ready. Tonight, she considered taking it to the next level.

That was until she strutted into the training hall. The last person Felicity had expected to see was the prince. Yet...she didn't know if that was true. She couldn't help but wonder if he had followed her or chosen to be there anyway, but she felt his presence before she saw him, and it didn't do anything to improve her mood. Instead, her previous frustration was replaced by the guilt he'd made her feel—and the guilt of the memory.

"Your magic still needs to be expelled. Just like your frustration." Prince Alarian sat on a bench outside the ring.

"I know. I had planned to deal with it tonight." He was right, and she was aware of it. Not that she wanted to admit it. "But I don't need you."

"You keep saying that." He watched her closely. "But I'm here anyway."

"You haven't been around much. I've survived fine." She could sense his gaze tracking her movements as though he could foresee her next position. "I don't think I can do this tonight. I need to concentrate on my mission." It was a pitiful excuse, but she hoped he wouldn't question it.

She felt him move behind her, and she twisted around, her fist ready. He grabbed her wrist at a speed she'd never seen from him before. Her gaze narrowed, and she attempted to free herself, but he held strong.

"What mission is that exactly?" He stepped closer. "What have you gotten yourself into?"

"You're upset that I'm doing as your father asked?" She twisted her arm, disengaging from his hold and sent an arched kick in his direction. He stepped back to dodge it, but her fist met his shoulder, unbalancing him. He side-stepped with his back foot, catching himself. Felicity kicked again and he caught her foot with that unexpected speed and pulled, knocking her to the ground with a grunt.

"We both know the truth about Lord Gullist. What happened was luck and luck is dangerous for a spy to play with." He reached a hand out towards her, palm up. "Haven't you realized I'm trying to keep you safe?"

"What do you know about being a spy?" She slapped his hand away and pushed herself to her feet, brushing the dust off her pants. "Are you doubting me now? You brought me here, hired me for this job. Why do you seem upset I'm completing it?" He was making her question who she was. Everything about what she'd become. Felicity turned away, her magic rushing to the tips of her fingers. *Not now*.

"He wasn't guilty, Felicity." Prince Alarian's voice sounded distant.

She faced him. He stood tall, fists clenched at his sides.

"Your father gave the final judgment." She needed to get away from him. But he followed, his presence a heavy reminder. "You were the one asking the questions at the brothel," she added.

"I was trying to help. But with the answers he gave, you had nothing to pin against him—not enough." He stormed ahead, cutting her off.

"Obviously, I wasn't wrong. You heard Lady Fiadh's accusations." Felicity tried to move around him, but he sidestepped in front of her.

"You know as well as I do that she was mistaken." His tone a warning whisper. "This is a dangerous game you're playing."

She couldn't help it—she laughed. "As an assassin, the only thing I understand are dangers. As a spy, I understand the games. Don't get in my way."

He grabbed her arm, and she twisted again, this time unsettling him. Light blazed to her fingertips as she knocked him to the ground. Felicity's dagger was mere inches from his throat, her knee on his chest, pinning him down. He held tight to both of her wrists without an ounce of fear—the emotion always found in the eyes of those in his current position. Didn't he understand? She was a weapon.

"You should be frightened of me, Prince. Just because you knocked me down once doesn't mean I can't hurt you."

Prince Alarian cocked his head, and her magic sizzled, the light illuminating his face. "I never feared you, Starlight. And I never will. Even if you consider me the enemy."

His words unsettled her, and she stepped back, putting distance between them. "You should."

It was his turn to brush himself off as he stood. He didn't close the space. "But I won't." His voice was a whisper. "Because I see who you are. And I'm willing to wait for you to see the truth too."

"What is that supposed to mean?" Her mouth tightened as her magic fought for purchase—a dim light illuminated her skin.

He took one step towards her then straightened, and she saw the change wash over his face. "Why? Why can't you look at me and see the truth? See who I am?"

Alarian reached out a hand, grazing the light that radiated from her arm. Felicity closed her eyes, enjoying the sensation of the cool shadows as they formed under his palm.

Then she snapped her eyes open and pulled her arm away. "Because your kindness to me is a ruse you attempt to use on all the females. Remember, I know the real you. Drunk, brawls, gambling, secret conquests at a brothel to save face in front of your parents...you can't fool me." Even as she said the words, she considered all the times he'd proven the opposite. No. She couldn't go there. Couldn't try to make him out to be something worth more when he stood aside while his parents caused havoc.

"No," he growled. "You won't allow yourself to see me. You've spent time analyzing and observing each courtier—but not me. You only listen to gossip and take it as fact, but never take into consideration what you see in front of you." He stepped closer, and air seemed to vacate her lungs. "Why? Why won't you allow yourself to look past hearsay and half-truths?"

Her jaw twitched. "I don't know what you're talking about."

Now that he was in her space, she had to look up to see him properly. Her body went rigid. She inhaled, his scent ticking her senses, her body tingling.

He leaned down until his face was a breath from hers. "I think you do. I think you don't want to accept what you feel. That you feel—"

"What emotion do you see right now, Prince?" she all but hissed. "What is it you expect from me?"

"I can read you, Felicity. I know you're angry. But it's because deep down, you don't want to admit I'm right."

"You're wrong," she bit out. When did she lose control of this conversation? Her chest rose and fell as her heart raced. Light exploded from her as if her skin had been trying to hold it in but couldn't resist the desire to shine.

Felicity's arms splayed out, and her head fell back as the magic encased her. Then everything went dark, even the lights extinguished. She shuddered, and strong arms pulled her up from the ground.

She hadn't realized she'd fallen.

"You need help with your magic, Felicity. If you don't want it from me, get it from someone else."

"How did you know?" Her body went rigid in his arms, uncertain how to respond to his touch.

"Know what?" he whispered.

She rolled her eyes. "You knew something had happened in my room. The letter."

His jaw tensed, and Felicity's body trembled as those green eyes pierced hers. "It must have been a coincidence. What happened?"

With a deep breath, she considered telling him. About the Tower, the truth of her memories, about the dreams and the emotions slowly coming back to her. But she took too long. His words reverberating in her ears.

"That's what I thought." He let go and took a step back, dissolving into the shadows.

Felicity was alone. Standing in the training hall, in the pitch black of night, the prince's presence left a vacant sensation on her skin.

Chapter
35

All was quiet over the next few days and routines continued within the palace. Felicity hadn't been able to bring herself to do more than meander about and act like she was spying. Any actual attempt at it made the prince's words reverberate within her head.

Instead, she concentrated on piecing the puzzle of her mind together. A process gone ignored during the previous weeks. After repressing them for so long, she couldn't deny that her emotions were returning and that she would have to deal with them.

There was a knock at her door, signaling it was time. The dinner to mark the beginning of the Lughnasadh season was tonight. It was a tradition for the Light Realm to host the event that began with dinner and continued into midnight the following evening. Drinking, eating, and festivities ended with a final feast and more revelry. Extra guards had been placed on duty as the guests arrived, the king not taking any risks with the celebration.

Felicity opened her door. Ward leaned against the wall dressed in a hunter-green vest over a white shirt and brown leather pants. His dark hair was styled similar to the first time she saw him, wisps falling over his brow. "Ready?"

She inhaled a deep breath. As soon as she entered the hall, a heaviness settled on her shoulders and her eyes darted over their surroundings as they walked.

"Do you feel that?" She breathed, keeping her voice to a low whisper.

His jaw tensed and he nodded.

They arrived at the ballroom decorated in bright oranges and red-flowered garlands. Flowers in tall vases were placed sporadically throughout the room and in smaller vases on each table. They weren't ones she recognized from the still cursed garden.

The guests and courtiers were spread throughout the room, mingling in low banter, gossip, and laughter. The royal family hadn't arrived yet, their seats still empty at the head of a long table.

Lady Solfire caught sight of them, and her smile faltered before she crossed the room to meet them. "You look lovely, Lady Dwauer. Your dress is stunning."

"Thank you." Felicity waved her hand at the female. "You look absolutely gorgeous." She couldn't believe how easily the words came out. It was true though. Avyanna wore a gold dress that contrasted beautifully with her dark complexion. Her long orange hair framed her face in thick waves.

Ward's gaze settled on Felicity's deep blue dress, and he gave her a sideways grin as if remembering something. "You do look nice."

Then he bowed to Avyanna. "As do you, Lady Solfire." His grin evened out, and the female's cheeks reddened under his stare.

Before anyone could say more, a trumpet sounded. Each guest faced the entrance as a herald announced the arrival of the royal family. "Your Royal Majesties, King Roald, Queen Marquette, and His Highness, Prince Alarian."

The three walked into the room, the king and queen leading with Prince Alarian a step behind. As they walked down the center aisle, everyone lowered into a bow or curtsy. While Felicity held her own curtsy, a pair of buffed boots stopped in front of Felicity's line of sight and a hand was held out. Her heart quickened against her chest as Felicity dared to look up and meet the prince's flat expression. With the memory of their blood oath, she took his hand, releasing a low sigh. He pulled her upright and led her towards the front. Each gaze that followed them increased the tempo of Felicity's erratic heartbeat speed further, and she wondered if they could hear it. The prince's grip remained firm, and he only released her hand to pull a chair out for her—the seat beside his.

The King remained standing as his wife and son took a seat. He didn't spare Felicity a glance. "Please rise, my loyal subjects."

Everyone straightened and bustled to a chair. Felicity kept her gaze locked on the king, unwilling to look at the gathered courtiers—afraid of what she would see in their faces.

"We have had dark and difficult times during this past season. But let us look forward to the future with pride and strength. Our vision is being witnessed, our power felt. With these new beginnings, we will see the strength of our people along with the change of the season and a bountiful harvest." King Roald raised his tankard into the air, and others mimicked his movement. "Let's drink to tomorrow and the future."

And everyone did.

As tankards and cups met tabletops, many now empty, servers walked in carrying silver trays laden with plates of food. They took one to each table while others entered carrying more mead and wine.

With her new seat at the head of the table, more gazes than she recognized darted in her direction. Those who hadn't seen her before or heard her name began to whisper about the young female at the prince's side and the announcement he made by picking her from the crowd. Lady Mistward's gaze met hers only once and it pierced through Felicity's skin.

Prince Alarian sat beside her with stoic grace, his expression impossible to read. Everyone ate their roasted lamb with mint jelly, steamed squash—the last of the summer vegetables—and freshly baked bread that was still warm. While it smelled delicious, Felicity could only nibble at her food.

A server came by and refilled her glass of wine without prompting. The prince leaned in, and she felt the warmth of his proximity and the scent of rain. "We need to talk." She balked, surprised at how close his face was. "Tonight, as soon as possible."

She tilted her head toward him. "There is a party. You have guests." She swallowed and gave a small smile. Let any who watched them believe they were sharing words of adoration as lovers should. "And I shouldn't be up here."

"You were the one who told my mother that I would escort you to the ball."

"I—"

He opened his mouth to cut her off but froze as a whooshing sound, like a mighty gust of wind, sliced through the air. "Shit."

There was a loud crash in the hall as the walls of the ballroom shook. A boom sounded and everyone froze, some with forks halfway to their mouths while others shivered in their seats. A few turned to the king who sat still, his lips a thin line.

A guard rushed in, his armor covered in dust and rubble. "They've breached the walls. We're under attack!"

There was a moment of silence before everyone panicked. Screams splintered and echoed in the vaulted ceiling.

The storm had hit.

Felicity searched for Ward from her seat. He jerked his attention towards her and nodded, his eyes wide in surprise. He hadn't expected this to happen now either.

Some ran, others hid under tables, many screamed, a cacophony of pitches melding into blood-curdling fear.

Pushing herself up from the table, she turned when the prince grabbed her hand. "Come with me, please?"

The look, the pleading in his eyes, almost had her agreement, but she shook her head. "I can't." She pulled up her skirts and ran in the opposite direction towards Ward.

Ward grabbed Avyanna's hand, and Felicity followed them away from the crowd. Felicity dared a glance at the female. Although tears were present in the corner of her eyes, her expression was firm and she didn't detour, following Ward through the panicked room with ease.

He went through a side door, unnoticed by the guests who ran towards the way they came in. *Stupid sheep.* One of the first lessons she had been taught—always know all your exits.

"You're hiding in my room," he called back to Lady Solfire. "You'll be safe there."

"What about Lady Dwauer?" Avyanna lurched towards Felicity and reached out a hand. "She should stay with me."

Ward seemed to consider her words for a moment, and Felicity shot him a sharp look. He sighed. "She'll be safe in her quarters."

They reached his room, and Lady Solfire stopped before entering, gripping Ward's arm. "Send any healers my way. I'll set up any staff I can collect to help with those hurt."

Ward glanced at Felicity, a question in his gaze that he seemed to not deign important to have answered. He turned back to Avyanna, pulled her body close and kissed her. She wrapped an arm around him, deepening the kiss.

Felicity, hiding her smile, turned away to enter her own room.

Before she closed it, she heard the male whisper to Avyanna. "I love you."

And Avyanna's voice held a lilt of a smile. "Be safe. Come back to me."

The door snapped shut behind her, her mind turning to the task at hand. With only moments to spare, she stripped from the dress and threw open her trunk, pulling out what she would need. Felicity was strapping a sword to her back when Ward knocked twice. Without waiting for an answer, he came in with his eyes closed. "Decent?"

The sound of her dagger sliding into its place was her answer, and he opened his eyes. "To the passageways. Hurry."

"Will she be safe in there?" Felicity considered staying to protect the halls. Maybe she could get more of the innocent out. Meira, the staff...

He nodded. "My contact has been informed of the room's location. They'll know that anyone within it is to be left alone. I don't think they plan to kill anyone unless they attack first."

"You knew?" Felicity opened the door to the passageway and they both slipped in, sliding it closed.

There was the sound of flint hitting stone, and a blaze erupted on a nearby torch. He removed it from its place and took the lead. "They said during the festivities. For precautions, I planned to inform you tomorrow because I thought for certain it would happen when everyone was deep into the celebration. I don't know why they did it now."

With quick steps, near silent patters, they rushed down the stone passage. She cleared her throat. "How long has it been going on between you two?"

Ward grumbled a word or two under his breath. "Really? Gossiping now?"

"No." She shook her head. "Just curious."

"Two years." He made a sharp left.

"You've kept it a secret that long? Impressive. So...the time I interrupted for a study session—"

"I really don't want to talk about this." He cursed and she fought back a grin.

They reached a doorway, and Ward ran a hand through his hair. "They know to watch for you. At least my contact is aware." He grabbed her arm. "Remember your promise and be safe."

She nodded. "Don't do anything stupid."

He gritted his teeth as she slipped a mask over her head. Felicity straightened and with a nod, Ward pulled in a deep breath.

When the door opened to the study, they slid it closed, the bookcase clicking into place. He pressed his ear to the door leading into the hall. "Nothing." He touched the door handle. "What are you going to do?"

Felicity considered his question for a moment. Although she believed in the rebel's cause, others would need her protection. Without knowing the rebel's plan, she needed to steer clear and keep her identity intact if this all went to hell. "Try to get the courtiers and staff to safety."

Ward's grip on the handle tightened. "Good. They might be scared of you though."

She chuckled. "Then that should ensure their obedience."

He nodded and opened the door. For a moment, they stared at each other. Ward reached out and gripped her arm. Without another word, they ran their separate ways. She didn't ask him what he was doing, but she was worried he was running into trouble.

Felicity stuck to the shadows and lifted herself up into the archways when she had a chance. It gave her an opportunity to watch the crowd. Ward had been right—the rebels didn't attack unless someone attacked them first. They allowed those filing out of the ballroom to exit the castle, while others fought off the guards. The guards themselves were confused about the rebel's actions and a few stood back, surprised.

Felicity noticed many of the rebels had pitchforks and rakes, and some wore gardening attire. *That was how they had gotten in.* They had been working in the gardens for months now and learning the grounds. The king and queen had been too busy with the curse of the gardens to pay attention. Clever.

Lady Mistward came into view, her grip tight on her daughter's wrist, dragging her along. Though visibly shaken the young Miss Isleen also looked to be in awe of the activity around her. Her mother, on the other hand, was angry. She kicked and bit the rebel who was pushing her towards the door. A guard noticed her and stepped forward, brandishing his weapon.

The two came to blows, and Lady Mistward screamed and began to claw at the rebel, darkness overtaking her eyes. Felicity jumped from her hiding place, hoping to dispel the thought of using her magic, and landed in front of her. Lady Mistward balked and stepped back, almost taking her daughter and another courtier down with her.

"You need to get to safety." Felicity made sure her voice was low, unrecognizable. "Go."

She yanked the courtiers, flinging Lady Mistward in line with the others. Miss Isleen gripped her mother's arm and yanked her towards the door, following Felicity's orders.

A scream echoed from the ballroom. Felicity ran towards the entrance, about to push herself through when what she saw stopped her in her tracks. She watched with horror as Ward battled guards while the king stood nearby, talons beginning to elongate from his fingertips.

Rebels fought while two other guards ushered the remaining courtiers out. A rebel fell at the doorway, blood seeping from his wound, his green skin turning a putrid shade of vomit.

Felicity pushed to get past, but the fight seeped into the hall. The courtiers screamed, blocked from the exit with the battles waging around them. Guards and rebels collided, pitchforks slicing through limbs and flesh, swords carving at skin and bone. Her instincts told her to get to Ward—but she had made a promise to him. Her true identity needed to remain a secret if possible. But if anything happened to him...

Rushing to the front of the line, Felicity placed herself between the fighting and the courtiers. She pushed back guards and rebels alike in an attempt to force an opening for the frightened guests. "Hurry." She waved them towards the exit, drawing their attention.

The courtiers began to run. One tripped, her dress too long and catching underfoot. Felicity leaned down and pulled her up. A blade just missed Felicity's shoulder, forcing her to pull her own sword free. With a twist, she met the guard's weapon and pushed back, almost slicing a bystander's arm. Courtiers screamed and sped up, running faster towards the door. Pushing through the crowd, Felicity did what she could to protect them from rogue weapons. When the last was at the doorway, she ran back into the ballroom. Although the fighting still raged behind her, it had stopped inside the room. Rebels stood frozen, their weapons on the floor as the guards had rounded them up and pinned them into the corner.

In the center stood the king, sword extended, talons exposed. And at the end of his blade, Ward crouched on the ground, gripping his side where blood dripped and pooled on the floor.

Felicity inhaled and entered the room, removing her mask. The king looked up, and his eyes glittered red. "We were just about to discuss you." The door closed behind her.

Queen Marquette stood and stepped from her seat. She had watched the whole proceedings with a quizzical brow and lazy sneer. Judging by the relaxed way she walked, Felicity knew she had never felt an ounce of fear. Lady Fiadh stepped out from the shadows and took position beside the king, her eyes shining bright with curiosity.

"Ward is with the rebels?" Felicity's heart raced against her chest as she shot Ward a glare.

King Roald chuckled. "If you were as good as I was told you were, how did you not find the one right under your nose the entire time? What do you know of it, girl? Or are you one of them?"

Felicity straightened. "I'm a spy hired by you through my guild. I have no reason not to be loyal to them—so in turn, to you." The king didn't know she wasn't loyal to the Tower anymore...unless Prince Alarian had mentioned it to his father.

"Stupidity or lies," the king bellowed. "One way or the other, I'll be the one left standing tonight."

"I have no reason to lie to you, King Roald. My mission has always been my priority." She pushed her hair behind her ear and gritted her teeth. This wasn't going well, and she didn't want to watch as Ward was arrested—or worse.

The king smiled. "Sámhach."

Felicity stilled. Her gaze found the mark on the ground where Ward's blood pooled. The promise hanging in the air between them. Or maybe it was too late and the king knew everything. Why else would he cast the spell?

Out of her peripheral, she saw as Ward's arm was yanked from his wound and bound with iron behind his back. But Felicity kept her attention on that pool of blood and thought about the sacrifice he was making for people who didn't even remember his name.

Chapter
36-Ward

W ard could feel his body weakening with each drop of blood dripping from his wound onto the floor beside him.

He had been preoccupied for just a moment, the battle heightened outside the ballroom, and it was just what the king had needed to get the upper hand. King Roald's talons had sliced him open, hip to rib. It looked worse than it was. Ward would survive if he could get the bleeding to stop, but now, with the iron on his wrists, he wasn't allowed even a taste of his magic to quicken his healing.

He smelled her as soon as Felicity entered and regretted that his thoughts had even turned towards her. Lady Fiadh's sharp smile as she whispered Felicity's name under her breath made his insides flip. He thought he would vomit when the king enacted the spell.

It wouldn't matter now. Either way, the king would make sure he suffered. A traitor, the king had called him when Ward had attacked. As if Roald's act against Ward's family hadn't been the truly traitorous deed. He couldn't speak the truth—the curse forcing his silence. Even attempting to write it, to communicate who he was, only left the others confused and questioning if Ward had lost his mind.

He'd watched his father, the rightful king, thrown from the continent. He grasped onto every memory he could even as everyone else forgot, except the traitorous family, as the nameless curse swept over Talamh. Heard the incantation by the witch who had given her life for the spell that removed Ward's true identity all just days before he received word that his remaining family had been butchered...

Now, he had only one bit of hope left.

Each breath hurt, so Ward began the count in his head, trying to even his breathing as the sound of Lady Fiadh's heels against stone echoed in his ears. The queen stood and watched as if the entire ordeal had been a pleasure to observe. Ward's jaw clenched—he hated them all. Not just for what they had done to his family but for what they had done to his people.

The king barked orders, and Ward's head reverberated with each word. "You three, guard him. The rest of you take the rebels to the dungeon. We'll take care of them later. And bar the doors. Leave two at the entrance and don't allow anyone through. I don't want further interruptions."

"The battle is still continuing outside, Your Majesty. Should we send reinforcements?"

The roar echoing through the room was enough for the guard to bow and do as he was told.

Ward couldn't help the hint of the smile at the corner of his mouth. King Roald had just confirmed his own end. The rebels were prepared and ready for this fight. If the king didn't step in, that choice alone confirmed victory for Ward's compatriots. As far as King Roald was concerned, he had his prize. The traitor king didn't know he was giving up everything else to ensure Ward's punishment. Stupid male and his egotistical pride.

Ward had counted on the male's anger.

He looked up at the real traitor. Horns already curled from Roald's head, his teeth elongated. Roald hadn't gone fully to the beast—yet. That wasn't good. He must be planning to play for a while. "What was the plan tonight, Ward?"

Ward spit, hitting the corner of the king's boot.

The king's hand slashed across Ward's face, sharp talons slicing open his cheek before Ward hit the floor. He coughed, blood coating his mouth as he looked up at Roald. With a nod from the king, one of the guards stepped forward. They kicked and beat him until he spat up blood, and the metallic sting coated his throat and tongue. Ward groaned as the guard pulled him to a seated position and held him by the collar of his shirt. The other guard laid into him, one punch after the other breaking ribs and bruising bones.

Disoriented, Ward's head rang and darkness beckoned him. He closed his eyes, unable to keep them open any longer and slumped forward, willing himself to unconsciousness at the very least. He still could keep Felicity safe. Anger grew at the fact she was witnessing this. But she had made a promise. Maybe it was for the best she couldn't hear.

"Stop," the king ordered. "I want him to feel all of this." The king's boots clipped on the stone floor as he walked around Ward's body. "And we will do this over and over again. Don't worry—your suffering will not end tonight." He tsked. "After opening my home to you. Allowing you to stay here all this time."

Roald stopped in front of Ward again and smiled. "Lady Fiadh, tell me. Does Lady Dwauer have anything to do with all of this?"

Ward cleared his mind of Felicity's involvement. If anything, he could do that for her. Her scent of steel and summer sun overcame him, but Ward concentrated on the smell and taste of his own blood. He could protect her. He *would* protect her.

Lady Fiadh was suddenly close, her expression contorting as she leaned in front of him. It was terrifying to behold as it changed from amusement to pure terror to manic excitement all within a breath.

"His thoughts are muddled by the curse—" The female sliced her head towards Felicity. "She lived," the female hissed. Her eyes widened, unblinking as she tilted her head up to the king. "She's his sister—the one you thought dead. But she doesn't know it."

Through slitted, swollen eyes, Ward watched as Lady Fiadh walked away to take her position beside the queen. Ward inwardly cursed himself. He wasn't able to protect the knowledge after all.

"That can't be." The king shook his head as he began to pace. "She died beside her mother."

"It is the truth, My King. I saw it within his mind. He has protected this knowledge since her arrival." Lady Fiadh frowned. "Before then, just as we all did, he had thought her dead."

The king searched the room. "Where is my son?" He pointed at a guard. "Find him."

One guard holding Ward let go and ran to follow the order. Ward pivoted his head sideways to watch as the guard ran from the room. As the door slid open, the sound of swords clashed in the hall, and the guard's body fell back with a sickening crack, an arrow protruding from his eye socket. The guards nearby pulled his body in and slammed the door shut.

The king roared, his body contorting again, hair bristling, and his feet transformed into hooves. "You," he bellowed. "Side door. Find Alarian." One of the guards who had helped bar the doors closed ran to obey the order.

The guard's hold on Ward tightened. Darkness still called for him, but Ward couldn't allow it. Not now. Not with the truth still ringing through the air. Tears stung at the corner of his eyes.

Finally. Ward hadn't been able to utter the words, fearing that they would be carried on the wind. Maybe she would have believed him—maybe she wouldn't. It had taken him time to accept the facts even when they had been placed before him. She looked just like her mother—his stepmother. The one from the story. He'd hoped she would put the pieces together until he discovered she didn't have her memories.

At Advisor Boister's party, he had questioned it. She looked like the little sister he'd lost. The one he'd played hide and seek, doted on, and fought with. They had been inseparable, the gap in their ages nothing in the span of a fae life.

When Felicity had smiled that night, even if he knew for certain it had been fake as she stood beside the greasy Advisor Boister, Ward had known it had to be her. His heart shattered when she left. But it was safer that way—safer to pretend she didn't exist. Better for her to stay hidden from the palace and the brutal truth. Even if she was the only one who could possibly remember his name and break the curse.

Finding out she was the spy—the one hired to uncover those he was working alongside—had felt impossible to overcome. It seemed smartest to keep her at a distance. To push her away. Doubt had clouded his judgment and when she asked him if he disliked her, he couldn't pretend anymore.

His need to protect her, his desire to save her, his want for her to accept him. In the beginning, those had felt like wishes on the wind, flying out over the ocean to disappear into the horizon. Never to come true. Until they began working alongside each other, thick as thieves. She had chosen him—over her sense of duty, over her loyalty to the Tower she had known as her home—she had chosen to align with him. And life had felt worthwhile for a while. Instead of resentment and bitterness, the little sister he had thought he failed had survived.

But this—this was impossible to overcome. His dreams of a future, with her, with their father, came crashing to a halt. There was no future for him, but he could keep her safe. Somehow.

Ward shifted enough from his place on the floor to find Felicity. She stood, her gaze pinned to the space beside him, unmoving, not reacting to anything as she had done every other time that evil spell was uttered. Every fiber in his body wanted to scream her name. Wanted her to know the truth. No one else would tell her if he didn't. Definitely not the king or any others present in this room. The secret would die with him.

At least they had time together. To fight, to laugh—for him to see her come alive at moments when her guard was down, giving him a touch of insight into the female she would become without the Tower holding her back. When the time came, she would kill the king. Of that, he was certain. And at least she was aligned with his cause—their cause, even if she didn't know it.

The king pulled Ward by his tunic to his feet, the fabric ripping in his taloned grip, but the king only tightened his hold.

"I can look at the positive in this situation. This means I can kill you," he chuckled. "I keep the deal with your father. Even with you dead, I'll still have one of his children, alive and within my home confirming his exile is intact." The king's smile widened. "And she won't even know. It'll be easier with her in my employ—unlike dealing with you. It seems her mind has been wiped from the past. Her guild has done a good job training their weapons."

As his laugh echoed in the room, the queen joined in, and Ward bit his tongue to keep the smile from his face. *But she would live.* The thought repeated in his mind. What the king thought was *his* weapon would wield herself against him.

Ward was only sad he wouldn't be there to see it. But his death would be worth it. This last stand against the tyrant. He hoped, if she ever discovered the truth, Felicity would be able to forgive him.

"May I recommend that she be the one to deal the punishing blow, my husband?" The queen smiled from her seat.

Ward's stomach churned and he was certain his heart had stopped. Almost wished it so she wouldn't have to be the one to stop it herself.

The king dropped Ward on the ground. His legs didn't even attempt to hold him up as he crumbled, his face meeting stone and body jarring from the impact. King Roald took a few steps back.

He looked at Felicity and then back to Ward. "You are wise, my wife." The corner of his mouth rose as his gaze bore into Ward's. "Your sister will kill you and will never know it was her brother she executed." He gestured to the nearest guards and the male stepped forward with purpose. "Gag him and hold him up."

Tears now slipped freely. *But she would live*. The guard wasn't gentle as he fitted the gag in place, wrenching the thick cloth between Ward's teeth. He lowered Ward to his knees and moved around to stand behind. The guard bunched Ward's hair in his fist and rested a firm hand on his shoulder. Everything hurt now.

Then the side door flung open and Alarian stepped in—alone. "I heard you wanted to see me." Blood coated his once-white shirt and the blade hanging from his hand. Ward growled, spit catching on the gag and almost choking him. Alarian's gaze snapped to Ward for a moment then back to his father. "What are you doing, Father?"

"Dealing out punishments." King Roald glared at his son. "I'll deal with you in a moment."

The male stepped forward. "You can't kill him. If you do—"

The king's roar echoed throughout the room, from floor to ceiling, shaking the pillars. Alarian's protest was cut short when he found Felicity standing in the back of the room. If there was one thing Ward and Alarian agreed upon, it was their desire to protect her—even if she didn't need it. In this instance though, would Alarian stand beside her if it came to it?

Shadows expanded around the prince. "What the hell are you doing, Father? What is all this?"

The prince lifted his foot and the king held up a hand. "If you take a step or say another word, I'll have you dragged from this room. Or worse. Be patient for your punishment, boy. Right now, I have another problem to attend to." He gestured to one of the two remaining guards. The male strutted across the room and stopped next to the prince, his hand on the hilt of his sword. The king snarled, "You've been warned, Alarian."

Then Roald's sharp gaze turned to the spy—to Ward's sister. "Felicity."

Chapter
37-Felicity

"Felicity."

When her name was uttered from the king's lips, Felicity's attention turned from the blood-stained marble to meet his gaze. Memories tickled. Too many thoughts vying for attention. She pushed them all aside and took in the scene in front of her.

Ward was crouched before the king, his mouth gagged, and hands clamped in iron at his back. Rage bit at her, hot and searing, at the injuries, blood, and bruises marring his body before a calmness slid over her. The prince's fidgeting drew her attention for a brief moment, the guard behind him resting a hand on the hilt of his blade.

She turned her attention to the king. "King Roald." Somehow, she kept her tone even.

"Father, have you thought this through?" Prince Alarian stepped forward, his shadows rising behind him and blood dripping from the sword in his grip.

A guard grabbed the prince's arm, releasing his own sword from its scabbard. "Drop your sword."

Prince Alarian took another step and the king pointed a taloned finger at his son. The prince stopped, his lips a thin line, and Felicity could see the resentment in his gaze. The two males stared each other down, and Felicity was certain they were locked in a battle of their own.

King Roald turned away first, his body completing the transformation to the beast, his jaw shifting to an extended maw with yellow pointed teeth. Coarse hair sprouted under his clothes and in between seams as his body expanded, pulling at the last stitches of thread.

The king, who stood a few feet from Ward, turned to face her. "You have a duty to fulfill." His voice was more of a snarl. "Since you failed to bring him to me and I had to capture him myself, you're to execute Ward. Do you understand your punishment?"

His eyes narrowed, and she blinked once and nodded. "If the king commands."

The pain in her chest heightened, magic thrumming against her skin at what she was to do. A pulse beat heavily against her temple, and her skin felt aflame as anger mixed with her magic. It took all her self-control not to let it shine—not to let it out and sear the skin from their bones. She held it in check—she had done so this far. She could keep it contained.

But she'd made a promise to Ward and hated him for making her swear it. She didn't break promises. Felicity crossed the expanse between them with purposeful steps, the heel of her boots clicking against the stone was the only sound that echoed through the space. She stopped in front of Ward, her back to the king, but she sensed him move in close behind her.

"Ward, for your crimes against the crown, you're sentenced to death to be meted out by *my* assassin." She could hear the sneer in the king's voice, feel his primal heat against her back.

Felicity's sword rang as it was freed from her scabbard. Only a few guards remained, the rebels gone—no others to witness his end. He deserved a hero's death, not one hidden behind closed doors. Ward didn't deserve any of this at all. In these past months, he had stood by and supported her while she found her place within these walls. The only thing he earned was the chance for his identity to be restored. Her heart raced as Ward's brown eyes met hers and locked in place.

"I'm sorry," she mouthed, less than a whisper. He nodded, baring his throat to her, giving his permission. His forgiveness. Although his pain was obvious, he straightened and drew back his shoulders. Even in the face of death, he wouldn't show fear.

With a deep inhale, she cleared her throat. She was no longer a weapon used by another—she was death itself. As she raised her hand and feinted her sword, she yelled, "I name you Prince Kellan of the eight realms of the continent of Talamh. Son of King Bastien."

The clasp fell from her hand as her magic sputtered to life, expanding, filling her. She pivoted and light—heat—extended down her into the blade she held, engulfing it, becoming the conduit for her magic.

The prince said to practice. She had.

Her magic arced off the metal, sliced through the air and towards the king's body. She wasn't anyone's weapon—the choice was her own.

By the time the sound of the clasp hitting the ground trickled through the room, there was silence. No one moved, all standing in shock and awe. Then a large gust of wind surrounded them and King Roald, mouth agape, split down his middle with a squelching slip. Each half crumbled to the ground with a sickening thud, blood pooling from his severed corpse.

Felicity gasped for air as she faced Ward—Kellan. His wide eyes brimmed with tears.

"Prince Kellan?" A guard clutched his head, shaking it between his splayed palms. The one behind Kellan had let go of her brother's hair, his wide eyes stared at her.

"Brother," she breathed. Felicity turned and glared at the guard. "Free your prince now."

She didn't know if it was fear, shock, or the reminder of loyalty to the rightful ruler that had the guard fumbling to remove the iron manacles from Kellan's wrists. There was a heaviness in her limbs from the use of her magic. She had built it up inside, holding it back but at the ready so she wouldn't drain.

Shadows crept in the corner of her peripheral and she whirled around at the expanding darkness to search for the male it was from.

"Seize her." The prince's—Alarian's—voice ordered from her left.

Felicity raised her sword, and the remaining guards unsheathed their own. Alarian stepped into the clearing of the surrounding shadows and met her gaze. Instead of anger or pain visible in his expression, the expected response at a father's death, she found relief.

As the other guards inched closer, her light shone brighter. Kellan struggled to his feet, stepping between them, panting with the attempt. He gripped his side, a ferocity in his expression. His wind gusted to life and blasted at the guards.

"No," Alarian yelled.

Felicity raised her sword as the shadows drifted from the room, only wisps remaining around him.

"Stop." Both Alarian and the newly reinstated Kellan ordered. Each soldier froze in place, eyes darting between both males. Then the wind dissipated and Kellan stumbled. Felicity wrapped an arm around his middle, holding him steady. She pointed her sword at Alarian, the soldier who had been guarding him now unconscious on the floor.

"Prince Kellan is your rightful ruler. Claim your side now," she ordered the remaining guards.

They stilled and met each other's gaze before turning back to her, eyes wide and surprise etched in their expression. She knew she must be glowing. They moved to Kellan and Felicity's side, probably out of fear, but that would be dealt with later. Her body shuddered from holding up Kellan's weight. "Seize him," she said to the nearest guard. It hurt to make the order, but Alarian's actions had forced her hand.

The ex-prince's shoulders slumped as a human guard picked up the iron manacles and pulled his arms behind his back.

Kellan groaned. Felicity realized her heat was warming him, and she recalled her magic. He gave her a half-smile and a breeze cooled them both.

Alarian was pulled before them, the guards gentle, still confused as to what happened—the emotion etched on the fine lines of their faces.

"Do you have anything to say before we toss you in the dungeon?" Kellan lifted his head, his chin jutting out.

"You're making a mistake. I'm not your enemy—but my mother is. Find her. She still must be close." Alarian pulled against the guard's hold.

Felicity shifted in surprise. How could she forget? Distracted—damn it. Both Fiadh and Marquette were gone.

"We'll find her." She waved to one of the guards. "Search the grounds. Call for assistance from those in the halls. Tell them the traitor king is dead."

He left quickly and when the door opened, silence greeted him. It seemed that everyone was stunned by the broken curse. She thinned her gaze on the ex-prince, even as a heaviness settled on her shoulders and her chest ached. "Now what do you have to say for yourself?"

"Besides my bloodline, what are my crimes?" Alarian leveled his stare. "I've never done anything against the people or to you." He darted a gaze in Kellan's direction. "Or your brother."

Although Felicity's anger pulsed, an eerie calm overcame her. "Did you ever step in to aid these people?" Her magic sputtered. She was losing her hold on it, her body wavering—weakening. "You never tried to save them."

"Those are assumptions. Are you willing to make them?" His attention turned to Kellan.

With a look at the guards, she repressed the emotions scrambling for purchase. It took all of her strength to keep Kellan upright, and she knew she had no choice. This needed to end now or she'd lose the authority they held if she showed an ounce of weakness. "Take Alarian to his room. Call in someone to spell it so he cannot leave. We'll question him later."

She pointed to another and gestured him closer. "Release the rebels. Bring them to the throne room immediately and allow any others to congregate there as well. If any resist Kellan's claim to the throne, take them to the prison to be dealt with later. We'll decide if any need to be punished or relocated."

Felicity shifted her weight as a stretcher was thankfully brought in for Kellan. A guard assisted her in lowering him, her brother emitting moans of displeasure. "Call for the healers and collect all the injured into the throne room. Take care of everyone no matter who they may be or what side they claim to be on. I want them to be given the best care." Glancing at the king's remains, she sniffed. "And take care of that."

The guards nodded and one leaned over, pulling Alarian up and taking him away. The ex-prince shot a glance at her over his shoulder, and it took sheer will not to divert her gaze.

"Felicity, please. My mother and Lady Fiadh are a danger to us—to all of Talamh. I need you to listen…"

Felicity turned away. Alarian continued to call to her, words she couldn't comprehend with her own exhaustion as he was dragged from the room. Later. Right now, she needed to ensure that her brother would live.

When Felicity reached the hallway of their rooms, Kellan carried beside her, her feet were near dragging. Lady Solfire rushed down the hall to meet them. "What happened?" Her gaze softened, even if the fear and concern remained. "What happened, Kellan?"

With a critical eye she began to assess him as they walked while Kellan attempted to mumble out an explanation. The color left Avyanna's face during his recount, but as they reached his room, she called out supplies she would need to a passing handmaid. The guards laid him on his bed, a hiss from the male's throat as he clutched his gut.

Felicity tried to remain standing by his bedside, but Avyanna pointed to a chair. "Sit down before you collapse. You look as though you're near drained."

"She might be," Kellan groaned.

Felicity's eyes closed on their own. "Nothing that food and water can't fix." She peeled her eyes open to concentrate on Kellan.

Brother—the word felt both foreign and comforting at the same time. So much she would need to adjust to. But it felt right.

Avyanna sighed and turned to the guards. "Please ask someone to bring food and water for the…"

But Felicity stopped listening, her eyes fluttering closed again. They were safe. Now she could rest.

***

Felicity finally woke when it was close to noon the following day to find herself in her own bed. As if on cue, Meira entered with a tray of food, her eyes bloodshot and tears staining her cheek.

In hopes of not frightening her, Felicity slipped slowly from the bed. "Meira, if you prefer to leave, I will understand."

The female sniffed, gently putting down the tray. "No, of course not, Princess. I just can't believe all that has happened. That we forgot…"

Princess. With all that had happened, the reality of that title hadn't set in until that moment. But there were too many other things to consider before she unpacked those feelings. Emotions bubbled up inside of her. Relief, contentment, frustration…all of them scrambling for purchase with the memories that had fallen into place.

She shook her head, trying to dispel those thoughts and concentrate on the now. "But you came with King Roald. I don't want you to feel like you're being forced into—"

Meira tsked, interrupting her. "I came for Alarian. I was his nanny when he was a wee boy. The only reason the family brought me along is because the prince knew I had nowhere to go."

Felicity inhaled. "You never told me that."

Meira shrugged. "It wasn't my place, Princess. Not that it is now. He ensured I oversaw your care. Now I wonder if…" She wiped the tears from her eyes, her words trailing off.

There was a moment of silence as Felicity considered Meira's view. "It is your place. And if I give you a reason to think otherwise, then you remind me of this conversation." Felicity settled herself in a chair in front of the fireplace, watching the female. "And please don't call me princess. I don't think I can handle that right now. Now, what were you going to say?"

Meira fidgeted for a moment, looking between Felicity and the tray. With a sigh, she made her way across the room. "He asked me to watch out for you. You caught his attention. Prince…" Meira blushed as she pulled a dress from the armoire, and Felicity couldn't believe it had been such a short time ago when she had slipped into the passageway behind it. It was still pulled away from the wall a bit, left ignored. If Meira noticed, she didn't give any inclination as she went about her duties.

"What will happen to Prince…I mean…to Alarian?" Meira covered her mouth, her eyes wide.

Felicity shrugged, her hand stilling. With a deep swallow, she picked invisible lint off her nightgown. "I don't know yet."

"He isn't like his parents, milady. That I promise you," Meira whispered. The handmaiden entered the bathing room. She shot over her shoulder before disappearing from view. "I'll draw you a bath. You need it."

Felicity followed her into the bathing room and looked at her reflection. Flecks of blood still clung to skin and hair. The color in her cheeks, the point in her ears, the fine lines of her jaw. She had seen her reflection more than once in these past weeks within these walls. But she wasn't the same female who had arrived then.

And yet, the drop of blood staining her temple, dried in her hair—that felt more like herself than the title Meira had uttered. Analyzing herself, the memory of *his* fingers on her skin forced a gasp and her lips parted at the sudden warmth that rushed through her body.

"I'll be back soon with a dry towel and to help you dress, milady." Meira left the room, Felicity's attention on her retreating handmaiden.

Felicity was in a new world. One that she didn't know how to wade through. Especially with the information the handmaiden had just left for her to grapple with. There always seemed to be more to the ex-prince. *See me.*

Felicity shook and turned from her reflection, squeezing her eyes shut. "I know he isn't like them, Meira," she whispered to the empty room. "I know." And she would find a way to prove it.

Chapter 38

A week passed. Many were still surprised by the suddenly returned memories of their rightful ruler and the coup kept hidden by the curse, but a sense of normalcy was already beginning to settle over the palace.

Kellan found her sitting on a bench near the back gate of the garden that led to the bluff. The weeds and thistle had thinned a bit, no longer overcrowding the plants. Even the shrubbery was beginning to settle into a state of dormancy.

Before he could say anything, she met his gaze. "Any news on Marquette or Fiadh?" The two had been found at the gate but must have been prepared for an escape. After they left the palace grounds, Marquette had called her shadows and whisked them both away before the guards could catch up.

"No. Not yet." He rubbed the back of his neck. That little worry line was present between his brows. She wasn't going to like what he was about to say. "I just came from visiting Alarian."

She nodded, unwilling to form words on the subject. Whenever he had brought up the ex-prince, she'd gone mute. It annoyed Kellan, but annoying him had never bothered her in the past, so why stop now?

"Whenever I go, he brings up nonsense of children's tales and how important it is to find his mother. Otherwise, he won't speak to me and asks for you to either be present or to come alone." Kellan sighed. "If you won't go, I don't think I can justify keeping him there much longer. I will have to send him to the dungeon to await his trial."

After the people had been freed from the caverns, guards and advisors had been rounded up to undergo trials. Many would either be removed from the castle or given different positions to prove their loyalty over time. Others would be imprisoned for the multiple crimes they committed in the name of the traitor king.

After a few moments of quiet, she heaved a sigh. It wasn't that she didn't want to go to Alarian, it was more that she wanted to ignore what that would mean. Besides, she hadn't found the proof she needed. Or at least not enough that would pacify Kellan.

"I remembered more." She smiled at him, hoping he didn't broach the previous subject further. "Not much from before the Tower yet, but I think nearly everything from my time there." She took a deep breath and averted her gaze to the ocean. "And I keep having the same dream. I believe it's a memory of when my mother was running away with me."

Kellan sat down on the bench beside her and held out his hand. Bandages wrapped two fingers together, so she was careful how she gripped it. With his magic returned, most of his wounds already had closed and the bruises faded to a greenish-yellow under Avyanna's strict care. He squeezed her hand, beckoning her to continue.

"It's the only one where I see her—in every other memory, she is just a blur or shadow. She was beautiful even in her fear."

"Yes, she was. Do you remember the story of when father knew she was meant to be his wife?"

Felicity shook her head.

He grinned and looked out at the garden. "Your mother, Kaliana, was brought here with an advisor and his family from Saol. She was a lady in waiting and a daughter of one of the less prominent lords. During her visit, Father had been walking through the gardens with me, discussing the sadness of the flowers when he caught sight of a rose that had freshly bloomed."

Warmth fell over Kellan's features as he continued. "Father was surprised as nothing had bloomed within the gardens since my mother's death, everything on the verge of decay no matter what the gardeners attempted. It took him three days of walking the gardens at each toll of the bells before he found her. By the end of the advisor's visit, he asked your mother to stay. Less than a year later, they were married. He always claimed my mother had sent Kaliana to us." His smile faltered and he ran a hand over his face. "She was lovely. I have no doubt she fought hard for you."

Felicity nodded and lowered her gaze to their clasped hands. "She was human?"

"No, she was a demi-fae but she had more human qualities. I think that's why you were able to create a glamour easily."

It was another of the memories returned to her. She had never had formal training for her magic. The Tower's council had procured someone to teach her to use the glamour—not only to hide her identity but to learn to dispel enough of her magic to not wither up and die.

She and Kellan had discussed her magic in the days that followed the traitor-king's death. An apology had been on the tip of her tongue but before she could utter it, he told her he understood why she kept the secret. From him. From everyone. She hadn't broached the fact that Alarian had been aware. The scar on her hand was dim but still present. A reminder that parts of their oath still existed.

Felicity met his gaze. "I think my mother knew there was no chance to save us both. I remember running for the Tower. She had tripped and during the fall, I hit my head. I don't remember anything after that, but she must have left me at the Tower and then attempted to take them off my trail."

Ten years old. The Tower had always said she had been five, but it was just the fae aging process that had been the reason she was able to pull off the younger age. So much she still didn't remember from back then—before the Tower. She closed her eyes as an autumn breeze passed. "Tell me about Father."

Kellan squeezed her hand as she straightened. "He's gentle. A fair and just king."

Noting the tears forming in the corner of his eyes, Felicity bit her bottom lip. "The people loved him?" She was uncertain if she would be able to fight her own battling emotions, so she turned her attention to the distant waves. "You need to take his place for now—until we can find him." The search for where their father was exiled was already underway. The knowledge that Roald probably had the answer to their father's whereabouts was the only doubt Felicity had about killing him so quickly.

With a grimace, he followed her gaze towards the ocean, lifting his head to allow the breeze to brush over his face. "I don't want to. It seems wrong."

"I know nothing of leading. You have years more experience than I do, and we need to ensure that everyone Roald and Marquette had enslaved are returned to their families." Her jaw tensed, hoping he saw the truth and not her own hesitancy regarding the title she had been thrown into. "Then we have to begin the trials for the advisors and guards so we can attempt to uncover who is not loyal and remove them from the court."

He faced her. "Sounds like you are more prepared than you believe." He chuckled, nudging her gently with his shoulder. "Will you remain by my side? I can't do this without you."

"I was raised a spy—an assassin. What good will I be?" She lowered her eyes to the roses.

"Felicity, you're meant to be here." He pointed to the flowers. "Avyanna—" He cleared his throat. "I mean, Lady Solfire told me about what happened at tea. The garden is coming back for you." Kellan's smile widened. "You're meant to lead."

She straightened and searched her surroundings. The once dormant plants were bright green, life returning to their leaves and new buds ready to bloom. A daisy, already open, settled near her feet. Even the roses she had been concentrating on hadn't been there when she had sat down. It seemed ridiculous she hadn't noticed their sudden appearance.

With a deep sigh, Felicity raised her chin and straightened her shoulders as she met her brother's gaze. "Yes, Kellan. We'll do it together."

***

That night, Felicity pushed open the doorway to the armoire a crack. A scent wafted through the opening, and she released a long sigh. When she entered her bedroom, Kellan sat in a chair in front of the fireplace. "Where've you been?"

"I didn't know I needed to check in with you on my comings and goings." Her tone terse.

Kellan's shoulders slumped. "I can't help it." He gestured to the chair and she sat. It wasn't his fault, she knew that. It's not like he would stop her.

He regarded her for a moment. "I just got you back and we have been honest with each other up to this point. Is there a reason you feel the need to sneak out?"

She winced at the truth in his words. As much as they had begun to learn to trust each other and to fall into a sense of normalcy after the past fifty years of separation, their relationship was still tender. Neither wanted to push the other too far. Kellan released a loud sigh.

Felicity sat back into her seat. "Within these walls, there is always someone following me. I know they feel the need, but you have to admit having guards watch our every move is daunting."

"It is," Kellan agreed. "Hopefully once the trials are over and father has returned, we can cut back on the security. Until then, we need to be careful. Things are not exactly safe just yet."

"Safe?" She snapped out her wrist, the mechanism gave a shrill slice and a blade broke free by from the glove she wore. A gift from Lord Dimitri and Lord Lian of Aer with a request not to slit their friend's neck with it. "Please don't be the over-protective brother."

Kellan groaned. "It's hard—but I'm trying."

She clicked the blade back into place before she removed the gloves and stood to pull off her cloak. "I promise I have my reasons for sneaking out." Underneath the cloak was a dress that would be common among the high-class merchants. Felicity walked across the room, aware Kellan had more questions on the tip of his tongue and opened her trunk. "And I'm going to remind you to trust me and not ask for further details now. When I know what it is I'm looking for—if it goes anywhere—I promise you'll be one of the first to know."

He wasn't appeased but contented himself with her answer. "You know you don't make being your brother very easy."

"You don't make it easy to be your sister either." She removed the dagger from her calf and put it into the trunk before snapping it shut.

He sighed and leaned his head back in the chair. "But if anything happens to you out there, as the princess..." He trailed off for a moment and swallowed. "Without Father, it is more important than ever that we show a united front."

"I'm being careful." She winked at him, the gesture enough to have him shaking his head with a smile.

Kellan headed towards the door, and Felicity pulled out a pair of pants and a tunic from the armoire.

"Felicity?" When she turned to find him in the doorway, he continued, "Two things before I go."

By the look on his face alone, the way his brow crinkled, and the thoughtful tilt of his mouth, she knew where this was going and almost cringed as he continued. "You need to go see him. I have allowed him to stay within that room for too long, and I have done it for you. The people will question us if we don't have him answer for any crimes."

Felicity's jaw quirked. "One week, Kellan. That's all I ask. Just give me one more week."

"For what?" he whispered.

She could hear the ache in his voice and thumbed the fabric in her hand. "I promise. This will be my last request on the matter."

Kellan swallowed and nodded. "One week, Felicity. I can pacify them that long. But beyond that..." He didn't need to finish that sentence.

"Agreed." She gave her best attempt at a smile but knew it came across weak. "Thank you."

He turned to leave but Felicity stopped him. "You said two things."

"Oh, yes. My contact has responded but they haven't seen Marquette or Fiadh in Scáth and from the contents of the Shadow Realm's letter, I don't think they're hiding them."

Remembering the queen's story, Felicity had her doubts that they would either. "That means we still have no idea where they are."

Kellan nodded. "No, but do you remember how I told you that I had one contact with the rebels."

"I do." Felicity furrowed her brow.

"He's been searching for their whereabouts in the southern territories. No luck so far, but he should arrive in Koselig tonight. His name is Sloan and he's asked to meet with you tomorrow."

Felicity searched Kellan's face for any sign or inclination as to why but found nothing. "All right."

"I think you'll like him."

Her gaze narrowed. "If you are playing at anything..."

Kellan raised his arms up in mock surrender, a grin stretched across his face. "What do you think I'd be doing?"

She tossed the shirt at him, wishing it was something harder, missing him by a body length as he flung open the door and ran from the room.

Alone, Felicity bent over and picked up the shirt, hanging it in the armoire. Her gaze rested on the blood-stained cloak. She hadn't thought about it since the return of her memories. But like anything else from before her time at the Tower, she didn't know if it had been her mother's or not. Someday she would have her answer.

She changed into comfortable attire and sat at the writing desk she had delivered a few days before. She ran her fingers along the feather of the quill, eyes gazing over the notes on the parchment before her. Meira had brought by the dinner she had missed shortly after Kellan had left.

Her trip to the *Rose & Wisteria* that afternoon had been more fruitful than her previous visit. She had arrived in the merchant's clothes claiming to be looking for her partner Harlin.

Mistress Holaps hadn't been willing to talk at all until the pouch of coins dropped with a tinkle on her table. Then she opened right up. "Harlin came to meet business associates. There wasn't much out of the ordinary, to begin with. The females and women claimed he was well worth their time—and he took up a lot of it. Paid well too." Felicity ignored the pain in her chest as the mistress continued, "But then one day, he just stopped. He would come for his meetings still, eat, drink, play some games but didn't partake in the females or males. It was his last visit that was the most notable. He took one of the new girls to the room and neither he nor she came back. He still paid, though. But haven't seen either of them since."

After leaving the brothel, Felicity ventured down to the docks where everyone raved about Lord Harlin's generosity and business etiquette. During her questioning, not a single one could point her where he was or who he worked with or for. "He paid and brought in the goods. We don't ask questions as long as the money comes in."

The only evidence he existed was the ship he owned—or claimed to have owned. Felicity walked on the deck and searched it from bow to stern. The only thing she found was the hull filled with supplies: rations, blankets, clothes, and other provisions. No sign of cargo or sailors. A ghost ship.

Felicity recorded the last bit of her findings, then reread her previous notes for her trip to the *Rose & Wisteria* when she had shown up as Bruin's sister, worried about her brother's whereabouts. Downtrodden and wearing simple peasant attire, Mistress Holaps didn't even raise a brow of suspicion. She didn't recognize that Felicity had ever stepped foot into the establishment before. That time it took a lot more to get the woman to talk since Felicity couldn't obviously throw much coin at the female. "He came, he ate and drank. He sometimes took a female to a room and always paid, so I never complained."

"What did he discuss?" It was a small chance the mistress would talk and when her brow furrowed, Felicity knew her time was short. She broke into a fit of fake tears, blubbering into a handkerchief over her 'lost brother.' The mistress nearly kicked Felicity out then. "He's fine. Probably met a nice girl. We haven't seen him in weeks."

There had been no chance to ask those who were actually in the mistress' employ, so Felicity was left with breadcrumbs for clues.

You won't allow yourself to see me.

She had tried to ignore his words—to push them out of her mind like the memories she couldn't yet grasp. But it didn't work that way.

What was it she was supposed to see?

A knock sounded at the door, and Felicity placed down the quill and began to pile up the pages, thankful the ink had dried. "Come in."

Meira entered, carrying a tray with a teapot and cup. "I figured you might want something warm tonight. You should be asleep." The handmaiden tsked as she placed the tray down beside Felicity and poured her a cup.

Felicity smiled as she took the saucer. "Thank you, Meira. I guess I have a lot on my mind."

"Is there anything I can assist with?"

Felicity shook her head. "No, I don't think...." She trailed off in thought. "Well, maybe." She gestured to the seat across from her. "Please sit."

Meira considered the invitation, and Felicity was certain the female was questioning if the choice would be improper or not. "I insist," she added.

With pursed lips, the handmaiden took a seat, folding her hands in her lap. "What is it I can do for you?"

Felicity didn't know exactly how to word the question. After a moment of silence, the handmaiden fidgeting across from her, Felicity cleared her throat. "Did Alarian and his parents have a close relationship while he was growing up?"

Meira inhaled deeply and flushed. Nope, guess those weren't the right words.

"I don't mean to pry—or make you uncomfortable."

The battle waging in the handmaiden's expression was visible from the tautness in her mouth and the crinkle in her brow. Then with a resolved sigh, her shoulders lowered. "No, milady. They did not. You see, he was a strong-willed lad. Always had and probably always will be. They sent Rian away when he was young to live in Scáth."

Felicity noticed the nickname and the corner of her mouth rose. It fit him, even if she had never heard anyone else refer to him as such.

"Rian didn't officially return until they called for him about a year prior to...." Meira trailed off and met Felicity's gaze.

Felicity deigned to finish the thought. "The coup against my family?"

Meira nodded. "I never knew his feelings on the matter. He didn't need a nanny any longer, of course. But there was a heaviness that year. I don't know how much he was aware of what his parents were planning. But a year into your father's exile, he and the Que—I mean Marquette had a vicious fight and he left."

Felicity's gaze trailed to the fire in the hearth. The way the flames twisted and turned in the darkness reminded her of a night in a training hall. "Where did he go?"

"If the rumors are true...everywhere." Heat filled her face, a motherly love evident in her eyes as she spoke. "I have said too much."

"Please, Meira. I'm trying to help him." Felicity was surprised at how true those words were. "To do so, I need to know everything."

Meira's brow creased deeper. After a few moments, the female sitting in resigned silence or deep thought released a long sigh. "Most of the word we received was gossip and hearsay. His parents were angry and claimed he was dragging their name through the mud. About a year and a half prior to your arrival, he returned. It never was right between them, but both Roald and Marquette were resolved to his presence and treated him as a soldier—easily dispensable, someone to marry off, nothing more."

Felicity closed her eyes, the light dancing against her eyelids. "Thank you for your honesty."

"Do you know what will happen to him, milady?" Meira whispered.

"No, I do not." It wasn't enough—not enough to claim his innocence or know if she was on the right track.

But it was something more about the male she was slowly beginning to piece together.

Chapter 39

The hallway felt abandoned. Haunted. Felicity stood outside the door. Twice now, she had lifted her hand to open it, the spell already removed by the guard, and both times she had dropped it again.

It wasn't her strongest moment. It had been two days since her talk with Meira and, as much as she wished otherwise, she hadn't uncovered anything new about the ex-prince.

One of the guards cleared his throat, and Felicity shot him a glare that had him straightening and looking away. The female guard on the other side snickered between gritted teeth.

"If either of you says a word about this…" Felicity warned, then pushed the door open. Although it was late morning, darkness enshrouded the room. As she closed the door behind her, she stubbed her toe on something hard. With a silent curse, she removed the pendant from her neck, rested it in her palm and called her magic to it, emitting enough light for Felicity to see where she was going.

Dodging books and piles of dishes, Felicity crossed the room and pulled open the drape, allowing in a bit more light.

A hiss sounded behind her as she dispelled her magic. She whirled around to find a pile of blankets and parchment shift on the bed then still again, no other sign of life hidden beneath the mess.

Mess was an understatement. Felicity scanned the space and her jaw dropped. Except for the little trail Felicity had used to cross the room, there was little floor space visible. Clothes hung over furniture, books were piled on all the surfaces, and some had toppled over onto the ground. Parchments of notes were scattered and there was even a spot on the desk where ink had spilled, a puddle staining the rug underneath. The smell was almost as bad as the room itself. Dishes, rancid food left untouched, were piled near the door. Felicity was surprised there weren't mice scurrying about.

"You know, if you come to visit you could at least be polite." A guttural voice whined from the bed.

"Curses, Alarian?" Felicity stormed across the room and tore his coverings off. Her eyes widened, surprised at the sight of the male lying before her. His skin was milky white, not the usual sun-kissed, visible by his bare torso—and was that facial hair?

It took years for most males to grow anything beyond fuzz, but he must have been among the few exceptions. Or maybe it had to do with his earth magic.

Alarian pulled a pillow over his head. "Go away."

Felicity searched the room and sighed. She crossed back to the door and yanked it open. "I need you to find Meira and tell her to come as soon as possible please. Have her bring assistance and as many baskets as they can carry."

The guards looked at each other, and then the male nodded and ran down the hall. Felicity turned to the female guard. "How long hasn't he been eating?"

"It's not that he doesn't eat, milady. It's just that he doesn't eat much."

Felicity thanked the guard before closing the door and strutting across the room. This time she tore the pillow off his head. "Get up."

"I said go away come back when you're ready to talk, not whatever this is." He pinched his eyes shut from the light. "And close the damn window as you go."

"No." Felicity hit him with the pillow and he growled. "Why the hell are you doing this to yourself?"

Alarian chuckled. "Why do you think you can just waltz in here and order me around?"

Felicity gritted her teeth. "It's been maybe ten days and you look like a mess. What do you expect me to do when I arrive to this?" She waved her hand around to the chaos.

He pushed himself up and stilled. His gaze trailed over her from head to toe, then back to meet hers. "What the hell has happened to you?"

Her brow furrowed in annoyance. She turned on her heel, grabbing a nearby shirt.

"There is something in your eyes." He was watching her—she could feel it. "Something that isn't you."

Felicity's chest cracked a bit then. Not even Kellan had noticed the small shifts in her. The ones she had noted in her reflection. She stuffed the tunic against his chest. "You need to take a bath. Put this on for now, others are on their way."

Before he could comment further, she went to the bathing chamber and turned on the tap. The door opened while she was in there and Felicity heard the audible gasp as Meira entered.

"My word, Rian. What is this? I raised you better."

Felicity entered the room to find Meira had brought two others to help with the mess. The matron handmaiden walked across the room and looked Alarian up and down, clicking with disappointment. Another handmaiden stared at his bare chest, the tunic still in his hand and Felicity emitted a growl from low in her throat.

Meira stopped her tirade and both she and Alarian stared at Felicity. The ogling handmaiden dropped her gaze immediately.

A smile spread on Meira's face. Felicity turned away and busied herself with picking up a book off the floor. "Your bath is almost ready."

Well, curses—after the guards watched her fumbling, now the staff would spread gossip. Why the hell had Felicity come here again?

Alarian grabbed a set of what looked like still clean and folded clothes from his armoire. "I don't need any of this. Remember, I'm a prisoner. They don't have maids coming and cleaning up after their messes. And they certainly don't have princesses ordering them to take baths."

Meira opened her mouth and judging by the way her face burned crimson, she was about to give the ex-prince an earful. Felicity almost let him have it, but instead she grabbed a towel that hung over a chair and tossed it in his face. "If you didn't ask to speak to me, I wouldn't be here. But I certainly won't suffer through this conversation *and* your stench. Now get in there."

He grumbled as he crossed the room, and Felicity was certain more than one curse was sent her way as he sulked. Meira and the others began bustling about, picking up clothes and piling the dishes into baskets. "We have this, Your Highness. Please don't trouble yourself."

Felicity began to pick up the loose pieces of parchment. "It's no trouble, Meira. I need something to do." She felt the matron's gaze, but Felicity ignored it as she continued her task. She glanced over his notes, recognizing his handwriting. She frowned, realizing that they were mostly on the heartstones he'd spoken of that night in the brothel and the Countess's story came to mind.

After all the papers were piled on the desk, Felicity began working on the books. Most were marked with pieces of fabric, and Felicity found the remains of an old shirt he had torn for placeholders. Children's tales, myths, tomes on the history of the realms—most Felicity had never seen before, even in all of her studies with Kellan.

Meira and the others had made several trips before the floor was spotless. They finished making the bed, then dusted and swept up the last of the crumbs. Meira ordered the others to take the baskets out, and then turned to Felicity. "Is there anything else you need?"

After a final pass over the room, Felicity nodded. "Something for him to eat, please."

With a smile, the handmaiden curtsied, grabbed up the last basket and left. It took a moment for Felicity to realize that now she had no clue what to do with herself.

Alarian stepped out of the bathing room and stopped, surveying the clean space as he dried his hair with the towel. "I'll never find anything again."

Felicity let out an exasperated sigh and rolled her eyes. "You can't tell me you could find anything before. Trust me, I looked at the books and pages—there was no order to the chaos, and I kept your pages marked."

"What you see as chaos, I saw as sense." He fixed the button on his tunic and tossed the towel in a basket that remained by the door. "Why are you here, Felicity?"

He may be clean, his hair a bit disheveled, but he still seemed gaunt. A sallowness around his eyes. She blinked, looking away, then went with the excuse that had entered her mind this morning. "Do you know where my father is?"

Alarian stiffened, his shoulders taut. "You know Kellan never asked me that and I kept waiting for it. Instead, he just asked about Fiadh and my mother."

Felicity waited, even as he strutted across the room in silence to take a seat. She knew Alarian had been forthcoming about any information he had regarding Marquette and Fiadh. Even if it hadn't brought about any concrete location yet, she believed it was one of the reasons Kellan had been more patient with the ex-prince.

He settled in the stuffed chair and gestured to the one across from him. She swallowed, keeping her distance. It felt safer right now to stay away from him after her reaction to the handmaiden. "I'll stay standing."

Alarian sighed. "Yes, I believe I know the location of your father." He opened the drawer at his desk and then popped open a false bottom. "Here you go."

"What is this?" Felicity took the letter he held out towards her, her brow furrowed as she recognized the seal of the Tower. She despised her trembling as she broke the wax and unfolded the missive.

Prince Alarian,

Everything is in place, and she has the information you requested. There is little she knows of the Oileán islands, so it's best to keep that in mind. I doubt I need to tell you that she is more than capable of taking care of herself, but please watch over her. We entrust you to prepare her as best as you can for what's to come. For the future of the realms and her people.

She's become important during her time with us and though we did our best, she is still naive to the outside world. Help her to experience the wonders of the realms—she will learn quickly. Show her what the people have to offer. Teach her to be more than a weapon. We wish we could have done better by her, but we are what we are.

And she is what she is. We know this is not her rightful place but wish we could have held on a little longer. If things go as planned, I know she will have many questions. Make sure she knows we will be here waiting to answer them.

Protection and Peace,

The Countess

Her stomach churned and she looked up from the letter to meet his gaze. There was a lot to unravel from the missive but first thing first. "Where? Oileán? Is that where my father is?"

Alarian nodded. "I believe so."

Felicity smiled and turned to rush to the door. "Call for Kellan." Then she turned to the letter again, this time reading between the lines at what the Countess said. The woman had claimed she knew the Tower wasn't her rightful place. There was a sense of trust in her words that went beyond a mission to uncover the king's enemies. But—

"How?" It was the only word she could form. Then the pieces all fell together and her eyes widened. She reread the letter again. *For the future of the realms and her people.* Alarian's grin grew as he watched her. *See me.*

"You." She looked at the letter again then back up to him. The undercover meetings at the brothel. The ship at the port. His torn relationship with his parents. "You're—"

There was a knock at the door she wished to ignore as that damn grin of Alarian's expanded. The guard didn't wait, the door opening. "Your Highness, someone is here to see you and says it cannot wait. He claims—"

"Sloan?" Kellan interrupted the guard as he and Avyanna entered, another male directly behind them. "I thought we would meet in the drawing room."

Felicity gawked, her gaze shifting from the new arrivals to Alarian. "From the brothel, correct?" Just add a mask to Sloan and he would be the masked male who had sat beside Alarian, or Bruin, in the Wisteria room.

Alarian winked.

Avyanna folded her hands in front of her skirts. "What is going on here?"

"I have a similar question. Sloan, I know you asked to meet with my sister, but this is a bit forward." Kellan's gaze thinned on the ex-prince and the male.

Felicity took a step between them, drawing her brother's attention. "Alarian is innocent."

"What?" Kellan asked, a flutter of a breeze sliding across her skin.

Sloan chuckled. "That's what I came to discuss."

Felicity held up a hand to the guest, silencing him. She needed to get this out. "I've told you to trust me and be patient. Let Alarian go. In fact, he's even told me the possible whereabouts of our father."

"His parents cursed us, raised a coup..." Kellan growled, fists forming at his side and Felicity could almost sense the magic pulsing under his skin—like the still before a lightning strike.

"He's the other rebel contact in the castle."

Sloan outright laughed. "Contact. He's more than that. Alarian's the damn leader."

A funnel of wind exploded through the room. Felicity rammed into the bedpost. As quickly as it started, it stopped. She rubbed her back at the point of impact as she sat up to find Sloan had crashed into a dresser, papers fluttering to the floor. Alarian had toppled backwards into his chair and was attempting to stand again.

Lady Solfire, who only remained standing since she was in the center of the storm, couldn't hold Kellan upright as Felicity's brother fainted—falling to the floor in a heap and taking her down with him—drained.

The guards rushed in then, swords drawn. "Your Highness…"

She cut them off with a look then climbed to her feet, her body aching. "Is he all right?"

Avyanna ran a hand over Kellan's chest then head. "Yes. Just unconscious. It was too much. He'll be fine with a little rest." She smiled as she cradled his head in her lap. "But it's probably best you explain things in the meantime." Curiosity piqued the female's expression.

Felicity turned towards Alarian who had gotten to his feet, brushing dust from his pants.

Sloan ran a hand over his shaved head. "I didn't expect Kellan to take things so hard."

Lady Solfire sighed loudly. "He's been stressed. And this news was unexpected."

Alarian settled the chair back on its feet, a glint of metal visible at his ankle.

Felicity glared. "Kellan put an iron cuff on you?"

The ex-prince winced as he took a seat. "Can't blame him. I was a high-profile prisoner. Even if you allowed me to stay in my rooms, he had to make sure I couldn't leave."

Felicity shook her head an turned back to the guards. "Would you please send for some broth and bread for my brother? But first, get the key for the iron cuff."

The guards nodded, backing out of the room with wide-eyed and observant expressions.

No wonder Alarian had looked so haggard. The iron would have weakened him and torn away at his strength and magic after so many days.

She turned to face the ex-prince. "You've been leading the re-sistance against your parents. The letter indicated you knew who I was. How many other things..." She trailed off as pieces of the past few months began to fit together. Pieces of the male who she crossed the room to stand in front of. "You weren't stabbed over cards, were you?"

Alarian shook his head. *See me.*

"That means the Countess knew who I was. And somehow you did too?"

"I didn't at first. I had suspicions but they were confirmed by Kellan's response to you at the Tower. The Countess did know your identity, so those are questions you will need answered by her."

Felicity rubbed her temples. Thinking.

"That day on the bluff, when I removed my clasp…" That had been when his parents had attacked and killed so many rebels—the death of all those children. "What your parents had done. That was why you were upset."

All pride on Alarian's face vanished. "One of many regrets. The day on the bluff, that was a day I wished I could turn myself in to save every one of those innocent people. I hadn't been close enough to the attack to do so and found out after it was over."

"What about the warnings about your mother. What are you researching?"

Alarian cleared his throat. "Heartstones. She wants to find them to tear down the veil." Felicity and Avyanna gasped, sharing a glance before turning back to the male for more information. He shook his head. "This is very important, and I think your brother should be conscious for it. We need to—" The guards opened the door again, and Alarian immediately grew silent as a handmaiden entered.

Sloan assisted Avyanna with getting Kellan onto the bed. Her brother groaned, but the iron on Alarian's ankle made Felicity lose sympathy for Kellan who would probably wake with nothing more than a headache. A handmaiden placed food on the bedside table, enough for Alarian too, and Avyanna brushed back Kellan's hair. "He's coming to."

It was only a minute filled with silence before the guard entered and bent over to remove the iron at Alarian's ankle. Felicity watched as the guard wrapped his hand with a thick cloth to protect himself from the iron. "Give the key to me."

"Princess, I don't think—"

She shook her head, holding out her hand. "It doesn't affect me." Probably another thing from her mother's human bloodline. Iron didn't steal her magic and strength as it did for most fae.

He looked confused for a brief moment and then held out the silver key towards her. She bent down, unclicking the lock. The manacle fell with a clank to the floor. She scooped it up, dropping it into the thick bag the guard held out.

Once freed, shadows filled the space and Alarian's shoulders immediately began to relax as his magic spread.

Concern settled in Felicity's chest. There were so many questions she needed answered, things she needed clarification on. She opened her mouth to stop him as the shadows wrapped around his body. But shut it when he held out a hand towards her, his expression serious, that smile gone. "Come with me?"

With so much uncertainty, going with him now just might confuse her more. Confuse the feelings the male already elicited within her. Emotions she couldn't quite place and didn't fully understand yet.

But there were so many unanswered questions.

Felicity glanced at his hand, then back up to meet his hopeful gaze, that damn grin stretching across his face. No—it was dangerous to let him distract her right now. Not when she knew this was the beginning of more. The veil. Her father. The ever-growing list of questions the Tower still had to answer. The pieces of her past that were still missing. Marquette and Fiadh. *Princess*...

There was much to be done.

She was about to turn away when Sloan leaned against the bedpost. "Don't be long, Rian."

This caused her to pause—to reconsider. Her gaze settled again on Alarian's extended hand. He'd made such a request before and she'd turned away from him. Chosen her brother. It was a decision she would never regret.

But this—this was another choice that was solely her own. If she chose him now, what would happen next?

To Be Continued

Book Two of the Realm Curse Duology coming Spring 2024!

For updates, to find more from GW Prouse, or follow on social media check out:

Acknowledgements

Thank you, first of all, to you the reader for taking a chance with this book. I truly hope you enjoyed it. A Nameless Curse wouldn't be what is it today if it wasn't for my editor and ANC's biggest champion, Megan Amato. She's read ANC nearly as many times as I have it seems and I appreciate all the chats and brainstorming as I over-analyzed everything.

To all those who have taken time to read the book and give feedback: Ruby, Samara, Tania Lan, Michelle Tang, C.C. Tyler, and beta readers Alissa, Kayla, and Lori- THANK YOU! To my fellow Query Wenches and Shrew- Thank you for your awesome support in this venture (extra shout out to L.J. Thomas) by being sounding boards, giving feedback, critique partners and so much more! You're all awesome and I'm so happy I commented on a post so many years ago! To the Secret Writers Guild for all the sprints and chats throughout the years. To WWTS- I've learned more about *my* voice because of this group and my book is better for it.

The ANC Street Team who celebrated every milestone these past few months and shared posts, made their own, and screamed about this book. To the wonderfully commissioned art by Dominique Callegari (chapter headers) and Angeline Trevena (map) and Natasha MacKenzie for the gorgeous cover.

To my husband for understanding my sanity requires writing. You're my second brain when mine is scrambled so thanks for talking through plot holes with me. Also, because this is important- "I love you the most!" There, it's in print, so I win! Finally, to my kids for being my biggest cheerleaders and just asking about my stories. I love you!

About the Author

GW Prouse has a heart for travel and a love of the outdoors that inspires her settings and worlds. While she lives near the beach, she prefers redwood trees, fog covered lakes and mountain peaks. If she's not writing, reading, or rushing her family around to the countless activities her children can accumulate, she can be found riding her horse, hiking the hills, or cuddling up with her husband for a movie.